HERE'S TO BUILDING
A BETTER FUTURE!

Clyde

GIRL OUT OF TIME

CLYDE BOYER

GIRL FRIDAY BOOKS

This is a work of fiction. Names, characters, organizations, places, events, and incidents are either products of the author's imagination or are used fictitiously.

GFB GIRL FRIDAY BOOKS

Published by Girl Friday Books™, Seattle
www.girlfridaybooks.com
Produced by Girl Friday Productions

Cover design: David Fassett
Development & editorial: Reshma Kooner
Production editorial: Katherine Richards

ISBN (paperback): 978-1-954854-22-2
ISBN (ebook): 978-1-954854-64-2
Library of Congress Control Number: 2022919774

First edition

To Dulce and Jacob, my North Stars, my dearest family, and my reason for being here. And to the readers young and old, may this make you laugh and wonder and inspire you in uncertain times.

PROLOGUE

Anna Armstrong's plan was so simple, she wondered why no one had thought of it before. She stood at the edge of her bed with her arms held high and her knees slightly bent. All she had to do was find a high enough vantage point and then jump as fast and as far as she could. Her mom had taught her about gravity, and she had a vague idea about velocity. If she could leap fast enough and at the correct angle, she could break free of Earth's atmosphere, up and out toward the stars in the night sky. Her first solo flight into space.

Anna stood at the edge of her bed and began the countdown.

"Five, four, three, two, one . . . liftoff!"

The flight lasted exactly 0.86 seconds, enough time for Anna to make a noise like a rocket before falling to the hardwood floor with a thud. Dazed but undaunted, Anna rolled over and looked up at the stars she had glued to her ceiling and wondered if it was a trajectory problem or a lift problem.

Anna's second launch came two years later. She had learned a lot from her earlier mistakes and realized that she alone did not possess sufficient energy to break Earth's gravity.

She smiled, thinking back to her younger self. No, she needed a lot more power, and this time no cape. It only added drag.

So, what would provide enough power? A catapult? Helium balloons tied to a chair? No, where would she find that many balloons anyway? But the trampoline in the backyard might just do the trick. There were times she had bounced so high she was sure she had reached the tops of the trees that encircled her home. All she had to do was generate a little greater force and there was no telling how far she could go.

With the help of the neighborhood kids, Anna dragged the trampoline to the edge of her house. She climbed onto the roof through her bedroom window and looked over the edge. From her vantage point, the trampoline below looked so small. She licked her finger and checked the direction of the wind before inching her way to the edge of the roof. This time, she decided to count down silently to herself.

"Five, four, three, two . . . just one small step . . . one!"

Whoosh was the sound she made going down. *Boing* was the sound she made going up and out across the lawn. She tucked into a ball and spun a full circle before landing in a honeysuckle bush near the edge of the lawn. Dazed but undaunted, Anna rolled over and watched a jet fly overhead; the contrails made perpendicular lines in the blue August sky.

Anna's third attempt to reach space never came to be. She spent the summer after seventh grade working in her father's shed while her parents were far away on business. By now, she had learned of real space travel and solid fuels and rockets that could carry giant payloads to other planets. She might not be able to make it into space herself, but she could build a rocket.

And she was close. So close. After a month of experimentation and spent fire extinguishers and the smell of burning plastic, Anna had landed on the right mix of corn syrup, sugar, rust, and stump remover for rocket fuel. She had fashioned a rocket body out of PVC and fins out of balsa wood. There was even an attachment for her old digital camera to take video as the rocket shot into space. The launch was scheduled for July 20, the anniversary of the first moon landing and the day her mom and dad would be returning from their long trip overseas.

Anna sprawled out on the grass in the backyard and waited for her parents to return. The launch was meant to be a surprise, a Welcome Home message written out across the sky. Time passed and the shadows from the trees stretched slowly across the lawn until the entire launchpad was covered in shade, but there was still no sign of her parents.

From inside the house, the phone rang. She didn't pay any attention at first. But then she heard her Aunt Claire talking loudly, which was rare. Worse was the sobbing sound that drifted outside and the silence that followed. Anna silently counted down from five and then closed her eyes as the screen door swung slowly open. She was floating in space.

Anna didn't believe in magic or the ability to read minds. She was a girl of science, after all. But even before she saw her aunt walk across the evening lawn, even before the rare embrace, she had a sick feeling that the world she knew was over. Her parents wouldn't be coming home again.

—

Something had happened to her parents' taxi en route to the airport. "Roads are dangerous in that part of the world," someone had said to Anna. She just couldn't remember who had said it. So many people said so many things over the course of the next week that it all blended together into a distant hum. There was a funeral service for her parents, with more hugs from strangers who had lined up out the front door like people waiting for a ride at an amusement park. Then the final guests left, and the door was closed behind them. The voices disappeared and the buzzing mercifully stopped.

The next day, Aunt Claire moved into the guest room across the hall and then into her parents' empty bedroom a week later. Anna and her aunt said no more than a couple of sentences a day to each other. Like electrons that repel, the two could never seem to share the same place or time. As one entered a room, the other would leave.

More strangers visited through the long winter. Books and clothes were packed. Furniture was moved and pictures replaced until room by room, piece by piece, the house she grew up in was transformed into an alien landscape. She might as well have been living on the surface of the moon.

It wasn't that her aunt was a bad person or even selfish, she was just a stranger, and living with her didn't seem to make things any better. On the contrary, it made things worse. So when Aunt Claire sat her down one day the following spring and asked if she would like to stay with her Uncle Jack, at least for a while, Anna didn't even let her finish her sentence. She grabbed her Aunt Claire's hand and smiled for the first time in months.

PART I

THE GIRL

CHAPTER 1

Anna waited outside the airport terminal with a small red suitcase and a green spring jacket. She didn't carry much with her, just several changes of clothes, a pair of running shoes, and a laptop that contained the parts of her life she still cared about. She had left the rest of her belongings—all the things she had outgrown, from clothes to toys—in boxes stacked in the corner of her old room.

Uncle Jack was easy to spot. He was driving the same rusty green pickup truck she remembered from her last visit years before. Herbie, his golden retriever, sat on the passenger side of the truck. Neither of them seemed to have changed a bit. When she hugged Uncle Jack, he smelled of wood chips and fresh-cut grass.

"You sure know how to travel light." Uncle Jack smiled as he lifted her red suitcase with a single finger and tossed it into the back. "Or are you looking for a quick escape?"

"Hmm. Not sure yet," Anna kidded back. "I like to keep my options open."

She had always liked her Uncle Jack. He was tall and laughed a lot and liked to make things. His nose was slightly crooked from a momentary lapse of concentration and a line-drive baseball in high school. She remembered he was a lot younger than her dad had been, like eight or ten years, and he didn't have her dad's always-worried expression, which made him seem even younger.

Anna sat in the middle of the bench seat so that Herbie could ride with his head out the window, his ears and tongue flapping in the wind. It was a warm day for early spring, and the air circulating through the cab of the truck felt good as they drove deeper into farm country. It smelled good too, like dirt after a rain. They talked about baseball and the Cubs' prospects on opening day for the first half hour and science for the next. Her two favorite subjects. Uncle Jack didn't bring up her parents' death or give her that sympathetic look she had grown to hate—not once.

It was midafternoon when they reached the outskirts of Uncle Jack's hometown. A faded green sign with two bullet holes and a dented bottom corner greeted them with *Welcome to Smartt, Indiana—Population 2,503.*

"Smartt with two *t*'s?"

"Yeah, I know." Uncle Jack chuckled. "The irony is not lost on me, either."

On the outskirts of town, there were big-box discount stores and farm equipment retailers with flapping orange flags draped across shiny green tractors. A two-lane bridge overlooking a small winding river marked the passage between the newer and older parts of Smartt. The older parts had a lot more charm. They passed by the downtown area with a white town hall surrounded by brick storefronts and an outdoor farmers market. They passed by the county fairgrounds that contained large barnlike structures and rusted carnival rides covered by tarps during the off-season. They drove by two brick buildings that looked like Lego blocks surrounded by a football field, a playground, and a large garden. Kids were playing out front.

Anna figured this had to be her new school—or maybe a very nice prison. Same thing, in her mind. Four stop signs, a traffic light, and a couple of left turns later and they were on the other side of town.

"Yeah, I'm afraid that's about it. This isn't anything like Boston." Uncle Jack smiled. He must have been reading her mind. "But you never have to worry about traffic, and folks are nice for the most part."

Within minutes they were on the last leg of their journey, down a half-mile dirt road lined with trees and a long white fence winding down a sloping hill. Fields, with rows of sprouting crops, spread out like a green blanket on both sides. At the end of the lane, a row of large rectangular barns came into view. The sun reflected sharply off their tin roofs and solar panels, forcing Anna to squint. None of it looked familiar until the sun's angle shifted and she could make out the old farmhouse her father had grown up in.

As the pickup truck rumbled closer, she noticed at least a dozen strangers standing under the shade of the old bur oak tree that covered part of the sweeping front lawn. The crowd was staring at the truck as if they had been waiting for Anna's arrival. Next to the crowd were two picnic benches set side by side and lined with piles of food and pitchers of tea sweating in the afternoon sun.

"So how do you feel about surprise parties?" Uncle Jack asked. His mouth turned up in a crooked grin.

"They're fine as long as they aren't for me," Anna said, grimacing.

"Well, too late for that." Uncle Jack slowly rolled the truck to a stop near the front gate. "I just wanted you to meet some of the folks I work with here on the farm. I promise it will be painless."

Anna reluctantly stepped out and fanned her hand in front of her face as the cloud of dust that had followed the truck rolled past. As the dust cleared, she could see the faces in the crowd. They were friendly and smiling and staring directly at her. Anna recoiled and wanted to get back into the truck. From her list of irrational fears—spiders, clowns, and being the center of attention—being the center of attention was the thing she feared most.

"She's a shy one, isn't she?" said a short, stout woman with spiked gray hair and cloudy blue eyes. She had an accent, French or Italian—Anna wasn't sure. Somehow, that helped it sound less condescending.

Uncle Jack held his hands up.

"All right, all right. Let's not overwhelm her. Everyone, this is Anna," Uncle Jack said, motioning toward his niece. "Anna, uh—I guess this is everyone."

One by one, members of Uncle Jack's team came forward and introduced themselves. Anna didn't like crowds, but she prided herself on being able to memorize people's names. It was a game her mother had taught her. Anna would take a part of the person's name and combine it with a silly image or sound. Memory tricks. And the game had the side benefit of occupying her mind and reducing stress. The woman with spiked hair, a botanist from France, became "Faye the Gray who likes to make hay." There was "Kevin from Kenya," an engineer, and "Gladness from Tanzania," a veterinarian whose name was perfect just the way it was. There was a tall blond man, a seed specialist, whom Anna nicknamed "Liam from Sweden who breeds little seeds." There was a soil specialist from China—"Li Wei or the highway"—and various other agronomists, animal scientists, craftspeople, and makers.

"And this freeloader here is Dr. Ricardo Gloria, my research partner." Uncle Jack put his arm around the shoulders of a thin, lanky man wearing a flannel shirt and cowboy boots. Dr. Gloria was tan, with smile wrinkles that dusted the corners of his eyes.

"It's a pleasure to meet you, Anna," Dr. Gloria said, shaking her hand firmly. "Your grace and intelligence must have come from your mother's side of the family."

Anna paused for a moment, looked around, processed the last couple of minutes, then moved close to her uncle's side. She leaned in and said under her breath, "Uncle Jack, what kind of place are you running here?"

Uncle Jack looked puzzled for a moment, then burst out laughing. "I thought you knew."

"Knew what?" Anna asked.

"Ever hear of Thomas Edison, the famous inventor?"

"Of course," Anna said.

"And his team of inventors and craftsmen at Menlo Park?"

Anna nodded.

"We're kind of like that, only dirtier and not nearly as smart," Uncle Jack said. "You know this is a research farm, right?"

"I thought it was just Grandpa's farm," Anna said.

"Well, it was. Now it's the Armstrong and Gloria Regenerative Farms Research Center to be exact, brought to you by a healthy grant from Indiana University. Didn't your aunt tell you?"

"Aunt Claire didn't tell me anything except the time for my flight." Anna looked around at the crowd of people who were now sitting down and eating and talking among themselves. "You guys do real science here? I thought you were just a farmer."

"That's Dr. Farmer to you, and yes, we do real science," Uncle Jack said, arching his eyebrow and smiling. "I don't want to brag or anything. But we're kind of saving the planet here."

Over the course of the afternoon, Anna learned about each researcher's specialty, from dealing with a changing climate and soil erosion to drone maintenance and tool fabrication. She was taken on multiple tours, walking a network of paths that connected the barns, labs, workshops, and rolling fields that made up her uncle's farm. She ate food with strange textures and names she had never heard of and spices from countries she had never visited. She learned to sing several songs in foreign languages, not understanding the words but having a great time making the sounds, as Dr. Gloria and Uncle Jack played their guitars well into the evening. By the time the sky had shifted from orange to purple and the temperature had dropped by a good ten degrees, the party finally began to wind down. One by one, her new friends said their goodbyes before heading out to their own dormitories on the other side of the farm or driving into town to their short-term rental homes.

It was the most social interaction Anna had experienced in almost a year, and she was exhausted. As the last truck left, she slumped down on the porch swing and let one leg hang over the side. Lazily, she rocked back and forth, feeling the slight breeze shift across her face from left to right and back again. It was quiet, but a different kind of quiet than the vacuum silence that marked her time with Aunt Claire. This was a quiet filled with life all around her. The slight creak of the swing. Uncle Jack and Dr. Gloria's low-pitched conversation in the opposite corner of the deep-set porch. The stir of tall grass in the wind. The light chorus hum of early-spring katydids and crickets. Slowly, she closed her eyes and listened to one sound and then the other until each sound wove into a single note. Then sleep.

CHAPTER 2

Anna woke up in a panic around two o'clock in the morning. Nothing was familiar. Her bed. The darkness. The silence. Then, slowly, as her head cleared, she pieced together fragments of the previous evening. She remembered lying down on the porch swing for just a minute. She must have rocked herself to sleep. Somehow, Uncle Jack had carried her upstairs without waking her up. Anna was still in the clothes she wore from the plane trip, and a garlicky film covered the roof of her mouth. *Yuck.* She hadn't brushed her teeth before going to bed. A first.

Her bedroom was so dark she couldn't see the floor, the walls, or the door. All she could see was a single open window on the other side of the room, filled with more stars than she had seen in her entire life. Dead silence gave way to the hushed whisper of a night breeze through the trees outside her window.

Her eyes slowly adjusted to a kind of darkness she never experienced at her old home with its streetlights and ever-present city glow. She crawled out of bed and made her way to the window to peer out at the night sky. The air was cool and felt good against her skin. She breathed in the smell of grass and dew. The stars were so dense she could almost sense their movement, the heavens spinning slowly above her in an arc. She instinctively leaned to her left to compensate for the motion of the Earth.

From the corner of her eye, lightning flashed silently in pink and blue-white bursts on the horizon. A spring storm miles away, a contrast to the clear skies overhead. She waited for the rumble of thunder, but the storm was far enough away that all she could hear was the soft murmur of wind. Anna traced the line where the storm came to an end to meet a sea of stars.

The storm began to fade. It had been several minutes since the last flash. Anna yawned and started to turn back inside when a new burst of light caught her attention. This time the light was closer, just on the other side of the trees that lined the far end of the field. It looked like a flashlight or maybe a floodlight. Whatever it was, it was bright enough to create a halo above the trees. The light flickered, then disappeared.

Down below, Herbie ran in circles along the fence, looking out into the field and whimpering. Something was agitating him.

Anna leaned out the window. "What do you see, boy, what—"

Before Anna could finish, Herbie began barking into the darkness. He sensed it before Anna could see it. A pause. A heartbeat. Then, a circle of light rose silently above the line of trees a half mile away—a light so bright it lit the ground below it like the sun. From this distance, she couldn't tell if the light was the size of a basketball or a car. But there it was, impossibly bright and floating in midair. Anna felt her legs give a little. She stood frozen, her eyes the only part of her moving as they tracked the light's slow progress. The object shifted direction and floated out toward the middle of the field and stopped, flickering between brilliant white and red. Spotlights scanned the ground back and forth in a crisscross pattern.

Then, just as quickly as it had appeared, the light disappeared with an audible pop. Almost instantaneously, sparks burst in a line along the edge of her uncle's farm like a fireworks display. There were five flashes of light, spaced in equal distances, leaving behind five glowing pinpoints of ember that faded quickly. Silence again. No bugs. No wind.

Herbie had stopped barking and stared out toward the edge of the farm and the woods just beyond. Minutes passed. Neither of them moved. Slowly, the sound of the bugs returned. Not all of them at first—just a brave few. But within minutes the night was filled with a chorus of katydids and frogs. Anna leaned out the window and took in a deep breath of cool night air, held it in her lungs for a four-count, then exhaled—another trick she had learned from her mother to help calm her nerves. As her breathing slowed, her rational brain began to take over again. She could wake her uncle up. But what would she say? What would he think? There was an explanation for what she had seen, she was sure. There always was.

She crawled back into her bed and glanced at the clock on her phone, which read 2:45 a.m. As the rational side of her brain took over, her eyes grew heavier, and she felt herself fall into that space between sleep and consciousness. Before drifting away completely, Anna took a mental note to ask her uncle in the morning.

CHAPTER 3

The sound of a motorcycle idling in the driveway woke Anna from a deep sleep. Her bedroom window, lightly coated with dust, scattered morning sunlight across the room. Had she imagined the light from the night before? She wasn't quite sure. One thing she was sure of was that her feather bed felt really good. She buried her head deeper into the pillow.

From downstairs, she could hear the squeaky hinges of a screen door open and heavy footfalls of boots across the kitchen floor.

"Rise and shine!" Uncle Jack called out from downstairs.

Do people really say things like that? Anna groaned, rolled over, and groaned again before she flopped out of bed. She yanked a wrinkled sweatshirt from her suitcase and pulled it over the T-shirt she had worn the day before. So much for first impressions. It was her first day at a new school, and her expectations were already low. Different school, same result. She brushed her teeth, looked into the mirror, and turned her head to the side. Yep, her jawline could still cut paper, and her ice-blue eyes were set too far apart. An alien. The freckles that dusted her nose were less pronounced than they used to be, but they were still there. She pulled her mane of wavy light brown hair behind her ears and shrugged in resignation before heading out the bedroom door. The smell of coffee grew stronger with each step down the stairway.

Uncle Jack rushed through the kitchen, noisily opening cupboards and drawers and pulling out silverware with a clang. Herbie sat in the corner, happy and unmoving except for his eyes, which tracked Uncle Jack's every move.

"Sorry about being late for breakfast. Had a little trouble out in the field this morning," Uncle Jack said, pausing to rub the back of his neck. "I'm not used to actually making anyone . . . food. I've got eggs I can fry up, I guess. Some cereal maybe."

"Cereal's fine. Thanks." Anna smiled.

"You drink coffee?"

"By the gallon," Anna said.

"Me too," Uncle Jack said, smiling. "Must be a family thing."

Anna poured herself a cup of black coffee as Uncle Jack reached into the cupboard and pulled out a large plastic bag filled with seeds and grains and what looked like dried twigs from the forest floor.

"We made this cereal from stuff grown right here on the farm. It's nutrient dense."

"Mmmm," Anna said under her breath. "Nutrient dense."

"So today is your first day in a new school. Are you excited?" Uncle Jack placed two bowls on opposite sides of the kitchen table.

Anna shook out several clumps of fused bark and watched as a cloud of cereal dust mushroomed out of the bowl. Milk helped settle the cereal dust and made the chia seeds expand like little boats. She paused before taking the first bite. Crunchy, really crunchy, but she was surprised to find it tasted pretty good.

"Exshited ish not exactly the word I'd ushe," Anna mumbled through a mouthful of cereal.

"Oh, I see." Uncle Jack paused. "School's not your thing."

Anna gulped before continuing.

"School's fine. It's the whole, you know, social thing," Anna said, making air quotes around the word *thing*. Black seeds stuck in the gaps in her teeth.

"Well, maybe that will change. That's the great thing about moving to a new place. You can reinvent yourself. Be the person you want to be," Uncle Jack said, sitting down across from Anna.

Anna remembered her father saying almost those exact same words on her first day of middle school, a little over two years ago. Her father had talked to her the entire drive to school and encouraged her to give the kids and herself a chance. She remembered her dad's smile and the bubble of optimism that followed her from the car to the hallway and into her first class. Air started to leak out from that bubble within seconds as familiar faces from elementary school entered the room. Anna could feel some kids making faces. Some girls whispered just within earshot. Groups formed organically around Anna until she was an island left alone in the middle of the room.

Anna looked at her uncle and figured it was time to change the subject. "I saw a funny light last night. Just at the edge of the field outside my window."

Uncle Jack leaned back, his face puzzled. "Really? What kind of light?"

"It was weird. I don't know. But it was really bright. Herbie saw it too."

Before Uncle Jack could answer, the screen door squeaked open. Dr. Gloria stepped in and let the door slam behind him.

"Oh, good morning, Anna. I'm sorry to interrupt." Dr. Gloria sat down at the head of the table, removed his baseball cap, and sighed. "The good news just keeps coming, Jack. Looks like we found two more on the northeast side."

Dr. Gloria threw two small squares of melted green plastic on the table. Their edges were curled and singed black.

"No kidding," Uncle Jack said, picking up one of the plastic squares and inspecting both sides. "Hey, Anna. You're a maker, right? You know what this is?"

"Sure, it's a fried microcontroller."

"Yep. Any idea what could have caused this?"

Uncle Jack tossed the microcontroller back on the table. Anna picked it up and ran her finger along the GPIO pins that had fused together like knotted hair.

"Was it a power surge?" Anna asked.

"Good guess, but no. All our sensor stations run off the grid. Each unit is powered by aerogel supercapacitors and solar."

"Cheap capacitors then." Anna looked at her uncle through a hole melted in the center of the microcontroller.

Uncle Jack shook his head *no* again. "I can explain one sensor going down, maybe two. But not five of them, and not all at the exact same time."

From the moment Anna had seen the blown microcontroller, a thought had been forming at the back of her mind—or maybe more of an uneasy feeling, an intuition. The fried microcontrollers were related to the light she had seen the night before.

"Two forty-five a.m.," Anna said, sliding the microcontroller over to Uncle Jack. "That's when your sensors went down. Two forty-five a.m. Right?"

Dr. Gloria shot a quick glance at Uncle Jack, his eyes wide. They stared at each other for a moment, then a broad smile broke out across Uncle Jack's face.

"Yeah. Well, two forty-two, according to the sensors' log. How did you know?" Uncle Jack leaned forward.

"Remember that light I mentioned? That's when I saw it. Two forty-two a.m. When it disappeared, sparks broke out like fireworks. Must've been your sensors shorting out," Anna said. She pointed to the melted plastic on the table. "All at the exact same time."

"A light, huh? Weird." Uncle Jack looked lost in thought, then his head snapped up as if just struck with an idea. "You know how to solder, right?"

"Sure," Anna said.

"Good. We've got some work to do when you get home from school."

CHAPTER 4

So far, so good. Anna had survived the first half of the school day. When the lunch bell rang, Anna made her way to the last empty table in the cafeteria and sat with her back to the rest of the kids. She pulled out a book and put on her earphones and turned on her own personal invisibility shield. She was so focused on not being noticed that she didn't see the boy who had sat down directly across from her.

After consuming a quarter of a dry cheese sandwich, Anna finally sensed a presence. She looked up slowly. The boy, for his own part, wasn't paying any attention to Anna either and stared down intently at his phone. He was smaller than the other boys in eighth grade and wore thick, black-rimmed glasses. *One of the outcasts,* Anna thought. She knew them all too well. But this boy with his mop-like blond hair and crooked grin emitted a funny kind of confidence.

Suddenly he laughed out loud, startling Anna. He laughed again and shook his head.

"Classic," he said to himself.

Anna didn't bite.

He turned his phone to Anna and showed a photo of a

young girl dressed as Albert Einstein, with a full mustache and wild hair.

"Is this really you?" he asked.

Anna stared, unblinking.

"It *is* you," the boy said, laughing. "For what it's worth, I think you look great with a mustache."

"How did you find that picture?" Anna said sharply.

"I heard your name in class. Learned you're from Boston. Found your not-very-active socials. Easy-peasy." The boy smiled.

"Well, I'd appreciate you not stalking me," Anna said flatly.

"Oh, no. You got me all wrong," the boy said, putting his hands up in defense. "Consider me like the unofficial class yearbook. If you want to know what's going on—the people to know, the foods to avoid—I'm your guy. People are going to want to know who you are. I figured I'd help."

Anna wasn't sure what to think of this strange little boy, and it showed in her face. He didn't seem to notice, or if he did, he didn't seem to care much and kept on going.

"My name is Scout, but my friends call me Scout."

"Scout? Really?" Anna said.

"Scout the Third, actually. Doctor says I haven't hit my growth spurt yet." Scout began gnawing on a carrot stick like a bunny. "It's a pleasure to meet you, Anna."

He reached his hand out. Anna let it float there for several seconds before slowly reaching out and shaking his hand back. He seemed harmless.

"Nice to meet you too."

"So I hear you're some kind of genius. Your placement tests had you, like, at a college level or something."

"News travels fast, I see," Anna said.

"You're the new kid. So, yeah, you're a big deal, at least until our attention spans run out. And, since you're new, let me share some things they never bring up in orientation.

For instance, whatever you do, pack your own lunch on Taco Tuesdays. Don't ask questions. Just trust me."

"Okay."

"And another thing. Most kids are pretty nice around here, but some think they were put on this planet to rule over us peasants." Scout jerked his head in the direction of a pack of girls at the lunch table two rows over.

Anna started to look but Scout stopped her.

"Don't look at them. If you make eye contact, they might attack." Scout shook his head and grimaced.

Anna looked over anyway and was met by a fearsome smile filled with white teeth from the prettiest girl at the table. The girl's lips were curled up in a smile, but the rest of her face was unmoving, and she didn't blink, like a predator calmly waiting for her prey to move. She appeared to be the leader of the group of girls who surrounded her like a queen. Anna smiled back with the same fearsome smile and unblinking eyes.

"Her name is Blaire. The others sitting around her are Brittany, Bethany, Brianna, and Brooke. I kid you not," Scout said under his breath.

Anna leaned in. "The Killer Bs?"

"Exactly." Scout smiled broadly, clearly surprised he hadn't thought of that one himself. "Say, I like your style, sister. You and me are going to get along just fine."

"Anything else I should know?" Anna asked. She wasn't used to this much attention, but it wasn't altogether horrible.

"Plenty. See those guys over there?" Scout nodded to a group of boys in the corner of the cafeteria. "Good people to know in a pinch."

"You mean the jock table?" Anna asked.

Anna knew the popular kids from their body language and posture and easy confidence—and that they owned part of the cafeteria, and, most likely, the entire school. She had always avoided their type before, and for good reason. Kids like Anna and Scout were easy prey, picked off from the herd because they traveled alone.

Scout whistled over at the table and waved.

"No, really, you don't need—"

"It's no problem. They may look simple, but they're surprisingly friendly." Scout continued to wave until he caught their attention. "There's Max, Theo, Gus, and Guillermo Delgado Gloria, otherwise known as Del."

Their faces flashed past in a blur except for the last one, Del, the boy in the back with the faded sweatshirt and a smile so bright that it made her pause. Just as Del made eye contact, Anna's stomach cramped. It was an unpleasant feeling, and Anna didn't like it one bit.

She cringed and prepared herself for the verbal abuse she was sure would follow. Instead, most of the group smiled back at Scout. The biggest boy, the one named Max, nodded in greeting. One boy even waved back. No sarcasm. No over-the-shoulder snickers that masked their true intent. Their reactions were genuine, and Anna couldn't have been more surprised if she'd seen a small lamb playing kickball with a pack of lions.

Anna was still trying to make sense of this new place when two other figures popped into view. They moved so fast they made Anna lean back and shake her head. The two figures, both girls, sat down on opposite sides of Scout.

"Is he bugging you?" the tall girl asked. She didn't even look at Anna but glared directly at Scout instead, like an angry older sister. "He's been known to bug people."

The girl was a good head taller than Scout and outweighed him by at least thirty pounds, most of it lean muscle. She was pretty in a Viking kind of way with her short-cropped copper-red hair. The other girl was Scout's size and had a small Afro pulled back in a neat bun. She smiled serenely and seemed oblivious to the potential violence to her left.

"What's your name? My name is Lula. My friend's name is Fiona. I love your shirt. It's funny," the small one named Lula said, blurting out her lines without a break and so fast that they sounded like one protracted sentence.

It took Anna a couple of seconds to parse what she had just heard. Before she could respond, Scout jumped in.

"Geez, Hulk, will you give me some room here." Scout pushed his small frame against Fiona. She didn't budge an inch. "Her name is Anna, if you must know, and you are rudely butting in on our conversation."

Fiona ignored Scout. She seemed to have had plenty of practice.

"Congratulations, Anna. I hear you're officially the smartest kid in school." Fiona took a fry off Scout's plate and bit it in half. "I used to share that honor with Blaire before you got here. It doesn't bother me, but Blaire ain't going to like it."

"It was just a stupid placement exam," Anna argued. "Seriously, it's no big deal."

"No, I think it's awesome. Anything that gets ol' Blaire worked up into a frenzy is all right by me. We need more smart people around here anyway," Fiona said, directing her last sentence at Scout.

"And other things I never heard at my old school," Anna said, smiling. "Ever."

"Well, ladies, it's been lovely chatting with you. But I know you have to run along," Scout said.

The girls didn't budge. Scout glanced back and forth, shrugged, then slumped back in his chair, defeated.

"Where do you live?" Lula asked, her eyes big behind her glasses. "Can we come over and visit? Do you play any musical instruments? Maybe we can start a band."

"I'm not sure which question I should answer first." Anna giggled.

"Just pick one. You'll get used to it," Fiona offered.

"Well, I live with my uncle now," Anna said.

"With your uncle? That's funny. Why don't you live with your—"

It took exactly three seconds for Lula's brain to catch up with her mouth. But when it did, she found she couldn't go forward—or back—so she sat unmoving, her lips frozen midphrase.

"My parents?"

"I'm sorry. It's none of my—"

"It's okay. You didn't know." Anna shook her head. "My parents had an accident a year ago. A bad one. The worst. And, since the state of Massachusetts doesn't let me live on my own, I had to choose who would take care of me. My Uncle Jack or Aunt Claire."

Scout smiled meekly. Lula stared straight ahead, while Fiona looked down at nothing at all. Anna searched for a way to break the awkward silence. She hadn't talked this much to kids her own age since forever, other than some of the guys from her Little League team from her life before. But they were just friendly—like teammates, not friends. This felt good. Better than she had felt in a long time. But now she could sense the conversation slip away, and with it the hope that this time things would be different. Anna was overcome with the urge to pick her things up and retreat into silence.

Then Fiona spoke.

"I'm glad you chose your uncle," Fiona said, breaking the silence. "Otherwise, how could we start a band?"

A band, of all things. That made Anna smile.

CHAPTER 5

Anna gazed out the bus window and watched the switch-grass and yellow wildflowers pass by in a blur. She was one of the last students on the bus. The end of the route. In the distance, irrigation lines sprayed giant jets of water that caught the afternoon light in bands of color. The fields were freshly plowed, with only a hint of green from budding new plants. Dirt fields. Brown, orderly, and neat compared with the carpet of varying green colors that blanketed her uncle's fields. As the bus neared the lane leading to her home, Anna saw her uncle at the end of the road, leaning on his dirt bike with his arms folded and legs crossed.

A grin spread across Uncle Jack's face as the bus doors opened. He nodded in greeting to the bus driver, then took several steps forward and handed Anna a motorcycle helmet. The bus pulled away with the rumble of a diesel engine, grinding gears, and a cloud of dust.

"Hop on back." Uncle Jack motioned toward his motorcycle. "We've got some work to do."

Anna placed her arms around Uncle Jack's waist as he sped down the dirt road that led to the house. He shouted back that she was a good passenger and that she knew how to lean with the bike, but she could hear only every other word over the whine of the motorcycle's engine. Her eyes watered, and small bugs smacked against her face more than once, but Anna felt free, like she was flying.

Instead of heading toward the house, they took off down a dirt road carved with deep ruts from an earlier rain toward the edge of the woods where Anna had seen the lights the night before. The dirt road veered to the left, then ran parallel to the woods for a half mile until it reached a sloping hill. As they made their way to the top of the hill, a span of water came into view.

"Tyson Lake," Uncle Jack said as he pointed straight ahead. "It's been around since the Ice Age. When I was a kid, I used to imagine wooly mammoths walking around here."

The lake was small enough for her to swim across if she tried hard enough—but it had a network of inlets that doubled the size of the shoreline. Woods and large boulders framed most of the water's western shore, and farm fields and meadows lined the north.

Uncle Jack coasted downhill to a grassy clearing and parked the bike just beneath a cottonwood tree. The motor ticked to a stop as Anna hopped off and stretched her legs. Uncle Jack removed the bungee cords that held a small toolbox in place behind the seat and then handed the toolbox to Anna.

"See that sensor station over there?" He pointed toward a wooden post with a square green box bolted to its side about fifteen feet away. It looked like an overgrown bird feeder. "Let's see if you can replace the circuit board."

Anna opened the toolbox and found two identical circuit boards wrapped in plastic, a night-vision camera board, a cordless soldering iron, a drill, assorted screwdrivers, wrenches, a USB cord, and an empty pack of gum. She carefully pulled one of the circuit boards from its wrap and held it by the edges.

"A location sensor. An optical sensor." Anna turned the board over in her hands and looked at both sides. "What's this one?"

"Airflow sensor. Measures soil air permeability."

"These boards look custom. Did you print them yourself?" Anna asked.

"Right here on the farm." Uncle Jack squinted in the afternoon light. "I also had a couple of night-vision camera modules lying around the shop. Handy, huh? Figured you might be able to do something with them."

Anna nodded approvingly and then got to work. She removed the plastic casing of the sensor station and surveyed a nest of unattached wires.

Uncle Jack, for his part, sat down on a soft patch of wild grass and leaned back with his hands behind his head to stare at the spring clouds passing by overhead. A stiff breeze formed tiny waves on the surface of the lake, reflecting light that shimmered and shifted in rhythm with the sound of leaves blowing in the cottonwood tree. Minutes ticked by in silence as Anna worked.

"You know what I see?" Uncle Jack broke the silence.

"Some guy lying on the grass while his niece does all the work?" Anna shouted back as she gently placed the new circuit board in its housing.

"No, besides that." Uncle Jack pointed up to a cloud overhead. "See that cloud right there? It looks just like the *Millennium Falcon* from *Star Wars*. Serious, look."

Anna took a deep breath and looked up to where her uncle was pointing. "It looks like a clam."

"No it doesn't. And check this out—if you squint just right, the little clouds in front of it look like TIE fighters, too," her uncle said, sounding genuinely impressed. "How cool is that?"

"You know, this might go faster if you help me out."

"And deprive you of this learning experience? Nice

soldering job, by the way." Uncle Jack turned his head in her direction. "Oh, I forgot to ask. How was your first day of school?"

"Weird."

"Care to elaborate?" Uncle Jack asked.

"Let me see." Anna didn't look back as she began drilling holes for a small camera mount on top of the green box. "The principal was nice. Kids were friendly. And I think I might have actually made some friends today. So yeah, weird."

"Yeah, that sounds positively awful." Uncle Jack rolled over on his side and propped himself up on his elbow. "I don't think you should ever go back."

Anna couldn't help herself and smiled.

"Not to rush you or anything, but how long is it going to take to wire up this camera thing of yours?" Uncle Jack asked. "I'm getting hungry."

"Just need to configure the settings." Anna removed the laptop from her backpack and plugged in the USB cord.

"So, how are you configuring the camera?"

"I've set up a script that takes a picture every five minutes on its own. But I've also integrated readings from your sensors. Anything moves out here tonight or any sudden bright light and the camera begins shooting video. It also triggers a message on my phone. If someone is out here messing around, we'll catch them." Anna closed the mount with a satisfying click.

"So no thermal scan?" Uncle Jack smiled slyly.

Anna rolled her eyes. "Yeah, that's coming in version two."

CHAPTER 6

In the field outside her bedroom window, a lone figure crept slowly in the darkness toward the house. Its movements were jerky, like jump cuts in a film, and its arms were impossibly long and bone-thin. The creature wore a broad round hat that cloaked its face in shadows. The hat brim glowed white in the sharp moonlight. Anna stood frozen at the window for what seemed like hours—unable to move, to breathe, to do anything but stare at the intruder walking closer.

How long had she been at the window? She couldn't remember. She couldn't remember anything at all, like why the sky was filled with star formations she had never seen and why a gaseous cloud, the deepest color of purple, stretched across the southern sky. *Who put that nebula there?* The cornstalks in the field were at least five feet tall and swaying like waves in a dark green sea, even though the air was stale and unmoving. *They were just seedlings yesterday. Didn't know corn grew so fast.*

The moon, much larger than normal and twice as bright, sat low in the sky, just touching the horizon. Another creature appeared in the cornfield. A twin. It wore the same black outfit, the same hat, and walked with the same herky-jerky movements toward the house. The night was dead silent. No wind. Nothing except for a low-pitched hum that seemed to come from the two approaching figures in the field.

Anna knew they were coming for her.

Ping.

The sound came from nowhere, distant and muted.

Ping.

The sound was sharper this time—closer. The figures in the field seemed to have heard it too. They stopped walking at the same time. In perfect unison, the brims of their hats lifted, slowly revealing their bone-white faces in the stark moonlight.

Anna tried to scream, but her lungs felt frozen. Paralyzed.

Ping.

Anna opened her eyes slowly and blinked several times to clear her vision. She was lying in bed. Her pillow was covered in sweat, just like her hair. She was still disoriented, and her heart raced, but at least she was awake. Her bad dream was over. *That's what it was. A bad dream, right?*

Her phone was blinking on the side table: an alert from the sensor she had installed in the field that afternoon. The home screen read 1:45 a.m. It took Anna a moment to process what was happening, then her eyes snapped open wide. She hopped out of bed and made her way across the room toward her laptop. She stopped by her bedroom window. As much as she didn't want to look, she couldn't help herself and turned her gaze out into the field. For a moment she was sure she'd see those bone-white faces staring up at her. But the field was empty, and the moon was back to its right size and place in the sky. The night was alive with a chorus of crickets.

It felt so real, Anna thought, *more like a memory than a dream.* And, unlike most dreams, the images in her head showed no signs of fading. She took a deep breath and made her way to her desk.

"Let's see if this camera is working." Anna sat down and blinked, adjusting to the bright blue glow of her laptop in the darkness.

Anna cleared the messages from her screen and logged into her cloud drive. She yawned while waiting for the host to resolve.

"Come on, come on, come on." Anna impatiently tapped the Return key.

Several video feeds populated as text links on her screen. She clicked on the link titled *Lake Station*, but the video feed was black even though the counter below was ticking off milliseconds. Anna opened the settings for the remote camera and adjusted the light sensor. Anna started to make out a fuzzy white image moving slowly in a sea of black.

"There we go," Anna said to herself.

More fuzzy white images appeared. *Intruders!* As she adjusted the light settings, the figures became clearer, then snapped into focus.

"Aww, how cute." Anna couldn't help herself. A small deer stared directly into the camera lens. Its big fawn eyes lit up like shiny silver dollars. Behind the fawn was a group of deer drinking water at the edge of the lake. "So you're the little guy that triggered my camera."

For the next two minutes, the stream of images showed the fawn licking the camera mount, which made Anna giggle out loud. She absently watched the small herd graze for a moment and was ready to shut down her laptop when the small deer closest to the camera popped its head up in alarm. All the other deer followed suit. Then the deer were gone. Just like that. *Wow, they're fast.* All that was left was the blur of a small white tail exiting the camera frame.

"Where did you guys go?" Anna said out loud to herself.

Something had scared them, but what? The screen was blank again except for two faint red lights that appeared in the center of the video frame. They were so faint; Anna wasn't sure if they were early-season fireflies. But with each passing second the lights grew brighter, like a car driving toward the camera with its headlights on.

Anna didn't remember seeing a road on the other side of the lake, but she couldn't think of any other explanation. Suddenly the two lights stopped. Instead of veering left or right, the lights floated straight up. Anna let out a gasp and realized she had been holding her breath for the last thirty seconds. A ring of smaller red lights appeared in the next frame, circling the two original lights like a floating hula hoop. The object began to spin in a blur. Its bright light cast a strange red glow across the trees and the knee-high grass and the surface of the lake. A flash, then static. The camera went black.

Anna stared at the screen for a second, then realized she might still be able to see the real thing if she were fast enough. She stumbled from her chair and barely caught her balance by the time she made it to the window. She leaned out just in time to see a red light float silently along the edge of the trees.

Unlike the night before, the light didn't disappear but continued on a course away from the trees and up into the night sky. Anna watched the light climb at a sharp angle, growing fainter until it was swallowed up by a bank of clouds across the valley. The clouds flashed pink like cotton candy, then returned to dark silhouettes outlined by moonlight.

The light was gone. But now she had a record of its passing. Now she had video.

"Uncle Jack!"

CHAPTER 7

"So, what am I looking at here?" Scout asked.

He squinted down at Anna's phone with his back to the sun. Fiona and Lula took turns invading his space as they jockeyed to get a better look. The four sat on the rusted bleachers overlooking the school's baseball diamond. It was lunchtime, and a group of kids were in the middle of a pickup game of baseball. There were loud shouts, the crack of a bat, and clouds of dust kicked up as someone ran the base path, but Anna barely noticed.

"Gaaah, back off, willya? You're steaming up my glasses," Scout said, pushing back against Fiona while crouching over the phone to block her view.

"So, what do you think?" Anna asked nervously.

Scout scrubbed the video back and forth trying to make sense of what he was seeing. He squinted, then opened his eyes wide. He swiveled his head back and forth in sync with the direction of the video.

"I don't know, Anna." Scout shook his head and handed the phone back. "It's weird. I'll give you that. But it's also a little fuzzy. I have no idea what I'm looking at."

"That's pretty much what my uncle said. He also said it wasn't a drone—at least not one of his. So no one has a clue. . . ." Anna's voice trailed off.

Someone whistled sharply from the baseball diamond, enough to catch everyone's attention. It was the kind of effortless whistle that Anna had always wished she could do. The boy named Del, the one who made Anna mildly hyperventilate the day before, smiled brightly from third base and raised two fingers.

"Fiona! You're up in two," Del shouted, then looked directly at Anna. "Hey, new girl. You play?"

Anna froze. Of course she played. She knew she could hit as well as anyone on the field, except maybe for that moose named Max. She searched for the perfect words—the confident, charming string of words she would say in reply. The words that would make Del remember her past lunchtime, through the afternoon, and for the remainder of the year.

But the best she could muster was a half-hearted smile and something that sounded like a cross between a grunt and "Yeah," more of an expulsion of air than spoken word. Del shrugged and returned his attention back to the game. Opportunity lost.

"Yeah, yeah. I'll be right there," Fiona said, waving her hand dismissively. She looked back at Anna. "Can I see your phone again?"

Anna, still mortified, handed over the phone. Fiona and Lula leaned up against each other to replay the video. Lula shook her head in amazement. Fiona's grin spread as her eyes widened.

"This. Is. Awesome!" Lula said. "I think you have aliens, Anna."

Fiona handed the phone back. "So you've seen this light two nights in a row now, right?"

Anna nodded *yes*.

"So there's a chance we can see it again tonight," Fiona said, grinning. "Maybe we can head on over to the lake and look around. I know it's last minute, but are you up for a sleepover?"

"I'd love to, but what would the neighbors think?" Scout didn't miss a beat.

Fiona worked hard to ignore him. Lula just closed her eyes and shook her head. But Anna hadn't heard a word Scout said. She'd never had a sleepover. Dog sitting didn't count. This would be another first in a week filled with firsts.

"Yeah, that would be great." Anna smiled, the dull ache from earlier already starting to fade. "I'm sure my uncle won't mind."

"Sweet. Shoot me your address," Fiona said. "I'll text you before we head on over."

Scout looked back and forth between Anna and Fiona.

"Wait. Is this a bring-your-own-sleeping-bag kind of deal, or will accommodations be provided?"

CHAPTER 8

Uncle Jack had given Anna his old bike to use. It weighed a ton and was ancient and rusted. She had to stand up on the pedals and push down with all her weight to get it started, but once she did, the thing could really move. After dinner, she made her way down the dirt road to the end of the lane, then leaned the bike up against the white fence and peered down the road in both directions. No sign of her friends yet. Across the road, a cow absently stared at her while slowly chewing a large clump of grass.

"Hi," Anna said, half-waving.

The cow snorted in reply.

Anna looked down at her phone. No new texts. The air was still warm, and the flies that swarmed the cow looked like a halo in the evening light. Her shadow stretched far down the road. Anna lifted her arms to her side and watched her shadow wings unfurl. She began waving her arms, trying to make the motion smooth like a wave, when she heard a voice behind her in the distance.

"Nice noodle arms," someone shouted.

Anna jumped and turned. Scout was pedaling furiously to keep up with Fiona and Lula.

Their brakes squeaked in unison as the three friends rolled to a stop.

"Hey, Anna," Lula said, smiling.

"Hey, guys."

"Sorry, but it looks like we picked up a stray on the way here." Fiona nodded toward Scout.

"Don't worry. I've had my shots," Scout said, smiling.

Anna straddled her bike.

"My uncle says the best stakeout spot is the hillside over the lake. It's supposed to have a clear view of the valley from up there. Follow me."

The three girls pedaled down the lane side by side, just fast enough that they could still carry on a conversation. Scout followed, singing to himself while weaving his bike back and forth in a snake pattern.

As they rolled closer to the farmhouse, the research barns and greenhouses came into view, glistening in the evening sun. An autonomous electric tractor rolled slowly down the center of the barnyard like a giant green toy as a dozen people made their way along paths that connected the buildings. The end of the workday. Patches of conversations in multiple languages faded in and out as the friends rode their bikes through the center of activity. A small white drone buzzed twenty feet above their heads as it headed in a straight line to the fields in the north.

"Your uncle's place is huge." Fiona looked around the facility in awe. "I didn't know all of this was here. You can't see it from the road."

"Yeah, it's pretty cool. Some kind of research farm," Anna said.

"Wait! I'm an idiot." Fiona stopped her bike. "Your last name is Armstrong, right?"

Anna slowed down and looked back. "Yeah. Why?"

"Doh!" Fiona slapped her forehead. "Your uncle is Dr. Armstrong."

"You know him?" Anna leaned against her handlebars.

"All the kids in 4-H know him. He and Dr. Gloria judge the innovation event every year," Fiona said.

"4-H?" Anna asked.

"Yeah, 4-H. It's this youth thing for future farmers. Fiona and I took first place at the fair last summer," Lula said. She and Fiona high-fived.

"Future freaks, more like it," Scout said as he pedaled his bike in circles around them. "I thought we were supposed to be hunting aliens, come on!"

He quit circling and started pedaling straight toward the farmhouse.

"But that's not the . . . direction," Anna said quietly.

"He'll figure it out eventually," Lula said. "Let's go before he notices."

Anna stood up and leaned down hard on the bike pedal to gain traction. By the time she hit the dirt lane that led to Tyson Lake, she was moving full speed. The three girls laughed as they made their escape. Their bike tires flew over the deep ruts in the road as they sped uphill toward the setting sun. Warm wind whipped Anna's hair and made her eyes water. Within a half mile, they neared the top of the steep hill and slowly rolled to a stop. The valley opened before them. A dense patch of woods lined the lake in one direction. Farmland seemed to spread out forever in the other. A flock of starlings, silhouetted against the evening sky, whirled in constantly shifting patterns just above the light reflecting off the lake. Amid the quiet, in the far distance, they could hear Scout shouting for them to wait up.

"Think we should?" Anna asked.

Lula and Fiona shrugged. The three laid their bikes on the ground and stretched.

"By the way, did you know Dr. Gloria is Del's uncle?" Lula smiled knowingly.

A dull ache struck Anna just above her solar plexus. "Who?"

"Who?" Lula laughed. "Look at her acting like she doesn't know what I'm talking about."

"What?" Anna shook her head. "I don't even—"

"Even what? I saw your expression when Del called out to you today," Fiona said.

"You guys are crazy. I don't like him. I don't even know him. I don't know anybody."

Lula opened her eyes in disbelief and stared accusingly. "Oh! You're so lying."

"Well, I mean, sure, he's cute and all. . . ." Anna's voice trailed off. She frowned. "Was it really that obvious?"

"To everyone except Del. He's clueless. Always has been. Cute and clueless," Fiona said.

Anna buried her face in her hands. "Oh my God. I want to die."

"Cute and clueless. You girls . . . must be . . . talking about me." Scout rolled to a stop behind them. He was winded.

"Little legs couldn't keep up?" Fiona asked.

Scout fell off his bike in exaggerated exhaustion and rolled onto his back. Beads of sweat lined his forehead.

"Can't get rid of me that easily. I'm too"—he huffed, pausing for a breath—"fast."

Fiona pulled a blanket from the back of her bike and unfurled it over a small clearing overlooking the lake. The three girls sat down, legs crossed. Scout made his way over, and the four sat in silence for a moment, taking in the view before them.

"Oh man—I know where I'm hanging out this summer," Scout said, chewing on a long blade of grass and pointing at the lake. "The Armstrong public pool, right here."

"I think there's a height requirement," Fiona said. "Sorry."

"Ha-ha. You're hysterical. But seriously. This is sweet." Scout pointed down toward the lake. "You even have your own little island, Anna. We could totally throw a party there. Turtle Island."

A small hump of land, covered in trees and bush, floated a couple hundred yards from shore. Scout was right: it was small and looked like a turtle shell peeking above the water, but it seemed big enough for a campout.

Anna showed her friends where she had seen the light from the night before and pointed out the direction of her uncle's house just behind the patch of woods. They spent several minutes quietly surveying the sky, then boredom set in. The next hour passed as they talked about music, the other kids at school, the movies they loved, and the foods they hated. And just like that, they had forgotten about the mysterious light as the evening sky turned from a pale orange to a deep plum blue. Stars began to dot the sky behind them. Then the sound.

Lula was the first to hear it. She popped up and began scanning the sky for the source.

"Uh, can you hear that?" Lula said, sounding uneasy. She stared down at her arms.

"Hear what?" Fiona asked.

Anna felt the sound before she could hear it—a kind of static shock, as if someone had rubbed a balloon across her skin. The hair on her head began to stand up now. Her body itched.

"Whoa—that's weird." Anna stood up and began rubbing her arms.

"What the—" Scout jumped up as if someone had pinched

him. He began bouncing back and forth and laughing in a panic.

From nowhere and everywhere at once, an impossibly deep horn blared across the sky, followed by silence. The four friends stood unmoving. Seconds ticked by, but no one was willing to move.

"Uh . . . that wasn't me." Scout tried to smile.

"Shut up, Scout," Fiona whispered.

"Maybe it's—"

Another trumpet blast, but this time the pitch changed, becoming a sound like twisting metal that vibrated through their bodies. Lula jumped. Scout let out a squeal.

"Is anybody recording this?" Fiona shouted above the noise.

Anna started the video on her phone, but she didn't know where to point. The sound was everywhere. Another horn— that's the only way Anna could describe it—began to blare in a slightly higher pitch. Then another quickly followed. All three sounds ran into one another like the sky was ripping open.

The starlings that had been flying in synchronized patterns scattered. Their form dissolved into individual black dots, each flying in a different direction. Lula covered her ears and shut her eyes tightly. Fiona put her arm around her instinctively. Scout, still laughing, ran back to his bike. Anna kept filming, frantically looking across the sky for the source of the sound. From the corner of her eye, she saw a flash of light. She turned in time to see a figure in white on the far side of the lake: a woman floating a good twenty feet above the far shoreline. Anna dropped her phone. The woman vanished, and suddenly the sound stopped as an echo rolled across the valley like a departing wave.

CHAPTER 9

Fiona and Lula lay curled up under a pile of blankets and over a patchwork of pillows Uncle Jack had spread out on her bedroom floor. Anna was propped up on her side in bed. The lights were off, but the moonlight streaming in from her bedroom window was bright enough to outline their faces in blue. They spoke in hushed voices.

Scout had left minutes after the final echo faded away. No smart comments. Barely a goodbye before he pedaled away as fast as he could. He was shaken up. They were all shaken up. The three girls had planned to camp outside under the stars and watch for the lights, but now they were more than glad to be inside.

As hard as she tried, Anna couldn't stop shaking. It wasn't fear. It was a sense she had touched the unknown. Something not of this world. She wanted to tell her friends of the woman she saw floating by the lakeside, but the whole thing felt like a fragment of a dream now, and she couldn't find the words. She laid her head back against her pillow and let her arm hang over the side.

Lula reached out with her small, warm hand and held

Anna's arm. Anna quit shaking and smiled at her friend. Lula reached out with her free hand and locked fingers with Fiona. The three smiled at one another, their eyes lit by moonlight.

CHAPTER 10

The girls woke up with the sunrise. A hot pancake-and-eggs breakfast was waiting for them downstairs. When they asked Uncle Jack about the night before, he said he thought it was a weather phenomenon. He called it a sky quake, but he wasn't sure. Anna nodded in agreement, but she was sure he was wrong. The woman floating above the lake was no weather phenomenon. The lights, her dream, the sounds from the sky. All of it pointed to a larger mystery, and all directions pointed toward the lake.

Uncle Jack sat down and joined the girls for breakfast. The table was quiet at first. The three girls still had sleep in their eyes. But by the end of breakfast he had them all laughing with tales of Herbie, the farmhands, and the challenges of managing an international team. Soon after breakfast finished and plates were cleaned and stacked away, Fiona's mother arrived to pick them up.

Uncle Jack and Anna stood shoulder to shoulder as they waved goodbye from the front porch.

"I'm heading into town to run a few errands. Want to come

along?" Uncle Jack asked as he watched the car disappear from view.

"No, I think I want to explore here on the farm," Anna said. "If that's okay."

"It's exactly what I'd want to do when I was your age," Uncle Jack said. "Let me know if you need anything."

Anna looked up with a crooked grin.

"There is one thing. What's the fastest way to the lake from here?"

———

The dust from Uncle Jack's truck hadn't even settled before Anna was out the door and across the dirt driveway to the empty field just beyond. She carried a backpack, her journal, and wore a thin coat of insect repellent. Uncle Jack had given her a rundown of where to go and what to watch out for, and deer ticks topped the list.

An irrigation ditch about twelve feet across separated the far edge of the field and the entrance to the woods. Anna walked along the ditch, keeping pace with a small stick that spun and bounced along with the flowing water until she reached a wooden plank that served as a makeshift bridge. The plank bowed in the middle and creaked as she walked across the irrigation ditch like a tightrope artist, but it held.

Anna took a step into the woods and felt as if she had crossed a barrier. Sound was muted, and the temperature was a good five to ten degrees cooler here. Light filtered down from the canopy of leaves, making patterns on the forest floor. The deeper she made her way into the woods, the quieter it became, except for the snap and pop of fallen branches she stepped on. *How long had it been?* It felt like an hour, but her phone showed only five minutes had passed. Then, just ahead, she could make out a clearing.

The trees and brush opened as she made her way down a slight embankment, revealing Tyson Lake. She climbed her way to the top of one of the large boulders that lined the shore and looked out. Across the lake, she saw the sensor and camera she had set up two days before. To her right was a large meadow surrounded by trees and with no road access. She looked down from her vantage point and could see her reflection shimmering in the water below. The water was deep. *Perfect for diving,* she thought. She'd have to bring her new friends here the next time they came over.

Anna worked her way down the boulder. She picked up a large rock and tossed it as far as she could over the lake. The rock splashed off the water's surface with a deep, satisfying *kerplunk.* She picked up a smaller rock, round and flat, and skipped it across the lake, sending out a succession of concentric ripples. She started scanning the shore for more skipping rocks, picking up and discarding rocks as she walked, until she looked up and realized she had made it all the way to the meadow's edge. Her stomach tightened. This is where she'd seen the phantom woman the night before.

Wind rippled in waves across the tall grass and wildflowers. The whole landscape seemed to be shifting—or at least everything except a strip of grass that ran from the water's edge to the middle of the meadow.

"Weird," Anna said softly.

Across the clearing, a bird flew along the tree line, then disappeared for several seconds before reappearing above the lake as if someone had spliced out frames in a film. A glitch in reality. Anna blinked, took in a deep breath, then tried to take in the landscape without focusing on any one thing. Everything looked normal, but something felt off.

Then she noticed it: a small egg-shaped patch halfway

across the meadow. It looked like a smudge on a camera lens. She could see the grass move behind it, but something was definitely there. Transparent, almost like the air was thinning.

Anna picked up another rock and began tossing it back and forth in her hands. Something was out there. She was sure.

The meadow was at least three hundred feet across. Maybe four. The weird smudge-like thing was maybe halfway across. One hundred fifty feet away. She had thrown a baseball that far before, but the rock was a little heavier, and its edges created drag. Anna calculated the vertical angle of the throw and wind speed and figured it was a stretch, but doable. She spun her arm around a couple of times like a pitcher warming up, then took a deep breath. She brought her arm back in a smooth throwing motion and let it fly.

The rock arced gracefully across the sky a good sixty feet before it stopped in midair with a metallic ping. It seemed to float for a second, then fell straight down to the earth.

"Huh?" Anna said out loud.

Had she hit a bird? Impossible. The sky was completely clear. Anna picked up another rock and chucked it across the meadow.

Ptinnng!

The rock stopped midair, just like the one before, and fell straight down to the patch of unmoving grass. Part of Anna wanted to turn and run. The other part, the one that drove her to build rockets and leap from the edge of her house onto a trampoline, told her to move forward. Anna made her way out into the meadow. Ten steps in and Anna heard a dull hum and felt an electric charge. The hair on her arms began to stand up, just like the night before. Thirty steps in and her face banged into something rigid and cold and invisible.

"Owww!" Anna grabbed her nose and fell back hard on her butt.

She looked up, rubbing her nose. Nothing but sky. Anna

slowly reached out with her hand and touched an invisible surface. It felt smooth, almost wet, and cold like glass. But there was nothing there. *A glass wall?*

She began to move along the wall, tapping on the surface with her knuckles and trying to make sense of what she was experiencing. *Who would build something like this, and why?* The invisible wall seemed to curve as she made her way closer to the shoreline, but she couldn't tell. Her hand left no prints on the surface. There were no smudges, no imperfections. Then her left hand felt an electric charge emanating from the surface. It was the blurry patch she had seen before, but up close it didn't look blurry. It just looked dim, like the lights had been turned down slightly.

Anna reached her hand out toward the dim patch of air. As she neared the surface, the electric charge grew more intense, her fingertips tingling. Her hand felt resistance like a repelling magnet, then the tips of her fingers disappeared. Poof.

Anna let out a shout and yanked her hand back. The tingling stopped. She was afraid to look down at her hand, but she could feel the tips of her fingers. She held her hand in front of her face. All digits accounted for.

"Oh boy," Anna whispered.

There was no way she was turning back now. Not now. Not this close. She planted her feet and pushed both arms through to the elbows. The air felt the same on the other side. Her arms were still attached. All good. She shook her head and took in a deep breath before plunging her head through to the other side.

CHAPTER 11

Even at a very young age, Anna had learned to trust her rational mind—her own clear-eyed view of the world. But the second she peered through the invisible wall, that trust slipped away like the strength in her legs. She couldn't make sense of what she was seeing in front of her. Light reflected off shiny surfaces, and the dim hum from the other side of the wall was now a bright chorus.

The first thing she noticed was the house, but it didn't look like any house she had ever seen before; it was part cathedral, part modernist home, part alien spaceship. It rested on top of a small hill with grass lawns gently sloping down from each side. The exterior was made almost entirely of glass, with white stone columns and a dome-like roof. Set in front of the house, a crystal spire reached high into the sky, its surface shimmering like water and reflecting the clouds passing by.

Anna pulled her head back just to check if her eyes were playing tricks on her. On one side, there was nothing but empty meadow. She leaned her head back through the invisible barrier. On the other side were lights, a house, and a giant alien spire. She spent the next minute leaning back and forth and wondering who had broken the laws of physics before stepping on through to the other side.

Two objects buzzed up from behind the house and began chasing each other around the spire like hummingbirds playing tag. They moved so fast Anna couldn't quite tell what they were. Then one of the objects slowed down long enough for her to make out its form. It was the size of a small child. It had two arms and two legs, but its torso was rounded and fire-engine red. The object floated silently in midair like a buoy bobbing in water. Slowly, its dome-like head swiveled around, and two bright lights pointed straight at Anna. She wanted to turn and run, but her legs were frozen in place.

Like a blur, the object descended from the sky to just feet above Anna's head. A floating garbage can. It stared at Anna as if it were trying to make sense of her. Anna stared back, also trying to make sense of this thing floating above her head. It definitely wasn't human, but there were human markings along its side. Numbers and letters. And it suddenly clicked.

"You're a robot," Anna whispered.

The thing beeped a series of birdlike notes and then buzzed back up the hill to the other side of the house, out of view. The bright chorus suddenly stopped as if someone had turned off a switch, leaving Anna in silence. Nothing moved, including Anna, who stood paralyzed—afraid to run back, afraid to go forward. Just as she had worked up enough courage to move, another figure gracefully floated up from behind the house.

This time there was no mistaking the figure floating toward her. Even from this distance, Anna could tell she was a woman, her body a silhouette with the sun against her back. Anna shielded her eyes from the glare. The woman glided across the air like a surfer on water and landed gently within feet of Anna. She had jet-black hair and wore a white bodysuit that sparkled like the surface of water depending on how the light hit it. Even in the glare, Anna could tell she was the most beautiful woman she'd ever seen.

"Oh my. You can see all of this, can't you? Me. My home." The woman frowned. She took a step closer. "This is a problem."

Anna didn't like the sound of that and took one step back.

The woman must have sensed it and smiled gently. "Not for you, my young friend. The problem is mine. I won't hurt you."

"Are you an alien?" Anna asked, surprised by how small her voice sounded.

The woman smiled even more broadly. "That depends."

"On?"

"On where you call home. Are you from Earth?"

"Yes."

"Then no, I'm not an alien."

"What are you then?" Anna asked.

"A girl like you, just older. My name is Mara."

"My name is Anna," she said. "Where are you from?"

Mara paused for a moment and then lifted a finger. "That is an excellent question, but before I can answer any questions—I'm sure you have many—I will need you to do me a favor first. Will you promise to wait right here?"

Anna nodded, still trying to take it all in. She watched Mara float ten feet above her head, wink reassuringly, and then glide noiselessly away. Her boots left a trail of blue light behind her as she flew. The large glass window on the second floor silently slid open, and Mara disappeared into one of the bright corners of the house. Anna began to mentally catalog all she had just seen and check off viable explanations for each. If Mara wasn't an alien, it left few choices. Anna was either suffering hallucinations or completely nuts—or a combination thereof. Or her view of the possible had just expanded to science fiction and comic books.

Mara emerged from the house and glided silently back down to the ground. She wore a pair of skintight gloves. *She didn't have those before,* Anna thought.

"Before we begin, I need to verify something. Can you look directly into my palm for me?" Mara lifted her hand up like a cop stopping traffic. In the center of her palm glowed a pulsing white light that spun in a lazy clockwise motion.

Anna squinted and swore she could see her own reflection in the light.

"That's weird," Anna whispered under her breath. She found it hard to look away from the spinning light. It was so pretty. And now she noticed a green pulse and the calming sound of running water.

"I'm sure everything seems strange now." Mara's voice was distant. "But it will all make sense in just a moment."

"What are you doing to me?" Anna struggled to keep from falling asleep.

"I'm doing us both a favor. Trust me, it's better this way."

Anna felt herself slipping away, losing control, falling asleep. But she wouldn't give in. She took in a deep breath and began reciting digits of *pi* in her head, a technique she had used for years when she felt things were spinning out of control. *3.141592 . . . 65358979 . . .* fifteen decimal places in and the buzzing in her head slowly began to fade . . . *323846264338327.* Thirty decimal places in and her head had cleared completely. The face in the reflection was her own again. Anna blinked several times. Her image blinked back. The only effect of her recent spell was that she felt rested and wide awake.

"The neurons that assist in your short-term memory have been interrupted, effectively erasing the last fifteen minutes from your memory," Mara continued. "You'll be dazed for a couple of minutes. But I promise you, when you awaken, you won't suffer—"

"I'm not sleepy."

A look of doubt clouded Mara's face, but she continued. "The full effects of the memory interruption will have already settled in—"

"No, serious. I feel fine," Anna said.

Mara let her hand drop slowly and cocked her head to the side, like a doctor trying to get a read on her patient. She waved her other hand in front of Anna's face. "How can that be? Are you sure you don't feel sleepy?"

"Nope."

"No blurred vision? No dizziness?"

"Nope." Anna shook her head.

"Well, that didn't work." Mara sighed and then looked sternly at Anna. "You know you're making this very difficult for me."

"Can I ask my questions now?" Anna stood her ground. Her curiosity had effectively trumped any fear she may have felt.

Anna wasn't insane. She was sure of it. This was real, as implausible as it seemed. She crossed hallucinations from her short list of explanations and was left with one likely remaining scenario. The more she thought of it, the more she was filled with a growing sense of excitement—a sense her entire world was just about to change. Anna took a deep breath.

"You're from the future, aren't you?"

Mara's eyes opened wide in surprise. "What makes you say that?"

"Well, if you're not an alien, it's the only other explanation that makes sense. Robots that fly. Some kind of antigravity thing. A weird cloaking device around your house that no one can see. We're hundreds of years from any technology like this," Anna said.

Mara sighed. "Ninety-three years to be exact, at least for the antigravity boots."

"Ha! I knew it. I knew it!" Anna pointed her finger at Mara and burst out in laughter. "Antigravity boots? Did you just really say that? That is the coolest thing ever. No, wait, time travel is the coolest thing ever. Can I hug you?"

Anna wrapped her arms around Mara before she could respond.

"Sorry, I just wanted to make sure you were real," Anna said. She released her grasp and stepped back. "Okay, so where do we start?"

"By you turning around and going home to your parents and forgetting you ever saw me." Mara pointed toward the clearing in the forest.

"I can't." Anna's voice cracked. "I don't have any parents."

Anna realized she had never had to utter those words before—not in that way. They sounded empty and far removed, as if she were describing the life of a stranger. Mara let her arm fall slowly to her side. Her face softened as she stepped forward.

"You're an orphan?" Mara asked.

Anna nodded.

"Just like me," Mara said. She placed her hand on Anna's shoulder.

The two stared at each other for a moment. Mara's lips were pursed tight and she didn't blink. Finally, her face relaxed.

"I'll make a deal with you on two conditions," Mara said.

Anna allowed herself a small smile. "Yes?"

"One, I'll answer your questions if I can. If I can't, don't push it. I have my reasons. Two, you can't tell anyone about this place or about me." Mara counted off the conditions with her fingers. "Not a single person. Not a word. Ever."

"Ever? Really? Come on." Anna's shoulders slumped. "You want me to keep the single greatest thing that has happened to me a secret? I'll explode."

"Not a word."

"And what happens if I do tell?" Anna probed.

"I have some things a lot worse than the memory interrupter at my disposal. Do we have a deal?" Mara put her hand out.

At that moment, Anna would have agreed to anything to spend more time in this strange new world. She grabbed Mara's hand and shook it hard. "Deal. Now, where can we start?"

CHAPTER 12

Anna found herself in an impossibly large room with curved white walls and a tall ceiling. Light emanated from all sides like an artificial sun. To the east, a giant glass wall provided an unobstructed view of the lake and the trees just beyond. In the corner of the room grew a blossoming fruit tree; its top branches mushroomed out at the ceiling, and its white petals lined the floor.

Anna had never seen so much *outside* inside a home before. She swore she could even feel a breeze. She sat in a swivel chair and spun in circles, taking in a 360-degree view of the room. Mara sat across from her, behind a table that shimmered like liquid metal. Her robot floated just to her side.

"Here are the ground rules. You have fifteen minutes to ask me questions. After that, I'm going to ask SID to escort you to the edge of the woods, and you will never come back here again," Mara said.

"SID? You named your robot SID."

"Of course not. SID named itself. And it's not just a robot, it's the AI that makes this entire facility possible." Mara waved her hand. "The robot here is just one of the forms that SID can take."

<But the form I assume most often is that of Mara's friend and protector.>

SID's calm, otherworldly voice seemed to originate from inside Anna's head.

"Nice to meet you, SID." Anna waved her hand as she looked around the room to identify the source of the voice.

<Nice to meet you too, Anna.>

"Now. Let's get this over with. Like I said before, if I choose not to answer your question, I have my reasons. You persist and our conversation is finished. Understand?"

Anna nodded and threw her backpack on the ground.

Mara motioned to the small red robot, which was floating just feet away from the table.

"SID—timer, please," Mara commanded.

A small, thin shaft of red light floated inches above the robot's domed head. Holographic numbers floated above the light. Seconds started to audibly tick backward from fifteen minutes.

"See this clock? It's your timer. You now have fourteen minutes and forty-five seconds."

"Wait! I didn't know we started," Anna complained.

"Fourteen minutes and thirty-eight seconds." Mara pointed to the timer.

"Okay, okay. Can you at least make SID stop that ticking sound? It's distracting."

"SID, stop ticking."

Mara lightly tapped the robot's dome. Anna took a deep breath and tried to collect herself.

"All right. First question. What year are you from?" Anna asked.

"Based on your calendar? The year 2187."

"2187," Anna said absently. Then the reality of the date set in. Her mouth dropped open. "Really?! Over 150 years from now?"

"Is that a question?" Mara frowned.

"No. No!" Anna had carefully lined up her questions in her head, but now they began to crash into one another. Buffer overrun. It took a second for her to pry one away from the wreckage. "Uh . . . okay. Okay. I've got one. How far have we traveled in space?"

"By probe? By manned spaceflight? You'll need to be more specific," Mara said.

"Manned spaceflight then."

"Humanity has ventured into interstellar space," Mara answered.

Anna waited for Mara to continue. But Mara just sat quietly and tapped the timer with her index finger.

"Can you give me a little more detail here?" Anna asked.

"You didn't structure the question for greater detail. Here, let me help you. We have research outposts on Titan and Europa. Colonies on Mars. We have space stations throughout the solar system, several exploratory ships in interstellar space, and even a Disney Park on the moon," Mara answered.

"Yes!" Anna pumped her fist. "I can't tell you how much I wanted to hear that. Have you ever traveled in space?"

"Just to the moon for vacation. But I have two cousins who live on Mars."

"Oh man, that is so cool. Cousins on Mars." Anna wanted to ask more, but she knew she only had so much time left, and she had so many questions to go. "Okay. Next question. Are aliens real?"

"Yes." Mara blinked once, silent, then blinked again.

"Aaargh. You're killing me!" Anna rolled her eyes. "What are the aliens called? What do they look like? Are they friendly? Super advanced?"

"Which ones?"

"There's more than one?!" Anna's eyes opened wide.

"Think about it. There are hundreds of billions of galaxies. Trillions of stars. We have an untold number of habitable planets in the Milky Way alone. The universe is teeming with life. We've been able to see distant civilizations through satellite imagery. We've even been in contact with several alien races. The problem is they don't think in remotely the same way as we do, and we don't have a clue how to communicate," Mara said. "We're still working on that."

"Bummer. Okay. I've got another one. Why do you look so normal?"

"Please clarify 'normal.'"

"You're from the future. I figured you'd have cyborg hands. Laser eyes. Something like that," Anna said.

"Hmm. Let me see if I can explain it in terms you'll understand. Computer–brain interfaces were banned by all governmental agencies after widespread cases of psycho-terminus dissociative disorder."

"Huh?"

"Connecting with computers full-time is a good way to go crazy," Mara translated.

"Oh," Anna said softly. "Have we found a cure for cancer?"

Mara rolled her eyes. "Ages ago. Probably while you're still a young woman. By my time, we have a cure for almost everything. Well, not everything. There's still stupidity. We haven't found a cure for that, but pretty much everything else can be addressed through gene therapy."

"So does that mean people are immortal? Are you immortal?"

"No. Not immortal. Nature still makes sure we have an expiration date." Mara shook her head, a slight smile lifting the corners of her mouth. "But most of us can expect to live two, maybe even three times *your* average life span."

"Wow. You must have a lot of old people."

"I guess we do. But we don't think of it that way. People age differently in our time. Time is perceived differently."

"Living that long must really change things." Anna looked puzzled.

"Like?"

"If you live that long, what happens to marriage or work or families? Do people still get married?" Anna asked.

"With algorithmic precision."

"Huh?"

"Most marriages are arranged by algorithm. Math. It's surprisingly efficient," Mara said.

"That sounds awful," Anna said, her features scrunching up in a stinky face. "Are you married?"

"Oh my, no!" Mara tilted her head back and laughed out loud. "I opted out of the *algorithm* while I was still in university."

"Ugh, there's so much I want to know," Anna said under her breath.

"Then choose your questions wisely."

"All right, all right. Uh . . ." Anna tapped her fingertips to her temples, looked down and then back sharply. "Please tell me we've had more than one female president."

"President of what?"

"Of the United States, of course."

"Oh yes. That one. Well, that's complicated." Mara frowned. "More complicated than I have time to explain."

"Wait. Just how different is the future?"

"Frame your questions in a way I can answer, please," Mara said.

Anna felt a growing sense of pressure. Too much to learn. There was no way to get a complete picture of what the future looked like with so little time. *Wait . . . picture.*

"What does the future look like?" Anna asked.

"Look like?"

"Yes—your buildings, cities, plant life, people. All of it. You have to have pictures, right?"

"Now *that* is a good question." Mara smiled.

Mara drew a large circle on the surface of the table with her index finger. Wherever she touched, the surface seemed to melt and flow. Like metallic plants growing at high speed, organic shapes began to rise from the table's surface. Anna jumped back in surprise, then began to giggle in nervous wonder. It was the single greatest special effect she had ever seen.

"Welcome to my world," Mara said.

The forms were unfamiliar at first. Then, as the shapes grew, pixel by pixel, Anna began to make out miniature buildings and roadways built to scale. But the buildings looked unlike anything she had ever seen before. Some of the structures twisted like corkscrews. Others looked like crystal formations jutting up into the sky. Three of the buildings towered above the rest, thin shafts blossoming like lotus petals at the top. She looked more closely and realized the lotus petals were actually parks with trees and fountains. Gardens in the sky. Just above the cityscape, which now stood at least four feet tall, small translucent clouds floated by until they reached the end of the table and disappeared. The scale model was alive with life and light.

Beneath the clouds, giant airships floated between the buildings. Smaller airships floated in a line of traffic. On the ground below, there were parks and walkways surrounding a lake and a river. Anna leaned in and looked more closely. She could even make out tiny people moving along the water's edge and the pathways through the park.

Anna ran her fingers through one of the small clouds in front of her. The mist swirled around her fingers like an eddy in a stream and then re-formed to make a new cloud shape before floating away.

"What is this stuff?" Anna asked as she stared at her hand.

"Electrostatic carbon allotropes."

"Um . . . what?" Anna asked.

"Programmable matter, a kind of universal building material. It's easy for SID to fabricate out of simple elements. No need for storage. Almost everything we design is made of it, including the chair you're sitting on. This house. My clothes." Mara touched her left wrist, and her bodysuit instantly changed from white to red. "See, it can even change color and shape."

"Oh, that is so awesome!" Anna laughed.

"It's self-cleaning too. Comes in handy when traveling back in time."

Anna continued to scan the city, making new discoveries. Tiny birds flew in a flock above the lake. Boats hovered above the river. She was suddenly overcome with an overwhelming sense of hope. This was her own personal window into the future. Not an imagined future, but a real future with real people. No robot armies. No zombie apocalypse. Just a landscape more beautiful than she could have imagined.

"We actually made it." Anna looked up at Mara.

"Excuse me?"

"We survived."

"You mean humankind as a species? Yes, we did, I suppose. But that too is complicated," Mara said. "That's all I can say."

Anna wanted to ask what she meant, but she remembered her promise.

"What's it like? I mean, the world you live in, society. I know people are married off by algorithm—weird. You have rocket cars. You also have antigravity boots, programmable matter. And, based on what I see from SID, you have artificial intelligence. But what else is there?" Anna stopped herself.

"Wait. Let me rephrase that. What's the single greatest invention of your time?"

"Isn't it obvious?" Mara raised a single eyebrow.

"You mean time travel? When was it invented?"

"Very recently. I should know, since I'm the one who invented it." Mara allowed herself a smile.

"You?! You're the one who invented time travel?" Anna pointed at Mara. "That's amazing. How?"

"That answer will take longer than the time you have remaining, I'm afraid."

"Then tell me what you can."

"Let me see if I can give you the short version. For over a hundred years, researchers have been trying to get free energy from the vacuum of space—primarily for interstellar travel, but with no luck. That is until I found a shortcut."

"A shortcut?"

"I'd been working on energy extraction for almost five years. I tried superconductive materials, quantum vacuums. But, like many great discoveries, I stumbled upon mine by mistake. Instead of free energy, I created a rip in space-time instead. A hole that curved back along a temporal path, like a tunnel to the past or future." Mara made a spiral gesture with her index finger, then shrugged. "I learned to control it—sort of—and here I am."

"So you're just a tourist here?"

Mara's expression barely changed, but Anna detected a micro-expression—a small sign of sadness in her eyes, a downturn of the corners of her mouth.

"No. I'm afraid my time traveling days are over," Mara said.

"Wait. Are you staying here?"

Mara looked out the window toward the lake beyond. "I suppose I am. But it's more than that. I can't go home, Anna. There is no home to go back to."

"I don't understand."

Mara looked back from the window but still didn't make eye contact with Anna. She looked down at the scale model of her city instead.

"I wanted to try an experiment: to go back 100 years to the time of the great warming. I've always been fascinated by that time. I promised myself I would stay no longer than fifteen minutes. I'd interact with no one. The risk seemed so low. . . ." Mara's voice trailed off. "But, when I returned home to my time, my home had changed. It was gone."

"You mean like Armageddon?"

"No, not Armageddon. Everything looked the same. The city. My lab. Everything. Except—" Mara paused. Her eyes were glassy. "My parents didn't know me. Even worse, they didn't even know each other. By going back in time, I had somehow changed the future. A future where my parents never met."

"If they never met, then that means you were . . . never born," Anna said softly. "That's why you say you're an orphan."

"Precisely."

"Oh, that's so sad!" Anna paused. "Wait! Why don't you just go back and fix what you messed up, or find a way to get your parents together, like in the movies?"

"I tried, but every time I went back, I created a new future. Some worse. Some much worse. But none of them the same. You see, Anna, every time I traveled, I was changing the course of history. I changed whole families, people's dreams, their futures. I had no right."

"Then why are you here?"

"I had no place else to go." Mara looked up from the cityscape and smiled. "I asked SID to program a place and time at random for us to live out our lives in isolation. So it was chance that brought us here to this beautiful meadow, next to this beautiful lake. And, to make sure, I destroyed the very equipment that allowed me to time travel."

"So you really *are* stuck."

"Yes. And now I hope you understand why I can't be seen or interact with anyone, including you. I promised myself I would never deprive someone else of their future like I was deprived of mine."

"Well, it's too late for that. Based on what you just said, you've already changed my future. So . . ."

Mara looked over at the timer, which now read *0:00*, and then back at Anna. "I'm afraid it's time for you to go."

Anna pushed back in her chair and planted her feet as if she were trying to glue herself to the ground.

"No. I don't want this to end. There's too much I want to learn. Please!" Anna pleaded.

"SID. Can you escort Anna away?"

"Nooo!" Anna shouted. "Wait. Listen. If I found you, then someone else is going to find you. I can help."

Mara stared at Anna for a moment before responding. "You, help me? How?"

"The last two nights, I saw lights floating over the lake. Those were yours, right?"

"SID, what is she talking about?" Mara looked annoyed.

<Apparently, the cloaking device on our exploratory probes malfunctioned. Running diagnostics now.>

"We've never had a problem with our cloaking device before. Why now, SID?"

"So, that *was* you I saw last night floating across the lake. Ha, I knew it!" Anna said. "I wasn't imagining things."

<Apparently, the cloaking device around the perimeter of our compound also malfunctioned. There seems to be some external energy source that is disrupting our cloaking mechanism. I can't determine its source. But all systems appear to be functioning now. Continuing to run diagnostics.>

"For someone trying so hard to stay hidden, you're not doing a very good job." Anna shrugged. "Why risk sending out probes?"

"Time travel has consequences. When I traveled here a month ago, I may have inadvertently ripped a hole in space-time," Mara said sheepishly.

"A hole in space-time?"

"Several holes, actually," Mara clarified.

"Is that bad?"

"Well, it's not good."

"Wait. Is that what caused the sound last night?" Anna asked. "That sound like the whole sky was ripping apart?"

"I'm afraid so. Although I don't know definitively."

"You're right. This doesn't sound good. What's going to happen?"

"I'm not sure. I still haven't worked that out yet," Mara said.

"And what's on the other side of these holes?" Anna asked.

Mara shrugged.

"So for all you know, we could get sucked into one of them and all die. Are these holes in space-time hard to find?"

"Almost impossible. We can detect several disturbances in the valley, but we can't identify the source. They could be as large as a doorway or as small as a grain of sand. The lights you saw were probes that I sent out to locate the wormholes. But I guess that option is out until my friend SID here can fix the cloaking device," Mara said sternly.

"Or you can use my help after all," Anna said, smiling. "It's perfect. You're going to need someone who can travel all over this valley without raising suspicion, unlike you. I can be your eyes on the ground. I can be your partner."

Anna thrust her hand out to shake. Mara ignored it.

"No, I don't think that would be such a good idea."

"Why not? What do you have to lose?"

Mara looked long and hard at Anna.

"Well, I suppose it would be helpful to have someone on the outside," Mara relented. "And I can't risk exposure."

"Exactly. Right?"

"And I have a feeling you're never going to stop pestering me about this, are you?" Mara asked.

"Not a chance." Anna smiled from ear to ear.

"I know I'm going to regret this," Mara muttered, face buried in her hands. A moment later, she let her hands drop and looked directly at Anna. "Meet me here tomorrow afternoon."

"For training?"

"Or erasing all of your memories. I'll decide when I see you. Now go away before I change my mind."

CHAPTER 13

Mara stood at the edge of her deck that looked out over the lake like the bow of a ship. The strange little girl was gone—for now. It was the most interaction she'd had with another human being in ages—literally ages—and she was tired.

"Any idea how she was able to find us, SID?" Mara asked.

<I've traced several energy signatures of unknown origin that appeared at the same time the cloaking device failed. The troubling thing is these signatures only seem to have appeared when the girl was present.>

"Anna couldn't be the cause. Could she?" Mara asked.

<No. I did a complete scan. She's nothing more than a healthy young girl with a life expectancy of 91.6 years. But the statistical odds that our cloaking device only malfunctioned in her presence are less than 0.000001.>

"Well, I guess we'll find out more about her tomorrow." Mara leaned against the railing and let her head drop.

<Are you sure about this, Mara?>

"You think I'm making a mistake?"

<Do you remember what we're hiding from?>

"I know, SID. But this time feels different. I don't know what it is," Mara said.

<*You sound tired.*>

"I am. Maybe I'm tired of running. What's the greater risk? Bringing her into my life or not. Trying to solve this on my own or not," Mara said. "For now, let's just see."

CHAPTER 14

Anna returned to the meadow the next day. She looked out across the tall grassy field, afraid to move forward. What if none of this was real? She'd had this feeling once before when she was ten. She had been flying at night in her dream, just above the treetops and the houses that lined her street. Her movement was effortless as she bobbed and weaved through the landscape at a dizzying speed. Then she woke up, stuck halfway between sleep and awareness, still believing she could fly but realizing with a hollow feeling that her power of flight was quickly fading away.

She had that same gnawing feeling as she stood alone in the meadow by the lake. She feared the whole thing had been a dream. There was no woman from the future, no flying robots.

Anna took a step forward. Then another. Each step was faster and more desperate until she was in a half run. *No. This isn't right. It wasn't this far away, was it?* Before she could answer, she slammed hard into the invisible barrier protecting Mara's sanctuary.

"Ooof!"

The air was knocked out of Anna's lungs as she bounced

off the wall and fell straight on her backside. A repeat performance from yesterday.

"You might want to try knocking without using your head next time." Mara stood ten feet away, just behind a round opening in the invisible wall. She made no attempt to hide her amusement.

"You saw the whole thing. Why didn't you try to stop me?" Anna said as she brushed off the dirt patches on her elbows.

"I figured the wall would stop you soon enough." Mara smiled. "If you're ready to begin, follow me."

Anna felt a strange sense of vertigo as she passed through the invisible barrier to Mara's sanctuary. She followed Mara for several steps, expecting her to turn toward her house. But Mara headed out across a perfectly manicured lawn to the lakeshore instead. One chair and a metal table had been set up in the grass near the water's edge. On top of the table rested a pair of tennis shoes. A large willow fluttered in the warm afternoon breeze just feet away.

Mara turned to see Anna smiling from ear to ear. Her eyes were open wide.

"Why are you looking at me like that?" Mara asked.

"Because you're real," Anna said. "And I'm not crazy."

"I'm not so sure about that second part. And please stop looking at me that way. You're making me feel uncomfortable."

Mara sat down with her back to the lake.

"Where do I sit?" Anna asked.

"You don't," Mara said. "First things first. I want you to stand right where you are with your eyes closed."

"Is this a trick?"

Mara turned her head to the side and sighed impatiently.

"Okay, okay. I'm shutting my eyes." Anna closed her eyes and put her hands out for balance. "Now what?"

"Now lift your right foot off the ground," Mara directed.

Anna lifted her right leg. Ten seconds ticked by, and she

could feel herself start to lean to the side. She pinwheeled her arms for a couple more seconds before dropping her right foot to the ground.

"Fifteen seconds." Mara looked unimpressed. "Really?"

Anna opened one eye. "Is that bad?"

"So much for the balance test. On to the next," Mara said.

"Test? You didn't tell me I was going to be tested. What's me standing on one foot have to do with anything?" Anna asked, annoyed.

"You'll see," Mara said. "Can we continue?"

Anna frowned but nodded anyway.

"Can you do a plank?" Mara asked.

"Sure. That's like that push-up thing where you hold yourself up on your elbows, right?" Anna said.

Mara nodded.

"You want me to do one right now?"

"Please."

Anna lowered herself down onto the grass and sprawled out in a push-up position, her elbows under her shoulders and her body perfectly straight just inches off the ground. The grass was cool on her forearms.

"Like this?" Anna asked.

"Like that. Now hold it as long as you can," Mara said. "The clock is running."

One minute in and Anna's stomach began to burn.

"Is this some kind of . . . weird TikTok challenge?" Anna grunted.

"If by TikTok you mean that I'm timing you, then yes," Mara said.

"Forget it," Anna said under her breath.

Two and a half minutes in and Anna could feel the muscles in her stomach start to cramp. Her shoulders burned. Four minutes in and sweat poured down her face, down her nose, plopping onto the grass. She collapsed on her stomach with a groan.

"Ow," Anna moaned. "That hurt."

"Hmm." Mara frowned.

"Are we through yet?" Anna asked. She rolled over on her side and propped herself up on one elbow.

"Oh, no. *We're* just beginning." Mara shook her head. "So let's recap. You have no balance and limited core strength. And based upon our brief interactions, I doubt you possess the requisite focus and concentration."

"Are you always like this?" Anna asked as she picked herself up off the ground.

"If you mean truthful, then yes. It's not just me. SID has also been observing you from the house and has come to the same conclusion."

"And what is that?" Anna asked.

"You're not entirely hopeless, but you're close."

"Thanks for the words of encouragement, SID!" Anna shouted up toward the house.

"We're not here to make you feel good, Anna. We're here to prepare you. You volunteered, correct?"

"Yes."

"Then let's get started." Mara pointed to the pair of white sneakers on the table. "Do you know what these are?"

"Yeah, of course. Those are sneakers. What are they for?" Anna asked.

"For you. I chose an acceptable shoe style from your era. And I estimate your feet are twenty-four centimeters in length. The shoes will easily adjust themselves even if the fit isn't perfect."

"Cool!" Anna kicked off her own shoes and shoved them in her backpack before grabbing the sneakers on the table. "Are these made of that material you showed me yesterday?"

Mara nodded.

Anna slipped the shoes on with ease. The lining inside moved like a living thing as the shoe reshaped itself around her foot. She jumped.

"That felt weird." Anna giggled. Then her expression changed to mild surprise as she began bouncing up and down to test out her new shoes. "Wow, are these comfortable. I feel like I'm floating."

"That's the general idea."

It took a second for Anna to catch on. She looked at her shoes, then up at Mara. Her mouth dropped. "You mean these are—"

"Antigravity boots? Yes."

"No way!" Anna yelped. "How do you turn them on?"

"You won't be turning on anything—not until you're fully prepared. Until then, I will do the driving," Mara said. "Ready?"

"For?"

Before Anna could finish her question, she felt her feet slip from under her as if she'd just stepped onto ice. She looked down and saw an inch of empty space between herself and the ground.

"We have liftoff." Mara laughed. "Try to focus on your core. It'll help keep your feet from sliding."

Mara raised the angle of her hand slightly, and Anna rose another foot off the ground. Like a toddler on roller skates, Anna spun her arms in circles. Her legs pinwheeled back and forth. She quickly transitioned from surprise to fear to wonder— a combination of feelings that had her head spinning and her body shaking in uncontrollable giggles.

"Higher, higher!" Anna laughed.

Mara raised her hand again and Anna quickly shot up seven feet off the ground. She wasn't ready for the acceleration. Her stomach flipped, as if she were in a steep drop on a roller coaster, and she lost control of her feet. She floated in midair, her legs spread out in a perfect split.

"Whoa!" Anna laughed again.

"Remember your core."

Anna tried to regain her balance, but she had nothing to hold on to except empty space. There was a moment of stillness. The breeze stopped. She could hear her heartbeat. Then she toppled straight forward, gaining speed like a falling tree. The ground rushed toward her. She closed her eyes and gritted her teeth for impact, but she felt only the wind through her hair.

Slowly, Anna opened her eyes, only to find herself hanging upside down. Her body swung gently back and forth like a pendulum. She looked up into the bright blue sky and saw her feet were still snug in their antigravity shoes, and those shoes were still seven feet above the ground.

"I told you to use your core," Mara said.

"Yeah, I heard that. Now how do I get myself right side up?" Anna asked as she reached for her shoes.

"I'll let you figure that out." Mara smiled.

Anna rolled her eyes. She was going to protest again but realized it would do no good. She struggled and grunted to pull herself up. She pulled on her pant leg. She bent her knees and kicked her feet back and forth, only to flop back and float helplessly above the ground.

"Can I get a little help here?" Anna finally gave in. The blood was starting to rush to her head.

"No. You're doing just fine." Mara gave an enthusiastic thumbs-up.

The afternoon breeze picked up, and Anna felt herself begin to drift. *You've got to be kidding me.* She looked around for something to grab. She stretched her hands out toward the grass, but her fingertips were still inches away. Like a balloon drifting lazily on a summer afternoon breeze, Anna inched across the lawn and out toward the water.

"Will you help me, please?!" Anna cried out.

Mara bit her lip to keep from laughing. She walked casually past Anna and cut her off before she reached the water's surface. She looked down at Anna for a moment and grabbed Anna's legs. Instead of pulling her up, Mara gently pushed Anna in the opposite direction toward the house.

"Come on! Are you serious?" Anna shouted. She was spinning now. A leaf adrift in a stream. "Will you please get me down from here?"

Mara kept pace with Anna as she floated toward the house. "So, what have we learned from our first lesson today?"

Anna folded her arms in resignation and looked up as she spun slowly in circles. "That you have a warped sense of humor."

"Besides that."

Anna sighed. "Antigravity boots are really hard to use."

"You're getting warmer," Mara said.

"Okay, okay. I get it. I have a lot of training to do," Anna said.

"And?"

"And I have to listen to everything you tell me to do," Anna said.

"Very good."

"Now can you get me down?"

"Of course."

Mara clicked an invisible button on her wrist and Anna plummeted toward the ground. She reached her hands out just in time, tucked into a ball, and rolled easily back onto her feet.

"Not bad. That was a decent tuck and roll," Mara commended. "Maybe there's hope for you after all."

"Okay, what torture do you have planned for me next?"

Mara reached into a small pouch attached to her belt and pulled out what looked like a diamond-shaped bandage, only transparent.

"Give me your hands," Mara demanded.

Anna looked at her suspiciously.

"Give me your hands. I promise it won't hurt. It's just a communications device." Mara stepped forward.

"What do you call it?" Anna stepped back.

"An iCom." Mara took another step forward.

"iCom? That's kind of lame." Anna folded her arms. "I figured the future would have cooler product names."

"You're stalling. Give me your arm."

Anna shrugged and held her hands out. Mara took Anna's left hand and gently rolled an iCom out as if she were applying a bandage. It felt sticky and cold, but once it adhered to her skin, it was completely invisible. She did the same to the right wrist.

"Hey. Where did they go?" Anna held the back of her hand up toward the sun.

"They're still there. Just no one can see them."

"But if they're invisible, where are the controls? How do I use them?" Anna asked.

"You don't. I communicate with you, and only as needed," Mara said.

"So I'll see you tomorrow?" Anna asked.

"No."

"Then when?"

"When you finish your training," Mara said.

"Whe—" Anna started.

"Ah, ah, ah," Mara said, cutting her off with an outstretched hand. "No more questions. I recommend you go home and get some rest for now. You're going to need it. Tomorrow morning your training starts. Wait for my call."

CHAPTER 15

"**W**ake up, Anna."

Anna opened a single eye. The other was glued shut with sleep. Her bedroom was dark and empty. The only light came from the stars outside her window. But she'd heard something—someone.

Another weird dream, Anna thought.

"I can see you."

The voice returned, close and clear as if someone were whispering in her ear. Anna shot up in bed, her pulse racing. She strained her eyes in the darkness in search of the source.

"Who is it?"

"I am your conscience, and we need to have a word."

Anna suddenly recognized the voice. "Very funny, Mara. Where are you?"

"Look down at your wrist."

Mara's voice was clear and bright. Anna glanced down at her iCom. The transparent diamond that covered the back of her left hand was glowing blue.

"Ugh," Anna groaned. "What time is it?"

A holographic time display flashed bright blue numbers just above her wrist: *4:22 a.m.*

"Really?" Anna sighed. "I thought you said morning."

"The sun is eighteen degrees below the horizon at this very moment. That makes it the official beginning of morning. So time to get up."

"For what?" Anna yawned.

"For your first real day of training. I've provided a course for you to run. Just follow the map on your iCom. I'll go easy on you today. Five miles in fifty minutes. That'll give us plenty of time to work on your core and discuss physics before school."

A three-dimensional topographic map of the valley appeared just above Anna's hand—a running trail outlined in a faint blue light.

"Are you serious? You want me to run outside in the dark?"

"You'd better get used to it. The dark is where you'll be doing most of your reconnaissance."

Anna sighed heavily and rolled out of bed. She tossed on a pair of shorts and a sweatshirt and tied her hair back with a scrunchie.

"Can I use my antigravity shoes at least?" Anna asked. "They're the most comfortable thing I own."

"Of course. That's why I gave them to you."

Anna walked quietly down the steps, past Herbie sleeping in the corner, and across the kitchen to the entryway. She opened the screen door slowly, afraid she might wake up Uncle Jack. Afraid to have to explain why she was leaving the house. What would she even say? *Oh yeah—I'm in training for a top-secret mission with a woman from the future. Yes, there are wormholes and aliens and we'll likely be vaporized if she finds out that you know.*

The air outside was cold and motionless, the world completely still. In the faint starlight, she could see a cloud of condensation form as she breathed out, a sign the temperature was around forty-five degrees on this cold spring morning. She jumped back and forth on the balls of her feet and swung her arms to get warm.

"Anna?"

"Yes?" Anna kept bouncing.

"Look up."

Anna stopped bouncing and looked up into the night sky to be greeted by a cathedral of lights. She had never been outside this early in the morning, alone and in silence, to see this view of the universe.

"Wow. The Milky Way."

"Beautiful, isn't it? I'm watching it right now too."

"Yeah. It feels like the whole sky is moving."

"It is. Everything in the universe is moving relative to everything else. Everything except you. So, get moving." Mara laughed. *"Just follow the blue line on your map. I'll be with you the entire way."*

"Whether I like it or not, right?" Anna said under her breath, then took off in a fast trot, following the blue line down the dirt road and into the darkness.

CHAPTER 16

By the time school started, Anna had run five miles, performed pull-ups and push-ups until her arms gave out, and listened to an introductory tour of special relativity. She also rode her bike the three miles to school. By first period, her legs were rubber, and her hands began to cramp as she wrote. By second period, she had dozed off in the back of the room.

"Psst," someone whispered somewhere deep in her sleep.

Anna's eyes flickered.

"Psst. Armstrong," the voice said more insistently. "You're drooling."

Anna's eyes snapped open, and the sounds of the classroom and the bright light from the windows came flooding in. One seat to her left, Scout was silently holding back laughter. His lips were shut tight and curled up in a smile. He pointed to his chin, then at Anna.

Anna reached up and felt the trail of drool that led from the corner of her mouth to her chin to the puddle on her desk below. She quickly wiped her face with her forearm, then shut her eyes and prayed for the day to end.

Anna spent the rest of the day stuck between two worlds.

She would be midconversation with Lula or Fiona when Mara buzzed through on the iCom. No warning. Just boom. Mara's voice appeared in her head unannounced, giving orders or directions or new things to learn. And suddenly, Anna was forced to parse two simultaneous conversations and not look crazy in the process. No one else could hear Mara over the iCom. No one could see the lights or the holographic images projected above Anna's wrist. Mara said that was because the light signals and audio waves from the iCom were beamed directly onto Anna's retinas and eardrums. To Anna, it felt like she had an ever-present imaginary friend.

That night, just before sleep and in the darkness of her room, Anna received another call on her iCom. This time it was to play a game—at least that's what Mara called it. The rules were simple: All she had to do was stare at a small glowing sphere that floated six inches above her iCom. Any time her mind wandered, or if she tried to focus too hard, the sphere of light would fade. The best she could muster that first night was thirty seconds of uninterrupted focus, which she accomplished just before collapsing on her bed asleep, still in the clothes she wore to school earlier in the day.

So this is what boot camp feels like, Anna thought when she woke up on the second morning. As Mara barked orders, Anna began to fantasize ways of disabling her iCom, like putting the iCom on mute or cutting her arm off. She ached in places she didn't know could ache. It was a new dawn, a new path to run, and a new lecture on the nature of time.

By the end of the fourth day, people began to notice the odd behavior. Anna had ditched the bike and begun running back and forth from school instead—through the muscle aches, past the farm fields and irrigation lines and odd looks from farmers as they watched this strange new girl sprint home. One farmer even stopped his truck and asked her what she was running from, his face concerned. At home, Uncle Jack had noticed the quick spike in her appetite and predicted a growth spurt would be coming soon. Armstrong women tended to be on the tall side.

As the week rolled on, Scout volunteered as Anna's training partner and rode his bike along with her as she ran back and forth to school. Fiona and Lula joined soon after and the four became a familiar sight, a caravan of friends along the one-lane roads outside the town of Smartt. She wanted more than anything to tell her friends the truth—that she was actually wearing something called antigravity boots, that she'd been hiding a great secret and would be searching for wormholes sometime soon—yes, wormholes to other dimensions with her new friend from the future. But she was good at keeping her promises, even though she wanted to burst. It was the single hardest thing she'd done, harder than all the workouts, lectures, early mornings, and sleepless nights combined.

Mara began to change the cadence of Anna's morning runs. *"Sprint . . . now slow your pace . . . jump . . . sprint . . . jump."* She broke down why these movements were necessary—how they were perfectly calibrated to maximize Anna's conditioning and endurance. Anna was sure it was to maximize her irritation instead.

Each day Anna asked when they would meet again. And each day, Mara responded with the same answer: *"When you're ready."*

New movements and exercises were introduced. Some to develop focus. Some to improve flexibility and boost strength. Some to increase visual acuity, which Anna didn't even think was possible. Each movement had a purpose, and Anna performed them without fail, even though she felt and looked awkward, like a girl trying to put out a fire.

"Up, down, back and forth, focus, focus, focus." New things to learn and paths to run. She was given a crash course in classical physics the first month, then ventured into subjects no

schools would teach for more than a hundred years: reshaping neural networks in her head and allowing for brand-new connections. The days melted into one another as the end of school drew near. Temperatures rose and fireflies emerged, and the spring crops carpeted the fields in a bed of green.

Anna didn't notice the changes at first. They were subtle. But she soon found she was able to easily do pull-ups without the help of the wooden crate. She could run, even sprint, for miles without losing her breath. And the daily aches were long gone. She noticed lean muscles and cuts in her arms and legs that were never there before. Even her face began to look different, older.

The changes weren't just physical. She could now focus for extended periods of time, keeping the sphere of light suspended above her iCom without faltering. The world had slowed down for her, too. Things that had once moved by in a blur now came into focus—the flap of a bird's wing or the gait of a running horse. She remembered hearing about baseball players who could see the individual threads of a baseball spin as it left the pitcher's hand. And somehow over the weeks of training she had developed a similar ability.

Two months in, she no longer asked when they'd meet again; she no longer saw her training as a task to get through but just the way things were. A constant in her life, just like Mara's voice over the iCom.

Anna hadn't physically seen Mara in almost nine weeks, but over that time she learned to understand her quirky sense of humor and timing. She had grown accustomed to Mara's constant presence. Like clockwork, she knew when to expect Mara's voice over the iCom. So on that morning before the last day of school, when Mara failed to contact her as scheduled, Anna had a feeling something was wrong.

—

Mara hadn't called all day. No signal. No orders. No new course to run. The anxious feeling that started as a hollow pit in her stomach earlier that morning became a full-blown panic attack by evening.

Anna sat out on the front porch with her Uncle Jack as the sun set and the night sounds came out in full chorus. Fireflies circled the oak tree in the front yard like strings of Christmas lights. She tried to read a book but found herself stuck in a loop on the same paragraph for almost fifteen minutes. Her uncle sat across from her, pencil in his mouth and all his attention focused on the sketchpad in his lap. The porch light cast long shadows across his face.

"What are you working on?" Anna asked, trying to distract herself.

"I'm just doing a little math. I'm trying to figure out how much carbon we can sequester, or capture, over the course of a year," Uncle Jack said. "Want to double-check my work?"

Uncle Jack handed over his notebook. On the left side of the page was a systems diagram with inputs and outputs. On the right, a lot of really sloppy handwriting.

"It looks like you sketched this with your feet." Anna smiled.

"Don't grade me on neatness, just let me know if it makes sense." Uncle Jack laughed.

"The diagram makes sense, but—"

The sound of crickets stopped as if someone suddenly flipped off the volume. The air felt charged. A dry breeze rustled the leaves, but there were no other sounds except for the slight squeak from the porch swing. Herbie, who had been sleeping next to Uncle Jack's feet, started to whimper and looked nervously toward the horizon.

Uncle Jack and Anna exchanged a puzzled glance. From across the lawn, the fireflies started to blink in unison, on and off and back on again, like Morse code.

"That's strange." Uncle Jack rose slowly from his chair.

Anna felt it first: a static itch that raised the hair on her arms. She instinctively looked down. Uncle Jack must have felt it too because he was absently rubbing his arms.

"You feel that—"

Uncle Jack was cut off by a deep rumble like distant thunder, followed by the sound of a horn—a sound so deep Anna could feel it in her bones. She put her hands over her ears in surprise. The horn blast changed pitch, deeper now. It seemed to come from everywhere. The sound of two ocean liners ramming into each other. Twisting metal. Herbie began to howl in harmony.

Uncle Jack grabbed his mobile phone. He tapped on the screen and then paced back and forth waiting for the person on the other line to answer.

"Hey, RG. RG!" Uncle Jack shouted into the phone. "Are you hearing this?"

"Yeah, [*static*]. Everyone [*static*] hearing it." Dr. Gloria's voice on the speaker could barely be heard above the sound.

"Is it a weather event?"

"We have our drones out, but we're not [*static*]," Dr. Gloria shouted above the noise. "Wait—we're getting some crazy barometric readings! Holy cow! Sensors in the northeastern fields just dropped below twenty-six."

"That's impossible. There's not a cloud in the sky," Uncle Jack shouted back. "Can we track the origin?"

"Not yet. What the heck [*static*], Jack?"

"I don't know, but I'm heading over to the lab right now. Maybe the AEDT can identify where this is coming from. Call me back if you find anything." Uncle Jack tucked his phone in his pocket and looked down at Anna.

"Stay put. I'll be right back!" Uncle Jack shouted as he bounded down the steps.

Anna watched her uncle run in a full sprint across the yard

and out toward the barns. Just as he faded from view, her iCom flashed blue. The first sign from Mara in over a day. Anna waited until she was sure her uncle was gone.

"Mara! What's going on?!" Anna shouted into her wrist.

"The sound? It isn't me. Not directly," Mara said, her voice clear and sharp in Anna's ear.

"What do you mean, not directly?"

The horn blast began to trail off, followed by a rolling echo that she could almost see dissipate across the valley. Anna heard shouts from some of Uncle Jack's team. People were scrambling under the barnyard lights. Some were quieting the horses that were agitated by the trumpet blast.

"That was one of those tears in space-time you talked about, wasn't it?" Anna asked.

"I'll explain tomorrow. Wait for my call." Mara paused. *"Based on what happened tonight, this phase of your training is over."*

CHAPTER 17

Minutes later, as the last of the trumpet blast echoed across the valley, a shadow peeked its head above the surface of Tyson Lake. It stared out across the water, disoriented, unsure if it was swimming in a sea of stars. Long spiderlike fingers dragged across the surface, creating ripples in the water that disturbed the reflection of the stars and moon overhead. The creature could breathe here through its skin and mouthlining, but everything else felt wrong. It looked up into the heavens. The familiar planets and stars were gone, as was the gaseous purple nebula that served as a constant and comforting marker in the sky. The magnetic fields were all wrong too. And it felt so light here, like floating.

The shadowed figure easily leaped from the water, using only its legs to propel it, and landed silently on a small patch of land. So much lighter here, and warmer. Strange plants rustled in the night breeze. It reached out with one of its four fingers and touched a leaf, leaving behind a trail of green light. Time to plant. It made a soft clicking sound in its throat as small black scales began to unfurl down the lengths of its arms, like a bird opening its feathers. Slowly, lights began to float out from underneath those scales like small phosphorescent dandelion seeds—little blue and green lights that caught the breeze and began to float lazily across the lake.

Visible only in silhouette, the creature watched and listened as the lights skimmed across the water's surface. Some lazily descended into the water, where their lights were extinguished. Other lights spun around each other, darting and bouncing off one another, like birds playing. A few made a direct line to the far shore, where they landed on the ground to form a straight line of light that pulsed in the distance. A signal to follow. The shape leaped into the water and headed to the far shore, barely making a sound.

CHAPTER 18

The last hour of the last day of school dragged on forever. Time was broken—the kids were all sure, as was the teacher, who repeatedly tapped on the side of the clock in a futile attempt to hurry time along. Finally, the bell struck noon, and the kids exploded from the classroom like horses from the starting gate.

Anna, Fiona, and Lula headed for the Ivanhoe Diner right after school. They talked about the sound from the night before as they walked down cracked sidewalks lined with weeds toward the fairgrounds. Fiona was sure it was the same sound they had heard months before. Lula wondered if it had anything to do with climate change. Anna stayed silent. A rip in space-time might be a little difficult to explain.

As they turned the corner, they were greeted by a large neon medieval knight perched atop a run-down drive-in that had seen much better days. The Ivanhoe Diner was a local landmark and a tradition for students on the last day of school. Most of the kids in town had come up with the same idea, and by the time the three friends made it to the front door of the cafe, all the seats inside had been taken.

The three ordered their food and took it outside to a small bench near the entrance. Inside, the diner was all chaos and music blaring and loud voices. Out in front, it was quiet enough to hear the flies buzz in the heat.

"Congratulations, you guys. We're officially high schoolers," Lula said, lifting her strawberry shake in a toast.

"Yep. And look at us. Still on the outside looking in." Anna tapped her plastic cup in return.

"I hear there's a party at the quarry tonight. A high school party," Fiona said. "All the incoming freshmen have been invited. Even us, I guess."

Anna paused.

"I don't think I can make it." Anna kicked at weeds that had grown beneath the bench. "My uncle has plans, I think."

"Yeah, I probably can't either. My brother ruined it for me when he went to a quarry party last year. My parents found him shirtless in a tree," Fiona said.

Bam!

All three girls jumped at the loud crack against glass and quickly turned to see a figure laughing hysterically from inside the diner. It was Scout, his hands and face pressed against the plate-glass window.

"You're such an idiot!" Fiona shouted through the window. "You made me spill my onion rings."

Scout blew air kisses in her direction. Then, realizing he had an audience, he pressed his mouth against the window and blew his cheeks out like a puffer fish. For a brief moment they could see the exact contents of Scout's mouth, from silver fillings to a chipped tooth.

"Ewww." Lula's lip curled in disgust. "That boy is so strange."

Scout walked casually to the front door of the cafe and poked his head out. "What are you ladies doing out here by yourselves?"

"Avoiding you," Fiona said.

"Ha, I love you too, Fiona." Scout strolled outside with his hands in his pockets, then pointed to the onion rings scattered at Fiona's feet. "Are you going to eat those?"

When the girls didn't answer, he picked up one of the larger onion rings and knelt before Anna. He took her hand in his own and looked up into her eyes.

"Anna, will you take this onion ring as a sign of my devotion?"

"Sorry, Scout." Anna smiled and yanked her hand back. "You're a little too young for me."

"Fair enough." Scout stood up and tossed the onion ring out into the street. He wiped the grease on his pants leg. "So, are you guys going to the quarry party tonight?"

"Quarry is off-limits for me," Lula said. "Don't tell me your parents are actually letting you go."

"Are you kidding? I can do whatever I want." Scout picked up another onion ring and tossed it at a passing car. "And what I want is not to be pummeled by my older brother and his stupid friends. He told me they'd pants me if I showed up tonight. So yeah, I'm not going."

"What's the plan then?" Anna asked.

"That's what I came out here to ask you guys. The fellas are thinking about a game night at my house," Scout said. "All the cold pizza you can eat. What do you say, Anna?"

Anna's iCom buzzed. Although she knew the others couldn't hear, she'd learned not to react too quickly to avoid raising suspicion. The iCom buzzed again and Anna casually glanced down at her wrist, even though she wanted to get up and run out as fast as she could. She looked for a graceful exit instead.

"How quickly can you get here?" Mara's voice was urgent on the iCom.

"Uh . . ." Anna almost answered out loud out of habit. She

stopped just in time but forgot to shut her mouth, which now hung open like a dead fish.

"Hey, Armstrong. Are you having a seizure again?" Scout waved his hand in front of Anna's face.

"*I see you have company. Hmm, I have an idea.*" Mara paused. "*SID is accessing your cellular networks. Calling now. Answer your phone.*"

"Excuse me?" Anna tried to process the two simultaneous conversations.

"I asked if you wanted to come over tonight," Scout said slowly.

"*I said answer your phone.*" Mara's voice in her ear was impatient.

Anna's phone buzzed in her pocket. She was glad for the reprieve. She raised her index finger in a "give me a second" gesture and pulled out her phone. Mara was on the other end.

"*Tell your friends it is time for you to go,*" Mara said. "*Meet me at the lake in the next thirty minutes.*"

The line went silent.

If her friends had been paying close enough attention, they'd have seen Anna's eyes dilate less than half a millimeter and her pulse quicken. Even though Anna had no idea what to expect, her body was already preparing for what was ahead. Adrenaline had kicked in.

Anna shoved her phone in her pocket. "Sorry, guys. I have to fly."

She closed her eyes briefly at the pun. She couldn't help herself.

CHAPTER 19

"**Y**ou've changed."

"What do you mean?" Anna wiped the sweat from her forehead as she plopped onto the grass near the lakeshore. She had run the three miles to Mara's hideout in a little under twenty minutes. "And it's good to see you again too, by the way."

The ground felt cool under the shade of a willow tree bending gently in the afternoon breeze. She rolled over onto her back and looked up into a brilliant blue sky filled with billowing white clouds. Mara leaned over her with her arms folded. Behind her sat a table made of the same liquid metal Anna had seen months ago.

"I've been tracking everything about you for the past nine weeks. Your reaction time and the increase in your muscle mass. The significant improvement in your equilibrioception and theta and alpha wave activity," Mara said.

"My equili-what?"

"Your balance and focus," Mara clarified.

"Oh."

"But I wasn't prepared for how different you look." Mara

gave a slight smile. "You really surprised me, Anna. I didn't think you'd make it past the second day."

"I do feel different. Better," Anna said. "So, you really think I'm ready to fly?"

"Let's find out."

Mara reached for a silver rectangular box on the table and handed it to Anna.

Anna took the box and shook it out of habit, just like Christmas Day. It was light as air and cool to the touch. There was a small indent on the top of the box in the shape of a button. Anna placed the tip of her index finger on the indent, and the package came to life. The top panel retracted like a coil. Inside was a pair of translucent wraparound glasses.

"Wow. That was weird." Anna giggled.

"Go ahead and put them on." Mara seemed giddy. "I remember my first pair."

"It's not going to shoot lasers into my eyes, is it?" Anna asked.

"Not unless you want it to."

Anna removed the glasses and set the box on the table. They were weightless and almost invisible. No seams, no hinges. She slid them over her ears and onto the bridge of her nose, but they felt like nothing at all. She ran her finger along the edge and felt no gap between the glasses and her skin. It was an airtight fit, as if the glasses had been molded to the shape of her head.

"Thanks. But I'm not sure I get it. What are they for?" Anna asked.

"Just tap your right temple twice." Mara tapped her own temple to demonstrate.

"Like this?" Anna followed suit and tapped her temple twice.

Immediately, her senses were assailed with more visual stimuli than she could process at once. Blue and green streaks of vibrant color. Circles and geometric shapes. Numbers and letters projected on the surface of her glasses.

"Whoa!" Anna stepped back and shook her head. "What am I looking at here?"

"It's the other half of your iCom." Mara was laughing. "Now hold on for a second. Quit moving. You'll make yourself sick."

"Too late."

"Tap your left temple once," Mara said.

Anna tapped her left temple. The amount of visual noise in her field of vision was reduced by half.

"The numbers in the lower right corner of your glasses are your external readings: air composition, temperature, air pressure, gravity. Any number that exceeds a safe threshold will start blinking red. Make sense?" Mara said.

"Yeah, this is cool." Anna scanned the horizon, wide-eyed and open-mouthed. "What are the numbers in the lower left corner?"

"Those are your internal readings. Your heart rate, oxygen levels."

"Can you change the distance settings from meters to feet?"

"Absolutely not. Temperature maybe, but not distance and weight. Get used to the metric system. You're going to be using it sooner than you think," Mara said. "Back to your iCom. You can toggle through the numbers by tapping your left temple. Once you get used to it, you'll be able to toggle through the readings by just thinking about it."

"Oh, I get it. Just like the concentration games you've been making me play every night," Anna said. "So that's what you were preparing me for."

"Exactly," Mara said. "Now, see the blue circles? You can focus those targets on a distant object if you want to know its size, distance, and composition. That'll come in handy later."

Anna locked the blue target on Mara, and the display showed a distance of two meters. Anna looked down at her wrist. The diamond-shaped iCom, invisible for most of the past nine weeks, was now clearly visible, bright and glowing. Buttons and arrays of controls lined its edges.

"Hey! I can see my iCom," Anna said excitedly. "Does this mean I can finally control it now?"

"Yes."

"And I can call you anytime I want, all hours of the night, just like you did to me?"

"No."

"Which one of these buttons starts up my antigravity boots?" Anna asked.

"Hold on. First, I need to talk about the sole reason I'm allowing you to do this," Mara said. "Your mission."

"My mission. Oh, I like the sound of that." Anna giggled.

Mara waved her hand across the table. A semitransparent topographic map of the valley hung suspended in air. Anna could make out the lake, the forest, the quarry, the roads that crisscrossed the farmland, and the town of Smartt itself. Blue lines of light bisected the miniature map like haphazard flight patterns.

"Do you know what this is?" Mara asked.

"A map of the town," Anna answered.

"Yes. But notice anything familiar?"

"The blue lines. Wait, those are all the trails you had me run over the past couple of months," Anna said. "They're a pattern, aren't they?"

"More of a map. In the six hundred or so kilometers you ran, you covered almost every area of this valley. And every time you ran, I collected data of your surroundings. Fluctuations in energy readings, changes in atmospheric pressure, magnetic waves, anything that might help us locate an anomaly, like a wormhole."

"So I was your probe."

"Yes. Slower, but also less likely to be detected." Mara smiled.

"Did you find anything?"

"See this light?" Mara tapped on one marble-sized light suspended above the valley. "Based on the readings you helped me collect, this light represents the most likely location for our wormhole."

Anna leaned over the map and tapped the light. It shimmered to the touch. "It looks like it's a good mile above land."

"1,982 meters to be exact."

"Whew." Anna whistled. "That's really high."

"Yes, it is," Mara said.

"Wait, you want me to fly up there?" Anna's eyes opened wide.

"I don't expect you to walk."

"I thought I'd just be flying around the treetops." Anna laughed nervously.

"Your boots can actually carry you to a low earth orbit, so height is not a problem. Cold is, but not height," Mara said. "And don't worry. The boots have been calibrated for Earth's gravity. A safety has been built in to prevent you from decelerating too quickly or hitting the ground."

"So what's the plan then?" Anna asked.

"The plan is to investigate the area tonight and collect as much information as you can," Mara said. "I've mapped the course. You'll be flying over an area where you won't be detected. Think of this as a solo test run."

"That's it?"

"Straight up. Straight down. I'm hoping you find nothing at all. There's no reason a wormhole should exist on its own, let alone stay open for a long period of time. But if you do find something, under no circumstances are you to get too close. We have no idea what we're dealing with."

"I don't even know what I'm looking for. Is it big? Is it small? Does it make a noise?"

"You'll know when you see it," Mara said, then paused. "I hope."

CHAPTER 20

"So how do I get these things to work again?" Anna looked down at her antigravity boots. "What button do I push?"

Mara walked over and poked the tip of her index finger against Anna's forehead.

"This one." Mara laughed.

"Huh?"

"There is no button. You control your boots remotely using your iCom and this." Mara poked Anna on the forehead again. "Your mind. Trust me. It's a lot easier than you think."

"My mind. How?"

"Relax. Take in a deep breath like I taught you." Mara breathed in deeply and exhaled slowly. "Now see the fuzzy faint light in the center of your glasses?"

Anna made out the small diffused dot of light that seemed to float in front of her. "Yeah, I see it."

"Focus on it."

"Okay—focusing," Anna said. The minute she focused on it, the light became more distinct and locked into place. When she took her focus from it, the light became fuzzy again.

"Now picture lifting that light with your mind, just like the game we played."

Anna focused in on the light again and pictured it rising from the ground by several degrees. The light instantaneously followed her commands.

"And that's it," Mara said. "You're flying."

"What?" Anna looked down at Mara and realized she was floating several feet in the air. "Aaagh!"

Anna lost her focus on the light and plummeted three feet to the ground, like someone had pulled a trapdoor from underneath her. She lay in the grass for a moment and looked up at the sky, which was now darkening with large thunderclouds. The wind had picked up and blew Mara's hair across her face as she looked down.

"I thought you said this thing had a safety," Anna said.

"My mistake. I forgot to set it." Mara reached out and helped Anna stand back up. "Not bad for your first time. Let's try it again."

Anna shook her arms out and took in a deep breath to relax. She focused on the light in front of her again, and this time the light snapped into focus immediately. She envisioned it rising a couple of degrees, but now she was ready for the sense of weightlessness and held steady as her feet lifted off the ground. Her heart raced and the world grew silent around her as if all her attention had collapsed in on this one moment. Timeless. She could feel the breeze against her skin, the blood rushing through her body. She'd never felt more alive. She was flying.

She stopped her ascent at twenty feet and took in this new view of the world. Mara was running just beneath her, trying to keep up and laughing the entire way. Anna could now clearly see the other side of the lake and the thunderclouds rising across the horizon. She found that she could turn easily if she shifted her weight. Wherever she directed her center of gravity, her boots would follow. In seconds, she was spinning gracefully like an ice skater until her eyes filled with tears from laughing.

"Yes, I think you have the hang of it!" Mara shouted from below.

"Come join me!" Anna shouted back.

Mara looked up and nodded. She took one step forward and then glided up silently to meet her. Anna reached out and grabbed Mara's hands and the two began to spin slowly in the air. Anna let go and the two spun away from each other, tumbling and rolling in midair.

"This is magic." Anna smiled so hard it almost hurt.

"No, just science," Mara said.

"What if someone sees us?" Anna asked as she looked out across the lake.

"Don't worry. I've extended the cloaking device to cover the surface of the lake," Mara reassured her. "Okay, so it's obvious you're a natural at this. Let's see what you can really do."

Mara glided to Anna's side and lightly tapped her on the shoulder. "Tag! You're it."

Anna floated back, surprised. "What?"

"You're it! Now see if you can catch me." Mara laughed as she bolted out toward the lake, leaving behind a thin trail of blue light.

Anna took off in pursuit. Or at least she tried. She had quickly mastered navigating up and down and side to side, but she wasn't so sure how to do the pursuit part at all. She focused on the light in front of her, but the fastest she could go was a leisurely pace. Mara stopped about fifty feet away and floated in midair.

"Listen. I'm going to take a nap. Let me know when you're getting closer," Mara shouted over the wind that had turned to gusts.

Anna tried leaning forward and felt herself gain momentum. The more she leaned, the faster she moved. It was a sensation she'd felt once before, two summers back, when her parents had taken her to Hawaii, and she'd spent the entire month of June learning to surf. She remembered that feeling between falling and speeding forward as her surfboard rode the crest of the wave. It was a balancing act. A controlled fall that lasted as long as the wave carried her forward. She remembered it felt like flying at the time. Now that she was flying, she realized how right she was.

"Ha! That's more like it," Mara shouted back encouragement, then took off across the lake.

Anna leaned forward like a ski jumper catching air, instinctively finding the right body position for speed. Within seconds she was gaining momentum and making up ground. *Twenty meters from Mara. Fifteen meters.* The blue target in her glasses calculated the distance as she flew.

Mara looked back, her eyes open wide in surprise. She leaned back and slowed her pace just a bit as Anna barreled forward.

Twelve meters. Ten. Anna wasn't sure how fast she was going now. The world was a blur, but she knew she'd catch Mara before she reached the end of the lake. Anna reached her hands out. She was only a couple of arm's lengths away when Mara stopped suddenly in front of her—so suddenly that Anna had no time to react. She continued to barrel forward with just enough time to see Mara give a small wave and a smile as she flew on by.

Anna had no idea how to stop.

"Aaagh!"

Anna instinctively threw her hands out in front of her, but it did nothing to slow her velocity. The trees at the far edge of the lake were rapidly approaching. She had just enough time to elevate herself the fifteen feet required to clear the tops of the trees. As she passed the first line of branches, Anna locked eyes with an eastern bluebird that blinked once at the strange object flying by.

Partly out of instinct and partly because she remembered seeing the same thing in a cartoon years ago and it seemed to work then, Anna leaned back, put her feet forward, and dug in her heels. She decelerated so fast she almost cartwheeled midair. Anna adjusted her center of gravity and managed to stay upright until she came to a complete stop. She floated midair for a second to catch her breath, then looked back across the lake. Mara was several hundred feet away and doubled over in laughter.

"Looks like you figured out how to stop." Mara's voice faded in and out in the swirling wind. "Sort of."

Those who knew Anna well would have instantly recognized the look on her face. Her eyes narrowed. She clenched her teeth until muscles popped in her jaw. It wasn't anger but a sense of inevitability. Anna would simply never give up.

She focused her iCom's blue target on Mara again, then took off like a shot. *Eighty-one meters. Seventy-five.* Instead of going straight, Anna swooped down just feet above the lake. The wind was swirling in the air above, but down at the water's surface it helped to push her forward. She reached down and dipped her fingertips into the lake, leaving a spray of water in her wake. *Twenty-five meters.*

Mara barely had time to respond. She laughed out loud in surprise and veered back toward her house. Anna could see where she was heading and changed direction to cut Mara off. *Ten meters.*

Anna was almost directly beneath Mara now, close to invisible at this angle. She aimed for a point just ahead of Mara and jetted upward toward her friend. *Five meters. Three.* Anna stretched her arms out. Mara must have sensed the movement, because she looked down a split second before impact, her expression a combination of surprise and joy. The next second the two were tumbling in the air, Anna's surprisingly strong arms wrapped around Mara's legs.

"Ha! Got you. Now you're it." Anna laughed. She let go of Mara's legs and floated to a stop. "Not bad for a first try, huh?"

Mara smiled. "Not bad at all. But let's see how you do tonight when you're out on your own."

CHAPTER 21

Anna sat on the edge of her bedroom windowsill. She dangled her legs over the side, spit between her antigravity boots, and watched it fall twenty-five feet to the lilac bushes below. Anna looked up and saw one of the remaining clouds from the afternoon storm roll quickly across the sky, obscuring the moon for a moment. Her goggles picked up distance, temperature, and wind speed on everything in her field of vision. Sensory overload. She turned off the glasses display to take in the full expanse of the night sky instead.

Uncle Jack had gone to bed an hour before, and every exterior light on the farm had been turned off, right on schedule. No lights. No hum of motors. Just a chorus of frogs and crickets and the soft hush of a night wind. Her uncle wanted to simulate nature as much as possible, and turning the farm dark at night helped regulate the farm animals' circadian rhythms. On cloudy or moonless nights, she couldn't see her hand in front of her face. But on nights like this, especially after the evening storms had passed and the sky shimmered, she could read a book by moonlight—a light so bright that the trees around the perimeter of the house cast shadows across the lawn.

Anna looked back to the clock on her nightstand. The display read 11:05. She took in a deep breath and paused. What if the boots malfunctioned, or she lost focus, or the safety wasn't set, like before? Anna tentatively scooted a little off the ledge. She tapped on her goggles, and the display came to life. *This is it.* She felt like a tightrope walker—just stepping out into nothing with only a thin thread of wire separating her from empty space. Anna breathed in deeply to calm her nerves, then took her first step out the window.

If someone had been watching from the yard below, they'd have seen a young girl walk hesitantly in midair as if balanced on a transparent pane of glass. Her steps were awkward and slow at first, as if she were afraid the glass would break if she moved too quickly. *Just nerves,* she thought. Her first solo flight. She watched her pale shadow move across the lawn, and with each step her confidence grew. The boots worked fine. She worked fine. By the time her shadow reached the edge of the lawn, she was ready. Herbie playfully ran in circles beneath her, enjoying this new game.

Anna checked the settings on her goggles. Mara had already programmed the wormhole as a destination: 2.5 kilometers northeast from her home and over a kilometer in the air. All she had to do was follow the faint blue target and she'd be at the wormhole within minutes. But there was no rush to take the straight route—not yet, not when there was so much to discover from this view on top of the world. Anna leaned forward and felt the warm night air wrap around her as she glided up and above the barn rooftops and then out across the fields that circled her home.

Every second Anna ascended into the sky, the dense sound of crickets and frogs grew fainter until all she could hear was the wind rushing past her ears. She imagined this was what it must be like for a bird. Weightless. To fly without effort. Quietly riding on air currents or, for Anna, waves of gravity.

The valley opened up before her. Patches of woods ran like dark rivers. Each field was a colored square in a patchwork quilt. Tiny headlights from what looked like toy cars bounced down different country roads, heading in different directions, oblivious to one another or the girl silently flying above their heads.

The light atop the radio tower on the outskirts of town blinked red. Just past the tower, a grid of lights crisscrossed Smartt, creating a luminescent haze that floated above the town like a halo. To the east of Smartt, in a large circular patch of dark woods, small fires burned in a line. *It must be the high school kids at the quarry party.*

Anna veered off course and headed out toward the make-shift fires instead. A quick ten-minute detour to see how the other kids lived. She thought about her friends and what they would think if they could only see her now. *I'll make the party after all.* Within a minute, she was flying hundreds of feet above the trees that lined the quarry. But even at that height she could hear car stereos thumping and kids screaming as they jumped from the edge of the quarry to the dark waters below. She watched kids wander from campfire to campfire in small packs. Some danced. Others drank. *So, this is high school.*

She slowly descended to the tops of the trees. From this distance, Anna could hear a tangle of muted conversations and make out the faces of some of the kids by the light of the fire. Anna recognized one of the girls, Katie, a waitress at the Ivanhoe. She spied two of the Killer Bs, Brittany and Brooke— or was it Bethany? They all looked the same to her. The two Bs seemed to be holding court in front of a group of upper-classmen boys, completely comfortable and in control of those around them. Anna didn't know how they did it. It was just the natural order of things for girls like the Bs. Flying in the sky without a net? Anna made that look easy. Talking with upper-classmen? That was terrifying and incomprehensible. It was a mystery as deep and dark as the wormhole she had set out to find.

Anna had felt invisible for most of her life—an outsider looking in. What would the kids think of her if they could see her now? A superhero. The girl who could fly. All she had to do was fly a little lower and announce herself to the world. The fantasy played out in her head. The shocked expressions. The shouts of encouragement from the high school kids. The adulation. *"Look up in the sky!"*

Then Anna realized one of the boys, dressed in a letterman jacket, was looking straight up at her, his expression confused, half-drunk, and totally terrified. He pointed a finger at her but was unable to string together any words that were recognizable. Before he could alert the others, Anna shot straight back and out of his line of sight, leaving the boy rambling to his friends about the beautiful girl he just saw—an angel flying in the sky.

Anna's heart thumped as she glided silently above the trees.

A voice came over the iCom. It was Mara. *"That was stupid."*

"Yeah," Anna replied quietly. "I guess you saw that."

"Did you get it out of your system at least?"

"Yeah."

"Do I need to mention the danger you'd put us in if you got caught?"

"No, I've got it. Sorry."

"Good. Now back to work."

Anna checked the display on her goggles and set herself back on course. She changed her flight path just enough to fly straight up and through a small stratus cloud. Mist fogged her glasses and cooled her skin for a moment, then she popped out of the top of the cloud, leaving a small swirl of condensation behind her.

Anna smiled. "I've always wanted to do that."

"Just stay on target."

Anna was close to a kilometer high now. The temperature was definitely cooler at this altitude, and she regretted not wearing a jacket. Something to remember for next time. Her goggles flashed a green alert. She was within two hundred meters of her destination, but there was nothing but clear skies, the moon, and the Earth's horizon in the distance. Maybe Mara's calculations were off or maybe no wormhole existed at all, as Mara had hoped. Just an aberration in her initial readings. Anna spun slowly to scan the entire sky. She moved so slowly it took almost a minute to complete a full circle, like the minute hand of a clock.

"Are you sure this is the right place?" Anna asked over her iCom.

"Positive."

"Well, I'm positive there's nothing here," Anna replied.

Then a flash of light caught the corner of her eye. In a section of the sky just beneath the Big Dipper, stars seemed to bend in a circle, like light along the edge of a ripple in a pond. Anna cocked her head to the side. The bend of light followed her. Now that she focused on it, the ripple looked more like a lens from a magnifying glass that had been pasted in the sky.

"Wait. . . ." Anna slowly glided toward the lens. "Are you picking this up?"

"Picking what up?"

"Straight ahead. I can't explain it, but I'm looking right at it." Anna glided closer, but the bend of light kept its distance. An optical illusion. "You have to be seeing this."

"Anna, are you sure? I'm not getting any readings from your iCom."

The bend of light suddenly doubled in size. It now looked like a large glass bubble, allowing light from the stars and the moon to pass through. It was hard to judge the distance, but Anna knew she was getting closer.

"Whoa!" Anna laughed. "You have to be seeing this. I'm getting a closer look."

"Anna! Wait. . . ." Mara's voice was broken up by static. *"There's . . . [static] . . . reading . . . wait."*

"Mara. You're breaking up." Anna tapped her iCom but the static persisted. "I just hope you're getting this."

The static grew louder as she glided closer to the bend of light. The display on her goggles began to glitch with random numbers and symbols. Then the display went dark.

"Mara? I can't hear you. Mara?" Anna paused midair. It was dead silent at this altitude.

The orb began to glow as light swirled around it. She was only feet away. *How did I get so close so fast?* She glided cautiously around the orb, edging closer and closer. As she neared, the light from the orb grew brighter. Traces of pink and white flashed across its surface. A hole in the sky. From a distance, she had no idea how to gauge the orb's size. Up close, she realized the orb was approximately four feet in diameter. Just big enough for her to fit through.

She floated straight above the orb and stopped, frozen in midair.

"Oh . . . my . . . ," Anna whispered.

At this angle, the orb was no longer a transparent glass bubble but a window that opened to a world brilliant in sunlight. Anna leaned in closer. Her brain had a hard time processing what she was seeing. But it was unmistakable. She was looking into a different world.

Through the window of the wormhole, Anna could see a vast ocean broken up by a chain of islands and atolls. Without perspective, she had no idea how large the islands were. They could be miles wide or feet across. But she did see waves crest against the alien beaches and sloping mountains covered in red and green vegetation. The sky on the other side was a pink-ish color, like a sunset.

Anna turned her gaze away from the bright light and blinked. It took her eyes several seconds to adjust to the dark-ness of her own world. She turned her back to the glowing orb and looked down to her own valley and out toward home. She saw the moonlight reflect off Tyson Lake in the distance and thought of Mara. She'd be worried by now and expect Anna to return. But apparently, Mara had no way of communicating. No way of knowing if Anna was okay. No way of tracking her.

Which meant Anna could do what she wanted, and what she wanted more than anything was to reach out into this new world she had just discovered. Just for a second. To be the first. *To boldly go . . . one small step . . . to infinity and beyond.* Anna turned back to the light of the wormhole and glided closer. She reached out with her left hand and watched her fingers bend and elongate as she reached into the light, like a reflection in a funhouse mirror.

So far, she hadn't been torn into subatomic particles. *That's a good sign.* She reached in even farther, up to her elbow, and all she felt was a gentle breeze against her skin on the other side. It was the perfect temperature. Warmer. Anna closed her eyes and took a deep breath before submerging her entire face into the orb as if it were a pail of water. She paused for just a moment, feeling the warmth of the alien sun against her skin, then opened her eyes.

CHAPTER 22

Anna held her breath, afraid to test the alien atmosphere. She leaned in as far as she could—half of her body floating in this new world, the other half still floating above Earth. With her one free hand, she shaded her eyes from the glare of the alien sun. A star, larger and brighter than our own, lit up the afternoon sky—or at least it felt like the afternoon, with the color and angle of the light as it was. Just beneath the bright sun, a smaller red star floated above the horizon.

Wow, a binary solar system.

Anna looked to her left and saw a chain of islands lined up across the vast ocean. Small marshmallow-like clouds floated just below and above her. Her lungs began to burn, but she couldn't pull herself away from the panoramic view of this alien planet.

The display on her goggles flickered to life, surprising Anna and forcing her to exhale the little oxygen she had left in her lungs. She frantically pulled her body back through the hole and found herself floating in the familiar night sky of her own world. She gulped in air and tried to adjust to the darkness of home. Her goggles flickered and went dark again. Something about the wormhole didn't agree with her iCom.

Anna floated in midair as her breathing returned to normal—and then it hit her. She was the first to see an alien planet up close. The first! Anna Armstrong. But it wasn't enough, and she knew it. She wanted to be the first to *explore* an alien planet. There was no question in her mind. She had proved the temperatures wouldn't freeze her skin, nor would the atmospheric pressure crush her to mush. *Hurdle one.* Jumping through the hole wouldn't be any different than a quick jump into the deep end of a pool. Just submerge yourself for a while and swim around the bottom. All she had to do was hold her breath.

One . . . Anna took in several big gulps of air to oxygenate her blood.

Two . . . She reached into the orb with both hands, then took one final deep breath.

Three . . . Anna pushed through the hole and off into an unknown world.

For a brief second, she felt like she was swimming through water, then she emerged on the other side. Immediately, her iCom flickered to life. Numbers played across the screen, letting her know the exterior temperature, 80 degrees Fahrenheit; wind speed, 17 kmph; and atmospheric composition, 24 percent oxygen, which was higher than on Earth but perfectly safe. All of her readings were within the safe green zone, but she continued to hold her breath until her lungs began to itch. She exhaled the last of her breath, then sipped in a quick gulp of air. So far, so good. The air felt normal and even tasted a little sweet, like the clearest of spring days. She allowed herself to take in another gulp, then another, until she was breathing normally. *Hurdle two.*

Anna checked the coordinates on her goggles and took a snapshot of her location. If she was going to explore, she wanted to make sure she had a way to get back. She looked down and saw speckled light reflect off the ocean's surface. To her left was a chain of small islands. To her right was a large landmass that spread off into the horizon. That looked like the best place to start her exploration.

She knew she wouldn't have long to explore. Mara would now be officially freaked out. But she couldn't pass up this chance. Anna looked back one more time to make sure the wormhole was still there. Through the bent light of the wormhole, she could see the familiar moon and stars and night sky of her own world.

The air currents were a lot bumpier here than at home, and she had to shift her weight constantly to keep from being tossed around. Maybe it was because of the ocean or the altitude. As she glided closer to land, she could make out more detail of the mountains and the vegetation. Two rivers meandered on opposite sides of the tallest peak, merging just before flowing into the ocean.

Anna was now close enough to make out a flock of white birds—or birdlike animals—riding the air currents along the edge of the shore. About a half mile off the shore, a group of ocean creatures broke the water's surface, popping in and out of the water like a school of dolphins. The altitude gauge on her dashboard read 86 meters. From that height she estimated the animals playing in the water were the size of small elephants—at least she *thought* they were playing until she noticed a shadow just beneath the water's surface closing in behind them. It looked like an enormous rock at first, but it moved at a fast clip and was propelled by four giant fins. The shadow was on the hunt. She focused her iCom on the leviathan to get its readings. It was almost 100 meters long—a little bigger than a football field—and big enough to snatch her from the sky, even at her current distance. Anna quickly changed her course up and out toward land.

She could hear the roar of the waves, fifty to sixty feet high, as they crashed on the rocks of the beach; they were twice as big as anything she had seen in Hawaii. As she made her way over land, the deafening crash of the waves gave way to a strange chorus of new sounds. Anna felt like she was trying to pick out words from a foreign language. She wasn't sure where one noise stopped and the others began. Tweets, squawks, deep thundering hums. The world was alive with sound and movement.

Beneath the canopy of trees that lined the mountain, she could make out quick flashes of alien life. A great long arm covered in white fur swung gracefully on the branch of a tree. Two eyes peered between fan-shaped leaves. Smaller red animals, like jellyfish, swung from tree to tree in a pack, their movement like water flowing in a stream. There was so much to see—so much that was alien—that the images began to blur in Anna's mind no matter how hard she tried to hold on.

Anna followed the path of one of the rivers, past a series of cascading waterfalls to its source at the top of the mountain. At this height, clouds swirled around the mountain like water flowing around a rock, and the wind buffeted her from side to side. Water vapor formed droplets on her skin and hair. But once she cleared the mountaintop, the wind gusts stopped and a great valley opened up in front of her. The land was flat as far as she could see. No hills. No mountain ranges in the distance. Just an uninterrupted flat plain dotted with enormous trees that mushroomed hundreds of feet into the air, their branches leaning toward the ocean like sentries pointing toward a faraway destination. Underneath the shade of their giant canopies, four-legged animals grazed on rust-colored and lime-green grasses.

She slowly descended until she was just feet off the ground but far enough away from the tree and the herds of animals to be safe. She had no way of knowing if they were carnivores, omnivores, or herbivores and didn't feel like testing it out. The ground looked safe enough—no quicksand or giant insects or gaping holes ready to suck her underground. Anna landed gently on the surface. The first thing she noticed was that the soil felt a little softer than soil at home, almost spongy.

Anna ran her hand along the blades of waist-high red and green grasses, which felt soft like fur. Was it her imagination or were the grasses bending and reaching out toward her as she walked through the giant meadow? The sun was warm and the air dry. In the distance, she heard beautiful singing unlike anything she had heard before. Were the animals talking with one another? Was this their music? The sound worked its way into her head and resonated in her chest. Her shoulders relaxed; her eyes half closed. Anna found herself smiling and swaying with the grass as the light from the alien suns warmed her skin.

Then something flapped against her face. Feathers.

"Aaack!" Anna swatted her hand in front of her face.

A birdlike creature fluttered around her head, swooping and swirling as if trying to get her attention. Another birdlike creature landed on the ground near her feet and looked straight up at Anna. Anna looked straight back, surprised to see something so familiar in this alien landscape.

"What are you doing here, little fella?" Anna smiled. "You look just like the birds we have at home."

Then she realized it *was* a bird from home. She didn't know the type of bird, but she was sure she had seen it before. There was no mistaking it. The bird seemed to respond to her voice and joined its friend in fluttering around her playfully.

"How long have you been here, you poor things? Did you fly through the same wormhole I did?" Anna asked softly, afraid she might scare them away. "You'd never be this friendly on the other side, would you? You must sense I'm from home."

The two birds began to tweet loudly and swoop and swirl

around her head. Something was agitating them. And, just as quickly as they'd appeared, the two birds took off like a shot in the direction of the closest giant tree.

"Was it something I said?" Anna called out.

Then it hit her. The silence. The beautiful song that had filled the air was gone. The air was still. Anna looked around nervously. The animals under the canopy of the trees had disappeared. All bad signs.

Anna held her breath as she strained to hear any approaching sound. She watched her two bird friends take off in a straight line toward the tree, only to disappear in a gap in the trunk. Then she realized all the animals had made their way into the base of the cavernous tree trunk, barely visible. Hidden and protected. *What are they doing?*

A loud thunderous groan broke the silence and made Anna jump. The groan was followed by a terrible and great sustained crash of wood twisting and snapping. The branches of the giant tree somehow began to twist and fold and collapse, wrapping around its trunk in a protective cocoon. Each tree that dotted the horizon moved in a similar pattern, closing their giant branches like bird wings. How could anything so big move so quickly?

The grass that swayed in the breeze just moments ago began to collapse in circles at her feet. In a giant rolling wave and a quiet hush, grass flattened against the ground as far as she could see until the ground looked like a green and red carpet. In seconds, the entire landscape had changed. Alien and incomprehensible.

The temperature had also changed: 90 degrees and rising, according to her iCom. Sweat began to trickle down Anna's back. Ninety-five degrees, now 100. The air that smelled sweet like spring just moments ago began to turn stale. Anna sniffed and her lip curled up in disgust. Sulfur. A breeze began to blow from across the valley, but it was hot and dry and quickly became a full-blown gale.

Oh man, what had she been thinking? Anna wanted to kick herself. How long had she been gone? Where was she? Anna tapped her iCom and mapped the location of the portal that would lead her back home. The display read 21 kilometers away. She plotted a course back to the wormhole, and a blue target appeared on the screen. She turned and readied herself to fly when something in her peripheral vision caught her attention.

A figure, dressed in black, stood alone in the distance. It wore a round white hat that reflected the sun like a halo. *It can't be,* Anna thought. And suddenly she felt she was in a dream remembering a dream. She had imagined these creatures months before—the creatures in the field outside her window. The figure's impossibly long and thin arms swayed back and forth as if it were searching for something. She was sure of it. It was searching for her.

From this distance, she could barely make out its face. White like bone. Two dark holes where eyes should be. Suddenly, the figure stopped and raised its head. Its eyes locked with Anna's, and then it began to run toward her in herky-jerky movements. Too fast. Anna couldn't move her legs; she couldn't feel her legs. She was frozen.

Before it could reach her, the creature stopped and opened its mouth, a round black hole that seemed to take up more than half its face. A silent scream. The creature made no sound, but somehow Anna could hear it speaking to her. A voice deep within her head. Words without language. It was unmistakable. The creature told her:

Run!

And just like that the creature vanished. She was left alone. Anna felt like she was losing her mind.

In the far distance, clouds on the horizon began to part and disappear at a great speed. It reminded Anna of an old grainy film she saw of an atomic bomb blast and how the resulting shock wave parted the clouds in the sky. Just like now. Something was parting the clouds in the sky, and it was heading directly toward her.

"Oh no. . . ."

It started with a rumble, like jet engines in the distance, growing louder and louder until the sound vibrated in her chest and made her head throb.

"No, no, no, no, no!"

Anna instinctively turned and ran in the opposite direction of the sound. She was able to clear ten paces before she was hit hard with a wall of air that tossed her dozens of feet into the air. She was spinning now, lost in an air current, unable to tell which direction was up or down. The roar of the wind was deafening. She was stuck in some kind of alien windstorm, and it took all she had not to put her hands over her ears and scream.

Her lungs began to itch. From the corner of her iCom display, the oxygen sensor blinked red: 19.5 percent and dropping. At this oxygen level, she had minutes left before she would pass out. The more she struggled against the wind, the more she was tossed like a rag doll. The wind speeds were well over 130 kilometers per hour and rising. At this rate, she'd be tossed out far across the ocean—far enough away from the wormhole that she'd never find her way back. She'd be stuck here forever on this alien planet. That is, if she survived at all.

It was like being caught in the undertow at the beach. There was no fighting it. She forced herself to relax and lean in the direction of the wind even though her body was racked with panic. At least she was being blown in the direction of the wormhole. Now it was a matter of aiming herself perfectly at the wormhole and hitting it straight on while going well over

150 kilometers per hour and spinning out of control. Easy—like hitting a bullseye in a hurricane.

The first obstacle was the mountain range that was fast approaching. Anna flattened herself out and used her arms and legs to ride the air currents over a mountaintop. Just as she stabilized her flight, her body was hit with a crosscurrent and she began to tumble out of control. No matter how hard she breathed, she couldn't take in enough oxygen. She was close to blacking out, but she couldn't stop now. Anna used her core to stabilize the spin and was back on course. But the spinning and lack of oxygen were taking their toll.

At this speed, Anna calculated she had seventy-five seconds before reaching the wormhole, but her lungs were already burning and she wasn't sure if she could hold on that long. She tried to relax and conserve oxygen. *Focus. Focus.* Anna rode the air current along the mountain range, just clearing the peak before being shot out into empty air like a cannonball.

Her iCom showed the wormhole straight ahead of her, but she was beneath it by two hundred meters. She needed to climb at a six-degree angle if she had any hope of reaching it in time. She used the little bit of strength left to adjust her arms and legs like ailerons on a plane, even though her body was being rocked from side to side. *Five degrees. Four degrees.* Forty-five seconds to go. Anna wondered why her iCom display was growing dim—then she realized she was blacking out. *Two degrees.*

Almost in line. Almost. Come on.

Anna's vision began to blur. Twenty-five seconds to go. The blackness at the edge of her vision began to constrict like a lens closing on a camera. Blurred colors streamed past her. Ahead was a tapestry of black, speckled with points of light. Her arms and legs grew limp. The last thing she remembered was the roar of the wind. Then nothing.

PART II

THE SHADOW

CHAPTER 23

The Shadow sat perched in a tree at the edge of the woods. It had been sitting perfectly still for the past twenty-four hours, waiting for any kind of sign that could lead it home. This strange new place was tiring, with its bright lights and heat. At home, the air was cool and the sky dark all the time, but here the sky would turn bright without warning. The light burned its skin and hurt its eyes before thankfully turning dark again. The Shadow didn't know how it had arrived here or why. But it ached for home.

Then a sound cut through the silence—a sound only it could hear. The Shadow turned its head to the sky and saw a flash of light. Anyone else who'd looked up at that moment would have thought it was a meteor or an unusually bright star, but the Shadow's vision was far sharper, especially at night.

The first thing the Shadow saw was the light and a stream of dust, then a small figure falling from a hole far up in the sky. The falling figure was limp and its arms and legs unresponsive as it plummeted toward the ground. The Shadow could tell it was hurt. It also knew that the falling object emerged from the same kind of hole that had brought the Shadow itself to this world. Maybe this was the way home.

The Shadow leaped from the top of the tree to land silently on the ground below. It took off in the direction of the falling body, leaping over fallen trees and ravines and dashing across empty fields. All the while, it kept its focus on the falling object. Maybe it was too focused on the object—or it was unfamiliar with this strange new world—but the Shadow didn't see the two bright lights barreling toward it as it ran. When the Shadow did notice, it was too late. It turned and was blinded immediately. Pain seared through its head, and it stood frozen in its tracks.

A thin, protective lens rolled down across its eyes, which allowed it to see in the bright light but did little to lessen the pain. When its vision cleared, the Shadow could make out a figure just behind the two lights. The strange figure opposite the Shadow was sitting in what looked like a yellow shell or a box. The creature's eyes were small. Its skin pale and pink. The two stared at each other for what seemed like minutes. The Shadow tilted its head and took a cautious step forward, then another. Suddenly, strange sounds floated out from inside the yellow box, and the Shadow panicked. The muscles in its legs coiled like springs and it leaped over the two lights, bounced off the top of the hard shell, and disappeared into the night.

CHAPTER 24

Katie Summerfield was having a really bad night. First, her boss had told her she needed to open the Ivanhoe Diner in the morning, which meant she had to wake up at 5:00 a.m. the day after graduating from high school. Second, her boyfriend had flirted with an incoming freshman at the quarry party. An incoming freshman! Third, the battery on her phone was almost dead; she had forgotten the charging cord in her boyfriend's truck, and she was still fifteen minutes from home.

She decided to take a shortcut from the quarry party by driving along the half-paved road that connected the Potter farm to the main highway. The road was still muddy from the afternoon rain, and Katie had some difficulty avoiding large puddles and potholes while texting—so much difficulty that she almost veered off the road twice while crafting a particularly long and poignant breakup text to her boyfriend.

She was debating with herself whether to push Send or not when a shape darted out in the road in front of her.

"Sugar!" Katie shouted as she slammed on the brakes.

Her phone flew from her hand as the car skidded to a stop.

"Perfect! Stupid deer," Katie muttered. "I bet I cracked my screen again."

She felt blindly along the floor of her car and found her phone wedged just beneath the emergency brake release. She picked up the phone, looked down, and for a brief moment felt things weren't a total disaster. No cracks on her screen, breakup text still pending.

Then Katie glanced up at the road in front of her. The figure she had mistaken for a deer was still there. But it was no deer. At first, she thought it was a kid dressed up in a Halloween costume, but then she realized its arms and legs were too long, too thin. And its skin shimmered black in the glare of the headlights.

"O . . . M . . . G." Katie whispered each letter.

The black-as-night creature stared at her, unmoving and silent. Its large platelike eyes blinked. Slowly, Katie raised her phone to eye level.

"Hey, Hooli . . . take a video," Katie whispered a voice command to her phone.

"I'm sorry. I didn't understand your command. Please try again," her phone replied at a volume that seemed to echo out to the hills and beyond.

"Hey, Hooli. Take a video," Katie whispered frantically. Her heart was racing. "Stupid phone."

"Searching for Wi-Fi hotspots in your area," her phone cheerfully answered.

"Shut up," Katie whimpered.

She could barely breathe and was almost too terrified to move. Her left hand trembled as she reached over to manually press the video record button on her phone.

"You're in luck. There is a Wi-Fi hotspot within three miles. Mapping directions now." The voice assistant on her phone sounded pleased.

The timer on the video camera ticked off the milliseconds.

She was getting this strange creature on film. The fear that had paralyzed Katie was slowly giving way to the realization that she was quite possibly going to be famous. Once she posted this video, she would be trending for days to come. Maybe a spot on television. Katie was counting the possible number of retweets in her head when the black creature took a step toward her.

"Ghuuug" was the sound that came from Katie's lungs. It was a totally involuntary response to a deep and primitive fear she had never felt before. It was also totally uncool, and she knew, even then in the grip of panic, that she'd have to edit that sound out later. If she survived.

The creature took another cautious step toward the car. Katie began fumbling for the gear shift with her left hand while she held her phone with her right. Her body twisted. She was whimpering now. Tears welled up in her eyes. Before she could put the car in reverse, the creature suddenly leaped toward it. Impossibly fast.

Katie screamed and dropped her phone again just as the creature landed on top of the car. She sat frozen, sobbing, straining her ears to hear the slightest sound.

"Proceed down Potter Road for a quarter mile, then take a left at Dewey Road."

The sudden sound of the automated phone assistant made Katie jump, but it was enough to get her moving again. She slammed on the gas pedal and sped away, not looking back—not even reaching for her phone.

CHAPTER 25

Anna dreamed of a distant plain. She stood in waist-high grass that swayed in rolling waves with the soft wind. Next to her stood a figure twice her height—the figure with the round white hat from the other world. Anna stood in its shadow. Its bone-like hand reached down to Anna as if it were beckoning her to follow. She looked up into its face and saw its eyes for the first time. What she thought were two empty holes were actually round discs filled with tiny spinning lights. No, not lights—galaxies were spinning in its eyes. Billions of stars, endless and outside of time. Without speaking, the figure told her:

It is time to go.

Anna opened her eyes and blinked.

A campfire burned bright in front of her. She was lying on her side on the softest pillow she had ever felt. There was a sudden pop from the fire, and sparks shot upward to slowly fade in the night sky. At the base of the fire, embers glowed red, and Anna smelled the most pleasant scent of cinnamon and cedar. At first, she thought she was still dreaming. But then she felt small hammers take turns pounding her forehead. *Nope, only reality could feel this bad.*

Mara sat across from her. Silent. Her arms crossed and her expression set like stone. Without moving her head, Anna scanned the area to figure out where she was. It took a second. Her head was still blurry, but she finally recognized the deck and fire pit outside Mara's home that overlooked Tyson Lake. She just had no idea how she'd gotten there. Anna knew she might be safe, but from the expression on Mara's face, she was still in trouble.

Anna went back to gazing at the fire in silence. Mara continued to stare straight ahead. Neither of them spoke for several moments. Both waited for the other to start. SID broke the silence, its voice bright over Anna's iCom.

<*Your readings indicated you suffered oxygen deprivation, but fortunately no cerebral hypoxia or heart and brain damage. I gave you a treatment of concentrated oxygen while you slept. You should be fine except for the severe headache and nausea. Isn't that good news?*>

Anna's head hurt so badly that tears welled up in her eyes and rolled gently down her cheek to be soaked up by the pillow.

"What part of straight up and straight down didn't you understand?" Mara finally spoke. Her voice wasn't angry or elevated, just tired. "I'm so mad at you."

"I know."

Anna looked up. Mara's eyes shimmered in the firelight. The two sat in silence for another minute.

"I don't know if it means anything to you, but I was worried sick," Mara said quietly. "I thought I'd lost you."

"I'm sorry."

"I didn't think I'd feel like this, but I do. I've been alone for so long I'd forgotten what it's like to care about someone. To have a friend. To have something to lose."

"A friend?"

Mara smiled as a slightly quizzical look crossed her face. "Of course, a friend. But it doesn't change the fact that I'm still mad at you. You're all I have, Anna."

Anna smiled. The pounding in her head started to fade. The ice had broken.

"How did you find me?"

"It wasn't hard. I just looked for a girl falling from a hole in the sky. There aren't too many of those around," Mara said. "Your boots slowed your descent just like I said they would."

"Yay," Anna said meekly.

"Once your system was back online, I took over control of your boots and guided you back here."

Anna smiled. The idea of her floating around the countryside upside down in the dead of night made her want to laugh, but her head still hurt too much. "I wonder what the cows must have thought seeing me float across the fields."

"'Oh, look. What an obstinate, thickheaded child.' If I'd known you were going to fly around the entire valley instead of straight to the wormhole like I told you, I'd have wrapped you in a cloaking device. I'll need to work on that." Mara paused for a moment, then sighed. "Was it worth it? Going through the wormhole to the other side?"

Anna thought about what to say next, then smiled broadly. "Yeah. Yes. A thousand times. There is so much I want to tell you—so much that was different in the world I saw. I'm afraid I can't remember it all."

"Was it beautiful?"

"It was the most amazing place I've ever seen. Oceans like our world, with giant animals just below the surface of the water. They had to have been three or four times as big as a whale. There were dense forests and craggy mountains. I saw trees the size of skyscrapers."

"I may be mad, but I'm also envious. I wish I had been there with you."

"I'm sorry I made a mess of things. Were you able to get what you needed at least? The data you were looking for? I'd hate to think the whole night was a waste."

"Yes, I was able to find data. Lots of it. I just don't have a clue what most of it means. There were no energy signatures. No gravitational waves. Nothing. Based on what I saw, there is no reason the wormhole should've ever existed in the first place. It takes a tremendous amount of energy to open a wormhole, and even more to keep it stable."

"I don't understand," Anna said.

"I'm beginning to think my time travel here didn't cause the wormhole after all. Which means some other force caused it." Mara's voice drifted. "And made it disappear almost at the exact moment you fell from the sky. But I had nothing to do with it, and that's what concerns me."

Mara stared absently at the fire in front of her as if she were still processing that last sentence. Anna used the pause in the conversation to work up the nerve to sit upright. She took in a deep breath and pushed herself up to a seated position. She was still light-headed, but the pounding had stopped. She held the pillow close to her chest for comfort.

"On to other good news. Do you remember once asking me what we might find on the other side of these wormholes? Well, I think we found out tonight." Mara leaned forward. "SID? Can you pull up the video posted to social media earlier?"

A large rectangle of light, translucent and slightly curved like a TV screen, floated feet off the ground between Mara and Anna. On the left side of the screen, a large browser window appeared with a blurred image and a Play button.

"What is this?" Anna asked.

"It's footage captured earlier tonight from a local girl

named Katie Summerfield. SID, can you play the video please?"

It took a moment for Anna's eyes to adjust to the dark and blurry image. But as the video started to roll and the image cleared, the almost pitch-black figure snapped into view. Humanlike but definitely not human. Pie-sized eyes. A round head with no perceivable mouth or nose. Black skin that seemed to absorb light. Feather-like structures swept back from its round head. Anna jumped when the figure hurtled toward the video camera. The picture froze, then went blank.

"Close screen, SID," Mara asked.

"Ohhh, that's not good," Anna whispered. "What are we going to do?"

"I've scanned your town's police channels, phone lines, and social media feeds. It looks like some of the locals are already on the hunt for the creature as we speak. If it's found, it will change your world in profound ways."

"Do you know what it is?"

"No." Mara shook her head. "All I know is that it's not of this world."

"So it's an alien. A real-life alien and proof that life exists elsewhere. And we're not going to get a chance to learn more about it because half the town is hunting for it! Have you seen the road signs around here? They're covered in bullet holes. That creature doesn't have a chance." Anna jumped up. "We have to find it before it gets hurt."

"Or *someone* gets hurt. We have no idea what this creature can do or how it thinks. It could be dangerous. I'm not letting you continue this on your own." Mara sighed. "It's time I join you on the other side of this wall."

"What about all that 'putting the future at risk' stuff?"

"Considering this video already has ten thousand views, I'd say the chances of stopping changes to your timeline are . . . zero. I'm more concerned about the future of *you* at this moment," Mara said. "It'll be much more efficient if we work together anyway. And safer."

"Awesome! It's about time." Anna smiled. "But wait. What happens if someone sees you or tries to talk to you? This is a small town. People will notice. My uncle will notice. And, no offense, but your future-girl outfit doesn't exactly blend in."

"Hmm." Mara frowned.

"You could wear a disguise?" Anna offered.

"A disguise doesn't explain why an adult is spending a good part of the day hanging around a child. That would look suspicious."

"Yeah, good point," Anna said.

"I need a reason to spend hours of time at your house without causing suspicion," Mara said.

"How about being my tutor?" Anna offered. "No one would be surprised if I were working with a teacher."

"A teacher?" Mara worked it around in her head. "That's not a bad idea. It would explain why I'm around. But what kind of teacher?"

"Hopefully a patient one. You can just say you're tutoring me for college prep."

"Perfect. I'll work on a story tonight. Then we should get started in the morning. . . ." Mara's voice trailed off.

A silence floated between them—a different silence than before. Mara looked expectantly at Anna, not sure what to say. Her face filled with something Anna hadn't seen before: doubt.

"Are you okay?" Anna asked.

"Yes, I just . . . can't remember." Mara shook her head as she stood from her chair. "I can't remember what it was like to be outside. I mean really outside. With other people."

Anna smiled. "I'll be there with you."

Mara sighed deeply, then returned the smile. "Yes, you will."

CHAPTER 26

Ba-da-doop.
 Ba-da-doop.

Anna rolled over in bed and willed her eyes to open.

Ba-da-doop.

She still had a trace of a headache, and the morning light seemed too bright and hit at odd angles. The bedroom window was open and the curtains rolled in the breeze, exposing a bright blue sky and a late-morning sun.

Ba-da-doop.

Anna looked over at her phone on the nightstand. 11:15 a.m. It buzzed with a new text message.

"Stop already," she moaned.

Ba-da-doop.

Anna grabbed her phone and squinted to focus. Forty-two messages in a group chat with Scout Master, Fi0na, and L00L-A.

Ba-da-doop. Forty-three messages.

Anna's fingers felt thick as she typed her response.

Anna-kin: Slept in late zzzzzzzzzz. SRY

Scout Master: Did you see my text!?!?!?!

Anna-kin: Which 1

Scout Master: All of them. We r being invaded! Did you see Summerfield's video?

Fi0na: Why is HE on this chat?

Fi0na: Heading out to Potter rd later where Katie took the video. Wnat to come?

L00L-A: Lol

L00L-A: we sound like the scooby gang

Anna-kin: Sure. I'm bzy this morning. But meet me at my place this evening. Sounds fun :)

She signed off with a smiley face but didn't feel much like a smiley face. She yawned as she made her way downstairs. There was muffled conversation in the distance, but the voices didn't register. Nothing registered except the desire to crawl back into bed. She yawned one more time for good measure and turned toward the kitchen.

No one was there. For a brief moment she headed toward the refrigerator out of habit, then realized she didn't have an appetite. She glanced out the window to see where the voices were coming from, then froze. Her heart skipped.

Uncle Jack was in the front yard with his back to the house. Across from him stood Mara. She was wearing a brilliant white shirt with the sleeves rolled up and a pair of worn blue jeans. Her hair was pulled back in an ornate braid spun with mathematical precision. She was radiant.

Anna opened the screen door and stepped out onto the porch. Uncle Jack heard the hinges squeak and turned.

"Hey, she's alive," Uncle Jack said. "I was just going to come drag you out of bed. No need to thank me for doing your chores."

Mara glanced up at Anna with a knowing smile and winked.

"Good morning, Anna. It's a pleasure to finally meet you face-to-face." Mara preemptively walked over to Anna and extended her hand.

Anna shook Mara's hand in return, her face showing a combination of confusion and an oxygen deprivation–hangover headache.

"I'm surprised you didn't tell me we were going to have a visitor today." Uncle Jack smiled, his face flushed. "And what's this about an Albright Fellowship? That sounds amazing."

"Yeah—amazing." Anna looked over to Mara for help.

"It's part of the Albright Fellowship program, where they match gifted young students like Anna with teachers like me," Mara explained without missing a beat. "Anna had agreed to meet on a daily basis over the summer—that is, if it's not an inconvenience to your family."

"Well, considering the family is just me and Anna, there's no inconvenience here. I just wish Anna would have told me sooner." Uncle Jack looked down at himself, a little embarrassed. He was covered in streaks of dirt and grease. "If you're interested, I could show you around the farm later. That is, after you two have finished and I shower, of course."

"I'd like that very much," Mara said.

Anna detected a different tone in Mara's voice—lighter and more playful. And Uncle Jack was goofier than usual, unable to stop smiling and holding on to glances just a second too long. There was an uncomfortable pause when the two seemed unsure of how to finish the conversation or where to go next. Anna wasn't sure if it was because this was Mara's first encounter post-exile or if there was something else. Uncle Jack smiled again and made an awkward wave before heading inside the house. Anna waited for him to leave.

"Albright Fellowship?" Anna asked. "Is that even a thing?"

"It's a thing now. SID and I created it last night. It even has a website in case someone gets nosy."

Anna looked behind Mara and noticed a new motorcycle in the driveway.

"Wait. Did you create that too?" Anna pointed.

"Of course not. I bought it this morning. I need a form of transportation other than flying, don't you think? And I always wanted to ride one of those things."

"But how? Where did you get the money?"

"It was a lot easier than you'd expect."

"You stole?"

"That sounds so harsh when you say it that way. Of course I didn't steal. I just generated cryptocurrency and created my own bank accounts. Anonymous and untraceable," Mara said. "Come here, I have something for you."

Mara walked over to her motorcycle and removed a metal box that had been strapped to the rear seat with bungee cords; it was a box like the one Mara had given her yesterday, only slightly larger. She handed it to Anna, who immediately held it to the side of her head and shook it.

"What is it?" Anna asked.

"Part three of your training. Now, go upstairs and try them on. We have a lot of work to do today," Mara said. "And bring your goggles down with you after you change."

Anna bounded upstairs while trying to place the tip of her index finger into the indent at the top of the box. She finally made contact, and the top of the box instantly slid open. Anna flipped the box over and dumped its contents onto her unmade bed. Laid out in front of her were a pair of gray jeans and a white long-sleeve shirt with seamless red stripes running down the sleeves. The fabric glistened with iridescent light as she held it up in front of her.

She tried on the jeans first. No surprise, a perfect fit. But the fabric felt much softer than jean material and almost weightless. The shirt was weightless too. She stood in front of the mirror and was surprised by the figure in front of her.

Like Mara had said yesterday, she had changed. She wasn't the beanpole with a mop of light brown hair she had been her entire life. For the first time, she was able to look at herself—really see herself—without cringing. A faint smile crossed her lips. Then she remembered the goggles.

Anna rummaged through unfolded clothes in her dresser drawer and grabbed her goggles. Before she headed downstairs, she glanced out her side window. Down below, Mara was sitting on her knees beneath the shade of the old bur oak tree. She seemed to be lost in a dream. Her hand moved slowly back and forth across the grass. Her gaze focused on the ground beneath her. It was strange seeing Mara in this new context, away from the protection of her hidden fortress.

The noon sun bore down hot as Anna walked across the lawn. But the material in her new shirt reflected the heat and kept her cool. As Anna crossed the line of shade from the leaves above and joined Mara at the foot of the tree, she felt a marked decrease in temperature.

"What are you looking at?" Anna asked.

"I've counted over twelve different species of insects in the last two minutes. Twelve," Mara said wistfully without looking up. "I could sit here for hours and watch this procession of ants. There's so much to learn."

"Sounds like fun. Now, what did you want to show me?" Anna held out her goggles.

Mara ignored her, leaning back against the tree and looking up into the network of fractal limbs and branches above her head. Pinpoints of sun broke through the leaves as they fluttered in the light breeze. She closed her eyes and breathed in deeply.

"Are you okay?" Anna asked.

Mara smiled but kept her eyes closed. "The air feels so different here. In this time."

"You mean the farm smells?"

Mara chuckled and opened her eyes.

"No. I'm talking about the sheer diversity of smells and sounds. Just life." Mara sat up tall. Her attention back. "Now let me take a look at you. How do the clothes feel?"

"Kind of weird, like I'm wearing nothing," Anna said as she held her arms out and shrugged.

"You'll get used to it. Now put on your goggles."

Anna wrapped her goggles behind her ears and jumped. The red lines on her sleeves glowed like neon stripes. She held her arms up and admired the light show.

"Whoa, that's new," Anna said.

"Just wait. Now tap the small divot just above the right lens of your goggles."

"Here?" Anna ran her finger along the frame until she felt a small divot she hadn't noticed before.

"Yep. Right there."

Anna pressed the divot and felt a tight suction form around the edges of her face and underneath her chin, as if someone had just shoved a giant plunger against her face. She instinctively grabbed for her face in alarm, and her fingers tapped against a hard, transparent surface. She moved her fingers along a faint seam that ran around her forehead and ears and down her face to under her chin. It was a transparent mask. A perfectly fitted mask. Anna could hear her own breath.

"What the heck is this?" Anna shouted. Her own voice sounded loud in her head. She tried pulling at the edges of the seam, but the mask felt welded to her face.

"Don't even try. When activated, your mask has an almost impenetrable seal. Trust me. That is a good thing. In zero-oxygen environments it provides approximately twelve hours of oxygen," Mara said.

"Well, thanks for telling me that now! Might have come in handy last night when I almost died of *oxygen deprivation!*" Anna stood up and put her hands on her hips.

Mara ignored her as she flipped on her own mask. It was almost invisible except for the slight seam that ran around her forehead and underneath her chin.

"Okay, now we match," Mara said.

"Huh. I can barely see it," Anna said as she reached out and touched Mara's mask.

Mara swatted her hand away.

"That's the point. The less people see, the better. Which brings me to this." Mara stood up, placed her hand on her iCom, and smiled. "Ready?"

"Ready for wha—" Anna stopped midsentence.

Mara was gone. Vanished. The spot she'd occupied just seconds before was empty. Anna instinctively flung her arm out where Mara had just been standing and hit a solid, invisible object that felt like a wall of muscle.

"Oof!" Mara grunted through her iCom. "Please don't do that, Anna. I'm invisible. Not permeable."

Anna laughed out loud while still poking the invisible figure in front of her with her index fingers. "Invisibility. That is awesome! How did you do that?"

"If you quit poking me, I'll show you," Mara said.

Anna felt a small static surge over her body, then looked down. There was just empty space where her legs had been. She waved her hands in front of her face, but there was nothing there. A phantom limb. Disoriented, Anna felt herself stumble backward only to be caught and steadied by an invisible hand.

"Invisibility is a little disorienting at first, like flying, but you'll get used to it," Mara said. "There are a couple of different cloaking settings. This setting here—no one can see you. You can't even see you."

"It makes it kind of hard to grab ahold of stuff." Anna reached out to the tree but misjudged the distance and jammed her invisible index finger into the trunk. "*Ow!*"

"If you hold still for a second, I'll show you a different

cloaking setting—the one you and I will be using most often," Mara said.

Anna heard a slight buzz, then Mara instantly reappeared, this time surrounded by a neon light-blue outline. Anna looked down at her hands and legs. Her body was outlined with the same thin blue line.

"Why am I glowing?"

"You're not. Our visors have been set to bypass the cloaking device. As long as I have my visor on, I can see you and you can see me. But to the rest of the world we're invisible."

"So no one can see us?"

"Or hear us. Our masks block out the sound of our voices. The only way we can hear each other is through our iComs. We are effectively ghosts to the rest of the world. Want to try it out?"

Mara took two steps away from the oak tree and gently floated twenty feet above the ground, her body a silhouette against the sun. Anna looked nervously past the tree to the barnyard, where farmworkers busily hustled between research barns. No one seemed to notice the figure floating in the air just above their heads. Mara motioned for her to follow.

Anna took a couple of bounding steps, then floated to Mara's side. It felt glorious to be flying again, especially in the light of day. She looked down and expected to see her shadow, but there was nothing there except gravel and dirt from the driveway, brightly lit in the noonday sun. She looked over to the house. She was eye level with her bedroom. Her brain tried to process this new perspective: different angles and patterns on the roof, hidden from her previous earthbound view. She silently glided over to her bedroom and placed her hand on the window to peer in. She could see her hand, but there was no reflection in the glass.

"Come on," Mara called out. "Let's get to a higher vantage point."

Anna kicked away from the house like a swimmer pushing off from the side of a pool and joined Mara as they glided
several hundred feet above the ground. Warm air wrapped
around them like a blanket, and the horizon opened before
them as they ascended. Bright green patchwork fields, irrigation lines, and a loose grid of dirt roads lined the valley
floor. Anna could see the entire shoreline of Tyson Lake from
this height. Across the lake, Mara's home, invisible to others,
shone like an alien outpost—the white dome and crystal spire
reflected light. Anna figured that Mara's house must use the
same cloaking setting.

"This should be good. Let's stop here," Mara said.

She placed her hand on Anna's shoulder and slowed them
both to a stop. The two bobbed in the air currents like swim-
mers on the surface of a lake. Anna was mesmerized by the
view and the quiet. This wasn't like flying in a plane, where
circular steel walls box you in and the view out the window is
like watching the sky through a small TV screen. Up here like
this, there was nothing but sky in all directions.

"Can you show me where the creature was sighted last
night?" Mara asked.

"The quarry is about ten miles that way. Potter Road
should be about halfway in that direction," Anna said, pointing. "My friends are headed over there this evening to check it
out. Should we wait?"

"No. That may actually prove useful. Look for footprints or
tracks. Anything that might help us," Mara said.

Mara casually laid back with her hands behind her head
and looked up into the brilliant blue sky. Anna tried to do the
same but did a cartwheel first before finding her center of balance. After a moment of spinning back and forth, she was able
to come to a stop with her body in a supine position. She im-
itated her older friend and placed her hands behind her head.

She looked up into the sky, no ground in sight, and felt adrift on an infinite blue sea.

"This is sooo weird. We're literally floating on air." Anna smiled.

"I do this sometimes when I just want to think. It feels like a blank slate up here. Helps to clear the mind," Mara said. "So, let's talk about last night. What can you tell me about the creature we saw in the video? Its characteristics."

"Its characteristics? I don't know. It was dark."

"Really? That's all you could piece together?"

"Uh, well. It had two arms, two legs like us—but not like us."

"Your powers of observation are astounding." Mara grinned.

Anna frowned.

"Okay. It had super big eyes." Anna paused. "And it seemed to be sensitive to light."

"Go on."

"Which means it probably evolved in a dark environment, right?"

"Exactly. And what was the world like that you visited last night?" Mara asked.

"Really bright. It had two suns, and with the way they were positioned, it was probably bright and sunny most of the time," Anna said, then paused again. "Okay, I get it. You don't think this creature came from the same world I visited last night."

"Which means there is another wormhole in our area."

"Great. We're leaking all over the place," Anna said.

"I don't know how we missed it, and that's what troubles me," Mara said quietly. "While you're out with your friends this evening, I'm going to run some different models with the new data we collected last night."

"Do you think anything else made it through the wormhole?" Anna asked. "Like another, you know . . . visitor."

"I don't know. But it's possible," Mara said, then turned to face Anna. "I want you to be careful tonight. Promise me that you will be careful. If you see anything—I mean anything— out of the ordinary, I want you to contact me at once. This is a search mission, not a capture."

"I got it."

"No. I don't think you do."

Mara spun in a half circle to an upright position and shoved Anna's shoulder, knocking her off-balance and sending her spinning like a leaf in a current. Anna flailed her arms until she regained her balance.

"Hey, what did you do that for?" Anna shouted.

"Because I don't believe you. I know exactly what you're going to do if you see the creature. You're going to try to communicate. You're going to get too close." Mara folded her arms.

"How do you know?"

"Because it's exactly what I would do if I were you," Mara said. "Which means I can't stop you. So you'd better at least find a way to protect yourself."

Mara glided over. Before Anna could move, Mara grabbed ahold of both her wrists and turned her palms down.

"Are you going to throw me again?" Anna flinched.

"Not yet." Mara smiled. "Now, take a look at your iCom. See anything different?"

Anna looked down and saw something unfamiliar: a tiny, pulsing red diamond on the bottom corner of each iCom.

"That's new."

"I just activated your defense mode," Mara said as she let go of Anna's hands. "Triple-tap the diamond with your index finger."

"Does it matter which hand?"

"Either hand. Just triple-tap."

Anna tapped the red diamond on her left wrist three times. Three holographic shapes outlined in red appeared above the back of her left hand: a circular ring, a sine wave, and a starburst.

"Cool! This is just like a video game. What's this do?" Anna asked as she flicked the red ring.

Instantly, the display disappeared, and a strange pressure formed around Anna's fist, like someone had dipped her hand in concrete.

"Do you always act first and then ask questions?" Mara asked.

"Pretty much," Anna said. "Hey, why does my hand feel funny? It's like I'm wearing a tight glove."

"That's your first defense. It's a vortex cannon. It fires pressurized air."

Anna pointed her arm out and closed her right eye like she was sighting a gun.

"Nice. How do I shoot it?"

"Watch me," Mara said as she held her arm straight out in front of her. "Point your arm where you want to fire, like this, then double-clench your fist. That primes the cannon. When you want to fire, just clench your fist again."

Mara clenched her fist, and a small ringlike puff of vapor burst from her hand in a blur, so fast Anna could barely track it. Mara held both her arms out in front of her and began firing off vapor rings in rapid succession, her hands pulsing like an air machine gun. Vapor trails began to form in front of them like small wispy clouds.

"Wow! That is awesome. Let me try it." Anna held her arm out.

"Do you want me to finish showing you—"

"No, I've got this."

Anna held her left arm out in front of her. She double-clenched her fist and could feel pressure build. She relaxed her hand for just a moment, then clenched her fist again. Anna immediately felt the pressure release from her hand—an explosion—and then she was spinning in the air, hurtling backward. The sky and ground kept taking turns in her field of vision. After multiple spin cycles, she was able to regain her bearings and stop her washing-machine motion. Her stomach felt queasy. She allowed herself to float for a second just to make sure she didn't throw up first.

"Newton's third law, Anna," Mara called out from thirty feet away.

How did she get all the way over there?

"Ugh. I know. I know. For every action, there is an equal and opposite reaction," Anna said as she glided back to Mara's side.

"Would you like me to finish showing you how it works?" Mara asked.

Anna nodded, her face still a little green.

"You need to plant your feet using your antigravity boots. It takes some practice to get the timing down, but once you do, it's second nature," Mara said. "Want to try again?"

Anna nodded. She tapped her left wrist three times, swiped the red ring, and then held her arm in front of her. She focused on her right boot and tried to visualize planting her foot. She double-clenched her fist and felt pressure steadily build around her hand.

"What if I just keep clenching my fist?"

"The longer you clench your fist before releasing, the more powerful the vortex," Mara answered. "You want to be careful, though. The objective is to incapacitate your opponent or buy yourself some time, not to blow it to pieces."

Anna planted her foot, then fired. She felt a recoil in her arm but stood firm. She tried again, this time with both arms, and within a minute she was firing small blasts of air just like Mara had been doing moments before.

"See? It pays to follow instructions."

For the next two hours, Anna practiced turning her invisibility mode on and off at will. She learned how to fire not only pressurized air but also sonic waves and ultrabright light bursts of rapidly changing wavelengths that could temporarily blind an opponent—and in some cases induce vomiting. Anna questioned whether that last part was necessary.

The light in the sky had shifted, and now the westerly sun cast small shadows that dotted the landscape below. After her final practice run, Anna rolled over onto her stomach midair, exhausted—her arms out to her sides like she was floating facedown on a raft. Her head was clearer now, but she was parched.

"Does my iCom have anything else awesome—like a bottle of water or a sandwich?" Anna asked.

"Oh, I'm sorry, Anna." Mara laughed. "I didn't realize the time. You must be starving."

"I am. Next time, can we bring a picnic?" Anna asked.

Mara glided to her side.

"That sounds like a great idea. A picnic in the clouds. That would be a first for me too."

Anna smiled. She was kidding when she said it, but the idea of sitting on a cloud and eating sandwiches and cheese and sliced apples hundreds of feet above the ground sounded like heaven. She scanned the farm below her. A red-tailed hawk was riding the same wind currents just one hundred feet below, circling in a wide arc above the trees that lined the lake. At ground level, toylike figures bustled back and forth across the barnyard.

"Hey, look! That's Uncle Jack down there. See? And Dr. Gloria," Anna said as she pointed to the ground. "I can tell it's Dr. Gloria's hat even from here. That's funny."

"You want to know how you can tell for sure?" Mara asked. "Hold your index finger down on the temple of your goggles. Watch me."

"Like this?" Anna asked. A symbol appeared on the right upper corner of her goggles.

"Now slide your finger back. It works like an optical zoom," Mara said.

Anna slid her finger back along the frame of her goggles. The numbers increased from 1× to 100× as her lenses zoomed in so close to the top of her uncle's head that she could count individual hairs. She could even hear her uncle talking now, clear as day.

"Are you kidding me? I have super vision and hearing too?" Anna looked over at Mara and could see the pores deep in her friend's skin. "Oops. How do I turn this off? I think I see your insides."

"Just double-tap the right upper corner of your goggles." Mara laughed. "You know, in no time you're going to be able to activate these controls by just thinking about them. You just need to practice."

"Do you have anything else to show me?"

"I think that's enough for now," Mara said. A sly grin spread across her face. "But if you're not too tired, do you want to have some fun before we stop for the day?"

CHAPTER 27

Mara and Anna glided down to just feet above Uncle Jack's head, so close that Anna could reach out and ruffle his hair. He was cleaned up now and smelled like soap. He was even wearing a new shirt, and his hair was neater than usual. Dr. Gloria walked by his side. A large cowboy hat offered shade from the hot afternoon sun. Both of them looked down at the ground as they talked.

Anna swooped down in front of her uncle, missing him by inches. He mistook the sudden fluctuation in air pressure as a bug buzzing by and absently swatted the air in front of his face. Anna had spent a good part of her life being invisible to the other kids around her. She remembered what it felt like to smile at someone who didn't return her smile, that hollow feeling that came from being not just looked past but looked through. But now that she was actually invisible, she felt a strange sense of power and a faint but perceptible sense of guilt.

"It's like having a superpower. I can literally spy on anyone without being detected," Anna said over her iCom.

"Hmm. Maybe I should have spent a little more time with

you on the ethical implications of this technology," Mara said. She kept a safe distance.

"I know. 'With great power comes great . . .'"

Anna stopped midsentence. Dr. Gloria had started talking, and she wanted to listen in.

"We've known each other a long time, Jack," Dr. Gloria said. "So I hope you don't take offense to what I'm about to ask you."

Uncle Jack slowed his pace. He looked concerned.

Anna leaned in to hear.

"Of course. You can ask me anything," Uncle Jack said.

"Are you actually wearing hair product?" Dr. Gloria stifled a laugh. A broad grin brightened his face.

Uncle Jack looked away and closed his eyes, embarrassed. He took in a deep breath and then smiled back. "Why yes, RG. I am wearing hair product. Thanks for noticing."

"I just don't think I've seen you this cleaned up. At least not since our grade school pictures," Dr. Gloria said. "This doesn't have anything to do with a recent visitor to the farm, does it?"

"Visitor?" Uncle Jack wasn't very good at playing coy.

Mara flew down by Anna's side. She was leaning in now too, positioning herself closer to the conversation.

"Gladness said she spotted a woman with Anna earlier today. Said she looked like an Amazon goddess," Dr. Gloria said.

"Ohhh, yeah. That visitor." Uncle Jack rubbed the back of his head. "Anna's new tutor, Mara. She is a little tall."

"Tall? That's all you have to say?"

Anna could sense where this was going and put her hands over Mara's ears.

"Lalalalalalalalala."

Mara pushed her hands away. "Stop it. I want to hear this."

"But what about all that ethical implications stuff?" Anna asked.

Mara kept Anna at a distance with one hand and signaled for her to shush with the other.

"Did you see her?" Uncle Jack asked.

Dr. Gloria shook his head *no*.

"She rides a motorcycle, RG. A motorcycle. And she has a PhD. I don't think I've ever met anyone so cool in my entire life." Uncle Jack shook his head.

"And it doesn't hurt that she's beautiful. Gladness's words. Not mine."

"Nope, doesn't hurt at all." Uncle Jack squinted in the sun.

"You know, we shouldn't be listening to this." Anna tugged at Mara's sleeve. "This is a private conversation."

Mara ignored her.

"So, what are you going to do about it, Jack?"

"Just met her today, RG. I'm not doing anything about it." Uncle Jack turned and picked up his pace as he headed across the barnyard. A signal this conversation was over.

Dr. Gloria had to run to catch up. Anna and Mara split in different directions and glided quickly away, just in time to let Uncle Jack, oblivious to their presence, march straight between them. They glided back together and floated several feet behind.

"All right, all right. No pressure, Jack." Dr. Gloria laughed. He had to half jog to keep up. "Though Lord knows you could use a push."

CHAPTER 28

Mara had been gone for several hours, and the evening sun had cast long shadows across the barnyard when Anna received a text from Fiona. Her friends were on their way. Anna texted back that she would meet them at Potter Road in fifteen minutes tops.

Anna wrapped her backpack around her shoulder and headed out on her battle cruiser of a bike. Pedaling was easy now, especially after months of training and antigravity boots on her side. Her tires hummed across the hot asphalt as she made her way down the back roads. There was no one in sight. No cars. Only cows, irrigation lines, and farmhouses set far back from the road. She still wasn't used to this much empty space, but she was getting used to the different rhythms and constant hum of katydids and crickets.

She passed through pockets of warm and cool air that formed near irrigation lines and swatted at swarms of gnats that popped up in clouds along the road. She passed through the outskirts of town and avoided the large trucks that rumbled down the main roads. Within fifteen minutes she was at the turnoff to Potter Road. She looked up at the road sign to make sure. Surprise. It was filled with small buckshot holes but still readable. She had arrived.

Anna looked down the single-lane road. Waist-high weeds with purple and white flowers lined both sides, and evening bugs danced like little flecks of dust in the waning sun. The day's heat had dried any leftover puddles from the earlier rain. Less than a quarter mile away, Anna saw her three friends by the roadside, their figures blurred by the waves of heat that rose from the broken asphalt.

By the time Anna met up with her friends, they were already off their bikes and exploring the area. Anna made a satisfying skid to a stop and let her bike fall with the others along the roadside.

"Find anything yet?" Anna asked.

"I think these are Katie's skid marks from last night. They look pretty fresh," Scout said, squatting next to two dark tire tracks. "My skid marks would have looked a little different if I had seen that bug-eyed thing, if you know what I mean."

Fiona and Lula were on opposite sides of the road. Lula was walking in the open field, while Fiona wandered toward a patch of woods to the left. They were sweeping their hands back and forth through the weed patches and waist-high grass and looking intently at the ground for any traces of the creature. Anna walked to the end of the tire tracks and knelt down. She could feel the heat rise from the asphalt.

"So if Katie stopped here, then that shadowy thing was standing over there, right?" Anna pointed to a spot twenty feet down the road. "And facing in your direction, Lula."

Lula lifted her head up and made her way over to the side of the road. "I haven't found anything except a couple of broken beer bottles and a dirty sock. No footprints. Nothin'."

"I haven't found anything either. Except maybe the missing

match to the sock you found, Lula," Fiona shouted back. She was looking at the ground as she walked, then suddenly stopped. "Wait!"

Anna stood up from her crouched position. "What is it? You find something?"

Fiona bent down and disappeared into the deep grass, the top of her head the only thing visible.

"Yeah. This is weird. Come see," Fiona shouted back, her voice muffled.

Anna, Lula, and Scout jogged across the road and into the tall grass. Fireflies rose like tiny missiles all around them, only to flicker out and disappear as they walked past. They reached Fiona, who was still crouched down.

"What do you think?" Fiona looked up.

The ground was sandy and the topsoil dry, even though there had been recent summer rains. If the light had been hitting any differently, Anna wouldn't have noticed the two faint bean-shaped impressions in the dirt, twenty inches apart. On closer inspection, she realized it was part of the same print.

"A footprint maybe? But that'd be an awfully big foot," Fiona said. "Maybe some anthill or something."

"I don't know. Lula weighs less than a loaf of bread, and look, even she makes a deeper impression in the dirt," Scout said.

Anna walked away from her friends and toward the woods, swaying her arms back and forth to clear a view through the grass. Fifteen feet away, she found another footprint in the very same shape.

"Hey! I found another one. I think they came from that direction." Anna pointed to a path that disappeared into the shadows of the trees. "Let's see how far the trail leads us."

The four made their way to a barbed-wire fence that carved a jagged line separating the woods from the road.

Many of the rotted wooden posts had toppled over, and long stretches of the fence were covered in deep brambles. The wire was rusted, but the barbs were still sharp. Fiona reached over and carefully pulled the top two lines of wire apart so her friends could pass. Anna hunched over and was ready to squeeze through when she noticed a piece of torn black fabric hanging from one of the metal barbs. The shape was uniform and looked like a small black feather, but there were no wrinkles or discolorations, just a jet-black surface that looked like a hole in space.

"What the heck is that?" Anna leaned in closer. Even inches away, the small feather seemed to absorb all light. "That's trippy."

"Hold on. Let me try my phone." Lula turned on her phone light and shone it directly on the feather's surface. "That's crazy. It looks like a hole in the air. Go ahead, Scout, touch it. I dare you."

"No, you touch it." Scout took a step back.

Anna knew instinctively that the black object wasn't from this world. She looked over at Lula and Scout, who were playfully pushing each other closer to the fence. They had no idea what was at stake here, and she wanted desperately to tell her friends what she knew. But she couldn't. Not yet.

"I'll touch it, you big cowards." Anna laughed.

She set her backpack on the ground, pulled out a small plastic bag, then withdrew a pair of utility tweezers from a Swiss Army knife. She grabbed ahold of the feather's edge and twisted it free from the hooked barb. The material felt spongy but firm, and even up close there was no perceptible sign of light. If anything, it was the absence of light. She held it up and looked at it from different angles, then put it in the plastic bag and sealed it shut before shoving it into her backpack.

She squeezed through the gap in the fence that Fiona had

forced free. Lula and Scout quickly followed. The four friends walked single file down a small dirt path that led to the edge of the woods and then disappeared into a haze of dark shadows and thick bramble.

"Watch for ticks," Scout said. "You go first, Fiona."

Anna followed the dirt path into the woods. It was noticeably darker, but enough light still made it through the thick branches that she could see the path, her feet, and several steps ahead. They had walked for thirty feet when Anna stopped. A premonition. She felt like she was being watched.

"Why are you stopping?" Scout said. "I don't see anything."

"Me neither." Lula stood close to Fiona's side. "But I feel something."

Suddenly, a small dim green light flickered in front of them. A blossom of light on the end of a plant.

"Ha. You guys are funny. It's just fireflies," Scout said.

"Wait." Anna held her hands up and leaned closer to the green light. "That isn't a firefly."

Up close, the leaf looked as if it had been painted with a brushstroke of fluorescent green paint. The light slowly grew brighter as Anna moved closer, like someone raising the dimmer on a light switch. Then a blue light flickered right next to it, then another. Lights began popping to life in a row—some on rocks or fallen limbs, some on leaves, until a line of green and blue glowing lights stretched ten feet in front of them along the path. The lights pulsed. Several flickered and changed color. Anna reached her hand out and the light grew brighter in response, making her giggle. The forest floor glowed in a magical light. A fairy ring.

"Anybody filming this?" Fiona said, her face alight in the green glow. "It's beautiful."

"So beautiful." Lula shook her head in disbelief as she filmed the glowing lights in front of her. "Can you feel that?"

Lula was right. But it wasn't a physical sensation. It was

more of an emotion, a sense of calm and quiet. The closer she came to the lights, the greater the sense of calm.

The four stood mesmerized and silent for what seemed like minutes—even Scout. Each connected to the others, each swaying in rhythm to the pulsing lights. A small, nearly imperceptible movement. Anna could almost sense what the others were feeling. No need for words.

Then, from a distance, the sound of a stereo broke the reverie, its thumping music growing slowly louder. Anna figured it must be a passing car. She looked over at Scout, his mouth still open. The glowing lights from the forest floor reflected off his glasses. Then the passing car honked its horn, Scout blinked, and the reflection of lights in his glasses suddenly dimmed to darkness. The lights faded and left them in the dark shadows of the heavy woods. The four friends shook their heads in unison as if awaking from a nap.

"Scout, get out here!" a faint voice shouted from the roadside. The stereo was still blaring.

Scout closed his eyes and groaned.

"You gotta be kidding me."

"Scout! Don't make me come get you." The faint voice sounded more agitated.

Anna headed to the edge of the woods and peered out between the hanging branches. A pickup truck filled with a half dozen high school boys was idling in the middle of the road. One of the boys was dragging her friends' bikes and lining them up in a neat row in front of the truck. Anna pulled back and hid in the shadows.

"Who is that?" Anna whispered.

"That's my sociopath brother, Tyler," Scout whispered back as he nervously rubbed his thighs. He seemed smaller than usual.

"I know it's you, Scout. I saw your stupid little bike," Tyler shouted out. He wore an old sweatshirt with its sleeves torn off and a faded, stained ball cap turned backward. A bush of long-ish brown hair poked out on the sides, and his skin seemed too tight on his muscular frame.

"What's he doing?" Anna asked in a hushed voice.

"Well, knowing him, he's getting ready to run over our bikes," Scout whispered.

"Your brother wouldn't actually do that, would he?" Anna asked.

"Oh yes he would," Lula said. "That boy is crazy."

"Oh no he won't," Fiona said loudly as she ran out into the clearing. "Hey, Tyler! You better not be touching my bike."

Fiona swung her arms in wide arcs as she stomped forward. Her anger acted like a force that dragged her friends behind her, through the barbed-wire fence and out into the clearing.

"What did you say, Fiona?" Tyler stepped forward. He bobbed his head up and down in an attempt to be menacing, but it made him look like a strutting rooster.

"I said you better not be touching my bike, or you're going to be hearing from my brothers!" Fiona kept barreling forward.

The threat stopped Tyler in his tracks, which made Anna wonder just how scary Fiona's brothers must be.

"Just like my wuss little brother to be hiding behind his girlfriends," Tyler shouted.

Tyler's friends snickered on cue. The kid on the driver's side opened the rusted pickup door. A .22-caliber rifle lay across his lap. An empty beer can rolled out slowly and clanked off the asphalt. Scout ran forward and grabbed Fiona's arm to stop her. She looked over her shoulder, startled. Scout smiled back.

"Thanks, Fiona, but I got this," Scout said. He stepped out onto the road to cut his brother off. "Hey, Tyler, how about being a prince and giving us a break today?"

"What are you doing out here anyway, you little turd?" Tyler looked down at his brother. He fake-punched the air in front of his brother's face, but Scout didn't flinch. He must have had practice.

"We're just leaving, Tyler. Just leaving," Scout said as he edged his way toward the front of the truck, but Tyler cut him off before he could reach the bikes.

"I know why you're here. You think you're gonna find that thing Katie saw last night." Tyler stepped forward, his face inches away from Scout's. "Well, forget it. It's mine."

Scout paused. He looked down at his feet and shoved his hands in his pockets. He was trying to keep it together, Anna could tell. But something was going on under that expression. The muscles in his jaw were popping as he ground his teeth. His lips twitched back and forth. His eyes grew wider as he slowly raised his gaze to meet Tyler's. A look of frustration and pent-up anger. Then the dam broke.

"Yours? *Yours?!* I didn't realize you were so hard up, Tyler." Scout stood on the balls of his feet. "Ever think of dating someone from your own species?"

The response was immediate. Tyler popped Scout hard in the chest with his open palms, knocking him to the ground. Scout lay there for a moment, stunned. He rubbed his chest, trying to get oxygen back in his lungs. His eyes began to brim with tears, partly from pain and partly from humiliation. Two of Tyler's friends jumped from the back of the pickup truck and stood behind Scout to block him from running away; one had sleepy eyes and a cigarette hanging from his open mouth and the other one, with thin blond hair, looked nervously toward Fiona. *There must be history there,* Anna thought.

"Hey, Hanson. My brothers aren't going to like this," Fiona shouted at the nervous kid.

"Butt out of this, Fiona," Tyler shouted back.

Scout suddenly realized he was trapped. Backed into a corner, Scout's posture changed. He pulled his shoulders back and puffed out his chest. He even smirked back at his brother as if realizing he had nothing left to lose. Anna's stomach was in knots. Scout looked so small. She couldn't tell if this was a real threat or an ugly sibling rivalry, but she looked down at her iCom and engaged the defense mode just in case.

"I have an idea. Why don't you and your primate friends go groom each other and let us go back to what we were doing?" Scout spit out.

The words seemed to float in the hot evening sun, long enough for everyone to take them in and shake their heads in disbelief. Scout was fearless but doomed. He was the yipping dog that had to get the last bark in.

"You don't tell me what to do. You don't ever tell me what to do." Tyler grabbed the back of Scout's hair and yanked hard.

"Ow, ow, ow!" Scout cried out. He tried pulling free, but his brother's grip was too tight.

"Hey, Billy. Give me your cigarette." Tyler looked over at his sleepy-eyed friend. "Let's see if a cigarette can burn twice. Hold his arms."

Billy took one last drag before handing the still-burning cigarette to Tyler and then pinned Scout's arms to his side. Tyler pulled up his brother's shirt to reveal his stomach, a row of skinny ribs, and two small circular scars on his left side.

Lula desperately motioned for Fiona to call her brothers.

"Hey, Tyler, come on. You're not serious," the mousy one called Hanson said nervously.

Tyler shot him a look that froze Hanson in his tracks. His eyes were rimmed red.

"Stop!" Anna screamed loud enough to get Tyler's attention—as well as everyone else's within a half-mile distance.

Tyler turned his head and tried a half smile, but it came across as a sneer. "You're the new girl. Not half bad, but you got a big mouth."

The way he looked at Anna made her skin crawl. She pumped her fist twice.

"Let him go." Anna took several steps forward.

"Or what?"

"Or I call the cops. I don't care if you're Scout's brother, but I'm pretty sure assault is still illegal." Anna kept walking until she was within striking distance.

"It's not illegal if it's an accident." Tyler lowered the cigarette closer to Scout's exposed stomach.

Tears worked their way down his little brother's face. Scout was openly sobbing now, and his glasses sat crooked on his head.

That was enough. Anna leaped forward faster than anyone expected—faster than anyone could even see. She knocked the cigarette from Tyler's hand and placed her fist within an inch of his chest. She paused just long enough to register the look of surprise on Tyler's face and pumped her fist one more time. Anna instantly felt a satisfying recoil in her hand.

The blast of compressed air knocked Tyler off his feet and threw him back against the side of the pickup truck. He slumped to the ground in a daze and moaned, strands of Scout's hair still in his grasp. Scout was no longer crying. He was too confused to cry as he absently rubbed the back of his head. Everyone looked confused. Tyler's friends were unsure if he had tripped or if he was just playing. The thought that Anna was capable of knocking him off his feet didn't even register. None of them had a clear view, and everything had happened so fast. Billy and Hanson leaned over and started to laugh, thinking their friend must just be playing.

Anna didn't wait. She shoved Scout toward their bikes and waved for her friends to follow. Fiona and Lula kept their distance as they circled to the front of the truck. Scout was the first on his bike. His handlebars wobbled as he pumped his legs furiously. Fiona and Lula were right behind. Anna stood up on her pedals, pushed down hard, and within seconds she had caught up with her friends. She looked back over her shoulder

to see if they were being followed, but no one seemed to notice they were gone. They were too focused on Tyler, who was
now up on one knee and shaking his head. No lasting damage.
That's good. He looked up and made eye contact, his face a
combination of rage and fear and disbelief, but he didn't make
any attempt to stop them from leaving. Also good.

Anna turned away. The safety of the main road, where
traffic and people and witnesses would be, was less than a half
mile ahead. No one said a word as they pedaled as fast as they
could; no one looked back until they turned the corner and
made their way to town.

CHAPTER 29

Anna sat at her desk and looked out her bedroom window. The sun had set, but the air felt hot and stagnant and the earthy smells from the barnyard hung heavy in the air. She stared at the black feather she had found earlier in the day. It lay at the bottom of a glass jar on the edge of her desk, in safekeeping until she could drop it off at Mara's in the morning for analysis.

For the past hour she had been sketching images from the alien world she had visited the night before. There were gaps in her memory, but the more she sketched in her journal, the more connections began to form. There was the jagged shape of the coastline. The leviathan just under the surface of turquoise waters. The small round eyes ringed in yellow and blue that peeked out from under the jungle canopy. The giant trees, like skyscrapers. She skimmed through her journal, and the last page gave her pause. Staring at her from the white page was a tall sticklike figure outlined in jagged pencil strokes. Set deep in its bone face were two eyes made of spinning constellations. The other sketches in her journal were fixed memories. This page still felt like a dream.

Anna closed her journal and walked over to the window. She hung one leg over the ledge into the night air. She leaned back against the windowsill and absently began scrolling through the messages on her phone. Fiona and Lula had reached out an hour before on group chat, two-word messages followed by a string of emojis, but from Scout there was radio silence. Anna texted a quick message to Scout directly. No reply.

She remembered the look of humiliation on Scout's face. There was anger in that look too—and a lot of fear. But it was the pair of glasses that sat lopsided on his head that broke her heart. She had never seen that side of Scout before. He was annoying, sure, but also funny and confident and unflappable. She wondered what it must be like to grow up in that house of his. What happened when no one else was around? The more she thought about it, the madder she got.

She looked at her phone. Still no reply. Time for drastic action. She tapped in his number instead. The phone rang five times. Anna was ready to hang up when she heard Scout on the other end of the line.

"Anna? Why are you calling?"

"I didn't feel like texting," Anna said.

"Oh."

"Are you all right?" Anna asked.

"Never been better." Scout's voice was muted.

"I just wanted to thank you for sticking up for us today. That was pretty brave," Anna said.

Anna could hear Scout shuffling in his room. A brief pause.

"You think so?" Scout said.

"Yeah, I think so. I also think your brother is a jerk," Anna said.

"You ought to try living with him," Scout said evenly.

"Can he hear you right now?"

"Nah. He took off with his idiot friends. Probably out

drinking by the fairgrounds. He was in one foul mood." Scout paused. "Hey, Anna. What happened today?"

"What do you mean?" Anna knew exactly what he meant.

"All I remember was Tyler getting ready to burn me. You jumped at him. Next thing I know, Tyler is on his butt and I'm missing a handful of hair," Scout said.

"Trust me. I did not touch your hair," Anna said.

"No, serious. Did you do that?"

"I may have pushed him. But not a lot. I think he just tripped and we got lucky."

She knew she had to be more careful in the future.

"I guess." Scout paused again. "You know I wasn't hurt or nothing today. I don't know why I was crying."

"Yeah. I know," Anna reassured him. "Hey, Scout. Those scars on your side. Did your brother do that?"

Anna looked out her window and watched a single blinking light move slowly across the sky. A plane. She didn't push for an answer. She didn't try to fill in the blank space and gave Scout time.

"Yeah," he finally said.

Anna could feel her chest tighten and her teeth clench. It was like she was channeling Scout's anger. Maybe it was the look on Scout's face that she kept replaying in her head, or maybe something inside herself—the sense of unfairness—but she couldn't let this slide.

"Where is your brother again?"

"Probably down by the fairgrounds. Why?"

"Nothing. Just want to make sure we stay out of his way," Anna said. "See you tomorrow?"

"Sure. See you tomorrow. Night, Anna."

Anna shoved her phone in her pocket and took off downstairs. She had no intention of staying out of Tyler's way. Not tonight.

———

Anna opened the screen door slowly with one hand to prevent it from squeaking. In her other hand she held a carton of eggs she'd pulled from the refrigerator. Uncle Jack might notice, but hey, they lived on a farm and eggs were easy to find, right? She tiptoed across the front porch and made it down to the dirt lane before she glanced back over her shoulder. No sign of life anywhere on the farm except for the yellow light that streamed from her bedroom window.

Anna took several running steps, then silently glided above the treetops, her fingers tracing the leaves in the top canopy as she flew by. Within minutes she was flying several hundred feet above Smartt and following the few streetlights that ran down the middle of the town. There were lights from the gas station and mini mart. The red neon sign outside Ivanhoe's shone like a beacon. At the edge of town, as the lights gave way to open fields, there was a large section blocked out in shadows. The fairgrounds.

Even from this distance she could hear a stereo blasting below. She zoomed in with her goggles and scanned for the source of the sound. Tyler's pickup truck sat alone at the edge of the large parking lot. Its headlights were on and the doors were open. Tyler's friends took turns throwing rocks at a pyramid of beer cans. She could hear their conversation, a series of shouts straining over the loud music blaring from inside the truck cabin. They were talking about the shadow creature and how it was going to make them famous, how it was going to make them money—enough money to get Tyler out of this stupid town. He also told them that it was his shot to take when the time came. No one else. It took a second, but Anna suddenly realized what he meant. This was a hunting party.

Anna positioned herself directly above Tyler's pickup. At two hundred feet, an egg dropped from this height would hit around 77 miles per hour. She wanted to get back at Tyler but not hurt him. She turned on her cloaking setting and then floated to fifty feet above the truck. Anna opened the carton and took out a large brown egg. She closed her left eye to focus on the target below her and then guided herself until she was in a straight line just above Tyler's head.

Bombs away.

The egg silently sailed down and 1.763 seconds later hit the ground, narrowly missing the top of Tyler's head. *Grrr. A miss.* But at thirty-eight miles per hour, the egg disintegrated with a loud thwack as it hit the pavement and sprayed yellow slime in a six-foot radius.

Tyler leaped from the pavement like he'd been shot from a cannon and landed in the back of his truck. He cowered in the corner. The big one named Billy looked down at his pants legs covered in yolk and held his hands out in horror as if he'd just been shot. His other friends stopped their game of beer-can toss. Tyler warily peeked his head above the bed of the truck.

"Who threw that!" he screamed angrily.

I did, Anna said to herself. She grabbed another egg from the carton and glided over several feet. She adjusted her aim to account for the wind and then let the egg drop. This time, the egg found its target and exploded like white shrapnel off the top of Tyler's head.

"Owww!" Tyler shouted as he looked around frantically. "Who's doing this? I'll kill ya. I swear! I'll kill ya."

His friends remained frozen. They exchanged glances but were unable to move or even speak. Such easy targets. *Thank you for your service,* Anna said to the open carton as she turned it over and let the remaining eggs fall all at once in a cluster.

Thwack! Thwack! Thwack!

Egg bombs shattered in quick succession, coating Tyler and the top of his truck in egg yolk. Tyler screamed in anger and began blindly thrashing his arms as Anna paused to take in the carnage in all its glory. Not one of Tyler's gang looked up. They scanned the horizon frantically. They looked at one another like they were ready to rat out one of their own. But at that moment, as she flew quietly away back to her home, Anna realized no one had ever looked up. No one ever looked up.

CHAPTER 30

M inutes later and halfway across the valley, the Shadow sat huddled in a drainage pipe that ran under a one-lane dirt road. Water trickled in a small stream near its feet. The Shadow had learned to avoid the vehicles with four wheels and bright lights, just as it had learned to avoid most of the inhabitants of this new world, especially those who walked upright. Worst of all were those who traveled in packs.

The minutes ticked by and the Shadow remained motionless until it was sure it was alone. It turned its head to the sky as if listening for something. The star patterns in the sky were different here on this world, but their consistency made them fairly easy to navigate. It leaped from the roadside out into the field and scurried silently through thick dogwood bushes and over fallen tree limbs like a fog moving across the valley floor. Once the Shadow reached the edge of a small wood, it leaped effortlessly onto the lowest branch of a tree and climbed to the top limb.

Its skin was black as ink, a total absence of color. Anyone walking by would just see a continuation of the night sky. From its perch, the Shadow looked out across the valley, its head swiveling almost 360 degrees. To the south, a thin haze of light pulsed above the town. To the east, about a half mile away, sat a farmhouse shrouded in darkness. The Shadow made a high-pitched sound, inaudible to the human ear, and waited silently for a response. Seconds passed and then, from the direction of the farmhouse, a dog howled in return.

The Shadow leaped from its perch and landed harmlessly on the ground thirty feet below. It sped on all fours across the grassy knoll in the direction of the howling dog. In a little over a minute, the Shadow reached the edge of the large dirt driveway that encircled the farmhouse and crouched behind an ancient, rusted tractor covered in weeds and knee-high grass.

The farmhouse was silent and dark except for a curtain that flapped through an open window on the second floor. Across the driveway, an old Australian shepherd wagged its tail playfully. The dog made a low, gruff sound—almost like an old man mumbling—and pawed at the ground in an invitation to play.

The Shadow emerged from behind the tractor and glided across the driveway toward the dog. The dog, famous in the area for chasing anything with four wheels and barking at the rustling of leaves, rolled over quietly in return and looked up expectantly as the Shadow approached. The two creatures stared at each other for a moment, then the Shadow reached out and scratched the dog behind the ears. Within seconds the dog was asleep and happily dreamed of chasing small lights that floated in the night sky.

The Shadow stood unmoving, taking in all sounds and smells and changes in the wind. It was hungry and growing weak. It knew it needed to eat soon but could find no food here that would sustain it.

Then a new sound emerged from the second-story window—a low rumble followed by a hiss. The sound grew louder as it repeated the same pattern: rumble then hiss, rumble then hiss.

The Shadow made its way toward the side of the house, through a set of bedsheets hung out to dry in the night breeze, then leaped twenty feet straight up to the windowsill on the second floor. What the Shadow did not see was a small glass object, an ashtray, that rested on the edge of the windowsill. When it landed, the Shadow's left foot struck the edge of the ashtray and sent it flying across the room to crash against the far wall. The rumble and hiss the Shadow had gone to investigate was gone, now replaced by a startled moan, then silence, then a scream.

CHAPTER 31

The next afternoon, Anna swung gently in a hammock stretched between two beech trees in the backyard. She lay with her notebook open on her stomach, her eyes half-closed and her hands propped behind her head. The temperatures had crept up to the high nineties. But the air was a good ten degrees cooler in the shade, and gently swaying back and forth in the hammock created enough of a breeze to keep her comfortable.

From a distance, Anna could hear the thrum of a motorcycle engine coming closer, followed by the high-pitched whine of a downshift, then quiet. A moment later, Mara's voice came over her iCom.

"Where are you?"

"Come around to the back of the house," Anna said. "You can't miss me."

Anna propped herself up in the hammock as Mara walked across the back lawn. The slight movement made the hammock swing in a wide arc.

"What is that thing?" Mara pointed straight ahead.

"You don't have hammocks in the future?" Anna asked.

"No," Mara said, shaking her head. "It seems structurally unstable. Is it used for protection from ground animals?"

Anna laughed.

"No, it's used for being lazy. Come join me." Anna scooted over and patted the hammock in invitation.

Mara reluctantly stepped forward, then paused to assess the proper landing sequence. She raised her left leg up like she was going to straddle the hammock, then set her foot back down. She turned around and tried to lean backward into the hammock, then stopped, frustrated.

"Forget it."

Mara gave up and decided to use her antigravity boots instead. She floated gently off the ground and landed softly next to Anna's side. She squirmed in the hammock, trying to get comfortable without knocking them both to the ground. After a minute she was able to find some kind of equilibrium and lay still, looking up at the leaves fluttering above her head.

"Now what?" Mara asked.

"Nothing. We just relax."

"This is the opposite of relaxing, Anna."

"Give it time." Anna smiled as she hung her leg over the side and gently began rocking. "Did you hear about the sighting last night?"

"I did," Mara said.

"My uncle knows the guy. Some old farmer who lives out just past Potter Road," Anna said. "Said he woke up to find some shadow creature staring at him through his second-story window. How's that for freaky?"

"He also said that when he turned on the light, the creature was completely featureless. No face. Just blackness—his words," Mara said.

"How do you know that?"

"I read the police report this morning," Mara said. "Just after I analyzed that black feather you found yesterday. I think the old farmer was telling the truth. Whatever you brought me this morning is not of this world. It's organic. But SID couldn't find anything remotely like a DNA sequence we know of. And I don't think it's a feather either."

"What is it then?"

"Best that I can tell, it's some kind of scale that absorbs about 99.98% of all light. It uses small nanotubes on its surface to somehow trap light. That's the reason the old farmer just saw a black space," Mara said.

Anna paused.

"Does that mean the creature is invisible at night?"

"Yes. I would think so."

"Good," Anna said. "Not for us. I mean for the creature. It's gotta be lost and scared. After what I saw yesterday, it has every right to be scared. Scout's brother wants to frame it on his wall."

"I'm afraid he's not the only one," Mara said quietly.

"How do you know?"

Mara tapped her iCom to display a holographic map of the valley in bright blue lines above her wrist. On the lines, little pulses of light glowed bright then faded away like raindrops hitting the surface of a window.

"See this? This is a time delta I had SID create. It tracks all police scans, news events, any kind of digital communication for this entire area."

Anna traced her finger along the blue lines, then stopped at one of the small pulsing lights.

"Oh. So that's how you know. You track people's conversations?" Anna said. "That's a little creepy, Mara."

"Not all conversations. Just the conversations that have changed," Mara said.

"Changed? What do you mean?"

"See those little glowing dots? Each one represents a change to your timeline. Events, messages, conversations that would never have happened if I hadn't appeared in your time. Changes that cause new actions and reactions, rippling out like waves in a pond. The changes could mean nothing to your future—or everything. I don't know."

"So these are people, right?" Anna pointed to another dot that pulsed bright on the map then slowly faded away.

"In a way. Yes. They're more like communication records. But I suppose you can see them as people," Mara said. "Before I came to your time, I collected a digital record of all communications originating from this area. Well, from many areas. Each record points to a person, a place, like a digital footprint. I asked SID to create a scan that flags any changes to these records. Make sense?"

Anna felt her world shift. She knew Mara had an understanding of the future, but not at this level of detail or at this scale. Police reports, electronic communications, private conversations.

"That means you know everyone's future, then. Uncle Jack's. Mine. I mean, that's the only way this delta scan of yours could work, right?" Anna said as she propped herself up on both elbows. "Of course you know. I can't believe this. Why didn't I think of this before?"

"I'm sorry. I should have been more careful in explaining this. The delta scan knows *traces* of your future. The digital records. Not your total future," Mara explained. "But listen, Anna. I've chosen not to look at these records more than I need to. Especially yours. The more I know, the greater the chance of changing your timeline."

"So you know what college I go to. Every text message I've ever sent. My first boyfriend. Everything," Anna said.

"I could find out, but like I said, I've chosen not to. So don't bother asking," Mara said. "The less I know—"

"I know, I know. The less of a chance you have to screw up my timeline."

"I used to think that there was an inertia, an almost physical force that kept things moving forward in time to where they were supposed to go. Time may meander a bit, but things always end up at the same destination," Mara said. She stared at the leaves moving in the afternoon breeze overhead. "But that's not how it worked out for me. My destination didn't just end when my parents failed to meet. It never existed. I just don't want the same thing happening to you."

Anna lay back with her head next to Mara's.

"Mara. I—I don't think you're looking at this right." Anna struggled to find the words.

"At what right?"

"Well, maybe all of it. I've been thinking about the whole timeline thing since you mentioned it the other night. And it's really been bugging me, and I didn't know why. But I think I'm beginning to figure it out," Anna said.

"And?"

"I don't think it really matters if my timeline changes. Not to me. As far as I'm concerned, this is all just happening for the first time. Meeting you. Learning to fly. No broken timelines. No lost futures. Just the one I have now." Anna smiled as she shook her head. "If you think about it, Mara, it doesn't matter to you either. It's all new every day."

"You can't be serious." Mara frowned.

"I know you lost your parents because of changes to your timeline. I'm not making light of that. Trust me, of all people, I know," Anna said. "But instead of looking back and trying to keep everything the same, maybe you should be looking forward. Maybe you should be thinking about how to make the best of the future you have. From right now. With me."

Tears lined the bottom of Mara's eyes. She looked up and blinked and took in a deep breath.

"The past is not to be messed with," Mara said.

"I know."

"Changes only mean one thing: a series of branching alternatives, each one leading to me being alone, without a home. Or, even worse . . ." Her voice trailed off.

"But you're here now."

Mara's eyes softened and a faint smile crossed her lips.

"Maybe you're right."

"Of course I'm right. So now that you have one, what are you going to do with all this future?" Anna asked.

Mara laughed at the absurdity of the idea—a future.

"First things first," Mara said. "Let's start by finding the creature before anyone else does."

"Yes," Anna said, nodding. "And then we help it find its way home, right?"

"If only it were that easy. Even with the data you found the other night, we're no closer to finding the wormhole. So we have no idea where this creature came from. Throw in that the creature is effectively invisible at night and doesn't appear to travel by day." Mara let her voice fall. "No, not easy."

"So what's the plan?" Anna asked.

"I was hoping you'd have one." Mara smiled.

"No. Serious."

"I guess you and I are going to continue to go out at night and search for a needle in a haystack. Not much of a plan, but it's all I have." Mara sighed. "Well, that and I also set up the delta scan to immediately alert us if it picks up anything on the creature. So we'll need to be ready and fast—and probably very lucky."

"Any idea how we capture the poor thing without harming it?" Anna asked.

"I'm working on an exopolymer net. It's the size of a small ball, but it expands fast when it nears its target. The net will immobilize the creature but also keep it safe. We just need to get close enough."

"Exopolymer?"

"Think of it as a biodegradable ball of goo," Mara explained.

"Oh," Anna said. "Do I get the delta alert too?"

"Of course. I'm not doing any of this alone anymore."

"I'm glad you included me. Makes me feel like a superhero, like we're using the Bat-Signal or something," Anna said as she leaned against Mara's arm.

"I have no idea what you're talking about." Mara laughed, wrapping her arm around Anna.

Even in the heat, Mara's shirt felt cool. Future-girl fabric. The two sat rocking for a minute, silent except for the slight breeze that flowed through the leaves like a hush above their heads. Anna could hear Mara's heartbeat, slow and strong, almost keeping time with the sway of the hammock.

"You're right. This *is* nice," Mara said.

Anna smiled to herself.

"You know. This is the first time someone has held me since my parents died."

Mara instinctively drew Anna closer. It surprised her.

"You know I used to prefer working alone, isolated in research, instead of having to interact with other people?" Mara said softly.

"Yeah." Anna giggled. "You kind of give off that vibe."

"But something happened when I was out there, lost in time. It was more than loneliness. The longer I was gone, the more I felt like I was fading away. My memories. My sense of place. Fading to nothing. But being here with you makes me feel more real than I've felt in a very long time."

"Me too."

"So, speaking of futures. What do you plan on doing with yours?" Mara asked.

"Easy. I want to go to space," Anna said without hesitation. "Oh, and save the world."

"Of course you do. Any specific order?"

Anna giggled and shook her head.

From around the corner of the house, Uncle Jack made sure to make enough noise to get their attention. He turned the corner carrying a large tin container. Near the top of the tin can was a frost line and beads of condensation that dripped down the sides. Two spoons stuck out the top.

"Hey! I hope I'm not interrupting," Uncle Jack said as he walked to the edge of the beech tree. He took turns holding the tin container with one hand, then the other, shaking his free hand from the cold. "You guys look cozy."

"We are," Anna said. "Whatcha got there?"

"Oh yeah. I forgot. I don't know if you know. Well, how would you know," Uncle Jack stumbled. "What I mean is that our farm hosts a series of exhibits at the county fair every year. That's just a couple of weeks from now. People from all over the world come to see our work on regenerative farming."

"And . . ."

"Oh yeah. In addition to all the learning exhibits and the innovation competition we run, we also prepare different foods from our sustainable crops. This here is strawberry ice cream that Faye made. It's from an old French recipe and uses a varietal called a mignonette. I'm sure I mutilated the pronunciation." Uncle Jack grinned. "They're resistant to fungi."

"Fungi resistant? Sounds delicious," Mara teased.

"Want to try some?" Uncle Jack asked, holding the tin can out in front of him. "I brought you both a spoon."

Mara and Anna both swung their legs over the side of the hammock, then leaned in to get a better look. A mound of light pink ice cream with big red chunks filled the tin can.

"I've never had a strawberry," Mara said without thinking.

Uncle Jack looked confused.

"You've never had a strawberry? Seriously?"

"I mean the variety you mentioned, the mignonette," Mara said, trying to recover.

"Oh yeah. Here in the States, most strawberries look like

golf balls. Taste a little like them too. The problem is we breed them that way." Uncle Jack shook his right hand from the cold. "You guys might want to try some before my hand freezes."

Anna fished her spoon around until she was able to snag one of the larger strawberry chunks and then shoved the entire too-big bite into her mouth. The sides of her cheeks spread out as she began fanning her open mouth.

"Coooo—" She laughed as she tried to say "cold," but the roof of her mouth was frozen.

Mara took her turn next and cautiously dug out half a spoonful with just a sliver of strawberry. This would be the first food she had eaten in this time—at least food that wasn't prepared by her food replicator. She tried to think back to a time she ate something that had grown directly in soil or been prepared by human hands. She couldn't. Her entire life, from infancy to adulthood, all her food had been prepared to order by a replicator. No waste. Efficient. Fast. How would her body respond? Was her microbiome capable of processing this type of food in this way?

She slowly placed the tip of the spoon in her mouth and immediately felt the back of her mouth water as the combination of cream and strawberry washed over her tongue and triggered emotions from a distant evolutionary past. She didn't move or make a noise. She just closed her eyes and let the ice cream melt slowly in her mouth. A combination of fat, fruit sugar, and a tiny hint of salt. Never in her life had she tasted anything like this. So many different flavors and textures at once. Sweet and tart and cold. Words failed her. *So, this is what a strawberry tastes like.* She finally opened her eyes, only to see Uncle Jack staring at her with a concerned look.

"Brain freeze?"

Mara didn't answer but shoved her spoon back in the tin container, this time with no hesitation. She searched for a larger chunk of strawberry, hit the jackpot, then shoved it in her mouth. She let the frozen strawberry melt on her tongue. She noticed her eyes watering but didn't try hiding it.

"I take it you like it." Uncle Jack smiled. "You know, we didn't have to add much sugar because there is so much naturally occurring in—"

"Shhhhhh." Mara held up her hand.

Her focus was solely on the mound of ice cream in front of her. She took another spoonful, then another. Silent. The rest of the world had disappeared. After a moment she began to slow down, her stomach already feeling the first signs of being full. She wiped her mouth with the back of her sleeve and looked up. Uncle Jack had a quizzical look caught between amused and impressed. Anna was just laughing.

"Well, I guess I know what to get you for your birthday," Anna said.

Mara looked up, a little embarrassed.

"That. Was. Amazing," she said.

"I'll be sure to tell Faye. She'll like that," Uncle Jack said. "Consider this an official invitation to the county fair. I hope you can find some time to make it."

"I'm sure I will."

"Okay then." Uncle Jack nodded for a moment, and then, unsure what to do next, he turned to leave. He took one step toward the fence, then stopped to look back. "Listen. I, uh, was wondering since you're new around here and all, would you like to have dinner with me?"

"You mean now? Here? That's not necessary. The ice cream was more than sufficient," Mara said with a straight face.

Uncle Jack laughed nervously. "No. Sorry. I meant to ask if you'd like dinner with me. Here at the house. Maybe this Friday around 6:30?"

Anna swiveled her head back and forth—from Mara to Uncle Jack then back to Mara—and felt as if she were watching two separate conversations with separate meanings and levels of understanding. Uncle Jack was smitten. That was obvious. Mara, on the other hand—the smartest person she had ever met, a genius—was completely oblivious to the subtext of the moment. *This is going to be fun,* Anna thought.

"Will you provide more food like this?" Mara pointed to the melting ice cream.

"I'll try," Uncle Jack said. He had forgotten about the cold freeze on his hands.

"Then yes." Mara looked him straight in the eye and smiled.

"Great. I guess it's a date then," Uncle Jack said. He took one step back, then another, ready to bolt before Mara changed her mind. "Well, I'll let you two get back to your studies."

"Just leave that here before you go." Mara pointed to the ice cream.

Uncle Jack handed over the tin container and wiped his hands on his pants. He nodded, then jogged toward the front fence, where Dr. Gloria stood waiting.

Mara dug her spoon around for a missing chunk of strawberry, then stopped.

"One question, Anna. What is a date?"

CHAPTER 32

Mara sat alone on her deck and looked out across the lake. The sun was setting behind her and cast a warm glow across the meadow, the lake, and the fields beyond. Silently she watched the mirror image of clouds and their reflection off the water's surface slowly roll by. She closed her eyes and breathed in deeply. The air was warm and smelled of summer grass.

<Mara?>

SID's voice broke the evening calm. Mara ignored it.

"This is the most wonderful smell." Mara opened her eyes and leaned back in her seat to look up at the darkening sky.

<You decided not to tell her.> SID modulated its voice for the greatest receptivity.

"Today was a very good day. Can we just leave it at that?"

<Based on the substance and direction of your earlier conversation with Anna, this afternoon would have been the optimal time. She has the right to know. It impacts her too.>

"And what should I tell her, SID? The future is not what she thinks it is."

<No, I'm referring to your situation. She believes she has a

future with you. Don't you think you owe it to her to be more forthcoming?>

Mara paused before replying.

"How long have we been doing this, SID? Over three years?"

<1,105 days to be exact.>

"Okay. For the last 1,105 days, we've traveled to how many destinations?"

<Twenty-six.>

"And the pattern has been like clockwork, correct? We arrive at a new destination and anomalies appear in the time delta almost immediately. Within a week, trumpets sound in the sky. Wormholes open up. Creatures escape from other worlds. Chaos. And then what happens, SID?"

<We detect the presence of the Others.>

Mara had no idea what to call them. SID could only detect changes in energy signatures. But Mara saw those creatures in real life and in her dreams—images of featureless bone-white creatures that felt so alien she could find no better word. *The Others.* From the first moment in the distant future, when she saw one across the street staring at her with eyes containing spinning galaxies, she knew that these creatures were hunting for her.

Her initial encounter with the Others came on her first day of time travel. She had just returned from her maiden trip, which lasted no more than fifteen minutes and served as a test run to prove she could travel to a specific time and location with precision. It seemed to have worked so well, and SID's numbers proved it out. Time travel was possible. She ran from her lab, excited to tell her father and mother. She carried images from the past on her iCom as well as a small extinct flower she'd plucked from the ground during her time travel as evidence.

She struggled now to remember what her old home looked

like, but she would never forget the expression on her father's face when he failed to recognize her that distant morning. Her father refused to open the door for her. Worse yet, he looked frightened of her. A quick scan of the network revealed what she was beginning to fear herself. There were no records of a *Mara Banjoko Lee* anywhere to be found. She didn't exist. Disoriented, she stumbled down the steps of her father's residence to the sidewalk and began walking in no particular direction for hours until she reached an unfamiliar intersection and saw the apparition that would change her future course.

She remembered how the Other stared at her from across the street. Silent as stone. Pedestrians were oblivious to its presence. No one else could see it but her. She knew it. The Other raised its arm and pointed its sticklike finger at her, then opened its mouth in a soundless cry that reached deep inside her chest. It told Mara that she didn't belong there—or anywhere—in a language she didn't understand but felt. It told Mara that it was time to leave her life behind and follow. Mara instinctively understood what that meant. It wasn't death. It was nonexistence. She had broken the natural order of things and it had cost her everything. And so she ran.

She fled back to her lab and grabbed all that she could: data records from different destinations and times, the replicator, the fabricator, and SID. She set course for a distant future where she could do no more harm; instead, she arrived in a foreign landscape with no sign of humanity except for an occasional ruin—the edge of a building rising above a dusty plain or a dead satellite still streaking across the sky, sending messages to no one. She wasn't sure if humanity had reached the end of its road or found a new home out in the universe. This future Earth was the perfect place to hide, but she was utterly alone except for the strange animals dotting the landscape who bore little resemblance to their evolutionary past. SID had always been by her side in her research—a voice to bounce ideas off and help correct her sketchy math. Now, in this isolation, SID became something more. A friend. It was SID who first recognized the damage that complete isolation and separation had on Mara and recommended they find a new place in time.

That new place was an equatorial village in the time of the great warming, but conditions were worse than history had taught her. She saw firsthand the human toll from climate collapse, so different from history's sterile charts and data. She tried to help those around her with the knowledge she had brought from the future. Mara befriended a group doing their best to help humanity survive, and for a brief moment she felt she could belong. Then came the sounds from the sky, and the anomalies, and the rips in space and time. Soon the visions of the Others followed, along with rumors of bone-white creatures lurking on the outskirts of town. Mara and SID decided it was time to go.

But at each destination, the same pattern occurred. The more Mara interacted with her surroundings, the faster the visions and the sightings of the Others appeared, until she decided that it was better to remain hidden behind cloaked walls. She also quickly determined another pattern. The greater the number of wormholes in her vicinity, the faster the visions came, which led Mara and SID to believe that the Others used those holes to track her down across time and space. They researched ways to scan for those tears in space-time. They came close, but they never had enough time. The Others always returned. And Mara was forced to quickly break down whatever she had built, remove all traces, and then set out for a new place in time to hide. The pattern repeated itself again and again.

Until now.

"This time is different, though, isn't it, SID? We've been here for almost five months. That's three times longer than any other place and still no sign of the Others. Why is that?" Mara asked.

<*I don't know what the Others are. I don't understand their motives. But perhaps they've grown tired of searching for us.*>

"Or maybe they've lost our trail."

<*Perhaps.*> SID paused while processing the right tone and intonation. <*Is this the reason you haven't told Anna?*>

"I think so."

<*You really believe we have a future here.*>

"I didn't think so until today. Anna helped convince me otherwise. Is it wrong to hope, SID?" Mara asked.

<*I don't understand hope. I understand probabilities. And our probabilities for survival greatly improve if we can identify the source of the anomalies and close the wormholes once and for all.*>

"You can't fool me, SID." Mara smiled and stared up at the first sign of evening stars. "I know you want to stay here as much as I do."

CHAPTER 33

Anna leaned against the windowsill, her chin on her folded arms and her knees bent on the hardwood floor. She looked out her bedroom window at the dirt road that led to their home. Friday evening. Date night. The clock on her phone read 6:38 and still no sign of Mara. Fiona and Lula leaned over Anna's shoulders to get a look too.

"Maybe she's just running a little late," Lula said.

"Mara is never late. She's never wrong. She knows exactly what she's doing," Anna said.

"I saw the spread your uncle is making downstairs. He sure is going all out for Mara," Fiona said.

"Yes, he is."

"Poor guy. He has it bad, doesn't he?" Lula said.

"Oh yes, he does," Anna said.

"Love stinks," Lula said absently.

From down the lane, the three friends could hear the faint whirr of a motorcycle engine followed by a rising dust cloud lit bright by the evening sun. Over the slight ridge, Mara emerged on her bike, her open jacket whipping in the wind. She pulled the motorcycle up to the front fence with a slight skid on gravel and shut off the engine as the dust cloud rolled past. She paused for a moment, her hands in her lap, and Anna was afraid she was going to turn around and ride away. Then Mara removed her helmet, dismounted her bike, and started the long walk to the front door.

"She just rode through dust and wind and her hair looks perfect," Fiona whispered.

"Annoying, right?" Anna whispered back.

Mara looked up to Anna's bedroom window and saw that she had an audience. She gave a quick wave and took in a long, deep breath. Anna gave an overly enthusiastic smile and big thumbs-up in return.

Mara walked to the front door and paused. The air was rich with savory smells that came wafting out from inside the house. The screen door was already open. She lifted her hand, closed her eyes, and knocked on the door.

CHAPTER 34

J ack opened the door before Mara could bring her knuckles
down a second time. Her hand hung midair. Her eyes
slowly opened.

"Hi," Jack said.

"You startled me," Mara replied.

"I thought I heard you pull up. Please, come on in," Jack
said as he moved aside.

"I'm sorry I'm late." Mara stepped into the foyer.

She surveyed the room. The Armstrong house was old, especially for this era, but if you looked closely enough you could
see newer layers from successive repairs and additions. It was
brighter and more open than she expected at this time of day.
Bay windows brought in bright light that created patterns
across the floors and the walls scuffed with several generations
of wear. This was so unlike the sterile, self-healing walls of her
childhood, where marks and stains would repair themselves
within minutes. These walls had memory. On the doorframe
of the coat closet, she saw faded pencil marks that ran verti-
cally from the floor. It took a second to decode, but she realized these pencil scratchings marked the passage of time and

the growth of several generations of kids. *Jack was a child here*, she thought.

"Has Anna showed you around before?" Jack asked.

"Yes, but she didn't give me much detail. You've lived here your entire life, haven't you?" Mara said.

"For the most part. I've spent a good amount of time overseas, but yeah, this is home." Jack glanced around the room. "The living room over here was part of the original home built about 120 years ago. I knocked down a bunch of walls to open the place up and I'm pretty sure I've ticked off my ancestors in the process. The morning room over there with the piano? I built that in the last couple of years. It's one of my favorite rooms."

Mara walked past the living room into the open morning room. Large wall-to-wall windows framed the green rolling hills and pastures and groves of trees just beyond the backyard. It was like a study in contrast and light. Sunset caught the corner of the room. *They have no idea how beautiful this time is.*

She made her way to the old white upright piano on the far wall. It too was covered in scuff marks and history. She stood over the piano and absently tinkered with several chords, an old song from her childhood that was still over a hundred years from being written. She paused and let her fingers rest on the keys as the final chord echoed through the room and down the hallway. It had been so long since she had heard that sound.

"You play piano too?" Jack shook his head. "What can't you do?"

"I don't really play. I haven't played . . . for years. Muscle memory I guess." Mara smiled.

"Well, your memory plays beautifully."

Mara looked to the row of picture frames above the piano. They looked like they had been lined up chronologically, with the oldest photos to the left. A smiling young couple looked back in black-and-white, and Mara saw elements of Jack in both faces. The large eyes and long eyelashes from the woman. The sharp jawline and long neck from the man.

"Your parents?"

"Grandparents," Jack said.

"Handsome couple."

"This one here is of my parents," Jack said as he pointed to a faded color image of another young couple, with a toddler in the mother's arms. "And that little guy was my big brother, Sam. The one with the big ears, like a car with its doors open."

"Anna's father?"

"Yeah. Anna's father. It's a shame, but I don't have any pictures of Anna's mother here. I really should. She was something. Beautiful, smart. A whole lot like Anna." Jack seemed lost for a moment, as if he were looking at these photos for the first time in a very long time. "I miss them both."

"I see a lot of Anna in you too. Your enthusiasm. Your desire to make a difference." Mara smiled warmly. "She really loves you, you know. She's lucky to have you."

"Yeah. I wasn't so sure at first." Jack chuckled. "I wasn't ready for this. To be a legal guardian. I guess that's what they call it. I think we both were a little lost after my brother died, but Anna has really helped me piece things back together. And now I can't imagine her not being in my life."

"That makes two of us." Mara gently touched Jack's arm.

"Uh, well. We better not let dinner cool off too much." Jack motioned toward the hallway.

They made their way back to the kitchen, where the dining table was set for two. Matching plates, a centerpiece of yellow and blue wildflowers, and several large white serving trays with food lined the table. Uncle Jack waited for Mara to sit down first.

"Okay, I guess I should give you a quick breakdown. Dinner

tonight was a collaborative effort. I made the whitefish. Well, let me expand on that. I caught, cleaned, and grilled the white-fish. Ricardo and his wife, Itzel, contributed the quinoa salad. It's pretty amazing, but fair warning, it has a kick." Jack smiled.

"A kick?"

"You know—spicy." Jack fanned his mouth. "Gladness made the chapati bread. It's a childhood favorite of hers from Tanzania, and it too is pretty amazing. Faye made the dessert. A peach pie. Once again, one of her family recipes. Oh, and the wine is also from Faye. Organic and French, so . . ."

Mara took one of the whole fish from the serving tray and laid it on her plate, followed by a scoop of the salad and one of the round flatbreads still steaming in a covered basket. She tore off a chunk of the bread first, and it released more steam with a rich smell of butter and salt. The texture was flaky, and the flavor was buttery and smooth with a hint of something else, maybe nuts. She closed her eyes and let the flavor rest on the middle of her tongue. She chewed slowly in silence. When she opened her eyes, Jack was staring at her again.

"Good?" he asked.

"Very."

She used her fork to create a combination of flavors next, spearing a piece of tangerine, avocado, and kale from the salad. She placed the whole bite in her mouth and let the food rest there without chewing. Sweet, tart, buttery, and a sense of heat. Real heat, but not unpleasant. She sampled the fish next. Another first. Real fish, not synthetic. Delicate and slightly sweet with a complement of garlic and spice. She went from dish to wine to new dish, sampling in silence and thinking to herself that of all the things the people of her time had lost, this one was the least appreciated. *Food.* Simple, whole food grown in soil or caught in the wild and prepared by hand.

"You're a quiet eater, if you don't mind me saying," Jack said.

"Where I come from, we don't talk during dinner. We rarely even eat together, and if we do, it's only out of convenience," Mara said. The wine made her cheeks flush.

"Really? That sounds awful. Food is a social thing here. If you think about it, it's the very reason for this farm's existence," Jack said. "I'm curious, since you mentioned it. Where *do* you come from?"

Mara paused. "Come from?"

"Yeah. I know so little about you other than you're brilliant and ride a motorcycle and really, really like food." Uncle Jack smiled. "I was hoping to get to know a little more about you."

Mara froze; her arms hung limply by her sides. She didn't respond for five to ten seconds. An eternity. She just stared straight forward trying desperately to recalculate the course of this conversation. She had practiced different types of questions and responses with SID earlier in the day and prepared for multiple scenarios. She had memorized her backstory. But for some reason all that preparation went out the window the second she fully engaged with Jack.

She stood from the table without saying anything and turned toward the stairs.

"Are you looking for the restroom?" Jack called out.

"No. I forgot something. Anna. I'll be back." Mara headed up the stairs, leaving Jack alone at the table looking confused.

Mara raced up the steps, clearing two at a time, and knocked on Anna's door. The door swung open. Inside the room, Lula and Fiona were sitting on the floor listening to music from someone's phone. Anna leaned against the door.

"What are you doing here?" Anna whispered. The music helped drown out the conversation.

"Your uncle is asking personal questions," Mara said under her breath.

"What did you expect?"

"I don't know. Not this. I froze?" Mara looked desperate.

"Are you serious?" Anna shrugged in exasperation.

"Very." Mara returned the same look of exasperation.

"Do what you used to do, I guess. I mean, what did you do when you went on a date before?" Anna asked.

"We don't have dates—at least not like this. There were no personal questions. No inquisition. We already knew everything about each other from our social streams. Our entire history. There's no mystery. And meetings were arranged by algorithm. I told you that."

"I didn't think you were serious."

"Help me find an exit. Tell your uncle I had to leave."

Anna shut the door behind her and joined Mara in the hallway.

"All right, all right. Just calm down," Anna said as she grabbed Mara by the arms and looked her square in the eye. "You're not leaving."

"Then help me. Come downstairs and join us."

"No. But I have an idea. When he asks you a question, just tell him *part* of the truth—the part you're comfortable saying," Anna said.

"That's your idea?"

"You're not very good at this, are you?"

"You mean deception? No, I am not. It might surprise you to know, but there is little need for deceit in the future."

"All right. Make the conversation about him then. Guys love talking about themselves. You ask the questions. *You* take the offensive," Anna said firmly.

"I take the offensive?"

Anna nodded in affirmation.

"Okay. Okay. That might work." Mara took in a deep breath. "But stand by your iCom. I may need an emergency intervention."

Anna smiled. It seemed to help. Mara took in another deep breath and turned to head back downstairs.

"My uncle flusters you a little, doesn't he?" Anna said lightly.

"Yes, he does," Mara answered without looking back.

———

Mara reentered the kitchen and sat down quietly at the table. She took another bite of bread followed by a longer drink of wine. She set the glass down and smiled.

"Everything okay?" Jack asked, his expression worried.

"Yes. Yes. I had forgotten to tell Anna about a deadline for the Albright Fellowship, but we're good." Mara took another drink of wine.

One deception down.

"Whew. I thought it was me for a second," Jack said, laughing nervously.

"So, you asked me where I was from."

"Yeah, I was just curious—"

"Boston."

"Boston? Oh, just like Anna. What a coincidence."

"Yes."

"Well, you sure don't sound like you're from Boston. To be honest, I couldn't tell where you're from. England, maybe Europe. Is that where your family is from?" Jack asked again.

Take the offensive, Mara thought.

"Are you trying to determine my genetic composition and heritage?" Mara leaned in.

"Uh, yeah. That sounded pretty insensitive now that you put it that way. I'm sorry." Jack leaned back.

"No need to be sorry. I'm 15 percent Northern European, 31 percent Southern European, 15 percent Manchurian and Mongolian, 12 percent South American, 10 percent North African, 7 percent West African, and 10 percent Southeast Asian, including traces of Denisovan and Neanderthal base strands," Mara said, then took a bite of the fish and followed it with more wine.

"Wow. That is oddly precise." Jack laughed. "I'd love to go to one of your family reunions."

"That would be a trick. We're pretty distant. My full name is Mara Banjoko Lee and I'm a research scientist. I have advanced degrees in integrated physics and biology and a brother and a sister." Mara sipped her wine again and looked down, slightly disappointed at her now-empty glass. "But enough about me. I want to know more about you."

"Okay. Ask anything you'd like."

Mara poured herself another glass of wine, leaned in, and smiled. Her cheeks felt warm.

"How do you intend to save the world?" Mara asked.

"Well, that's a pretty big question. I'm not sure where to start," Jack said. He poured himself another glass of wine in return.

"Start at the beginning. I have all night."

"Okay. Let me see. I never set out to save the world. I never intended to be a farmer. In fact, it was the last thing I wanted to do. Farming is hard and it doesn't make any money and you're at the mercy of nature and commodity prices. I went to college to study electrical engineering and planned on doing development work overseas."

"Is that where you met Dr. Gloria?"

"Oh, no, I've known RG since kindergarten, and we've been kind of joined at the hip ever since. In fact, we were even roommates in college," Jack said.

"So why did you return here to your family farm?"

"RG and I decided to work overseas after college. Since we had agricultural backgrounds, we were placed with farmers in Malawi. Setting up microgrids, upgrading farm equipment. Anything to help increase yield. We had all the naive confidence of youth and thought we were making a difference.

But it didn't take long to figure out that we weren't helping. In some ways, we might have been making it worse. We were exporting ways of working that didn't make much sense there." Jack shrugged.

"I'm sure you did some good?"

"Maybe, but the whole system is rigged against the small farmer over there. Actually everywhere, I guess. From seed to fertilizer to the equipment they're forced to buy. We were just helping those farmers get into debt faster. It was there in Malawi that RG and I realized that food and farming may be at the very heart of a lot of our issues today. From the environment to health to social justice. And these farmers were just victims of a crappy system like everyone else. So we came home, and I asked my dad to convert the farm into a research facility to see if we could help address it," Jack said.

"And?"

"And, after a couple of years of me preaching, he finally gave in and said yes. And that's the start of the Armstrong and Gloria Regenerative Farms Research Center and our goal to save the world, like you said." Jack smiled. "I wish my mom and dad had been able to stick around to see this place, and Anna. They'd be proud I think."

"So how are you doing?"

"With?"

"Your mission. Have you fixed the broken food system?"

Uncle Jack laughed and leaned back from the table. "Yeaaaaah. Well. I wouldn't say fixed. But we've made some headway. We've introduced open-source seed programs in developing regions. Even some here in the US, of all places, along with some lawsuits. We've open-sourced our designs for farm equipment. We've helped mentor regenerative farming programs in over a dozen locations. It's a start."

"It's not enough."

"Excuse me?" Jack looked genuinely surprised.

"It's not enough. We have three decades at most to draw down emissions, especially from farming. Six decades to preserve topsoil," Mara said. "Fifty-seven years to be exact. After that, there is no soil for food."

"Well, we're not certain how long we have—"

"I'm certain." Mara looked straight ahead, unblinking.

"Okay. I see you are."

"I can help," Mara said.

"I appreciate that, but physics ain't farming, Mara. People problems aren't so easy to break down, and the food system is ultimately a people problem."

"Maybe you're just using the wrong models," Mara said.

"Maybe we are, but there is no one simple solution and no one model. What we have instead are a whole bunch of complex problems all butting up against one another," Jack volleyed back.

"Then let me start with one," Mara shot back.

"One what? Problem?" Jack gave a half smile.

"Yes."

"Okay. Water. Regions throughout the world are depleting their water tables faster than they can be replenished. How do we increase the availability of water with drought increasing year over year?" Jack asked.

He poured Mara some more wine and smiled. He was having fun.

"I'll start working on it tonight." Mara raised a single eyebrow and smiled back. This is what hope felt like—what purpose felt like. Like she had said before: if she was going to make the most of this new future she had, she would start here, on this farm.

"Wait." Jack was taken aback. "You're serious."

"Of course I am."

"I mean *serious* serious? You want to join us?"

"Yes." Mara nodded and chuckled.

"What about your work at the Albright Fellowship?"

"Easy. I can do both," Mara said.

Jack spent a moment assessing where the conversation had gone. Not where he expected, that was for sure. And he couldn't decide if she was teasing or if she really meant to work with him here on the farm. But the resolute look in her eyes gave him his answer. Questions like for how long and for how much didn't seem to matter at this moment. She was just going to be part of his life in some capacity for the foreseeable future, and that was more than he had hoped for. He raised his glass.

"Well then, welcome to the team, Mara Banjoko Lee," Jack said.

She raised her glass in return. They sat for a moment and let the silence set in. Mara then placed her elbows on the table and rested her chin on top of folded hands. She turned her head to the side and traced aspects of Jack's face with her eyes.

"You are so unlike anyone I've ever met," Mara said.

Jack looked away for a second, then looked back.

"Yeah. I've never met anyone like you either."

"Your face is all wrong," Mara said, still tracing the contours of his face with her gaze.

"Excuse me?"

Mara reached across the table and ran her finger along the crooked edges of Jack's nose, an imperfection never seen in her time. He stared down at her hand, which was warm and smooth. His eyes crossed.

"Were you born this way, or was it some kind of mishap?" Mara said as she traced the other side of the bridge of his nose.

"Really?" Jack felt his heart sink. "It's that bad?"

"Not at all. It's quite charming."

"Okay, I'll take charming." Jack smiled, a little relieved. "It was a line drive I took straight to the nose when I was playing baseball in high school. It's what I get for not paying attention.

My dad set the break after the game, and it's been just a little crooked ever since. I don't know. I kind of like it."

"May I see your hands?" Mara asked as she reached out her own.

Jack paused just for a moment, not sure where this was going, then reluctantly held out his hands. Mara turned his palms over and ran her fingers along his hands. His nails were clean, but no amount of scrubbing was going to get rid of the calluses and deep-set work lines.

"These are calluses, correct?" Mara asked.

"You're definitely not from around here." Jack laughed.

Mara shook her head *no* and held on to his hands. Jack could feel the strength in her fingers.

"Somehow, all these imperfections just work," Mara said.

"I'm glad they're good for something." Jack chuckled. "Say, you want to go for a walk? I have something I've been working on that I want to show you."

Mara nodded and allowed Jack to take her by the hand as he led her past the kitchen, through the front door, and out into the late evening air. Temperatures had finally cooled just a bit, and fireflies blinked lazily at eye level. The two walked slowly past the front fence and into the barnyard. Most of the crew had headed home for the day, and the farm was silent except for the evening sounds, once so foreign to Mara. Jack let go of Mara's hand and motioned for her to stay there as he walked over to the fabrication shed, opened the door, then stepped back.

"What is this?" Mara asked.

Jack signaled for her to wait one more minute; a broad grin spread across his face. He reached into his back pocket for his phone and began typing commands. He looked back at the open door shrouded in darkness. Suddenly a warm golden light appeared at eye level from somewhere back in the shadows. The light floated lazily toward the door and out twenty feet into the night air. It was a Chinese lantern decorated in red and gold; its glow lit up the side of the building and the ground just below. Another lantern appeared, then another, until the sky above their heads was filled with spheres of light gently bobbing in the light breeze. The two looked up, their faces aglow.

"You planned this?" Mara asked.

"I did, but I wasn't sure if I was going to show you. It depended on how the evening went." Jack reached for her hand again. This time she wove her fingers between his and squeezed back. "I was originally planning on launching these at the fair. Looks pretty good, doesn't it?"

"You're trying to impress me, aren't you?" Mara asked.

"Maybe. Is it working?"

Mara grabbed his other hand. She hadn't expected this, or wanted this, but here it was just the same. She leaned into Jack, into this world where people held mysteries and imperfections, and kissed him beneath the light of the Chinese lanterns.

———

Back at the house, three young friends leaned against one another in Anna's bedroom and looked out a darkened window into the barnyard at the magical lights and the embracing couple. Anna hadn't expected this—at all. But, like Mara, now that it was here, she was glad.

CHAPTER 35

The next two weeks passed in a haze of summer heat and windless days, the drone of crickets and cicadas an ever-present soundtrack in the background. Anna practiced flying every chance she could. The more she flew, the more her body adapted to a completely different set of mechanisms and movements. She learned about air currents and how to ride the afternoon updrafts. If you could read the changes in temperature and humidity just right, air had a noticeable texture. No longer confined to a flat plane, even her vision began to change as she learned to better judge distances and angles and shadows.

Flying became a game in which every surface was a challenge. She learned to land gently on tree limbs or leap from fence post to fence post or ricochet off barn walls to gather momentum. She practiced flying through the woods—learning to speed up in a clearing and roll, pitch, and yaw like a bird to avoid tree branches. She sat on the uppermost branch of an old elm for a good part of one afternoon and watched how a group of starlings would dive, roll, and quickly ascend to defend their nest from a Cooper's hawk.

She would fly with Mara when she could, primarily in the late evenings or after the farm had gone dark and Anna could sneak out quietly from her bedroom window. Herbie could sense when she left—even when she was invisible—and let out a friendly bark, thinking this might be some new kind of game. Anna loved the nights. The valley would open up before her with a scattering of lights like a miniature set for a film. The lake reflected moonlight, and the woods were dark and impenetrable. But for all their searching, there still was no sign of the creature, and the sightings around town had stopped. Both began to wonder if it had found its own way home or disappeared altogether.

During the day, Anna would swim at the lake with her friends, jumping off the boulders along the shore to cannonball into the waters below, then drying off on those same boulders under the heat of the sun as puffy white clouds passed by.

Now that she was part of the Armstrong and Gloria Regenerative Farms Research Center, Mara was given a renovated shed near the edge of the grounds to set up her own office and lab. The floors were concrete but clean, and the walls were recently covered in drywall. Wooden tables, freshly cut by a CNC router and assembled by hand, lined the far wall and filled the room with the bright smell of cedar. She set up a server farm with components ordered online and installed a simplified version of SID on the local network. She built a modified version of a fabricator and hacked a mobile phone that allowed her to directly access her iCom without drawing attention, all the while cursing the antiquated tools she was forced to use.

In the afternoons, she would walk with Jack. They held hands, awkwardly at first, but as the week wore on, the initial fumbling and walking out of sync gave way to a natural cadence. Conversations focused almost entirely on the farm and research. Each day was the same. Mara would ask a series of increasingly complex questions until she reached the limit of Jack's understanding, and then she'd take a mental note for later. Now the question was how much she could reveal—and in what order—to help Jack and his team further their research. If she was to make the most of this future, like Anna said, she would start here on this farm.

During this process, she learned as much about Jack as she did about his work—his enthusiasm and optimistic view of the world—and found it contagious. Jack learned as much during all their sessions as he did his entire time in school. Dr. Gloria started making jokes that Mara might be a spy. But it was Gladness who came closest to understanding the truth.

An Angus cow was giving birth in the western pasture, and Dr. Gloria asked Mara and Anna if they wanted to join Gladness on the hilltop to watch the process unfold. By the time Dr. Gloria dropped them off near the shade of an old red oak at the edge of the property, the Black Angus cow was lying on her side. Her eyes were open wide and her breathing labored. Gladness observed the Angus from a short distance. She looked up and smiled at Mara and Anna in acknowledgment, then returned her gaze back to the cow.

"Why is she out here all by herself?" Anna asked.

"It's part of their nature."

"It looks distressed. Aren't you going to do anything?" Mara asked, concerned.

"Oh no, not yet. It's a *she*, by the way, and her name is Suzie." Gladness smiled, her eyes bright. She gave the cow distance, and everyone else followed suit. "This is all part of the bonding process. As that little one moves around inside her, hormones are released that trigger the maternal instinct. You jump in too quickly and you just mess things up."

"How long does poor Suzie have to be like this?" Anna asked.

"As long as it takes, my dear," Gladness said as she absently swatted at a buzzing fly. She had been through this dozens of times before in Tanzania and had developed an intuition about when a cow was in true distress and when it was just the natural cycle. "But the water sac broke about fifty minutes ago, and from the way mama is breathing and the contractions, I'd say the little one should make an appearance within the next ten minutes. Fingers crossed."

"How *little* is the little one?" Mara asked.

"Seventy-five to eighty pounds, most likely," Gladness said.

"Thirty-four to thirty-six kilograms. That's incredible. How can her body possibly support that?" Mara asked. It was less of a question to anyone else and more of a thought she said out loud to herself.

Gladness chuckled.

"Well, bovids, or cows, have been doing it this way for millions of years, and it usually works out just fine," Gladness said. "I see you're more comfortable with the metric system. Most Americans still have troubles."

"The imperial system is a relic of another time, a mistake that took far too long to address," Mara said absently, her focus on the strange process unfolding before her.

Gladness tilted her head and a quizzical look crossed her face.

"I'm usually very good with accents. But for the life of me, I can't place where yours is from," Gladness said.

Mara knew she needed to be more careful with this one. It took some control to not respond too quickly or defensively.

"It's a product of a lot of travel, I guess. To be honest, I'm not quite sure where I come from anymore," Mara said with a hint of a smile.

"Isn't that just the way it is nowadays?" Gladness said as she shook her head and sighed. She paused a moment before going on. "I hope you don't mind, but I couldn't help but overhear your conversations with the others over the past couple of weeks."

"You mean my persistent questioning or lack of understanding?" Mara tried to laugh it off.

"Oh, no. Just the opposite. I've never heard anyone with such a command over so many different subjects. You talked about soil conservation with Li. Botany with Faye. Amazing, really. You seem to know a lot about many things—except for maybe the mothering behavior of the Angus cow, that is." Gladness winked at that last part.

Just then, Suzie's eyes opened wide and she let out a tired bellow. She began snorting through flared nostrils followed by a series of labored breaths. Whatever line of questioning Gladness had planned was suddenly put on hold, and her full attention was now back on the cow in front of her. She took a cautious step forward. *Perfect timing,* Mara thought.

"Something's happening," Anna said excitedly.

Suddenly, two small hooves emerged from the cow for just a moment—then receded. Suzie let out another bellow.

"Oh my God! Were those the baby cow's feet?" Anna asked.

"I certainly hope so," Gladness said.

For the next couple minutes, small hooves would appear then disappear as Gladness coaxed the cow along with a soothing singsong chant of *"That's a good girl."* Mara and Anna stood transfixed, their faces mirror images of each other as they not only watched but felt part of what was taking place in front of them. They grimaced in empathetic pain when Suzie bellowed, and their eyes opened wide in awe when more of the calf appeared. They giggled and exchanged glances. Even their breathing was in concert. Without thinking, Mara reached out her hand and Anna gripped it in return. Minutes passed as Suzie continued to bellow intermittently—then a nose poked through, then the head, and then suddenly the full calf appeared; its small body lay covered in afterbirth on the ground.

The jet-black calf looked so small and fragile in the dirt. Its eyes were open, but the rest of its body lay unmoving. Anna stepped forward to make sure it was alive, but Gladness motioned for her to stop.

"Give them time," Gladness whispered.

The calf blinked and then its lungs expanded as it took its first breath. It lifted its head in its first attempt to stand. Seconds before, Suzie looked too tired to move. But with this first sign of life from her offspring, she was quickly back up and cleaning her newborn calf with her tongue. With each passing moment, the calf gained strength, just as her mother gained strength in return.

"I think I'm more exhausted than Suzie." Mara laughed.

She exhaled for the first time in an hour and relaxed her shoulders and arms. Imprints from her tight grip still showed white marks on Anna's hands.

CHAPTER 36

Finn Olsen was driving home after closing up shop at Wilderman's Feed Store when an image flashed in his head. The sliding bay door in the warehouse out back of the store was open. He was sure of it. *Dang it if I didn't leave it open.* It may have just been a crack, but that was more than enough for squirrels or possums or a wide variety of varmints to squeeze their way in from the small woods that abutted the warehouse. At nineteen, Finn was the youngest manager that old man Wilderman had ever trusted to lock up the shop, and he wasn't going to do anything to break that trust. Not now. Not with college and tuition dues coming up and a chance to finally leave this town just around the corner. With six siblings, his family couldn't spare a penny.

Finn turned his pickup truck around and headed back to the feed store. He looked down at the clock on the dash: *9:20 p.m.* He still had time to lock up, get back home and shower, then make his way over to Millersville to meet the others at Bacci's Pizza. The sun had set, and just the tips of the trees captured the fading light, like candles.

Minutes later, he pulled into the gravel parking lot of

Wilderman's and turned off his stereo. The warehouse out back was now covered in shadows, and the sky was dark purple, the color of a deep bruise. His intuition was right. He had forgotten to shut the bay door. He got out of his truck and left the passenger door open. This would be fast and there was no need to lock it. Gravel popped under his feet as he made his way across the empty lot. Keys jangled at his side. He was talking to himself in a low voice with his head down, as he sometimes did—engrossed in an internal dialogue about the night ahead—when he stopped cold. He felt a chill that made his shoulders shake, even though temperatures were still in the high eighties.

Finn lifted his head slowly. It was nothing but shadows behind the crack in the sliding bay door. No sound. No movement. But still, something didn't feel right. He tiptoed up to the door even though he wasn't sure why. He peeked his head through the gap. In the dim light he could make out a rounded shape: bags of cow and horse feed covered in tarp. He was ready to close the door when a black shape streaked in front of his line of vision. It moved fast—almost too fast to see. But it was unmistakable. Four misshapen limbs scurried silently along the concrete floor like a giant crab across the sand.

He jerked his head back out of the shadows and stood frozen in front of the warehouse door. He took in small gulps of air. It was all he could manage. His chest felt like it was being squeezed tight in a vise.

"Nope, nope, nope, nope, nope, nope. Uh-uh," Finn whispered as he shook his head.

From inside, a ticking sound echoed through the cavernous warehouse, a sound like a stick being dragged across a picket fence. *Tick—tick—tick—tick—tick—tick—tick—tick— tick—tick—tick—tick—tick—tick. Or a rattle*, Finn thought. That's all it took to break the spell, and Finn took off in a run for his truck without looking back.

He slammed the truck door behind him and immediately rolled up the windows and locked both doors before slumping back in the cabin seat. He started the engine. The headlights shone bright on a row of steel gates stacked in front of the warehouse, their shadows creating twisted shapes against the warehouse wall. He paused to look at the still-open bay door, afraid of what might come crawling out. Finn grabbed his phone from his back pocket and dialed 911. Two rings.

"911 operator. What's your emergency?"

Finn fumbled. He hadn't thought this far in advance. "Uh, I want to report a break-in. I think."

"What's your location?" the dispatcher asked.

"Outside Wilderman's Feed Store. I mean out back. Near the warehouse."

"I know that place." The dispatcher's voice brightened. "Wait, is this Finn? I thought I recognized your voice."

"Ma'am?"

"It's Mrs. Chaffin. Roy's mom. You boys played football together."

"Yes, ma'am."

"Do you need me to send someone out?"

"I don't know. I think so. I think something's in the warehouse." Finn rubbed his forehead.

"You mean someone?"

"I don't know."

"Okay, Finn. I'm sending someone out there as soon as I can. You want me to stay on the line with you?"

"Yes, ma'am."

CHAPTER 37

A halo of blue light flashed above Anna's iCom. Startled, she dropped the book she had been reading and shot up in bed. A holographic map of the valley appeared just above her wrist, followed by a pulsing blue dot. Based on the placement, the pulse of light looked like it was just west of the town center, near the railroad tracks. A thin blue line traced a path to the pulse from her current location. This was it. She knew it. She ran to her dresser and pulled out her goggles before turning off the lights and locking the door.

"I just picked up a 911 call from Wilderman's Feed Store," Mara said over the iCom. *"I'll meet you there. Are you ready?"*

"Yeah," Anna answered. Butterflies in her stomach. She activated her cloaking device. "I didn't think this time would ever come."

She hopped up onto the windowsill, her feet perched on the ledge for just a moment, then stepped out into the late evening sky. As her body fell forward, she leaned in and caught the air, a sensation between a sustained fall and acceleration. Faster and faster she flew, her body no more than twenty feet off the ground, until she made her way to the railroad tracks and followed the path west. The wooden planks beneath her passed by in a blur.

As she drew closer to her destination, a fifty-foot yellow grain loader peeked above the tree line like a toy erector set. At the end of the grain loader, along a rusted crane arm that extended over the railroad tracks, a body, outlined in blue, sat crouched in silhouette. It was Mara resting high above the ground. She was scanning the area. Anna landed gently by her side on the metal overhang and assumed the same crouching position. The evening light was now just a thin faded line on the horizon. The rest of the sky was dark and speckled with early-evening stars.

"I believe the creature is in the warehouse," Mara said. "And see down there—I think that's the person who called 911."

She pointed to a pickup truck fifty feet below, parked in an empty gravel lot between the feed store and the warehouse. The headlights were on and the engine was running. Inside, the driver's face was lit up from the dashboard lights. Even without zooming in with their goggles, they could see he was scared. His eyes were wide as he looked nervously from side window to side window.

"Hey, wait. That looks—I know that guy. That's Fiona's older brother, Finn," Anna said.

"I think we have about ten minutes before the authorities arrive. Maybe fifteen if we're lucky. That doesn't give us much time. I thought we could go through the skylights on the roof, but they appear locked. We'll need to go through the bay door in front," Mara said. She turned to face Anna. The lines of her jaw were tense. "Before we go in, remember what we discussed before."

"I'm not supposed to get too close to the creature."

"And why is that?"

"Because we have to assume that it's dangerous."

"Exactly. Guide the creature toward me. I'll try to incapacitate it with light, maybe sound if needed. We don't know how
it will respond. But hopefully, once it's incapacitated, we can
immobilize it with this," Mara said. She held up a small, perfectly round white sphere.

"Your ball of goo. You have more than one of those things?"

"One should be sufficient. I've tested the targeting mechanism multiple times. It'll work."

"Okay, so we capture it, then keep it safe at your place until
we find its home. Right?"

"That's the plan. Ready?" Mara asked.

Anna nodded.

"All right, then. Follow me down to the entrance and listen
for my directions. I mean it. Listen," Mara said. "Nine minutes
and counting."

Mara stepped off the metal scaffold and glided down toward the front of the warehouse. She landed gently in front of
the open bay door, with Anna following close behind, invisible
to everyone but each other. If Finn had been paying attention,
he'd have seen a small cloud of dust kick up where their feet
touched the ground. Light from the truck's headlights cut a
sharp line through the gap in the bay door and out across the
warehouse floor. The rest of the warehouse, fifty feet wide and
one hundred fifty feet deep, was shrouded in darkness. Mara
stepped through the door and into the shadows. No sign of
movement.

She levitated several feet off the ground to avoid making
a noise herself, then floated slowly toward the ceiling. The
warehouse looked empty from this angle. Maybe the creature
had escaped through another entrance? She signaled for Anna
to move to the far wall. They would float on opposite sides of
the warehouse and scan for any signs of life between them.
Even with the aid of the goggles, it was difficult to differentiate
shapes in the darkness.

They moved slowly, keeping each other in their field of vision. Anna was halfway across the span of the warehouse when she heard a faint crunching sound, like someone chewing ice.

"Mara, can you hear that?" Anna whispered into her iCom.

"Yes, it's coming from your side. Remember, not too close. I'm coming over."

Anna ran her hand along the wall as she descended to floor level. Her feet landed softly on concrete. The cracking sound was louder here and appeared to be coming from between two large shelving racks, each one twenty feet in height. Anna slowed her pace, then peered around the corner.

A dim ray of light shone down from the skylight above, providing just enough illumination for Anna to make out a shape. She couldn't tell if it was a box or a sack. She stepped closer. Then the shape moved. What looked like long legs unfolded from a crouched position to standing. Joints unhinged at odd angles. In its hands, the creature held a white cube. The crunching stopped. Anna had interrupted its feeding.

"Anna! Step back!" Mara shouted over her iCom. She was floating down from the opposite end of the aisle with her arms spread wide like an angel.

But Anna couldn't move. Her brain was working too hard processing what was in front of her. Long arms and legs. Small body and an olive-shaped head as black as night. There were words typed along the white cube it was holding: SALT. The creature was eating a large block of salt, the same kind they give to horses and cows, and white dust covered its chin and chest. Slowly the creature turned its head in Anna's direction. *Impossible*, she thought. Somehow it sensed her even with her cloaking device on. Then all at once black scales spread out in a fan around the creature's head and shook like a rattle. *Tick—tick—tick—tick—tick—tick—tick—tick.*

Scales on the creature's arm opened, and small green and

blue lights slowly wafted out like dandelion seeds and floated toward Anna. Fairy lights. The fear that had gripped her quickly melted away as the small floating lights grew closer. A wave of calm and visions of dark, still waters. Her eyes grew heavy. Something in the lights made her—

"Anna! Move!"

Anna's eyes snapped open from her daze. She was only out for a few seconds, but in that moment the creature had leaped to the shelving rack and was now quickly scurrying up the side. Mara tried following it, but the thing moved too fast. Anna flew to the top edge of the rack to cut the creature off. She held her arms out to block it.

On top of the shelf, the creature sat crouched on its hind legs, its head pivoting back and forth. Although it couldn't see its pursuers, it sensed it was trapped. Mara moved forward cautiously, gliding slowly along the top of the rack. The creature sensed movement and its scales fanned out in response, a black halo around its head—*tickticktickick*.

Mara held out the white spherical ball in her palm. It rose slowly to hang in midair, then began to spin as it locked on its target.

"Keep its attention, Anna. Just a moment longer," Mara said quietly over her iCom. "Three."

Anna waved her arms and tried to whistle. The creature turned its head sharply, aware of Anna's presence but unable to see her fully.

"Two."

The creature began to sway its head back and forth. It took one step toward Anna.

"One!"

The white sphere shot out toward the creature and erupted in a small, silent explosion of translucent goo. But the creature was already gone in a blur.

"Where did it go?" Anna shouted as she looked frantically around.

She strained to see into the shadows and the corners of the warehouse. Nothing made a sound except the liquid goo dripping down the sides of the rack to the floor below. The green and blue lights began to fade beneath her.

"I can't see."

"Stay still, Anna. Don't move," Mara whispered. "It's right above you."

Above me. How can that be? Anna looked up. Fifteen feet above her head, the creature's limbs splayed out against the ceiling. Its skin was the absence of light, so dark it looked like a cutout silhouette. It moved slowly across the ceiling. A lizard scaling rock.

"You gotta be kidding me," Anna said out loud.

"Close your eyes. I'm going to use the bang lights to incapacitate it," Mara said as she drifted closer.

"No. Not yet. We don't know if the lights will hurt—"

"Close your eyes, Anna."

"It's scared. I can feel it. Trust me," Anna said.

Anna turned off her cloaking mode and opened her arms, an outward demonstration that she meant no harm. Later, in a moment of quiet and with time to think things through, she'd look back and realize how foolish that gesture was. In nature, open arms could be a warning or the first step toward violence. Without a common language or understanding, any sign could be misconstrued as a threat. The creature snapped its head toward Anna now that it could see her. Scales fanned out across its head and its limbs and began to rattle. A high-pitched wail, completely alien, seemed to emanate from its entire body—the sound of a thousand metallic bees echoed back and forth through the warehouse.

"Now!" Mara shouted.

Anna closed her eyes just in time. A series of bright light pulses exploded in the back of her brain, followed by an afterimage of black stars set against a blanket of white snow. She blinked, disoriented, and shook her head. The black stars began to fade. The white snow disappeared. She rubbed her eyes from the aftereffects of the bang lights and looked up just in time to see the creature fall limp from the ceiling straight toward her. Mara raced to catch the falling creature, but Anna was closer. She opened her arms and prepared for the heavy impact that never came. The creature, weightless like paper, fell into her arms. Its body the size of a small child. Its long arms and legs hung limp at its side.

"Anna, be careful!"

Up close, Anna could make out features she was unable to see at a distance. The shape of the creature's face was almost human: a small bridge of a nose, a tiny mouth, and two large black eyes shaped like almonds. Its ears were holes surrounded by thin ridges in a half circle. She leaned in closer to see if it was still alive. The creature blinked back, and Anna almost dropped it in surprise. The creature blinked again; a reflective lens covered its eye. Anna could feel wiry muscles like rope begin to tighten and move.

"Uh, I think it's awake," Anna said, unsure whether she wanted to hold on to the creature but afraid to let go.

Just as Mara flew down to assist, the creature flipped and uncoiled like a spring, easily breaking Anna's hold and crawling up onto her back. The creature's legs wrapped around her waist in an impossibly strong grip. Its hands grabbed the sides of Anna's face with soft rubbery fingers like suction cups. Suddenly, an image of an alien landscape—rocks, lights reflecting off standing water, and an infinite night—flashed in her mind.

Anna's brain tried to process the two different sets of images and sensations. That's when the panic set in.

"Aaaaahhhh!" Anna screamed as she began flying in no direction at all, spinning and twisting in an attempt to get the creature off her back.

Anna flailed her arms and kicked out at nothing. *Outside.* That was all she could think of. She had to get outside. She twisted her body toward the entrance. The creature's fingers dug deeper into her temples. Up ahead, from the open bay door, the truck headlights appeared to grow brighter, the line of light expanding out across the warehouse floor. *The lights.* She just needed to make it to the lights. Anna leaned forward and made a straight line for the exit.

Just as Anna broke the plane of light, the creature loosened its grip. This was her chance. Anna spun quickly just as she shot through the open bay door into the blinding brightness of the truck's headlights. The creature sensed the light and kicked away, knocking Anna off balance.

The last thing Anna remembered was tumbling in the air. Then her back hit gravel hard. She bounced once then twice in a somersault before skidding to a full stop on her butt. Dust billowed up around her in a cloud. She coughed, blinked her eyes, then looked up. *Seriously?* was the only thought her brain had time to process.

Headlights sped toward her. Her pupils dilated in the approaching light as she brought up her hands to cover her face. She prepared herself for the impact, but the truck skidded to a stop just feet away.

Slowly, Anna allowed her arms to fall to her side. The truck engine ticked in the silence as dust rose like smoke in the headlights. Anna sat dazed as she heard footsteps in gravel come closer, then a body stepped in front of the headlights.

"Anna? Is that you?"

CHAPTER 38

Finn sat nervously in his truck. Mrs. Chaffin said it would only be a moment longer. That was ten minutes ago, and that moment seemed to drag on forever. *Come on, come on.* He rolled the window down just a crack and strained to hear any sign of the creature he saw earlier. Silence, except for the crickets and night sounds that drowned out all other noise.

"You still there, Finn?" Mrs. Chaffin said on the line.

"Yes, ma'am," Finn said. "How much longer?"

"I just got a call back from dispatch. Someone should be there in less than five minutes. Can you hold tight?"

"I'll hold tight, but I—"

Suddenly Finn was cut off by the sound of an unearthly scream from inside the warehouse. Surprised, Finn shouted out loud too. Not a scream—more of a grunt, like the kind he made in football practice when he tackled someone. His hands lashed out and hit the truck horn, causing him to shout out loud again.

"Are you okay, Finn?" Mrs. Chaffin tried to sound calm, but Finn could hear the edge in her voice.

"I, uh, don't know. I've never heard anything like that before. I gotta tell you, this doesn't feel right."

He stared at the opening in the bay door and took the truck out of neutral. At the first sign of anything, he was ready to press the accelerator and make a quick exit. He sat frozen, his eyes dry. He blinked once and caught movement from just behind the opening—a passing shadow. He blinked again and two figures exploded from the bay door like acrobats spinning and tumbling in the air. One was a shadow as black as night, the other a young girl dressed in gray pants and a white long-sleeved shirt. The black shadow spun once in midair, then landed lightly on all fours as it hit the ground running—if that's what he could call it. Its arms and legs moved at strange angles as it disappeared around the edge of the warehouse, faster than any living thing he'd ever seen move. The young girl spun helplessly in the air and bounced hard off the ground and rolled toward the truck.

Finn accidentally punched the accelerator and headed straight for the girl, who was now sprawled out on her butt and hunched over on the gravel. She looked up, her eyes bright in the headlights. Her face registered a brief look of surprise, followed by a sudden realization that she was about to be hit by a half-ton truck. The girl instinctively brought up her hands in front of her face in defense just as Finn slammed on the brakes. Gravel and dust flew as the truck skidded to a stop five feet in front of her.

Her hair hung down in knotted strands across her eyes and cheeks, but her face was unmistakable. It was Anna. The new girl. One of his little sister's best friends.

"Anna? Is that you?"

Finn ran over to her side. In the truck cabin, he could hear Mrs. Chaffin's frantic voice over his phone's tinny speaker.

"Oh . . . hi, Finn," Anna said as she looked up in a daze.

"What the heck is going on, Anna? Are you okay?"

"Oh boy. You can see me?" Anna said as she rolled over onto one knee. She had forgotten she'd turned off her cloaking mode. "That's not good."

"Of course, I can see—" Finn's voice was cut short.

A tall woman in a white bodysuit slowly glided out the warehouse door, her body floating feet above the ground. Floating—as if this night couldn't get any weirder. She stopped midair and locked eyes with Finn. Beautiful. Radiant. Terrifying. His mouth dropped open. His feet froze in place.

"It's okay. We're not going to hurt you," the woman said calmly. Her voice soothing like a song.

She raised her right hand like she was waving to a distant friend. A soft green light emanated from her palm. It seemed to spin slowly at first, then began to pick up speed, followed by the sound of running water and the feeling of sunlight on his face. His body relaxed as his head rolled to the side. In his mind, he shut his eyes. A perfect time for a nap. In the far distance, he could hear the distant echo of approaching sirens. Then nothing.

CHAPTER 39

Anna lay awake in her room. She stared up at the ceiling with her hands behind her head and listened to the old oak tree sway with the wind just outside her window—a hushed sound that ebbed and flowed like waves. The moon, a bright disc, peeked through the unfurling curtains.

Although she was bone-weary and it was past midnight, she couldn't sleep. She rolled over in bed and was reminded with a fresh jolt of pain of the doughnut-size bruise on her butt. Her knees and palms throbbed from where she had bounced off gravel like a rubber ball.

Hours had passed since she had encountered the creature, but she could still feel its fingers pressed against the sides of her head. Not a phantom sensation—it was something real, like a residue or a burn mark without the pain. The second it touched her temples, the creature had taken up residence in Anna's mind. That was the only way she could explain it. She'd felt the creature see this world through her own eyes and listen through her ears. Shared sensations.

And in turn, Anna had sensed what the creature was feeling: frightened and disoriented. Tired and hungry, not just for food but for connection with its home and its family. She remembered the creature touching the sides of her head and how, just like that, the channel in Anna's brain had flipped. New images had been projected onto her field of vision. She'd been flying through the cavernous warehouse but also standing on a distant shore looking out across the black emptiness of an alien sea. Two places experienced at once.

As she lay in bed, new images started to flood her field of vision again, as if her brain had just now been able to unpack all that it had experienced—a prolonged delay after pressing Play.

In her vision, she stood motionless in ankle-deep water that was neither cold nor hot. Even now, Anna could feel the water lap against her legs in small waves. It felt real. Not imagined. A shared memory of the creature's home world.

Black reeds waved in shallow tide pools, and stars reflected off the water's surface. Green and blue lights, like the ones she had seen at the warehouse, floated just feet above the water in a slight breeze. The air smelled of salt. Just along the horizon hung a giant dust-red planet that took up almost half of the night sky. It looked like Jupiter with its big colored bands and spinning storms. But it wasn't Jupiter. Anna was standing on a distant moon, orbiting a planet that no human had ever seen. An alien landscape. Shadow creatures moved nimbly across the sharp coastal rocks, their silhouettes a stark contrast to the brightness of the giant planet in the sky. She could feel the creatures' presence. They approached from all sides, but there was no sense of danger. In fact, she felt just the opposite. The creatures were humming in unison—a beautiful sound—not quite a song or spoken language, but a way of communicating just the same.

The creature was trying to tell me something.

One of the shadow creatures suddenly appeared in front of Anna. It was taller than the others, and the featherlike scales around its head were adorned with pulsing green and blue lights. The creature pointed its long finger to a sheer cliff that towered high into the night sky behind her. Intersecting steps and pathways weaved their way to the top of the cliff, each lit by a different color light. At the very top of the cliff a flash of warm light caught Anna's eye. A familiar light. A small orb spun in the sky and bent the light of the stars around it—the same doorway to another world she had seen just weeks before. The wormhole.

"Is that how you entered our world?" Anna asked out loud in her vision.

Suddenly, Anna felt herself being dragged through the wormhole. She looked down and saw the Shadow's hands where hers should be. A memory, but not hers. She was experiencing what the creature had experienced, seeing through its eyes. Just ahead she could make out a dim light as she was pulled through the wormhole, then she felt the rush of water around her. She was swimming now in a dark and cold body of water. She couldn't breathe. Her lungs itched. Then she broke through the surface and looked out across a site she knew so well. *Tyson Lake.* Somehow, she was home under the familiar stars of her own world. Just in front of her was the small island that Scout had once said looked like a turtle shell.

This was it. The Shadow was showing how it had entered this world. It was lost and disoriented and didn't know its way back. But Anna did.

The wormhole we've been looking for all these months—it was in my backyard the entire time.

With a snap, Anna could feel her body pulled back to this reality, back to her bedroom. Disoriented, she shook her head and blinked her eyes, focusing on the shadows of leaves moving across the far wall. She took a deep breath and activated her iCom.

"Mara, are you awake?"

"*I am. Is everything okay?*" Mara answered.

"I think I may have figured it out. Meet me on the island in Tyson Lake in ten minutes. I'll explain everything when I get there," Anna said.

CHAPTER 40

Anna could see a glow like a campfire on the southern edge of the island as she flew across the lake. Mara was waiting for her. A small soft light floated just above her hand like a beacon and lit the ground beneath her feet.

The two sat down on a patch of grass surrounded by thick bushes and tree roots that dipped into the water like long fingers. It was quiet here on this tiny island. The only sound came from the slight waves lapping up against the shore. The moon, almost full, reflected off the water's surface in shifting bands of light. Mara sat silently and looked out across the lake as Anna described her visions. When Anna finished, Mara leaned back and shook her head.

"It's possible to reconstruct a picture of someone else's visual experiences," Mara said.

"It's more than that, Mara. I could actually feel what it was like on the Shadow's planet. The temperature of the water. The smell of salt. I was there. Really there," Anna said.

"So you really think the wormhole is here?"

"I'm certain."

Mara put on her goggles and motioned for Anna to do the

same. Both activated their full masks, their faces lit by a faint light that traced the interior seal. The red stripes on Anna's sleeves glowed neon red. Mara stood from the grass patch and offered her hand. Anna pulled herself up, and the two looked down into the darkness of the water.

"All this time and it was right here. I never thought to look in water," Mara said as she shook her head. "I don't understand any of this, Anna. How the creature talks to you. How the wormhole stays open on its own."

"I have an idea." Anna grinned. "Let's go find out."

Anna dove headfirst into the lake. The light from her mask lit up the water in front of her, making the flecks of algae luminescent. Pondweed drifted back and forth with the slight current. Anna looked up just in time to see Mara dive in, her silhouette against the light of the bright moon shimmering on the surface. The two held hands as they floated side by side underwater.

"You're the expert here. What should we be looking for?" Mara asked over the iCom.

"I don't know. It's hard to describe. Bending light, maybe, like you're looking through a fishbowl," Anna said.

Anna let go of Mara's hand and began to swim slowly along the edge of the island, shining the light from her mask on the sloping shelf. Mara followed just behind. A fish darted out from one of the crevices and startled them both. Anna looked more closely and realized it wasn't just a crevice but a shallow cave leading under the island.

"I don't see anything—" Mara started.

"Wait," Anna cut her off.

Anna swam in closer. The cave wall was made of granite, not soil, and it receded under the island by about five feet. It was a shallow recess, no more than four feet high and five feet across, but tucked far enough under to prevent anyone seeing it from the surface. The light from her mask illuminated all four walls in a white glow. Anna's eyes opened wide. Her pulse quickened. This was it. There in the center of the shallow cave spun a dark orb, three feet in diameter. The color was different from the wormhole she had seen weeks before—almost black, with flecks of shimmering light. The edges bent the light around it, and Anna could feel a deep hum in her body as she drew closer.

"It's beautiful," Anna said softly. Her fingers touched the outside rim of the orb; the bending light distorted the shape of her hand.

"What is it?" Mara asked as she floated just outside the cave.

"The way through." Anna turned around and smiled.

She squeezed herself against the side of the cave to give Mara a clearer view. Mara placed her hand on the top edge of the cave to keep from bumping her head and peered in. She wasn't sure what to expect. She knew what the physics should be. She had modeled what a structure like this *should* look like. What she wasn't ready for was how she felt. A deeper emotion than excitement or even fear.

"Be careful, Anna. We don't know what this is," Mara said.

"Sure we do. Remember? I've done this before." Anna placed her hand on Mara's shoulder.

"How does it maintain its shape without collapsing in on itself?"

"I don't know. It just does," Anna replied.

"This makes no sense. I don't see any impact on the surrounding area. No apparent energy source," Mara said as she squeezed farther into the cramped cave, her hand unconsciously drawn toward the spinning orb. "What do we do now?"

Anna wasn't used to seeing Mara this way: hesitant, unsure, the one seeking answers. But she knew what her friend wanted.

"We explore," Anna said.

Mara paused. "Yes, we do. Against all good judgment."

"That hasn't stopped us before."

Mara looked at the orb and the sides of the cave.

"We can't fit through at the same time," Mara said.

"Then I'll go first. I've had practice," Anna said. "Just hold my hand. If anything happens, you can pull me back."

Mara nodded *yes*.

"I can't tell you how much I've wanted to do this. Imagine. Another world. There's so much to learn," Mara said as she turned to face Anna. "I'm glad I'm not doing this alone."

"Me too," Anna said. "Ready?"

"Check your oxygen levels and your vitals. Be ready to pull back at the first sign of trouble," Mara said.

"Don't worry. I've learned my lesson. Ready?"

"Yes. I'm ready."

"See you on the other side," Anna said, then began counting down out loud. "Five . . . four . . . three . . . two . . . one . . ."

Anna reached her right hand into the orb and held on to Mara with her left. There was no resistance at first, just like before. Then, suddenly, Anna felt a sharp pain, as if her arm were being yanked out of its socket. Something had grabbed ahold of her on the other side. She looked back toward Mara for help, but there was nothing there except darkness and spinning flecks of light. She felt Mara's hand tighten around hers but couldn't see anything, not even the end of her own arm. The darkness wasn't an absence of light—it had substance and weight.

She couldn't see Mara, but she felt her pull hard with both hands now—so hard her own fingers started to turn numb. But the force on the other side of the wormhole was even greater. Slowly, Mara's fingers began to slip. Anna screamed out, but there was no sound except her own racing heartbeat in her head. One last desperate pull from Mara on the other side and then Anna felt herself spinning. Her tether to her home world was gone.

Anna couldn't see any farther than inches in front of her face, but she could sense that she was tumbling forward. Alone. Then the darkness gave way to a night sky filled with an endless sea of stars. Anna had enough time to glimpse a giant dust-red planet that filled the far horizon and a gaseous purple nebula just beyond before she felt herself plummeting in thick air.

Something is wrong. Her chest hurt and her arms and legs felt like lead. She could feel the blood rush through her head, pumping harder than it ever had before. *Too fast. I'm falling too fast.* She was spinning helplessly just feet away from a sheer cliff of jagged rock. If she hit at this speed, she'd be dead on impact.

She focused on her antigravity boots and struggled to turn herself upright. At home she'd be flying forward, riding gravity faster than she had ever flown before. But here, she was only able to slow her descent. She strained to fly upward, her hands grasping at air. All her focus was set on breaking free of the force pulling her to the ground.

Anna looked at the corner of her goggles and scanned her environmental readings. Warning lights flashed red across her display. *Air composition: methane, argon, carbon monoxide, ammonia.* All at unbreathable levels. Her blood pressure was twice its normal level. One reading she had never paid attention to before stuck out: $g = 37.17 m/s^2$. The acceleration of gravity was more than four times what it was on Earth. Her antigravity boots were struggling against this world's gravitational force, just as her body struggled to breathe.

Sweat poured down her forehead and into her eyes. Her muscles ached, but she was able to slow her descent to less than a couple of miles an hour. A slow-motion fall. She reached out and grabbed ahold of an outcropping of rock. Even at this slow speed, her body slammed hard against the cliff wall, knocking the wind from her lungs. Still, she held on. With her antigravity boots on full ascent, she was able to hold on without breaking her arm. Anna leaned her head against the rock and closed her eyes. *Think.*

She couldn't fly upward. She had oxygen for another twelve hours, but she didn't know how long her heart or lungs could last in this gravity. Her limbs, even her head, felt like heavy weights. She thought of Mara and began to sob quietly despite herself. *Had she been pulled into the wormhole too—or cast out into another world?* One thing she did know was that Mara would be frantically searching for her. As much as she wanted to just let go, she couldn't quit now. Anna took in a long breath—as much as she could take in at once—and then released it slowly. She took another slow breath, and then another, until her head cleared enough for her to open her eyes.

Anna hung from the rock cliff with one hand and looked out across the horizon. This world might be slowly killing her, but she found it beautiful. Straight ahead was a dark ocean reflecting the light of the dust-red planet floating in the sky. Sharp rock formations jutted out of the ocean like giant black stalagmites. Far down below she could see a shoreline covered in thick vegetation, teeming and pulsing with green and blue lights that cast a glow well out into the water. The trail of vegetation and light followed the coastline until it disappeared in a straight line—too straight to be a result of natural causes. The cliff she was hanging on to was part of a massive structure, a sheer rock face that extended for miles in either direction. She had limited perspective since the landscape was so unlike her own, but she estimated the cliff to be at least two miles in height; she was halfway down its side.

In the far distance, miles down the coastline, she saw a different set of lights than the ones below. These lights were green and blue but also orange and white, and they were arranged in perpendicular lines that looked like city streets and buildings. The Shadow's home. An alien city.

Anna looked at the cliff wall just beneath her and noticed a set of lights that snaked their way down to the surface below. It was a thin trail that zigzagged its way up and down the face of the cliff, and it was no more than fifty feet away. Anna grabbed on to the rock overhang with both hands. She would swing her body toward the trail and use her boots to slow her speed just enough to land—or miss it altogether and plummet to the ground below. She tried using the increased gravity to help with the force of the swing, but it felt like someone was hanging on to her legs. She swayed once, twice, then flung herself toward the trail below just as her fingers began to slip.

She strained against the force pulling her down with just enough thrust that she felt like she was floating in slow motion. *Twenty feet.* She was going to make it. *Ten feet.* She prepared her legs for the impact.

Slam!

She felt her body hit the flat surface of the trail and then she rolled hard against the cliff wall. Her shoulder ached and she could barely catch her breath, but at least she could lie back to rest. The trail was no more than four feet across, flat and polished as if worn down through centuries of use. Anna rolled to her side and looked over the edge of the cliff. Water, edged with a blue-green glow, lapped up against the shoreline in gentle waves a mile below.

"Oh, that's a long way down."

Anna rolled onto her back and looked up into the alien night sky. So many stars, so bright and clear, scattered densely in strange formations. Her brain automatically identified patterns and created forms. A trail of stars looked like a whale. Another trail formed the shape of a starfish. She could be on the other side of the Milky Way or in another universe altogether. But her way home, the wormhole, was just a mile above her. Only a short hike in crushing gravity away. Gathering all of her strength, Anna rolled over onto all fours and then up to a bent knee. She could feel the bands of muscles in her legs and core strain to lift her body upright. Legs shaking, she took one step up the steep trail and almost collapsed, grabbing on to the cliff wall to hold herself steady.

"Just a mile hike. Easy . . . peasy," Anna said out loud just to hear her own voice. The first human voice in this strange world.

Twenty feet up and Anna could feel her hands and feet start to swell. Fifty feet up and she felt a warm trickle just above her lip. *A runny nose?* Then she experienced the sharp taste of iron. Blood.

"Not good," Anna said as she reached up to wipe her nose and slammed her hand against her face mask.

The pulsing blue-green lights on the trail ahead began to grow dim.

"Huh?"

Why are they getting dim? I didn't do that.

"I don't feel so—" Anna said just before collapsing.

She was aware enough to know she was falling—even aware enough to know that the force would hit three to four times greater than it would at home—but she was unable to stop her fall. Thankfully, she passed out before impact.

In her sleep, Anna could feel the blood rushing in her head. She heard the humming she had heard earlier that day when the Shadow had tried communicating with her. *Had it been that day? Or was that another life?* She was floating now, just above the trail. Maybe she was having an out-of-body experience. She had heard this happened to some people when they died. But there was a pressure against her arms and legs that grounded her to this place, and she wasn't floating as much as she was being carried. The humming sound and the rocking motion soothed her. Then she fell asleep in her sleep.

Minutes later, maybe hours or days, Anna didn't know—
she was stuck between consciousness and sleep—she felt a
light through her closed eyelids, like she was looking up into
the sky while lying out at the beach. But the glow was blue-
green, and a soft humming noise replaced the sound of crash-
ing waves.

Anna's eyes flickered open. She was on her back under a
grove of short, squatty trees no more than fifteen feet tall. The
trunks were thick like a baobab tree. In fact, it looked like a
baobab with its thin fractal branches. Small flat leaves fluttered in a soft alien breeze. But the humming came from the
lights, not the wind. The tree was filled with a shimmering
blue-green glow, bright enough to light the clearing around
her like the day. But the lights didn't just circle the trees. They
looked like they were part of the trees, like pollen.

A dark figure kneeled over her. Anna blinked to clear her
eyes. Scales, like feathers, fanned out around the creature's
head. Each scale was adorned with lights. *The shadow creature
from my vision.* Behind it stood four other creatures with similar markings.

*They must have carried me down here to the beach. Ugh,
the wrong direction.*

The tall one was applying a compress of black sand and
leaves and orange light to her shoulder. Her head wasn't
pounding as badly as before, and her blood pressure readings
on the iCom were still elevated but lower than the danger levels she had registered on the cliff.

"Hi," Anna said meekly. Her throat felt dry and raw.

The scales on the creature's arms flared open, and dandelion lights floated gently out to form a circular pattern that
floated in the air above Anna's head. More lights floated from
its arms to cluster together in a dense swarm.

"Is this how you say hi?" Anna asked.

Suddenly, the lights began to spin and realign to form

a perfect outline of a human face. It was her face—an exact likeness with her mask, matted hair, and a trail of dried blood from her nose.

"Wow," Anna said as she tried to push herself up on her elbows, still exhausted. "But seriously—I look better than that. You caught me . . . on a bad day."

The tall shadow gently placed its hand on Anna's shoulder and guided her back to the ground to rest. It pointed to Anna's floating portrait in lights, then pointed down to Anna.

"Yes, that's me," Anna said, nodding.

The creature nodded back. *It learns fast,* Anna thought. Then the lights shifted to form a new pattern—the outline of a shadow creature, smaller in frame. The tall one pointed to the floating portrait made of light and then looked back at Anna.

"Yes, I've seen it," Anna said. She remembered to nod, even though her head throbbed. "It came through the wormhole just like me."

The tall one looked back to the others. The green and blue lights on their heads started to pulse, each creature taking a turn until all their lights pulsed in sync. The creatures continued to stare at one another in silence. Motionless like black stone statues. Seconds passed. Anna turned her head and looked out past the grove of trees and saw the water's edge. She was less than a hundred feet from the ocean. The waves were quiet and barely broke against the shore. At least a half dozen creatures stood in silhouette in the distance, watching and waiting, their outlines in sharp contrast to the light of the giant dust-red planet on the horizon.

The tall one turned back to Anna and stepped forward. The lights in the circle above her head began to spin into a new form, this time a large-scale model of the cliffs and the trails that led to the wormhole above. Anna pointed to the wormhole in the model, and then to herself, and then to the actual cliffs above her.

"I need to get up there," Anna said.

The tall one stared back, unmoving. The shape above Anna's head began to dissolve, and the lights scattered like glowing dust in the slight breeze. Suddenly, the tall one turned and ran toward the shoreline, out of her field of view. The other four creatures followed just behind, running in a single file, leaving Anna alone in the small clearing.

Anna tried rolling over but her shoulder ached, and she could feel her heart struggle to pump blood. She slumped back against the ground and stared up at the stars that poked through the clearing above her head.

Minutes passed and Anna could feel consciousness start to slip away. She struggled not to fall asleep, fearing she might never wake up if she did. She tried focusing on the things around her, taking in what she could. The feel of the coarse black sand under her hands. The soft humming sounds. The massive cliff wall in the distance. She noticed that the thick trunks of the alien baobab trees seemed to contract and expand as if they were breathing. It was a micromovement, unnoticeable unless you focused long enough.

Then Anna felt something slowly crawl across her leg. She tried kicking at it, but her legs felt glued to the ground. For a moment, Anna thought she had scared it away, whatever it was. Then she felt multiple legs, limbs, fingers—she didn't know—drag across her exposed ankles. Her skin crawled. She strained to lift her head to look at her leg. Her eyes widened.

There at the base of her legs floated a jellyfish-like creature, translucent and pulsing with green and blue points of light. Its body undulated in a wave motion from the center out. Dozens of dangling tentacles dragged across Anna's legs as the creature slowly moved up her body, leaving a trail of lights wherever they touched.

She tried kicking again, but the jellyfish creature easily floated away, only to return and continue its slow trek across her body. Tears began to well up in Anna's eyes as she closed them tight. *This isn't happening. This isn't happening.*

Slowly, the fear that knotted her stomach began to melt away. The muscles in her legs relaxed. Wherever the tentacles touched her, Anna felt a warm sensation. Pleasant and healing. The translucent jellyfish was now floating just over her shoulder, and Anna was able to get a clear view of its insides. Green and blue lights were connected by thin opaque threads. Pulsing neurons. The tentacles were made of the same opaque substance—almost white, like milk. The throbbing in her shoulder faded to a dull ache.

The lights stopped pulsing, and the jellyfish-like creature started to float away, revealing the tall shadow creature just behind it. It had returned. Just behind it stood almost a dozen other shadow creatures.

"You're back." Anna smiled, relieved.

The tall one came over and slowly raised its hand to Anna's face. The tips of its four long fingers spread equally apart in a diamond shape. It reached its hand down toward Anna, making her flinch. The creature paused and made a soft humming noise. A comforting sound. An assurance.

Then Anna realized that the creature wasn't trying to touch her face. It was framing a spot in the sky miles above, just on the edge of the cliff. It was where she came through. The wormhole.

"Yes. There. Can you take me there?" Anna asked as she pointed.

The tall one tilted its head to the side.

"Help me get home and I'll bring back your friend. I promise."

The creature stood unmoving for a good thirty seconds, lights floating around it in a swarm. Then it stepped gently forward, arms out to its sides. The tall one made another comforting sound, lifting Anna as if she weighed nothing and cradling her in both arms. Its head moved first in a 180-degree turn toward the cliff, then its body followed.

The tall one started to run, taking ten-foot strides with apparently no effort and holding Anna so steadily that she didn't feel any sense of movement other than the breeze across her skin. Behind them, the other shadow creatures ran in single file, their strides in perfect unison. As they neared the cliff wall, Anna looked up at the massive sheer rock. Black and jagged. The only way Anna could make out the edge of the rock miles above was the dome of stars that marked the boundary between cliff and sky.

They reached the trail at the base of the cliff in less than a minute. The tall one easily leaped across an outcropping of rock and a shallow tide pool and began running up the steep climb of the cliff trail without losing its pace.

Anna looked out across the ocean. Her head was heavy, but she wanted to take it all in. This world, so different. So many mysteries. Small swirling patterns, like eddies in a stream, covered the pale red giant that filled the horizon. Like Jupiter, storms must ravage its surface. The mass on this planet (or moon, or whatever she was on) must be great enough to stay in its orbit. Maybe two giant planets in a perfect state of orbital equilibrium.

The rock face passed by in a blur. Anna looked up and studied the face of the tall one. In the low light, Anna could only see its outline, a silhouette against the night sky above. She felt herself fading again. Her breathing labored. The creature looked down for a moment and then quickened its pace.

Minutes passed. The thin trail began to widen as they neared the end. No more lights as guideposts. Just darkness. Then the creature stopped. Anna looked up to see why and then realized they had arrived at the top. To her left, floating thirty feet in the air, was a spinning orb in a dome of stars. Light bent around the orb like a lens. The wormhole. To her

right, a flat plain opened up as far as she could see in this dim
light. A purple nebula spanned the sky just above her like
spilled incandescent ink.

Slowly, as Anna's eyes adjusted to the increased darkness,
she began to make out shapes across the plain. A field of alien
baobab trees spread out as far as the eye could see. But unlike
the trees down by the shore, these looked dead. Lifeless. In the
slight breeze, ashes floated from the trees like snow.

Suddenly she saw movement in the trees—a dark form,
tall and angular. The pale opposite of the shadow creatures. Its
body stepped forward in a herky-jerky motion. Then stillness.
A bone-white face emerged at the edge of the trees and floated
in the darkness. Stars spun in its eyes.

Anna struggled to make sense of it. The ghost-white apparition from her half-remembered dream. She looked to the
shadow creatures that had carried her this far, but they didn't
seem to notice the apparition, or if they did, they didn't care.
Then, just as suddenly as it had appeared, the ghostly face disappeared into the shadows, leaving Anna to wonder if she had
imagined it after all.

The tall shadow looked down at Anna and made another
soft humming noise, snapping her attention back to this moment. Then, one at a time, it looked into the faces of the dozen
shadow creatures standing motionless in a circle. There was a
pause as the creatures signaled to one another with light. Here
at the top of the cliff, on the flat plain that stretched forever,
was absolute silence. A place void of life, so unlike the shore
down below.

With a sharp, high-pitched command and a nod from the
tall one, the shadow creatures began to run in perfect unison
to the spot just beneath the wormhole. Two of the shadow
creatures linked arms. Then, like a wave, the other shadows
scrambled and climbed onto one another, creating a ladder
for the next one to follow, until they reached the edge of the

wormhole thirty feet above their heads. A living structure. Unmoving.

The tall shadow cradled Anna in one arm and pointed to the wormhole with the other. Anna nodded *yes*. *Home.* The shadow began to effortlessly climb on the backs of the others until it reached the top. Just feet away from the wormhole, Anna could now see the white flecks spinning around its edges. The shadow held Anna out with both arms.

Anna reached for the wormhole, her fingers distorting into elongated shapes as they entered the dark orb. The tall shadow held Anna even closer to it, and suddenly she felt herself pulled into the wormhole with the same great force she had felt before. In a dark flash, the world that orbited the pale red planet and the trees made of lights were gone. Anna floated alone in a vast darkness.

CHAPTER 41

Mara felt a strong resistance as her hand entered the wormhole, almost like magnets repelling each other. The harder she pushed, the greater the pushback. She was ready to ask if this happened before when she felt Anna almost yanked from her grasp.

"No!"

She grabbed on to Anna with both hands and pulled with all her strength. No use. Whatever force had ahold of Anna on the other side was pulling her deeper into the wormhole. Mara tried diving in headfirst but felt more resistance, like fabric stretching to its breaking point.

"No, no, no!" Mara cried out as she struggled.

Her fingers started to slip. She placed her leg against the wall of the cave to brace herself and pulled back with all her strength—then her fingers felt nothing. The last of Anna disappeared into the dense blackness.

"Anna!"

In desperation, Mara primed her vortex cannon and fired at the wormhole. The second she released, she knew she had made a mistake. Compressed air bounced off the granite wall and knocked Mara back out into the lake, her body spinning.

For the next hour, she tried to force herself into the wormhole until her muscles ached and sweat streamed down inside her face mask.

<Mara.>

She ignored SID's voice.

<Mara. You need to rest. You're not thinking clearly.>

"I can't lose her. I can't," Mara said.

<Anna survived the wormhole before. She can do it again.>

"Why did it take her and not me?"

<Mara. Please rest.>

———

Hours passed and still no sign. Mara sat at the edge of the lake, hugging her knees to her chest and looking out across the calm waters. Temperatures had dipped down to the low sixties, and Mara felt herself shivering, less from the cool air and more from an overwhelming feeling of tension and loss. Stars still lined the sky in the west, but a thin gold band of light outlined the trees in the east. As night quickly disappeared, so did Mara's hope for Anna's return.

Just then, bubbles floated to the water's surface off the island's edge. Mara caught her breath. She looked down into the water. The ripples caused by the bubbles quickly faded away, leaving the surface once again like glass. Then more bubbles. Mara stood up, her legs numb from sitting for hours in the same position. This time she could make out a light.

Suddenly, the lake surface exploded, spraying water into the early-morning light. Anna flew free in the air for just a moment, her body arcing across the sky to land hard on the ground and roll to a stop near Mara's feet. Anna lay on her back and looked up into Mara's face.

"Hey," Anna said, her voice hoarse and weak.

Mara's legs buckled, a physical reaction to a sudden release of pent-up stress—relief cutting the strings that had been holding her up. She fell to her knees and embraced Anna hard.

"Ouch," Anna cried out. "It's good to see you too."

"I'm so sorry. I would have never left you. I don't know what happened," Mara said. "I tried to follow you. I really tried."

"I know."

"Are you okay?" Mara asked.

She placed one hand behind Anna's neck to support her while she scanned for injuries. Her young friend's clothes were still wet. Black sand clung to her shirt, and strange dewdrop-shaped leaves were matted in her hair. What concerned Mara most was the thick trail of blood that had caked above Anna's lip. Mara clicked the release on Anna's mask and removed her goggles.

"Whew—that's better," Anna said as she took in the cool early-morning air. "It feels good to breathe."

"You're bleeding," Mara said.

"I am? Oh yeah. I forgot," Anna said as she reached up to wipe the trail of dried blood. "I guess my body doesn't like hypergravity."

"What?"

Anna was ready to answer when she looked down at her arms and hands in the predawn light. Lights dotted her clothes and skin like a constellation of stars. Glistening blue and green lights. Traces from the world she had just visited.

"Anna. You're glowing," Mara said.

"Oh, Mara—do I have a story to tell you," Anna said, the strangeness and wonder of that distant world still reflected in her eyes.

CHAPTER 42

Anna rolled over in bed. From the intensity and angle of the light that seeped in through her closed eyes, she knew it was late. *Good*, she thought. *I need sleep*. She had every intention of lying in bed longer—then she felt a presence in the room.

Her eyes flickered open. Mara was leaning over her, sitting in a chair next to her bedside. She was holding a cup of some steaming liquid that smelled of orange and honey.

"How's my interstellar traveler doing this morning?" Mara smiled.

Anna tried to blink, but her left eye felt stuck and refused to open.

"Sleepy," Anna said softly.

"Here. Drink this," Mara said as she leaned forward, careful not to spill the cup's hot contents. "It has negatively charged ions. Just breathe it in."

Anna propped herself up on one elbow and winced. Muscle cramps worked their way up and down her legs and shoulders. She tried reaching for the cup, but the muscles in her arms felt like tight rope and ached.

"Ow, ow, ow." Anna grimaced. "I can't move."

"No surprise. That's what you get for wandering around in hypergravity all night." Mara laughed. "You activated muscles you didn't even know you had."

"No, I'm serious. Everything . . . hurts. Even my hair hurts."

"Microtrauma to your muscle fibers will do that," Mara said. "Come on. Drink up. It'll help."

Anna reached out for the cup with sore T. rex arms and held it under her chin. The steam warmed her face, and the bright citrus smell cleared her head of any lingering fog. She took a sip and felt the warm liquid, sweet and tangy, seep down her throat to spread through her body in a wave. Her muscles loosened like the unraveling of a tightly wound coil.

"Oh, that's good," Anna sighed, and took another sip.

"Yes, it is."

"What time is it anyway?" Anna asked.

"A little before noon," Mara answered.

"That was one long night." Anna stifled a yawn. "Did you get any sleep?"

"No, I took advantage of the quiet and installed a sensor near the wormhole. I also combed over the data from your iCom and ran tests on those lights that we found on you this morning."

"Seriously?" Anna asked. "I don't know how you do it."

"Stimulants and cognitive enhancers. And no, you can't have any," Mara said. "Not until your brain fully develops."

Anna pulled back the covers and sat up in bed. Her muscles were still sore but now loose enough to move freely. Her hair, on the other hand, was an impressive structure of tangles that seemed to defy gravity.

"So what did you find?" Anna asked.

"That Einstein was right about time dilation," Mara said.

"Time dilation?" Anna looked confused, then smiled faintly. "Oh yeah. That's that thing we talked about a long time ago. When you experience time differently because of gravity. Right?"

"The greater the gravitational force, the slower you experience time. Data from your iCom proved it out. Gravity on the planet you visited was 4.1 times greater than Earth's. So you aged at a slower rate last night. Not a lot, but it was traceable."

"That's so weird." Anna's eyes opened wide.

"Wait until you hear about the lights." Mara stood up and headed over to Anna's desk.

Anna saw a glass cube, ten inches wide, sitting on the edge of her desk next to her computer monitor. Purple, blue, and green lights pulsed in a spinning pattern. Anna walked over to the desk and leaned over the lights, her cheeks lit up by the glow.

"They're so pretty," Anna said as she lightly tapped the sides of the cube. With each tap, the lights glowed brighter in response. "Are these the lights you found on me this morning?"

Mara nodded.

"We're going to have to come up with a better name for our little friends here." Mara leaned over Anna's shoulder and tapped the side of the glass herself. "I was thinking of calling them sprites."

"You think these lights are alive?"

"I know they're alive—and unlike anything I've ever seen."

"But I thought they were just part of the shadow creatures, like their scales," Anna said.

"They are. But they aren't. Each sprite is a unique living entity and at the same time a symbiotic part of the shadow creature," Mara said.

"Like a parasite?" Anna asked.

"Oh, no. It's a positive symbiotic relationship. In fact, I think they're key to the shadows' survival," Mara said. "See how they glow? That's caused by a bioluminescent enzyme similar to luciferase in fireflies. But this enzyme can catalyze with ammonia, argon, carbon monoxide, and a whole slew of noble gases. Guess what it really loves?"

"What?"

"Oxygen. Sprites really thrive in our environment and reproduce superfast," Mara said.

Anna traced the glass cube with her finger. A line of purple light followed along.

"I've never seen a purple one before," Anna said as she looked up from the cube.

"For a good reason. The purple sprites are different from the others. They're a hybrid. Somehow you picked up some mushroom spores, either on your skin or your shirt. Probably from wallowing in the dirt yesterday," Mara said. "Our clever sprite friends here found a way to genetically recombine with the mushroom spores, which they also seem to love. And just like that, you have a new purple variant."

Anna stared wide-eyed at the sprites as they moved in infinitely complex patterns—fractals branching and converging as they pulsed.

"This is real. I mean, I'm looking at an alien life form," Anna said.

"Completely alien."

"Is it conscious?"

"Now that's a great question," Mara said. "I think it is, as much as I can determine what is conscious or not. But if it is, it's a completely different intelligence than our own."

"Can you communicate with it?" Anna asked.

"I already did." Mara smiled.

"You're kidding."

"I told you this was weird," Mara said. "SID noticed that when a sprite glows, it gives off a chemical signal so powerful it can even be picked up miles away by other sprites. SID also noticed a number of patterns in that signal and was able to determine that they aren't random but the basis for communication.

The sprites were actually talking to each other. I had SID reproduce one of the patterns in the chemical signal, and the sprite replied back."

"Wait. You understand what the sprites are saying?" Anna asked.

"Oh, no, I don't have a clue. But I know we've collected a lot of patterns and identified a pattern within the patterns. That's a start," Mara said as she leaned against the desk. "Something else: those chemical signals also contain neuropeptides, which allow them to tap right into our brains. Think about that. The sprites can affect what we feel—even what we see."

Anna stepped back. What seemed like magic now had a biological explanation.

"That's how the Shadow was able to communicate with me," Anna said.

"I think so."

"You said that these signals can be detected from miles away. Can we use them to track down the creature?" Anna asked.

"Yes. That's the most exciting part. We're no longer searching blind," Mara said. "The Shadow stays hidden during the day. But tonight, after the sun sets, you and I are finally going to get a chance to meet our alien friend."

CHAPTER 43

"Hey, Tyler. I'm thinking maybe we do something different tonight," Hanson said.

He looked out the side window of Tyler's pickup, his chin resting on his arm like a child bored on a long family drive. His thin blond hair hung down over his eyes as his gaze followed two teenage girls from their car to the entrance of the Ivanhoe Diner. The sun had just set but still cast a warm glow across the parking lot, and a breeze blew through the truck, clearing the cab of the stale smell of cigarette butts, oil, and decay.

"Do you have a car?" Tyler asked.

"You know I don't."

"Then *I'm* thinking you should just shut up," Tyler said. He looked at his reflection in the rearview mirror and combed his hair with his fingers. "I already told you we were going hunting."

"Yeah. About that. We've been going out hunting just about every night for a month. Ever since summer started, Tyler. And it's kind of getting monotonous," Hanson said. "Like, I'm starting to have dreams where all I do is drive around."

"Oh, I'm sorry. Are you bored? 'Cuz I can drop your ass off right here if you want me to," Tyler said.

"Nah. I just don't want to do this all summer. It's my last one here," Hanson said, still looking out the window. "Billy told me that Kendra Wilke is having a party tonight. She's not much to look at, but she's fun. I say we go over there."

"I have the truck. I say what goes. That's how it works," Tyler said, then pointed down at the empty burger wrapper on Hanson's lap. "Are you done with that?"

"Yeah, I'm done," Hanson said, sulking.

Tyler felt a hollow, tight feeling spread from his stomach to his chest. He didn't know what it was, but it seemed to come every day now. It wasn't fear. It wasn't sadness. It was something worse, and it made it hard to breathe. He had known Hanson his entire life, through all the changes and trauma and boredom of growing up in this stupid town, and the thought of him not being there felt worse than loss. Things were changing. People were leaving, and Tyler only saw a dark, empty expanse ahead.

"Listen. Let's go out for an hour. If we don't find anything, we head over to Kendra's," Tyler said. "Deal?"

"You mean it?" Hanson said, his eyes bright.

Tyler nodded reluctantly.

"Wa-woo woohoo!" Hanson let out a rebel yell and pounded the roof of Tyler's truck.

"Geez, Hanson. You're such a puppy dog." Tyler couldn't help but smile. "When Billy and Owen get here with the beer, we'll take off."

"I call front seat." Hanson grinned from ear to ear.

CHAPTER 44

The Shadow sat crouched just beneath the surface of the stream. It had found a spot almost five feet deep and hidden by a thick patch of cranberry bushes along the water's edge. It was cool here and away from the bright sunlight that hurt its eyes. But the solar cycle was almost complete, and the dim stars of this world would return, and it would be time to search again for the way home.

It slowly raised its head above the water's surface and looked out across the dimly lit forest floor. Glowing objects danced from plant to plant; these were new lights—some orange like embers, others purple like the color of the nebula back home. Each light pulsed in a pattern, a mesh network, sending out signals and listening for any sign in return.

Then the lights began to pulse erratically. Flashes of bright light, like firecrackers going off. The Shadow leaped onto the forest floor in a crouch and tilted its head up toward the sky. Something was happening. A signal from home. The lights began to vibrate now, leaving streaks of color as they swarmed back and around the shadow creature.

Slowly, scales opened and fanned out across its arms and

legs as the sprites nestled in like bees returning to a honey-comb. As the last sprite landed, the shadow closed its scales and began to process all this new information. New signals. Clear and strong. It was being called from miles away and knew exactly where to go.

Although the world beyond the forest was still lit by its too-bright sun, the Shadow couldn't wait any longer. It started to run.

CHAPTER 45

Miles away, Anna sat on the front porch with her sketch-book on her lap. She had brought down the glass cube from her room and set it on the wide arm of the Adirondack chair. The sprites had calmed their movement down to a steady pulse, and the glow of the lights was comforting. She needed it. All day long, she hadn't been able to shake this feeling that this night was the end of something—or maybe the start. Either way, she was anxious.

The sun was below the horizon, but the thin clouds above her head looked like cotton candy that had been set on fire. Another half hour left of light, maybe less, before she'd be taking flight. She breathed in deep. It was the first cool evening in weeks, and the breeze carried traces of lilac from the bushes on the side of the house.

Uncle Jack and Mara had gone into town for dinner several hours before, leaving Anna alone on the farm. Two quiet hours to herself, and Anna was grateful to be doing nothing at all. She knew it was going to be a long night ahead, and she needed her rest.

To divert her attention from the anxious feeling

hollowing out her stomach, Anna sketched in her journal, letting her hand and pen go wherever they wanted. But now she was stuck. The scale in her sketches was all wrong. No matter how hard she tried, she couldn't capture the sheer size and wonder of the things she had seen. The dome of stars. The pale red giant in the sky with twisting storms and ever-shifting bands of color. The sheer rock cliff that towered over the expanse of black ocean. The only thing she did get right was the squatty shape of the baobab-like trees and their fractal limbs.

Sketching was a form of meditation, a way to lose herself and think outside the edges. She would often return hours later and find unfamiliar elements in her sketches that her conscious mind couldn't recall. Still, Anna was surprised when she scanned her sketch of the dead baobab trees scattered along the alien plain and found a ghostlike face staring back at her from a universe away—a face she didn't remember drawing at all. Its eyes were black sockets filled with white lines. Galaxies spinning.

Bzzzz. Bzzzz.

Anna's phone buzzed and she jumped. Scout's avatar popped up in the middle of her display. She took in a deep breath, then poked his face with her finger.

"Hey, Armstrong!" Scout shouted. His face filled the screen, the camera so close that Anna could see his pores.

"That's nice, Scout."

"I need your honest opinion," Scout said. He thrust his upper lip into the camera. "You like a man with a mustache? Because I'm thinking of growing one."

Once again, Anna couldn't help herself and chuckled. It was needed.

"No offense, Scout. But I think I have a better chance of growing a mustache than you do," Anna said. "Why are you really calling?"

Scout pulled the phone back. He was staring at himself in the camera, tilting the phone to get the right angle.

"I was just checking in on you. Making sure you were okay and all," Scout said. He stopped posing and looked directly into the camera. "Did you hear about Fiona's older brother?"

"Yeah, she told me earlier today."

"Crazy."

He doesn't know the half of it, Anna thought.

"Yeah. Really crazy."

"There has to be an explanation, right?" Scout asked.

"There always is."

"Yeah," Scout said. He paused and looked at his phone. A puzzled look crossed his face. "Hey, Armstrong. Why's your face glowing?"

Anna looked down. The sprites were spinning wildly inside the glass, so fast the colors began to merge into one strobing light that was so bright it cast sharp shadows in odd angles across the porch.

Anna's iCom powered up on her wrist.

"Scout, I gotta go," Anna said.

"Hey, Anna, wait—"

Just as she closed the video call, SID's voice broke through her iCom.

<I've detected the creature. It's approximately five kilometers from the farm and moving fast in Anna's direction. I've provided you both coordinates and will continue tracking.>

Anna's heart skipped. This was it, but it wasn't supposed to happen this way. Not now. It was too soon. Something caused the creature to come out while it was still light outside.

"I'm on my way!"

CHAPTER 46

Tyler had the windows rolled down as they drove down the back roads outside Smartt. He howled along to a song blasting on the stereo, getting about every third word wrong, and banged his hands on the steering wheel like it was a drum pad. Hanson was used to tuning his friend out and watched the tall grass on the roadside pass by in a blur. Just behind his reflection in the side mirror, he caught sight of Billy's oversized truck driving up too quickly with its high beams on. The truck slowed down just feet behind and flashed its headlights as it swerved from side to side. Billy's truck kicked up a dust cloud as it veered off the road, balanced on the edge of the ditch, then corrected and edged back up on the main road.

"Why do we hang out with that guy?"

"Because he can buy us beer, which is more than I can say for you," Tyler said. "Speaking of—ask Owen to get me one."

Hanson opened the sliding rear window and peeked his head out the back. A pocket of wind turbulence whipped his hair across his face. In the far corner of the truck bed sat Owen, freckle-faced and pockmarked and the smallest of the group. His baseball cap was pulled down low around his ears to keep it from flying off, and he squinted his eyes against the wind.

"Hey, Owen. Hand me a couple, willya?" Hanson shouted above the turbulence.

Owen nodded, pulled out two beers from the case, and was ready to hand them over when he froze. Out in the field of summer wheat, a black figure was running fast and keeping pace with the truck. There was something in its movements, unnatural and disjointed, that made him shudder. His mouth dropped open. He struggled to find words that could make sense of what he saw, but he gave up trying and just pointed out toward the field while still clutching a can of beer.

Hanson looked up, puzzled, then out in the direction of Owen's frozen gaze. There on the far edge of the field was the creature. The target of endless nights of driving and hunting, false leads and close calls. It was real after all and moving unlike any animal he had ever seen. The creature bobbed up and down as it ran, its long arms and legs in full gallop. Its skin, black as night, was a sharp contrast against the honey-colored wheat.

Hanson turned quickly back into the cab, slamming his head against the roof.

"There. It's there! It's there!" Hanson shouted as he pointed frantically at the field.

Tyler looked out the side window. His heart skipped and the world slowed down. The bar was low, but he was the most cunning of his group. A natural hunter. His brain instantly tracked the creature's direction and speed. A map of the roads flashed in his head and different options played out as he plotted the best place to cut the creature off.

He calmly reached over and turned off the stereo.

"Get Billy on the phone and tell his fat ass to keep up," Tyler said coolly. "And grab the rifle."

He slammed the gas pedal to the floor. The tachometer

redlined as Owen lost his balance and rolled around the back of the truck like an empty beer can.

—

Less than a mile ahead, a rusty green truck was making its way down a straight stretch of road and going ten miles under the speed limit. Jack was taking his time. He was just returning from the Ivanhoe Diner with Mara and wanted nothing more than to extend the evening as long as he could. He glanced over. The windows were rolled down. Mara's hair billowed out in waves like a living thing, but she didn't seem to mind. The wind felt good to both of them and brought with it a faint hint of alfalfa and summer grass. The stereo played loud enough in the background for the two to catch the melody, but not so loud it prevented them from talking.

"What is this?" Mara asked.

"You mean the song? It's Hank Williams. 'On the Banks of the Old Pontchartrain,'" Jack said. "You like it?"

"I do. It sounds like a dream, but—" Mara's voice cut short, then she recited a line from the song. "'I left her alone without saying goodbye.' That's quite sad."

"Yeah. I don't think ol' Hank was a very happy guy, but I sure like his music," Jack said. "We can listen to something else if you want. I've got a bunch of different playlists. Soul from the seventies. Great stuff, like Bill Withers, Al Green. There's a David Bowie playlist. You pick."

"David Bowie. I've heard of him." Mara smiled.

"Well, all right. Good choice." Jack was ready to switch the playlist when he noticed two headlights rapidly approaching in the rearview mirror. "Huh?"

"What is it?" Mara asked.

"Someone's in a hurry," Jack answered, his expression puzzled.

Mara turned around and looked out the back of the truck. The approaching headlights lit up her face and dilated her pupils. A pickup truck was coming up fast and flying dead center down the middle of the road. She calculated the speed of the vehicle and the speed of Jack's truck and had just enough time to shout.

"Move!"

Jack was already in motion when he heard Mara yell out. He slammed on the gas pedal and edged toward the side of the road, his tires spraying a bloom of gravel. He looked out the side window and had just enough time to catch the driver's face as the truck flew by, missing him by inches.

Jack tried to steer the truck back toward the road, but the tires had hit the soft dirt on the side of the ditch. The truck tilted precariously. He looked over at Mara and for a moment thought she was floating, serene and calm, her hair unmoving. The second truck blew past just as Jack started to gain control. He could feel the back end fishtail and turned into the swerve; the back tires caught traction, and his truck bounced back up onto the main road. Old bolts rattled, the glove box popped open, and Jack almost hit the top of his head on the roof, but he didn't overcorrect and was able to get the truck under control. He slowed his truck and gradually rolled to a stop by the side of the road, his hands white-knuckled on the wheel. The engine ticked in the silence.

"You okay?" Jack asked as he looked over.

"Yes. What was that?"

"Just some stupid kids," Jack answered. "Some very stupid kids who are going to be hearing from me."

Mara was ready to respond when her iCom flashed blue. It was SID.

<I've detected the creature. It's approximately five kilometers from the farm and moving fast in Anna's direction. I've provided you both coordinates and will continue tracking.>

"I'm on my way!" Anna's voice came over the iCom.

"No," Mara said out loud, startling herself and Jack.

"I'm sorry. What?" Jack asked.

<I see you're with Jack. I'll call you now for a diversion, Mara.>

The iCom phone buzzed in her back pocket.

"My phone," Mara responded, glad for the reprieve. She read a text from SID—instructions for what to say next.

"Everything okay?" Jack asked.

"I'm sorry, but I need to get back to your place as fast as I can." Mara looked up. "It's family."

CHAPTER 47

Anna grabbed the goggles from her dresser upstairs and leaped from her bedroom window, dipping in a slight arc toward the yard below before flying up and out across the barnyard. She caught sight of several farm staff walking between buildings and quickly powered up her cloaking mode as she silently cleared the final barn. The valley opened up before her as she ascended into the sky. At this height, she knew she might lose several seconds in pursuit, but she'd gain perspective and buy herself some time to figure out what to do next.

She flew past Tyson Lake and its surrounding woods. She passed the soybean fields that looked like a brilliant green carpet in the fading evening light.

"How far, SID?" Anna asked over her iCom.

<Factoring in your speed and the creature's current location, you should have a visual any second.>

Anna broke the view in front of her into four quadrants, scanning her eyes back and forth across each quadrant for any sign of movement. From the corner of her eye, she saw two tiny trucks racing down one of the back roads. Even at this height, she could tell the trucks were moving fast. Dust clouds like

Morse code followed the second truck as it swerved on and off the road. Something in the speed and erratic movement made her pause. She zoomed in on the truck in front.

"Oh no," Anna said out loud.

Tyler was driving, his body hunched over the steering wheel, his eyes wild. The passenger in the front and the small one in the back both held rifles. The passenger in the second truck was leaning out and pointing his rifle into the wheat field. Two trucks. Three guns.

Anna's gaze followed the direction of the rifle barrel. On the far edge of the field, where the wheat abutted the forest's edge, the Shadow was running, its body bobbing above and below the wheat stalks like a jet-black fish swimming along the surface of the water.

"Mara! I'm going to need your help," Anna called over her iCom. "Tyler is here and has the creature in his sights. They look like they're trying to cut it off."

A moment's pause and then SID answered.

<Mara can't reply. She texted me to tell you to hold on until she gets there. Do not engage under any circumstances.>

Tyler made it to the edge of the wheat field and took a hard right onto a dirt service road. The second truck followed just behind. Anna was right. Tyler was trying to cut the creature off. The Shadow was fast, but not as fast as the truck barreling in its direction. In less than fifteen seconds, the creature would be reaching the end of the field, and Tyler would be waiting. Anna primed her vortex cannon.

"I'll be careful," Anna said into the iCom.

<Do not engage!>

Anna flattened her body and dove like a falcon toward the pickup trucks now skidding to a stop. She calculated the distance and angle of her dive. Not enough time.

Tyler had already opened his door before the truck had finished its slide, and he leaned out just like he had practiced a thousand times before. He drew his rifle out and mounted it on top of the roof in one fluid move. He closed one eye and placed his finger on the trigger. The creature was now in his view and moving straight in his direction.

Pop!

Anna thought she heard a firecracker go off. Sharp and loud.

Pop . . . pop!

She realized it was the percussive sound of rifle fire. The first two shots veered right. On the third shot, though, the Shadow dipped its shoulder to the left, and Anna wasn't sure if it had dodged the bullet or been struck.

She had one chance. Now twenty feet above the pickup truck, Anna fired her vortex cannon in Tyler's direction. There was a brief delay, then the ball of compressed gas expanded and hit Tyler like a giant hand slapping his back. His chest slammed hard against the truck as his rifle flew from his grasp to bounce off the hood and onto the ground.

Anna floated, invisible to all beneath her.

Looking down through the windshield of the pickup truck, Anna saw Hanson freeze. He looked disoriented and unsteady. His eyes were shut tight as if he were trying to wish the whole thing away. Then the pop of rifle fire from Billy's truck seemed to force Hanson out of his daze. He opened his eyes just in time to see the creature leap effortlessly from the edge of the field to the top of the truck.

Thwack!

The roof of the truck suddenly dented in with a deep thud. Hanson leaned his body out the side window and looked up to the roof. Just inches away, the creature knelt in a crouch, its arms and legs folded at odd angles. Its skin was an unnatural absence of color. Scales flared out around the creature's head as it turned to face its closest threat.

"Shoot it, Owen! Shoot it!" Tyler shouted. He had recovered enough to pull himself up to his knees by the side of the truck.

Owen was on his knees in the back of the truck. He lifted the barrel of his rifle, then froze.

The creature cocked its head and leaned forward. Its scales began to vibrate, its mouth opened wide, and a piercing, unnatural wail echoed out across the countryside. Owen looked into the creature's face—a black hole in the sky—and screamed. He dropped his rifle and leaped from the back of the truck to hit the ground running in a full sprint. His hat flew off as he passed Billy's truck, but he didn't look back. He wouldn't look back until he reached the paved road minutes later.

The Shadow's gaze followed the pale, noisy creature as it ran away—sensing its fear and panic—then quickly scanned the area, its head turning almost full circle. The signal to home was loud. The path was clear. It leaped from the truck in a high arc, passing over Tyler to silently land on the edge of the soybean field. Its arms and legs unfolded as it galloped along a small dirt path that separated the soybean field from the woods. Dust kicked up where its feet slapped the ground.

"I swear to God, none of you could shoot the side of a barn," Tyler shouted as he grabbed his rifle and jumped back into the cab of his truck.

"I didn't see you do any better, sure-shot," Billy lobbed back.

"Come on. Let's go!" Tyler said as he pounded the roof of his truck. "Go! Go! It's getting away!"

Tyler slammed his truck in reverse and took out a section of fence along the wheat field, wooden posts splintering with a loud crack, and then popped the truck into gear. He sped forward, flying over a small ditch and then out into the soybean field. His truck bounced up and down over the rows of dirt and vegetation. Billy's truck followed close behind.

From above, Anna could see Hanson clutch the truck's grab handle with one hand and his rifle with the other. His knuckles were white. His eyes blank.

Pop! Thwack!

Another rifle shot rang out, this time from the passenger in Billy's truck. He missed far right, really far right, as Anna could hear the bullet crack against a tree in the woods. She feared he was more likely to shoot someone in Tyler's truck than the creature.

Anna leaned forward and raced to catch up. Her body skimmed just feet above the plants, so close she could smell the freshly dug-up soil and the sharp chemical smell of pesticide residue. She primed her vortex cannon as she caught up to the side of Billy's truck and glanced over. He was just feet away, eye level, but she was afraid to fire while he was driving at this speed.

She frantically looked for other ways to slow the truck down—like taking the air out of the tires or dropping a log across their path—and realized she had no idea what she was doing. She sped forward and flew just above the hood, keeping pace with the speeding truck as she turned her body to face the front window. Anna flew straight backward as she looked directly into the cab. Billy was enjoying the hunt. His head was lowered, his eyes were narrow, and he grinned. At that moment, Anna wanted nothing more than to wipe that smile off his face—then she noticed the hood of the truck rattle just beneath her. The latch had come loose. Not completely, but enough to bounce up and down by less than an inch. *The hood. That's it.*

Anna's fingers were just able to squeeze under the hood. She searched for the release latch. She knew if Billy were to stop or suddenly turn, her fingers would be ripped off, but she continued to search along the edge until she felt a small hinge. The release. She strained to squeeze the hinge. Then *click*.

She had enough time to see Billy's eyes widen—his face registering what was happening before his brain could process what was going on—as the hood caught the wind and flew back against the windshield like a spring-loaded trap. Glass shattered but didn't break. Metal twisted and snapped. Billy slammed on his brakes and the truck fishtailed to the right and shuddered to a stop, the hood still sticking straight up like a sail. As Anna flew away, she looked back long enough to see Billy step out of his truck, throw his hat against the ground, and kick the side of the truck. *One down.* Without losing speed, she rolled her body forward and took off in pursuit of Tyler's truck.

The tires bounced off the deep, furrowed rows of soybean like a piston. The loose soil and uneven terrain slowed the truck down, but not enough. Tyler was still gaining on the creature.

Anna leaned to her right and accelerated up to the passenger side, bugs stinging her face like needle pricks. She flew at eye level with Hanson, avoiding the gun barrel pointed out the window. She looked forward and saw the creature was no more than twenty feet ahead.

"Shoot it, Hanson!" Tyler shouted.

Hanson didn't respond. He didn't move. Tyler reached over and slugged his friend's shoulder to get his attention. Hanson looked over slowly and loosened his grip on the rifle.

"I don't want to do this anymore," Hanson said.

This was her chance. Anna grabbed the rifle barrel and pulled hard. She could feel Hanson scramble to hold on as she yanked the rifle from his hands, but she had moved too quickly for him to respond. He was fighting ghosts. She flung the rifle as far as she could into the thorn-rimmed brambles that lined the foot of the woods. Hanson reached his arms out the window in desperation, his fingers flailing only inches from Anna's face, then he slumped back in his seat.

"What the hell, Hanson?!" Tyler shouted as he looked over in exasperation.

"Let me out," Hanson pleaded.

"You're not going anywhere." Tyler looked straight ahead. "Not until I kill this thing."

Tyler leaned forward and pushed the gas pedal to the floor. Metal tools rattled on the floorboard, and the rusted springs in the bench seat squeaked. The one remaining rifle bounced on Tyler's lap as Hanson looked over in horror. He was sure it was going to go off and spray his insides against the side of the cab. But Tyler didn't seem to notice or care. All his attention was on the black figure in front of him. The truck barreled forward, the right front tire now only feet from the creature's extended legs.

The remaining evening light was fading fast, and Anna suddenly had a hard time differentiating between the black outline of the creature and the dark crisscross of brambles and tree branches along the edge of the woods.

The creature skirted the headlights anytime the truck came close, like the cone of light was a physical barrier.

Tyler must have noticed this too, and he flicked on the 420-watt floodlights that sat on top of the truck, bright enough to light up a baseball field or stun a deer. But the light mounts had been twisted when the creature planted a six-inch dent in the roof, and they now shone at haphazard angles. The floodlight on the right shot almost straight up, like a beacon, while the light mounted on the left pointed directly at the far side of the truck and hit the Shadow straight on.

The blinding light burned past the creature's protective lens. The left side of its body seized up. The creature appeared disoriented, and its limbs no longer worked in sync.

It stumbled and fell forward into the brambles, its arms and legs wrapping around its body in a protective shell as it rolled to a stop.

Tyler slammed on the brakes and spun the steering wheel sharply to the right, making the truck fishtail out of control over rough mounds of dirt. Soybean plants flew in giant clumps as the truck tilted to the left, teetering on the edge of falling over. The truck seemed to float for a moment, its two right tires spinning in the air. Then the right side of the truck slammed back down with a heavy thud.

Hanson's head whipped forward and smashed into the roll bar. His body slumped in the seat.

Anna had just enough time to nudge her trajectory upward as the truck veered left. She used her hands to vault safely off the top of the truck as she flew past, but she bounced off at an odd angle and tumbled out of control in midair.

Tyler sat silent in the truck, his hands still on the wheel. His rifle was now at his feet and pointed up toward the roof. He looked over at Hanson, who was passed out in the seat next to him. A trail of blood ran down the side of his head and neck to stain his yellow shirt, but he was breathing. Tyler grabbed his rifle and looked out the front window. The left floodlight still enveloped the creature, now hunched over in a compact ball that reminded him of the roly-poly bugs he used to torture as a kid.

He stepped out of the truck and moved cautiously toward the creature, his rifle butted up against his shoulder, and pointed straight ahead. Tyler closed one eye and sighted the barrel dead center in the middle of the creature's back. He placed his finger on the trigger, then paused. All these weeks and he finally had his chance. It was his shot.

———

"Anna, can you hear me?"

Anna had recovered from her spin twenty feet away from the truck, disoriented and unsure if she had imagined Mara's voice on her iCom. She shook her head and looked up. Tyler was walking slowly toward the creature, his rifle held up to his shoulder, ready to fire. She primed her vortex cannon, then realized the blast might stop Tyler but could also cause him to press the trigger. She could try to wrest the rifle away like she did with Hanson. But that still might not stop Tyler from firing. There were no good choices.

"I'm sorry, Mara," Anna said over her iCom.

She flew forward and landed in front of the creature in a crouch, covering its back with her body and deactivating her cloaking mode. She held her arms out in a protective posture as the creature stirred behind her.

"No, Tyler. Please," Anna said.

CHAPTER 48

"I'm sorry, Jack. I'll explain later," Mara said as she ran from the truck to her motorcycle parked out front of the house.

"Are you sure I can't help?" Jack called out to her.

Mara hated not answering him and leaving him standing there confused and anxious. She would find a good explanation later. But not now. Nothing mattered other than getting to Anna before anything bad happened to her. She started her motorcycle and sped down the dirt road, racing to get out of Jack's line of sight before she took flight.

"Anna! Can you hear me?" Mara shouted over the iCom.

No response—the only sound came from the whine of the motorcycle engine and the wind buffeting her ears.

Night felt like a wave slowly rolling across the valley floor. Mara glanced in the side mirror. Behind her, the top of the Armstrong house disappeared beneath the soft rise of the hill and out of view. The road behind her was now clear. She leaned her bike toward a thick patch of weeds along the side of the road and let go of the handlebars as she silently took flight.

The riderless motorcycle followed along beneath her for the first couple of seconds on its own, forward momentum keeping it steady. Then the handlebars wobbled violently to the left then right before flipping in midair to land hard in the thick brush along the roadside.

"I'm sorry, Mara," Anna's voice came over the iCom.

Fear closed tight like a vise around Mara's throat and lungs and made it hard to breathe. She leaned forward and willed her body to go as fast as it could.

"SID! Where is she?"

<Anna is approximately thirty seconds away at current speed. Follow the coordinates I provided.>

Mara passed over Tyson Lake, the light from the newly risen moon reflecting off the water's surface. From this elevation, farm fields sprawled out in a square patchwork of varying shades of gray. Lines blurred. Then, just ahead, along the black line where the woods and the fields met, Mara could make out a cylinder of light pointing up toward the sky like a beacon. She zoomed in and saw the source of the light. She saw a young man with a rifle walking forward, his back lit up by a truck's headlights. The rifle was aimed at a figure crouched on the ground. It was Anna.

Mara wanted to scream, to lash out, but focused every bit of her attention on a spot just inches in front of the young man and sped downward in a blur. She covered more than a hundred feet in the time it took the young man to move one step forward. Within the next second, she had halved the distance between them. The young man took another step closer. Just a few seconds more. Mara had one chance to pull up from her dive before hitting the man at a speed that would kill them both. The ground raced up to meet her. She calculated the coming shift in gravity, the direction of her body, the air resistance, and her speed, then slowed her descent as she swung her legs up in a kicking motion.

The sudden deceleration caused her stomach to flip and her eyes to blur, but she knew she had to kick out now. The heel of her boot came down hard against the rifle barrel, knocking it out of the man's hands and away from Anna.

The young man screamed out at nobody and began flailing his arms blindly in a circle. Mara landed gently in front of him—making sure to stay out of his reach—and turned off her cloaking mode.

She raised her palm, and its pulsing glow seemed to calm the young man. With each pulse of light, the will to fight or even move appeared to flow out of his limbs like water.

"Mara!" Anna called out.

Tyler turned his head, surprised by the distant voice.

Mara signaled for Anna to be quiet while never losing eye contact with the frightened young man in front of her. She took a small step forward, her hands held up in front of her. A sign she meant no harm.

"Anna. Take the creature and go to the lake. Now," Mara said calmly. No sense of urgency in her voice. "I've got this."

CHAPTER 49

Mara watched as Anna cradled the creature in her arms and flew up and over the line of trees. The errant floodlight that pointed up like a beacon lit Anna's path as she flew out of view. Mara waited until her young friend disappeared, then turned to face Tyler again.

"It's okay, Tyler. It's over now," she said calmly, her hands still held out in front of her.

"How do you know me? I don't know . . ." Tyler's voice faded away.

Mara cocked her head. She had planned to just clean his memory and make short work of this, to leave him there alone with a dented truck and a hole in his life. But in the sharp glow of the floodlights, he looked so different. Younger than she expected. More afraid. The history she had gathered on him earlier—the citations and warnings, the altercations and struggles with school and himself and everyone around him—now started to make some sense. It wasn't time to go. Not yet.

"I know everything about you, Tyler," Mara said.

And she did. Even things he didn't know about himself or was afraid to say out loud.

"Are you going to hurt me?" Tyler's eyes watered.

"No. You do a good enough job of that on your own," she said.

"Then . . . what?" Tyler asked.

"I'm going to give you a chance at a fresh start. Would you like that, Tyler?" Mara said.

The light in her palm now began to gradually change color from white to green, and with it came the hushed sound of wind through thick pine. Calming.

Tyler's face started to relax. A slight smile crossed his lips.

"Yeah. I'd like that," he answered.

"In a couple of minutes, you're going to take your friend to the closest hospital. He'll be fine, but he's going to need some attention."

"Did I do that?" Tyler asked, a hint of sadness in his voice.

"It was an accident, but yes. You seem to attract accidents, don't you, Tyler? And there are more ahead for you too if you don't change course—far worse than this one. Accidents you won't be able to walk away from," Mara said.

"Then what do I do?" he asked, light reflecting off the rims of his eyes.

Mara paused. She had seen Tyler's past and future paths. His last couple of years had been a hazy state of inertia and boredom—stagnant, like the heat that hung heavy on a late August afternoon just before a summer squall ripped branches from the trees. She had seen the pictures in the newsfeeds and police reports. There would be the death of another, then the lost decade, and finally his own early death.

She would have work to do. Not tonight but in the coming months, and it still might not be enough. This new future she was part of held no certainty.

"This town isn't good for you," she said.

"I hate it here," he said absently.

"No. You hate *you* here," she said. "You need room to breathe, and this town holds too much weight for you. You need space and time to discover who you really are. You'll receive a message in the coming months. An opportunity to leave. You're going to take it, because you know it's your last, best chance."

"How will I know?"

"You just will. Trust me."

Tyler smiled. "Okay."

"And one last thing before I leave you."

Tyler's eyes closed, the smile still on his face. He could feel the synapses in his brain smooth over like a fresh dusting of snow. Before he disappeared altogether in this vast, white landscape, he felt someone speaking to him from a distance.

"Be nicer to your younger brother."

CHAPTER 50

By the time Anna cleared the trees, the creature had wrapped its long arms and legs around her and nestled its head tight against her shoulder. Its body felt light, like balsa wood. Scales fluttered then opened around the rim of the Shadow's head, as blue and green and purple sprites floated out and clung to its skin like luminescent dewdrops, vibrating and shaking in the wind. Anna could feel the glow against her own skin and smiled. The creature trusted her, and it was letting her know.

She dipped her right shoulder and glided closer to the lake's surface—close enough to touch the water with her hand. The last of the day's light was now gone, and the moon peeked just above the horizon, lighting the landscape in a dark blue haze. Anna looked down and saw her own dim reflection on the surface of the water as she sped toward the small black island in the center of the lake.

Anna slowed her trajectory as she drew closer and turned her body upright to land. The creature sensed the change of movement and leaned into the turn as Anna landed gently on the same patch of grass she had shared with Mara just the night before. The creature unfurled its arms and legs and sat back in a crouch. Its head tilted toward Anna in expectation.

"You're going to have to go swimming for a bit. Is that okay?" Anna asked.

Sprites circled slowly around the two of them like electrons in orbit, sending and retrieving signals from the surface of their skin. Specialized neurotransmitters and peptides communicated at a level outside language. The creature understood and stepped forward with its hand outstretched. It was time to go home.

Anna guided the Shadow to the shoreline and looked down. She flipped on her full mask, then made a diving gesture with her free hand. But it wasn't necessary. The creature knew what to do and where to go now. The two paused for a moment, their bodies in sync, and then dove into the lake as if they were one form, barely disrupting the water's surface.

The creature moved easily underwater, and Anna wondered how much time it had spent swimming beneath the surface of its own world's vast black ocean—and what mysteries lay underneath. Within seconds, they made it to the small cave just beneath the island's shelf.

The wormhole spun noiselessly in front of them just as it had the night before, and flecks of light circled the edge like shooting stars. The creature squeezed Anna's hand. It knew where it was. It knew where it was going. Sprites floated from the surface of its skin and spun in spirals toward the wormhole, where they disappeared like small petals down a whirlpool. Anna let go.

The Shadow didn't look back as it reached into the wormhole with both hands. There was a brief pause as the creature leaned into the dark orb and pushed against the surface tension, then its body disappeared with an audible pop, as if something had reached across space and time to yank it to the other side. And with that the Shadow was gone.

Anna floated just feet away—tempted to lean in for one last look—when the wormhole started to slow its spin. Its edges began to smooth and expand as the flecks of spinning light slowed down so much that they appeared to float like fixed stars. The orb was growing. A perfect circle, a smooth glass window, now the same height as Anna.

On the other side of the window, she could make out the pale red planet reflecting off the surface of an expansive black ocean. Then the view opened up even more, past the cliffs of the alien planet to the distant plains lined with dead baobab trees as far as the eye could see. Ash fell like snow across the landscape.

From a clearing in the trees, a figure stepped forward, bone white and thin. Its movements like jump cuts. The brim of its round white hat flashed bright as if from some internal light. Long sticklike fingers cast out orange and purple sprites like a farmer spreading seeds across the ground as it walked. Another bone-white figure appeared in a small clearing, and then another from behind a tree, each casting sprites far out into the sea of trees.

The stars in the sky began to spin in concentric circles. Then Anna realized it wasn't the stars that were moving—it was the planet spinning faster as time unfolded in front of her. She was witnessing the passing of days, maybe years, in seconds. The sprites cast out by the bone-white figures began to spread from tree to tree in a wave, lighting the landscape until the whole plain was aglow in life and light. The trees shook off their ash and began to breathe again.

She didn't know how or why, but Anna was witnessing the future—a time when the alien planet, the Shadow's home, was beginning to heal. She had been given a glimpse of this renewal for a reason, but she had no idea why or what it meant.

Suddenly the wormhole began to shrink in front of her until it was the size of a small black ball. Anna reached out with her finger and touched the edge of the shrinking black orb. She could feel the pull from the other side and heard a small, distant hum.

Then . . . *thwip!*

Anna jumped as the wormhole disappeared, leaving behind no trace.

CHAPTER 51

The moon sat in the western part of the sky, closer to dawn now than midnight. Mara sat on the edge of her deck, feet dangling over the side, and sipped a steaming orange broth.

Hours before, she had joined Anna on the small island in the middle of the lake. The two danced in circles under the night sky, celebrating the successful return of the Shadow to its world. For Anna, this was the end of a months-long journey, and with it came a sense of relief, not unlike the feeling of the last day of school. She flew home and collapsed on her bed in her clothes, the months finally catching up to her as she fell into a sleep as dark and deep as the alien ocean she had left behind.

But for Mara this wasn't the end. She wouldn't allow herself room to relax. Not yet. Not until she knew for sure and all the data was analyzed. She waited nervously to hear from SID and only managed two hours of fitful sleep before she gave up altogether and headed out into the cool early-morning air.

SID was still crunching numbers, running models, and scanning the environment. She would know soon whether this was really it. The end of the hiding, the running. She looked out across the lake. The steam from her cup held up close to her chin looked like mist rising from the water's surface.

<Mara?>

Her heart skipped.

"Yes, SID?"

<Do you want the long explanation or the short?>

"Let's start with the short."

<Sensors detected the closure of the final wormhole at nine thirty-two p.m. local time. Since then, we've been unable to detect the presence of a wormhole. No energy signatures. No anomalies.>

"They're gone."

<To put it in context, ever since we escaped from our own time and went into hiding, there hasn't been a single moment we didn't detect the presence of some energy signal. That is, until now.>

"Meaning?" Mara asked, but she already knew the answer.

<That you were right. This time is different.>

"That we're safe?"

<I believe so.>

Mara set her cup down on the deck and covered her face with her hands. She breathed in deep, smelling the spices from her drink still on her hands, and cried for the first time in ages.

PART III

THE OTHERS

CHAPTER 52

Anna stepped out into the barnyard to a cacophony of sounds and movement. Uncle Jack called the days leading up to the fair "controlled chaos," and it showed. The farm had the feel of a Hollywood set or a traveling circus setting up camp before opening night. Most of the farm staff were shuttling between buildings. Shouts and playful banter in multiple languages seemed to come from all sides, woven together with the sounds of farm animals and heavy equipment. There were several new faces too, helping assemble freshly fabricated tables, exhibition booths, and displays. The lot was scented with freshly cut wood. Kevin from Kenya was leading the build, while Gladness helped guide selected livestock to open trailers. Li Wei was pouring rich black soil into a glass display that looked like a giant ant farm, and Faye the Gray was waiting patiently for a small autonomous tractor as it ferried crates of newly harvested heirloom peaches and blueberries to the back of an electric truck.

Anna made her way to the end of the barnyard, smiling at familiar faces and making sure to step out of the way of the orchestrated ebb and flow of work. She walked down the shady side of a football field–sized greenhouse at the end of the lot, grateful for the reprieve from the morning sun, and made her way to Mara's shed.

She opened the door without knocking and was hit with a wall of cool, dry air. The room felt charged with ions, and the servers were running in the corner, filling the space with a hum.

"Hey, Mara," Anna called out. "You here?"

Mara peeked up from her desk. She was wearing goggles with large round lenses that made her eyes appear enormous. A broad smile lit up her face. In front of her was what looked like a tall stack of brass plates joined by glass tubes and wires.

"How long have you been hiding here?" Anna asked.

"Since dawn. I needed to explain my sudden departure last night to your uncle. I didn't want him to worry."

"Oh. That's right. I heard you had family issues." Anna assigned air quotes to the last part. "What's that you're working on?"

"Let me see. The quantum data plane, the control plane, and the control processor plane," Mara said as she removed her goggles.

"That's a lot of planes," Anna said, smiling.

"Especially when you're building by hand. SID is working on the quantum processing unit, but it's slow going. The design isn't the problem. It's the lack of materials from your time."

"Wait. You're building a quantum computer?" Anna asked.

"It's child's play, and I mean that literally. We played with them as children like you play with blocks," Mara said.

"Wow. A quantum computer. How's it coming along?"

"I don't know. Let's ask," Mara said, then looked over to the cylindrical speaker next to the computer monitor. "Hey, SID. How are we doing?"

The small green light that lined the top of the speaker

began to pulse and glow. SID's voice echoed across the room, clear and bright—and in a distinct Scottish accent.

"I've finished the first quantum processing unit, which will store up to one billion qubits. Sufficient for our purposes until we can refine the process. Instead of diamond, I opted to use a superconducting graphene material that can be replicated easily in this time. It's not programmable matter, but it will do. We should finish our quantum computer by this afternoon and have it running by this evening," SID said over the speaker.

"Why is SID speaking in a Scottish accent?" Anna asked.

"Because it sounds delightful, don't you think?" Mara laughed.

"No, seriously."

"Okay. So now we're being serious," Mara said playfully. "I've installed a simplified version of SID on the local network and have a need to interface in some way. The speaker patches into our iCom using components and materials from this time."

"Still. Why do you need a version of SID on the local network—or a quantum computer—when you have the real SID right here?"

Mara paused before answering.

"Because we have some big problems to address, and we need to do it fast. Big, incredibly complex problems that the computing architecture of your time can't address," Mara said.

"That still doesn't answer my question," Anna said.

Mara smiled, then stood up. "Listen. This is going to take a little bit. Are you up for a walk? I need to stretch my legs anyway."

Anna followed Mara out past the greenhouse and down a narrow dirt path lined with tall grass and orange hawkweed plants. The trail ran along the edge of the woods, filled with a chorus of bird calls, and meandered past a decaying wooden fence overrun by brambles. Heavy dew still hung on the vegetation and collected on Anna's pants legs as she walked. The air was humid and warm and filled with the smell of fresh soil. Mara stopped and took in a deep breath.

"Tell me. What do you see?" Mara asked as she pointed at the brambles—a tall, leafy cathedral made of interlocking blackberry bushes.

"A bush."

"Look more closely," Mara said.

Anna took several steps closer and felt, more than heard, a soft, almost imperceptible buzz. She paused and let her eyes focus on a single patch of small flowering plants. What looked static a moment ago was now pulsing with movement. Thousands of bees and wasps and butterflies and moths swarmed the brambles and danced from flower to flower.

"How did I not see that?" Anna asked.

"It's easy to miss. How many species can you identify?" Mara asked.

Anna laughed.

"I don't know. Too many to count."

"What if I were to tell you almost every one of those species doesn't exist in my time? The bees, butterflies, hummingbirds—even the blackberry bushes—were just historical records of species long gone, just as the dinosaurs are to you," Mara said.

Anna heard the words, but they were an abstraction, just sounds, and she found herself incapable of internalizing what they meant.

"I thought—"

"We survived? We did. But we lost so much in the transition," Mara said. She started walking again, with Anna walking numbly behind.

"But you showed me your world. It was beautiful," Anna said as she jogged to catch up.

"It was a bubble we created to protect ourselves from the damage already done," Mara said. "Have you heard of the Library of Alexandria?"

"Yeah, I think so. It was an old library that burned down, right?" Anna said.

"It didn't burn down, at least not at once. It took centuries for it to fall into decay. But the story is the same. At one time it was supposed to have contained the sum total of human knowledge, and its destruction ushered humanity into the dark ages," Mara said. "You are living in a similar moment, Anna. Right now. But the stakes are so much higher."

"I don't understand."

"We need solutions to an array of problems. But nature has already solved most of those problems through evolution. Energy production, resource distribution, water collection, waste management. The list goes on," Mara said. "Nature is like the Library of Alexandria, but instead of scrolls there are natural models. We just need to learn its language. Unfortunately, your time doesn't have the tools needed to unlock that language fast enough. And in my time, well, we learned that lesson after the library had already burned down."

"So that's why you need a quantum computer," Anna said.

"Yes, to better model the complexity of nature while there is still enough nature to model."

"But still, why don't you just use SID?" Anna asked.

Mara stopped midstride and turned around.

"When I decided to stay and work here on this farm, I didn't do it just to help your uncle. My timeline, our future, is no longer a fixed path. We have a chance to help rewrite the future—maybe even prevent the great warming or minimize it if we can. But this isn't going to be easy, Anna," Mara said.

"I don't know," Anna said. "You already know the future. Let's just fix it."

"Understanding the outcome doesn't always reveal the

cause," Mara said. "What if we pursue the wrong problems? In the wrong sequence? How much new science or technology can I introduce to your time? Too much too soon could destabilize society. Too little, and, well—"

"Well, what?"

"Well, there will be a lot of unnecessary suffering and loss," Mara said. "I'll have to strike a balance. The best path forward I can think of is to use materials from your time to build new and better tools. Tools that others can build—not just me—and adapt if necessary. That's how we'll scale. But we're going to need to do lots of experiments and get lots of people involved."

CHAPTER 53

U ncle Jack was up before dawn. Anna could hear him shuffling in the kitchen, and the rich smell of coffee worked its way up the stairs. She rolled out of bed and made her way to her window. A thin band of clouds lined the horizon, outlined in a sliver of light, and the rest of the sky was a deep purple, streaked with brushstrokes of pink and red. Dark silhouettes in the barnyard worked busily in the shadows—the farm staff in predawn light. The final day before the fair.

She headed downstairs and was surprised to find a cup of coffee waiting for her on the table. Next to the steaming cup was a single sheet of yellow notepad paper and a list of tasks for that night's kickoff dinner that ran the length of the page.

"All this for me?" Anna asked.

"That was the hope. Do you think you might be able to get some of your friends to help?" Uncle Jack asked. "Guests are coming in by evening time and we're shorthanded."

"Where are you going to be?" Anna stifled a yawn.

"Back and forth to the fairgrounds most of the day. Mara will be with me. But we should be finished by the time the guests arrive. Fingers crossed. Thanks for holding down the fort, Anna."

And with that, Uncle Jack was out the door with Herbie following. Anna sat down and placed her face over the cup of coffee, taking in a deep breath and letting the steam wake her up. In addition to food prep, something she felt particularly unsuited to do, she saw a request to greet guests as they arrived throughout the afternoon. There was a map for the tables and a seating chart for guests. Picnic tables would need to be set up throughout the front yard for the hundred-plus guests who would be attending—farm staff, family and friends, delegates from six countries. She did a double-take at the size of the list.

"How big is this thing?" Anna said out loud.

By eight o'clock that morning, Dr. Gloria's extended family had arrived bearing pots and pans of pre-prepped foods and crates of fresh vegetables. By 8:10, the kitchen had become a smooth-running factory. Anna learned how to properly cut onions and garlic from Del's father, Hugo, a local electrician and family cook. As she worked with him, she caught glimpses of Del in his expression, especially in his eyes and a smile that brightened the room.

As the morning progressed, more people shuttled in food until the staging area in the kitchen had expanded out into the dining and sitting rooms. There were wild-berry pies from Faye. A pot of Köttbullar from Liam. A large basket of Kaimati from Kevin. Red bean buns from Li Wei. As Anna moved between the rooms, different smells would waft by, shifting from savory to sweet and light, like wildflowers. Some sharp, some rich. Hints of spices and chocolate and roasting beef. By late morning Anna's stomach was grumbling, and she couldn't remember the last time she felt this hungry.

By early afternoon, Anna was grateful to escape the constant temptation of the kitchen and headed outside to set up the yard. Fiona and Lula arrived just in time to help arrange chairs and air out tablecloths and place name-card holders for visitors who would be arriving in the coming hours.

The three friends looked for their own name cards and saw that they were seated together with other teens at the far edge of the lawn. She scanned for familiar names and noticed that Del's name card was on the exact opposite end of the table from her. So did Fiona, who picked up Del's card and swapped it out for the seat right next to Anna.

"I saw what you did there!" Lula laughed.

Fiona shrugged innocently, and Anna said nothing but smiled.

"Geez. Some of these names are unpronounceable. I have an N-d-h-l-o-v-u from Malawi sitting next to me?" Fiona spelled out the letters on the name card. "I don't even know where Malawi is."

"It's right next to Tanzania," Anna said as she nudged her chair closer to Del's.

"Which is . . . ?" Fiona asked.

"Just north of Malawi." Anna laughed.

The sun beat down sharp and bright, and the three friends took frequent breaks beneath the shade of the bur oak to drink lemonade from tin cans that Mrs. Gloria brought out.

By early evening, most of the farm staff had returned from the fairgrounds and were cleaning up for the night's event. There was a brief pause as a quiet spread out across the farm. The kitchen staff was now down to a skeleton crew, the barnyards were empty, and the three friends sat lazily around the big kids' table arguing about the proper etiquette for greeting guests from different countries.

Anna was the first to notice the cloud of dust coming down the lane. Their first visitor. She straightened her shirt and tucked her hair behind her ear, only to be surprised to see Tyler's truck coming over the hill. The floodlight mount still sat crooked on the roof of his truck, its lights pointing in different directions like a chameleon's eyes, and the sides of the truck were streaked with dirt from the soybean fields two nights before.

Tyler pulled the truck to a stop and smiled as he gave a half salute to the three friends. Scout jumped out of the passenger side and didn't look back. He was wearing a shirt buttoned up to the neck, and his hair was parted sharply to the side.

"I'll pick you up by ten thirty," Tyler called out the window. "Have fun."

Scout raised his hand without looking back as his brother pulled away and headed back down the road.

"Have fun? Did he really just say . . . have fun?" Fiona said.

"Crazy, right? He's been like this ever since he got up yesterday. He even asked if I wanted to play catch." Scout shook his head.

"With a knife?" Lula asked.

"Yeah, no. A football. Go figure," Scout said. "I think he's planning on killing me in my sleep."

Anna stared at the truck disappearing down the dirt lane and wondered what had happened in those few minutes that Mara and Tyler were alone. Had she altered his brain? Made him docile? Replaced him with a bot? She made a mental note to ask later.

The sun began to cast long shadows across the lawn as the first guests arrived. Lights had been strung above the tables and around the perimeter, like Christmas, and added to the warm glow of the evening. Music drifted from the PA system that sat atop the front porch, which now served as center stage.

The four friends took turns guiding arriving guests to their tables. Many of the faces they recognized from the farm or around town, but others were new. Some hesitant, some expectant. Some were dressed in jeans and clean T-shirts. Some braved wearing a suit on a hot summer day. And some wore clothes with bright colors and unfamiliar patterns from their own countries.

Something in the color of the sky, the sounds of the yard, and the collection of unfamiliar faces reminded Anna of her very first day on the farm those many months before. She smiled. It felt like a lifetime had passed—like she had always known Mara, and how to fly, and that there were holes in space-time that allowed you to travel to other worlds.

Dr. Gloria arrived wearing jeans and dress boots and a brand-new cowboy hat he wore tilted back on his head. He began making the rounds, shaking hands and embracing old friends and dragging some guests from table to table to make introductions. Wherever he went, he brought a kind of energy that freed people from their seats and increased the pitch of their conversations until they competed with the din of cicadas and crickets on the periphery. By the time Uncle Jack arrived, the yard was alive with the murmur of conversations and movement.

As Anna headed back to her own table after seating the last of the guests, she caught sight of Del for the first time. He smiled when he saw her and maintained eye contact until she sat down next to him. Her leg brushed against his. She had set her chair too close. But neither seemed to mind. Neither one moved.

Fiona and Lula were in deep conversation with a young woman from Malawi, and Scout was entertaining the far end of the table. Somehow, against all odds, his quirky sense of humor and exaggerated intonation translated well across language and culture.

"It's good to see you, Anna," Del said. "Are you still running?"

"No, I decided to try flying instead," Anna said.

For a moment, Del looked confused and a little embarrassed, then Anna could see a perceptible light go off and a broad smile brighten his face.

"That's funny," Del said.

Before he could go on, the staticky squawk of feedback from the PA system cut through the evening air. People turned their heads and looked for the source of the sound. Conversations dropped midsentence.

Thump . . . thump . . . thump.

"Can you all hear me?" Uncle Jack asked as he thumped the microphone.

He stood on the front porch. He wore a clean white dress shirt, fresh from its packaging. Wrinkles from the fold cut straight lines down the front and back. He held the microphone with a tightly clenched fist as if he were unsure whether to speak into it or use it to pound in loose nails on the porch steps.

"Man, there are a lot of folks out there," Uncle Jack said. He paused as he looked from table to table. "I see a bunch of old friends here tonight, and some new ones too. I see a lot of smart people I can't wait to learn from this week, and some who are definitely better dressed."

"That doesn't take much, Jack!" Dr. Gloria shouted from the front table. His voice carried across the lawn. There were ripples of laughter from the crowd and some verbal affirmations, almost like a church sermon. Uncle Jack shook his head and grinned.

"One thing we all share—we're optimists. Am I right? Because we have to be. Otherwise, we wouldn't have chosen farming as a profession. For many of us, if we're not fighting a changing climate, we're fighting Big Ag or policies that promote bad decisions for the land and ourselves. It doesn't have to be this way. And I genuinely believe this group here, along with thousands of other small sustainable groups just like ours, can help turn agriculture around before it's too late. Can help transform our trade and our relationship with the soil, and in the process make the world a healthier and more just place. I promised to keep this short for your sake and mine.

But before I go, I want to thank everyone who made it here tonight, especially for you folks who traveled great distances. Take advantage of this week we have together. Share what you know and be ready to learn. At the end of the day, it's the connections and friendships we make here that'll make the difference." Uncle Jack placed the microphone back on top of the PA system and signaled for everyone to follow. "Now let's eat before we all pass out."

Lines formed near the food tables and snaked out into the yard as smells from the newly opened serving trays drifted on a slight evening breeze. Scout raced to the front of the line, with Fiona and Lula not far behind, leaving Anna and Del alone at their table.

The two sat close together, their knees still touching, but they looked in separate directions at the crowd of people on the lawn. An awkward silence began to form between them, and Anna knew if something wasn't said soon, that silence would grow into a wall that neither one could scale by the end of the evening. She turned to face Del.

"I wasn't expecting this," Anna said.

"You mean all these people? Yeah, me neither. Uncle Ricardo just asked if I wanted to come to some dinner," Del said as he turned. "And he said you'd be here."

Anna tried not to read too much into that last part, but she couldn't help it as a broad smile brightened her face.

"If you'd asked me earlier if meeting kids from Africa and Asia was on my bingo card tonight, I would have said no," Anna said.

"We're playing bingo?"

"No. I . . . uh. Sorry, it's just an expression," Anna said, then tried to change the direction of the conversation. "Are you going to the fair?"

"Oh yeah. The midway opens up tomorrow night," Del said. "That's usually when I go."

"Midway?"

"Yeah, midway. You know. That's where the carnival is. Arcades and games and stuff. There's also a concert stage, but nobody good ever performs here. The rides are pretty gnarly, though," Del said.

"Gnarly like in a good way or bad?" Anna asked.

"I don't know. Kinda both." Del shrugged. "Are you going?"

"I guess so. I know my uncle wants me to be there for some of the presentations," Anna said.

"The fair stuff should be done by then, so you're good," Del said, then paused. "Do you want to meet at the midway tomorrow night? Maybe we can walk around together. I'll steer you clear from the rides that get you sick."

Anna felt a rush through her body, a combination of euphoria and nausea, like a freefall when flying. She breathed in deep until the feeling ebbed away just enough.

"That sounds great," Anna said. She felt herself holding a look too long and turned away from Del and out to the yard. "You think we should go get something to eat?"

Del nodded, and the two stood up and headed toward the back of the food line. On the way, they passed their friends who were now returning to the table. Fiona winked knowingly as she passed. Lula smiled from ear to ear, her eyebrows working like handles. Scout was expressionless—mouth open and eyes huge behind his glasses—as he stared at the two walking by.

———

As the sun set, the lights strung around the perimeter took on a greater role, their glow lighting the grounds in a warm haze. Conversations became more animated with the cooler air, and there was a steady migration of people from table to table as the evening wore on. Groups shifted in size from large to more intimate. The younger kids gathered around the dessert table, and carafes of coffee needed to be replenished on a frequent basis, ensuring the night would go on for some time.

"Did you notice that little dynamic over there?" Jack leaned over to Mara and pointed to Anna and Del on the far side of the lawn.

"How could I miss it?" Mara said. "They're quite awkward."

"Aren't we all." Jack laughed. He then pointed to the front porch, where Scout sat alone, eating a second serving of rhubarb pie. "But I bet you missed that over there. The poor guy keeps looking over at Anna every ten seconds. You can set your watch to it."

"That's Scout, isn't it? I feel for him. I feel for all of them. How do they navigate this age with all this uncertainty? It seems inhumane," Mara said. She watched Anna from a distance and marveled at how much she had changed. "And the hormones don't help."

"No, they don't." Jack shook his head.

Mara pulled her chair away from the table and turned to face Jack.

"Jack, I know the fair is starting tomorrow, but I have something I need to do," she said.

"Is everything okay?"

"Everything is fine, but I was wondering if I could steal Anna away for a couple hours in the afternoon," Mara said.

"Sure. The schedule doesn't really pick up until Saturday, anyway," Jack said. "What's going on?"

"It's a surprise. Something I promised Anna a while ago, and I think it's time to make good on that promise," Mara said.

CHAPTER 54

Mara was standing near the shore of the lake when Anna arrived. The noonday sun beat down directly overhead, sandwiched between two towering cumulus clouds that billowed out in folds of white against a deep blue sky.

Anna descended softly, her feet lightly touching the ground as she landed. A metallic silver box sat on the grass just behind Mara, whose arms were folded across her chest. Her expression was unreadable. Stoic.

"What's going on? Everything okay?" Anna asked as she dropped her backpack to the ground.

"That depends. Are you ready?"

"For . . ."

"Lunch," Mara said as she allowed a grin to soften her face.

"Really? You had me worried."

"Today is a special day, Anna. I'm not one for celebrations. But considering the success of our recent work, I wanted to show you my thanks," Mara said. "Do you remember asking for a picnic in the sky?"

"Yeah, why?" Anna grinned. "Is that what the box is for?"

"Oh, no. That's a different surprise. Lunch is just the start."

Anna looked around the lawn and then back to Mara.

"I don't see any food. Are we going somewhere to eat?" Anna asked.

"Yes, we are," Mara said, then pointed directly up with her index finger. "Approximately two thousand meters straight overhead."

"You're serious," Anna said.

"Almost always," Mara said. "I created a floating terrace for us, where we can hang our legs over the edge and take in the view and eat. Sounds nice, doesn't it? It also serves as a good launchpad."

"Launchpad?"

"You'll see. Go ahead and open the box. I'll explain as you try it on," Mara said.

Anna kneeled over the box and placed a finger on the small indent in the center of the metallic surface. The top of the box slid back and revealed a white bodysuit, just like Mara's, folded neatly in half. The fabric glistened and shifted colors as she removed it from the box and held it in front of her. The top of the bodysuit had a hood and attached gloves, and the bottom had full leggings that would cover her feet.

"You want me to try this on here? Out in the open?" Anna asked.

"You could always change in the water if that makes you more comfortable."

Anna looked around skittishly then removed her shoes, T-shirt, and jeans and threw them in a ball near the box. She hurriedly put on the leggings first. The material felt slightly thicker than the shirt Mara had given her before, but it was just as light and pliable. The fabric wrapped around her like a second skin and formed a tight seal. No gaps or folds, just a perfect fit. There was a thin layer of soft padding that molded to the bottom of her feet. She pulled the top over her head and down to her waist with no effort, and just like the leggings, the fabric formed a tight seal once in place. The hood hung loose behind her.

"The fabric feels thicker," Anna said as she swung her arms back and forth across her body.

"That's to help regulate your body temperature and protect you from changes in atmospheric pressure," Mara said.

"Atmospheric pressure?" Anna asked. "Where are we going?"

Mara smiled and waited for her young friend to catch up.

"No, it's where *you* are going," Mara said. "Do you remember I once asked you what you wanted to do most in this life?"

"Yeah. Vaguely."

"And?"

"And, I said I wanted to go to—" Anna stopped. Her eyes opened wide, and her arms hung to her sides.

"Space?" Mara finished her sentence.

"Yeah—wait," Anna said. "You mean, like, space? Today?"

"That was the plan."

"So you're saying this suit will get me into space? It has everything I need? Antigravity boots?" Anna asked excitedly.

"Built right in. And radiation protection, thermal protection. Trust me, you'll be fine," Mara said. "The question is, how high do you want to go?"

"As far as I can," Anna said as she began bouncing on her toes.

"Safely."

"Sure, safely. But at least fifty miles. That's the altitude you need to earn your astronaut wings," Anna said.

"SID will make sure you track with Earth's rotation and that you don't wander off into the vacuum of space. That wouldn't be good," Mara said. "But you control everything else. Are you ready?"

Anna didn't wait. She flung her backpack over her shoulders

and shot up straight into the sky. Mara looked up at the streaking figure and shook her head.

"You might want to wait for me. You have no idea where we're going."

———

Anna could see the blue outline of the floating terrace from several hundred feet away. It was elliptical and blended in with the towering cumulus cloud. They both landed gently on the transparent surface. Below their feet, they could see lower-hanging clouds drift past, as well as a flock of birds and a green patchwork of forest and farmland. In the middle of the invisible terrace sat an old-fashioned picnic basket that looked to be suspended in midair.

Mara carried the basket to the ledge and opened it. Inside were two large sandwiches, two glass containers of water, almonds, sliced cheese, grapes, and assorted small pastries and chocolates.

"Did you make this?" Anna asked.

"Of course not. I ordered it from Ivanhoe Diner," Mara said. "The chocolate things are amazing, by the way. You should try them first."

"I like your priorities."

"Did you know that I had never tasted chocolate before yesterday? Cacao doesn't exist in my time."

"Really?" Anna said between mouthfuls. Chocolate lined her teeth. "That's tragic."

The two sat down and let their legs dangle over the edge and began to dig into their sandwiches, which contained goat cheese, sliced green apples, and salted ham. Another first for Mara, who closed her eyes after every bite.

"Do you have any advice for my first spaceflight?" Anna asked.

"No, you know everything you need to know. And SID will make sure you don't go too far off track," Mara said. "But I might recommend waiting a couple of minutes to let your stomach settle. Trust me on that one."

"How long can I stay up there?"

"It'll take you about fifteen to twenty minutes to make it to the edge of the thermosphere. Another fifteen to twenty to come back. You just need to make it back in time for the fair tonight. So I figure you can spend an hour or so up there. You'll be surprised how quickly time will pass," Mara said.

"Why don't you come with me?"

"Because *you* have the special suit," Mara said. "It's also something that may be best experienced in solitude."

"Are you just going to hang around here then?" Anna asked.

"Hang around here, enjoy the view," Mara said, then reached into the basket for one of the cherry tarts. "And finish off the rest of these."

Anna laughed, then wiped her hands on her legs. She reached behind and grabbed her backpack, opened it up, and pulled out her sketchpad and pencil. The breeze blew her hair across her face and made the pages of her sketchbook flutter so that she had to hold down the edges of one side with her elbow.

She looked out directly in front of her and watched the clouds slowly churn and shape-shift like milk in water. The cloud tower had grown since they'd arrived and now rose several thousand feet above their heads. And there they sat, in a canyon of rolling clouds. It felt like a childhood dream, where she could just reach out and scoop up a handful of cloud and eat it like candy. It felt like Mt. Olympus, and she was Mercury, flying high above the ground. She looked down at her sketchbook and realized she would never be able to capture what she saw at this moment. She decided it was better to just try to hold on to this feeling for as long as she could.

The two sat silent for several minutes, then Anna closed her sketchbook and placed it back into her backpack. Just as she leaned back, a stiff, cool gust of wind laced with moisture blew across their faces. Droplets of water frosted their hair and tickled their skin. Anna wiped her hand across her goggles and began to laugh.

"Well, that was a lovely damp rag," Anna said. "There's a lot of moisture in the air. Are you sure a storm isn't coming?"

"I double-checked before we left. We're good. These clouds will begin to thin out in another hour, so you should have a beautiful return," Mara said as she brushed her hands off and stood up. She reached down and offered her hand. "Are you ready? It's time."

"I think so." Anna giggled as she took Mara's hand and pulled herself up. "Is it okay to say I'm nervous?"

"I'd say something was wrong if you weren't," Mara said. "Here, put on your hood. You'll want to make sure it's a solid seal."

Mara helped place the hood over Anna's mop of thick hair, and just like the rest of the suit, the hood instantly formed a tight seal around her face. Anna activated her mask and heard an audible click as it attached to the rest of her suit. She ran her gloved fingers across the sides of her face, then down her sides. There were no visible seams. No exposed skin.

"How fast can I go?"

"I'll leave that to you," Mara said.

"I can't believe this is happening. Thank you, Mara. For everything," Anna said.

"Of course," Mara said. "Now go."

Anna took in a deep breath, clenched her fists, then looked up into the sky. "See you soon."

And with that, Anna shot into the air, her white suit a blur against the cathedral of clouds that swirled around her. Mara stared straight up, with her hand shielding her eyes, until the faint blue line that tracked Anna's progress faded to nothing.

"SID, can you tell me what she's seeing?"

———

Within seconds, Anna had raced past the top of the cumulus tower and was flying in the clear. The sun was blinding at this height, and the sky was a monochrome deep blue. She looked down. Just on the edges of the cloud bank, the rest of the world opened up, and Anna could make out vast swaths of farmland and rolling hills. She could see the shadows cast by smaller cotton-ball clouds rolling across the landscape. Lakes and small ponds, rivers and streams reflected the full glare of the sun in brief flashes like sparkling jewels.

It took her less than eighteen seconds to climb another mile, and Anna let out a shout of pure joy.

Within minutes, she'd passed through contrails formed by jets crossing the continent beneath her. She was now above the flight paths and ascending quickly. A mile every thirteen seconds and accelerating. Her body was a dart, barely registering any turbulence.

From this height, towns and cities became gray, crystal-like formations with sharp edges and odd lines. Roads and highways ran like threads, connecting the cities, until they blended into a landscape of green and brown, and signs of civilization began to lose their edges.

As more of the landscape opened up, Anna was surprised to see that there were no map lines dissecting the terrain beneath her. She laughed to herself at how she had been conditioned to look for boundaries. At this height, she saw no parallels or meridians, just a continuum of land and water. She had always prided herself on being a person of the world, but she never felt that physical reality like she did at this moment. She was an inhabitant of this entire planet, not a square on the map.

Minutes later, Anna could make out the Great Lakes hundreds of miles to the north—impossibly big, like oceans. From this height, she saw a world she had seen only in books, but those images didn't prepare her for this. The colors in those photos weren't nearly as bright, and they didn't reveal the myriad shades and contours, the dimensionality of a great space unfolding beneath her.

The sky was darkening, even as the sun shined brighter—a strange juxtaposition she didn't expect. She also didn't expect the absolute and total silence that enveloped her, that gave her a sense she was floating even though she was now flying at almost half the speed of sound. Her earlier elation gave way to a quiet sense of calm, and she thought of the little girl who once leaped off the edges of beds and the sides of houses in hopes of breaking free of Earth's gravity. But this moment was nothing like her earlier imaginings, with their flat primary colors and simple line strokes that represented topographical changes. Up here, she sensed the unfolding of geologic time. The topography swirled and flowed in countless shades of green, and the clouds looked like small wisps of foam clinging to the surface of an ever-changing landscape.

More minutes passed. The night-blue sky gave way to the great darkness beyond, and Anna could see Earth's horizon as a curved line for the first time. She was getting closer. Stars dotted the midnight-blue dome above her. Higher still and she could see Earth's atmosphere as a curved line too, but it looked so fragile and impossibly thin. How could so much exist within that delicate shell—all of her life and everyone and everything she had ever known contained within its limits?

She checked her iCom and saw she was now over sixty-seven

kilometers above her home (or forty-two miles, as she did the math in her head). Temperatures had dropped far below zero, but she couldn't tell. Her insulated suit constantly adjusted to the variations in temperature and radiation exposure. It had taken less than twenty minutes to travel this far, and she was now well into the mesosphere, the great in-between. No longer tethered to Earth but not yet part of space, Anna felt her connection to home loosen. It was a strange, humbling feeling. As more space opened beneath her and above her, her sense of self began to dissolve.

We really are wanderers, she thought. She remembered having this craving even as a young child, not just to break free of the confines of Earth but to discover new worlds and new ways of seeing. But now, so close to open space, she began to question whether that desire was something she was born with or more of a beckoning that originated somewhere out there, in the stars.

Her iCom showed she was now ninety-three kilometers above Earth—more than high enough to earn her astronaut wings, but she wanted to go even farther, to the very edge of space. She slowed her ascent but didn't notice a change in acceleration, and for a moment she wondered if she had gone too far. She closed her eyes and felt herself tumbling backward. Panic set in, and she looked to her iCom for reassurance. Her altitude readings continued to tick up. She was headed in the right direction after all, but now at a much slower pace. *A trick of low gravity.*

If she traveled just a little farther out, she knew she'd end up leaving this planet forever. Anna stopped her ascent and floated with her arms spread out to her sides. The endless sea of stars seemed to take on a depth she never saw on Earth—a three-dimensional image she felt she could reach out and touch.

The desire to keep going was strong, but a new feeling, even stronger, began to take hold. She missed home. Mara was wrong. She said time would fly by. Instead, Anna felt as if she'd been gone a lifetime.

She looked back down and had to reconcile two competing perspectives: how grand and immense the view was beneath her while being fragile and small and precious. She thought of what Mara had told her yesterday—about the rapid changes her world would soon see—and suddenly felt a desire to somehow protect it.

<Anna?>

SID's voice sounded unbearably loud in the quiet of space.

"I'm sorry, SID, but could you lower your voice?"

<Pitch or volume?>

"Volume, please." Anna had softened her own voice to a whisper. "What do you need?"

<You're now at the edge of space. I've limited your capacity to travel any higher as a precaution. But feel free to stay as long as your oxygen levels allow. It's quite beautiful, isn't it, Anna?>

"Yes, it is, SID."

<Signing off now until you return. Mara wants you to enjoy the view.>

Anna didn't respond. She wanted nothing more than to enjoy these final few minutes in quiet, to take in as much as she could before she returned home. Half of the world to the left of her, half of the world to her right. Then, suddenly, a red flash caught the corner of her eye.

Her first thought was that it had originated from inside her eye, a flicker across her visual field due to a change in pressure. Or maybe it was a meteor disintegrating off the mesosphere just beneath her. She looked to her left and waited.

Another red flash. This time there was no mistaking it.

It filled her line of vision for less than a second, like lightning, and left a fading afterimage burned on her eyes: a large elliptical ball at the top and tendrils that dangled beneath like a clump of roots that had been yanked from the ground.

"Wow! Did you see that, SID? I think I just saw red lightning. Is that even a thing, or am I going crazy?" Anna called out across her iCom.

Anna floated in silence, waiting for a response. The seconds ticked off, but still no reply.

"SID? Can you hear me?"

Still no response. Slowly, a crawling, hollow feeling began to work its way out from her stomach to her chest. She started taking in short, quick breaths. Another bout of panic began to set in, and a feeling of complete isolation, like she was floating adrift in the middle of the sea with no land or friendly face to be seen for thousands of miles.

"SID?!"

<Anna! Get back here as fast as you can. Mara is in trouble.>

CHAPTER 55

"**W**here is she now, SID?" Mara asked as she swung her legs back and forth over the edge of the terrace.

<*Just leaving the stratosphere and entering the mesosphere. Forty-eight kilometers and climbing.*>

"How are her vitals?" Mara asked.

<*Surprisingly steady. She shows no sign of elevated heart rate. Breathing is normal.*>

"That's my girl. Calm and collected as always," Mara said.

She looked out at the clouds swirling around her and the lush green farmland far below. The newness of open green spaces still thrilled her. In her time, there were no sweeping vistas outside the manicured safe zones. She thought of how quickly this would all change—the droughts and shifting climate. Even now, she could see some of the earliest impacts.

Mara took a final drink of water, placed the container back in its compartment, and closed the picnic basket. Just to the left, Anna's backpack lay open, and the corner of her black sketchbook poked out. As Mara reached over to close the backpack, a gust of wind buffeted her side and pushed the bag several feet away. The sketchbook fell out and slid to the middle of the terrace, its pages flapping in the wind.

"When will these gusts die down, SID?" Mara asked. "I was expecting a little calmer weather by now."

<*That gust was an anomaly, but not unexpected. It was likely a hyperlocal weather event that was never recorded. You should expect decreasing winds over the next hour.*>

"Can you tell me what she is seeing now?" Mara asked as she stood up to retrieve the contents of the backpack before they scattered to the wind.

<*The curvature of the Earth and the thin envelope of our atmosphere.*>

"That should change her life," Mara said softly. She picked up the backpack and the sketchbook and returned to the ledge. "Even though she's seen so much already."

She opened Anna's notebook and began flipping through its pages. The first few pages contained rough sketches of the farm and a surprisingly realistic version of Dr. Gloria, down to his laugh lines and cowboy hat. Anna was less successful with Jack, whose broken nose took on cartoonish proportions. There were sketches of Mara's home and the two of them flying for the first time together—silhouettes against a bank of clouds.

<*Anna will reach the exosphere in approximately one minute. I'm going to alert her that I'm limiting her ability to fly any higher. Do you have any message you want me to convey?*>

"Just tell her to enjoy the view," Mara said, then returned her attention to the notebook.

She flipped the page and saw a rendering of an alien landscape, so detailed she could make out the individual dewdrop-shaped leaves along the canopy of a forest. They were sketches of the first alien planet Anna had visited, and the drawings helped connect the myriad stories Mara had heard over the past month. One sketch showed small four-legged animals along the canopy, and another sketch that spanned two pages showed two cascading rivers and a towering crag of a mountain range. The next series of sketches revealed a great plain of grass and giant trees that rose hundreds of meters in the air like skyscrapers.

For all the wonders Mara had seen in her own life, she felt a twinge of regret that she was unable to travel alongside Anna during her adventures to other worlds. She had been close. She had touched the wormhole and felt its pull and seen unfamiliar stars on the other side, but even now she had no idea what force prevented her from entering.

<I've conveyed your message to Anna. She'll be returning shortly.>

"Thank you, SID. Just keep an eye on her. We want her home safely, and on time for—"

She flipped the page and stopped cold. A fear, deep and black, gripped her entire body as the winds suddenly died down to complete stillness. Silence.

On the page, staring back at her from a universe away, was an image of the Others.

"No," Mara whispered.

She flipped to the next page. Scrawled out in rough black strokes was a sticklike creature dressed in black, with bone-white skin and holes for eyes—holes filled with spinning star formations. Its mouth was gaping open and its finger pointed off the page directly toward Mara.

"No, no, no! This is impossible," Mara cried out to no one.

<Mara. What is it?>

She flipped to the end of the book and saw more pictures of the Others, peering out from behind strange, squatty trees and across space and time. She had been found.

"Why didn't she tell me?" Mara said.

<You're concerning me, Mara. What is wrong?>

She was still gripped by dread, but rising quickly beneath

it like a river was a sense of absolute loss and sadness. She felt paralyzed, unable to look up from the page.

"Why now?"

<Mara. Please.>

Mara didn't respond. The wind began to pick up again, this time in gusts that blew her hair across her face and buffeted her ears. But she didn't notice. Clouds began to swirl around the terrace. The sky darkened.

<I'm detecting a new energy signal, strong and very close. I estimate within one hundred meters.> SID paused as it tried to identify the optimal tone of voice to break through to Mara. *<I'm sorry, Mara. But I believe the Others have returned.>*

A new feeling began to run roughshod through her body as the winds kicked up even higher. Anger and frustration at the unfairness. She shoved the sketchbook back into the backpack and leaped to her feet. Within the last minute, the canyon of soft white clouds had turned into a dark gray wall, threatening her from all sides.

"SID! Get Anna on the iCom. Tell her to get down here now!"

Rain began to bounce off the terrace surface and poured off the edges in streams. A sharp gust of wind knocked Mara off her feet and forced her to activate her antigravity boots as the terrace tilted to the side like a boat in rough waters.

<I can't reach Anna. The energy signature is interfering with my communications.>

"Try again!" Mara shouted above the wind.

It took all her focus to not be tossed like a rag doll in the winds. A deep, low rumble emerged from within the wall of clouds like a giant ancient door opening. It echoed out across the canyon of clouds and forced Mara to put her hands over her ears. Balls of lightning began to pop like flashbulbs along the surface of the clouds—temporarily blinding Mara— followed by the sharp crack of rapidly expanding air.

<I was able to reach Anna, just for a moment. She's return-ing now.>

"Tell her—" Mara started, but was hit with a percussive wall of wind that spun her full circle. She struggled to stay upright. "Tell her to avoid the storm."

<I'm sorry, but I've lost contact again.>

"Can you track her?" Mara shouted.

<Yes.>

"Then find a way for me to get to her, now!"

<Taking over control of your navigation systems.>

Mara could feel the micro-adjustments in her antigravity boots as SID helped guide her toward a small clearing in the clouds. Even with SID aiding her flight, she felt helpless against the gale-force winds.

"I'm going to try to contact Anna myself," Mara said. She felt as if the air were being pulled from her lungs. She activated her mask and tried to steady her breath. "Anna! Can you hear me? Avoid the storm. I'll meet you on the northernmost edge of the cloud bank."

No response.

Mara strained to hear any sign from her young friend. But nothing. Anger welled up inside her again as her muscles tensed and adrenaline flowed, giving her a short burst of energy. She began to thrash against the wind like a swimmer against a riptide.

Then, just inside her peripheral vision, a figure appeared to float in the air just above her and to the right. Mara didn't need to turn her head fully. She knew who was there. Hovering less than a hundred feet above her was the Other. Its sticklike figure was a black silhouette against a wall of slate-gray clouds.

The world seemed to slow down, and even through the winds, Mara could hear her heartbeat in her ears. Two other figures materialized from the clouds and floated, unmoving and impervious to the winds, just behind the first.

"Why now?" Mara whispered, but somehow she knew the Others could hear. "I promise. I'll go. Just leave me alone and don't harm my friends."

The Others remained silent, like still waters. Flashes of light in the clouds behind them outlined their bone-white faces in an unearthly glow.

"Please."

Mara felt a tingling sensation build throughout her body just before the world came to an end. Jagged lightning lashed out and struck the floating terrace in an explosion of plasma, superheating the air and dissolving the small platform into a mass of tiny translucent cubes that quickly evaporated in the wind. The picnic basket and Anna's backpack exploded in flames as a wall of sound from the rapid expansion and contraction of air hit Mara like a blow to the head.

Dazed, Mara looked up. A swirling column of gray clouds began to circle her and the Others, faster and faster, until her body, in the center of the vortex, began to spin like a leaf caught in an eddy of a stream.

CHAPTER 56

"**M**ara! Can you hear me?" Anna repeated over her iCom. It had been eight minutes since Anna had heard from SID, and in that time she had covered almost the entire distance of her return journey. Her speed was now close to 375 miles per hour, her body a small blur, falling like a rocket in re-entry. During her descent, lights flashed erratically under the cumulonimbus dome just beneath her, like old war footage of cluster bombs. A storm was raging below her, and her friend was stuck in the middle of it.

How could Mara have missed so badly on the weather today? She knew every element of the daily weather, from wind speed to dew points to the amount of fine particulate matter in the air. Maybe she was distracted, or the data was corrupt. Either way, Anna wasn't going to let her friend live this down once they were both safe and on the ground.

She rapidly approached the top of the cloud dome. At this distance, the clouds looked like a living thing, swirling at impossible speeds. Anna broke the outer edge of the storm and immediately found herself flying blind in a dark gray fog. It took her a moment to adjust to the change in light as ice and water streaked across her face mask and blurred her vision. She checked her iCom for the coordinates of the terrace and felt a renewed sense of dread. The terrace was gone. She tried to lock on to Mara and was unable to find a trace or signal.

Anna instinctively slowed down as she tried to figure out what to do next. Mara would want her out of the storm and harm's way. But there was no way she was going to leave her friend behind, not while there was a chance she was still in danger. Anna played back her flight path and identified the location of her initial launch. Another fifteen thousand feet down and to the left. Anna pressed her arms to her sides to reduce drag and picked up speed.

Air currents rocked her body, but her suit protected her from the sting of rain and hail. The silence of her earlier flight was now replaced with the continuous rumble of thunder as lights flashed all around her, leaving afterimages like blooming flowers.

Four hundred feet to go and the clouds began to part, revealing a small clearing no more than a couple hundred feet across, surrounded by clouds spinning in a circular motion. In the middle of the vortex, she saw a figure struggling against the winds. It was Mara.

Anna was buffeted in all directions, but she maintained her course. Two hundred feet away and she could see that Mara was still conscious. Fifty feet and she locked eyes with Mara, who looked up with an expression of both surprise and exhaustion.

Anna looked at the spin of the vortex and tracked the direction of the wind currents on her iCom. She had to grab Mara at the right angle or she would run the risk of being sucked into the same twisting current. Anna followed the center of the vortex, where the winds were most calm, for as long as she could, then hurled herself in Mara's direction at the very last second.

Her arm reached out and caught Mara's arm like a hook, pulling her free from the spinning force. The two clung to each other as they hit the edge of the winds, and their bodies shot out toward the ground like rocks fired from a trebuchet. Anna pulled Mara even tighter, and Mara clung on now with both hands.

Free from the vortex, Anna began to gradually reduce their speed, though the winds still buffeted them from side to side. She looked over at Mara. The clouds were so dense that she could see only feet ahead, and the rain streaked their masks. Mara was silently mouthing words, but she couldn't hear. Anna tapped her ear and shook her head.

Suddenly, a streak of light reflected off Mara's mask. At first Anna thought it was another lightning strike. But the light was warm and sustained and fell at a precise angle. Sunlight poured through a clearing just above their heads as the clouds began to thin all around them. Anna looked up and saw more streaks of sunlight break through as the storm quickly retreated, faster than she had ever seen clouds dissipate before.

The two continued to fly, arm in arm, toward the rapidly approaching ground. The skies were now clear, and both could make out the lake and the shining spire outside Mara's home, but the two were still surrounded by the last of the falling rain that glistened in the sunlight like tiny drops on fire. Anna looked down. They were flying faster than the last of the downpour, and it created the illusion that the rain was flying upward, time winding in reverse. As Anna slowed down, the rain looked frozen in midair for a brief moment before natural order was restored and the rain continued its path downward.

Anna still held on to her friend as they lightly touched down on the lawn outside Mara's home. The grass glistened in the sun, and the last barrage of the rain pelted the lake in small splashing sounds just seconds later. Then silence.

Anna released her mask and pulled back her hood. Her

hair was matted but dry. She put her hands on her knees and tried to regain her breath, as if she had just finished a long race. She looked up, her eyes still wide-open in excitement, then broke out into laughter.

"That was awesome!" Anna said. She put her hands behind her head and looked straight up into the clearing sky. "Oh my God. That was amazing!"

Mara released her own mask and took in short, shallow breaths. She looked dazed. But it was more than that, Anna thought. Mara looked scared and disoriented, her eyes unable to focus on any one spot.

"Mara?" Anna asked. The smile on her face started to fade.

Mara didn't respond.

"Mara? Are you okay?"

Finally, Mara looked up as if she were hearing a distant voice. She took in a deep breath, shook her head, and tried to steady herself.

"Yes. I'm . . . okay," Mara said weakly. She even tried smiling, but it was a thin smile that didn't reflect in her eyes. "I think I'm just a little dizzy."

"What the heck was that? A tornado?"

"I don't know," Mara said.

"And did you see how fast the storm disappeared? That was crazy."

"Yes, it was."

"I guess I don't have to tell you this, but you really biffed it on the weather report." Anna smiled. "What happened up there?"

"I made a mistake. Somewhere. I don't know," Mara said.

"Well, mistake or not, that was still a lot of fun," Anna said. "And now I finally have something to tease you about. So, win-win."

Mara finally allowed a slight smile to cross her face. Her eyes softened.

"You're such a strange one, Anna," Mara said. The light reflected off the bottom edges of her eyes. "That's why I guess I love you."

"You're pretty weird yourself. That's why I guess I love you too," Anna said back. "So, what do you have planned next for me? An asteroid strike? Maybe an alien invasion?"

Mara stared at Anna for a good five seconds without responding. A faint smile crossed her face, both wistful and tired.

"No. I think I'm done for the day," Mara said. "Can you tell your uncle I'm not going to be able to make it to the fair tonight?"

"Yeah. Of course," Anna said, then instinctively took a step forward, bridging the distance between the two. "Hey, are you going to be okay? Because I can stay with you tonight if you want."

"I'll be okay. I just need some rest," Mara answered. "Anyway, shouldn't you be getting ready? I understand you're meeting someone at the fair."

"Oh yeah. I guess I am." She looked at the time on her iCom. "And great. It looks like I've only got about a half hour to get ready, and I have no idea what I'm going to wear. You think maybe you can print me up a really nice-looking outfit?"

"Not this time," Mara said.

"Fine." Anna reached down and picked up her pile of wet clothes she had discarded earlier. "I'll see you tomorrow then, right?"

Mara nodded.

"There's so much I can't wait to tell you," Anna said, then paused. "Thanks again for everything, Mara. I'll never forget today."

They smiled at each other one last time as Anna slowly rose into the air. Mara watched as she flew over the tops of the trees and out of sight, holding on to the image of her young friend for as long as she could. She turned toward her house and sighed deeply, partly out of exhaustion and partly for the long night she knew she had ahead.

<Why didn't you tell her, Mara?>

Tears welled up in Mara's eyes, and she found it hard to breathe.

"It's time, SID. You know what to do," Mara said, her voice flat.

<You can't . . .>

Mara turned off her iCom, silencing SID's voice and any further conversation, then shut the protective barrier behind her.

CHAPTER 57

Del was waiting under the neon-lit entrance of the midway when Anna and her friends arrived. He held strands of pre-purchased ride tickets that stuck out like dried yellow stems. Scout stood just behind him with his back against the archway and his legs spread wide.

"So, where do you want to start?" Del asked.

"This is all new to me. Go ahead and lead the way," Anna said.

They drifted through the entrance, flowing along with a procession of young families, curious farmers, and packs of roaming teens. Del and Anna took the lead, already lost in their own conversation, while the others followed paces behind. Scout bounced from foot to foot trying to maneuver to the front but was blocked at every turn by slow walkers and a flotilla of baby strollers.

"Hey, when did this become a thing?" Scout caught up to Fiona and Lula and nodded in Anna's direction.

"You mean Anna and Del?" Lula asked.

"Yeah."

"I think we're watching it happen in real time," Fiona said.

"I know. Isn't it romantic?" Lula said.

"No. Not really." Scout shook his head. "Seriously, I don't get it."

As they wandered aimlessly through the midway, wasting tickets on the rides with the shortest lines, the color of the evening sky transitioned from a golden haze to a deep plum. Anna looked up and saw the first sprinkling of stars. She had been up there just hours ago—really up there—and missed the quiet of space already. Something about the cacophony of sounds in this place—the screams and shouts and whirr of speeding rides—felt unreal. Time seemed disjointed and splintered. And, for a moment, Anna wished she had just stayed home with Mara after all.

Colored lights flashed from every surface and lit their faces in a succession of neon hues as they walked along. Anna looked over at Del, his tan face almost bone white in the harsh glare of the Whacky Shack, his head crowned by the lights of the Ferris wheel in the distance. He had said something, but she didn't hear it. Something in that light had made her uneasy.

"Are you okay?" Del had to raise his voice above the wooden clacking of the roller coaster. "I thought I lost you for a second."

"No, I'm okay. It's just hard to hear." Anna smiled back. But she wasn't okay, and she couldn't understand why. The last few moments with Mara had thrown her off, and a sense of unease had followed her home and to the midway and was only getting worse as the evening progressed.

"Want to go someplace else?"

"No. Maybe I just need something to eat," Anna said.

The five followed the smell of fried grease and funnel cakes as the off-key organ from the merry-go-round clashed with the music blasting from tinny speakers overhead.

The rides along the midway were all variations on a spinning motion—some fast, some slow, some in perfect circles, some with jarring whipsaw trajectories. They seemed to be building up a field of kinetic energy that Anna could feel in her bones. Her skin itched like static electricity.

"See that ride there? The Claw? I don't recommend eating before you get on that thing," Del said.

"Excuse me?" Anna asked, distracted.

Scout had caught up again and stuck his head over their shoulders.

"Yeah, The Claw, affectionately known as the vomit comet. Questionable safety record, but definitely the best ride on the midway," Scout said. "That is, unless you're afraid to go on it, Armstrong?"

Anna looked down at Scout. At that moment, she wanted nothing more than to throw her friend over her shoulder and rocket him through the sky in a series of barrel rolls to let him experience a real vomit comet firsthand. *Amateur.*

"How would you know, Scout?" Fiona said. "You can't even meet the height requirement."

Scout shoved Fiona, who shoved back harder in return, back and forth, escalating all the way to the concession stand, where Scout finally conceded defeat and rubbed his sore shoulder. The five settled on corn dogs and fries and ate as they walked toward the arcade, their fingers sticky with dripping mustard and no napkins in sight. As they turned the corner, they walked straight into a row of arcade booths covered in candy-striped awnings, and a gauntlet of carnival barkers were shouting out at any passerby within striking distance. Del stopped at the milk-bottle toss and wiped his hands on his legs.

"You want me to win this for you?" Del asked. He nodded toward one of the faded stuffed prizes that hung on the back wall.

Anna looked directly at Del for a moment. She knew he meant no harm, but she was irritated. The too-bright lights and the constant electric buzz of the midway had set her on edge.

"How about this? How about I win it for myself?" Anna said and plopped three wrinkled dollar bills down on the counter.

The barker swooped up the dollar bills with one hand and laid down three large softballs in return.

"Three! Three chances to knock down the bottles. Just step right up," the barker shouted out to no one in particular.

"Forget it, Anna. These games are rigged," Scout said.

The barker leaned over toward Scout.

"Why don't you let the little lady make that decision for herself?"

Anna picked up one of the softballs and tossed it up and down in her hand, estimating the weight and drag and resisting the urge to throw it at the barker's head.

"No, he's right," Anna said as she forced eye contact with the barker. "You're cheating. These balls are corked. I can tell. And the bottle on the bottom right—it's jutting out by almost an inch so it can absorb most of the force."

The barker was used to confrontations, but he seemed to be taken aback by this young girl's fierce gaze.

"Sorry, Einstein. No refunds," the barker said quietly as he looked away.

"No refund needed," Anna said.

She focused in on a spot no more than a quarter inch in size just between the two bottles on the bottom. She factored in the weight of the ball and the required force, then pulled back her arm and whipped it forward using her entire body for leverage. The softball hit with a dull thud as the lead bottles not only toppled but exploded off the entire base.

Anna's friends cheered in unison and clapped her on the back, as Scout pounded the counter and jumped up and down like a monkey. But something was wrong. She couldn't hear anything. Not her friends' voices nor the sound of the crowd. Nothing but a deep buzzing sound, like stray magnetic waves around a transformer box. The sound seemed to come from inside her head, blocking out all other sounds in the midway. Anna shook her head and thought her iCom must be malfunctioning. The buzzing was louder now and had shifted to a different point of origin, just across the alley near the entrance to the Hall of Mirrors. Anna turned as if in a dream and looked past her friends. There in the shadows that marked the entrance, a bone-white face appeared to float in midair. It stared straight ahead with deep-set holes for eyes and opened its mouth in a silent scream.

Anna blinked and the buzzing stopped.

Like the rush of air into a vacuum, the sounds of her friends and the midway returned, and the bone-white face was now replaced by the tired look of a middle-aged father escorting his two small kids out of the Hall of Mirrors. Only seconds had passed, but it had felt like minutes.

"Hey, kid! You want the jalapeño or not?" The barker held out the fluorescent green prize at arm's length.

"No, keep it," Anna said quietly.

"Anna?" Del asked. "Are you sure you're okay?"

"Yeah, I just think it's the noise," Anna said as she rubbed the sides of her temples. "Maybe I'll take you up on your offer to go someplace else."

"How about the Ferris wheel? It's pretty quiet at the top. Want to try that?" Del asked.

"Sounds good to me," Scout said as he put his arm around Del and Anna. "I call outside seat."

Fiona grabbed Scout by the collar and yanked him back with a tug.

"Did you not see the sign? No third wheels on any ride." Fiona looked down at Scout. "Maybe we can get some drinks while they're gone. What do you say, Scout? Your treat."

"And no rush, you two. Take your time." Lula gave an exaggerated wink as Fiona dragged Scout, still protesting, toward the concession area behind her.

Anna glanced back at the shadowed entrance of the Hall of Mirrors. Nothing. Those raw-boned figures were real, she knew it, and they had somehow followed her from her dreams and across the universe to finally arrive here. Del placed his hand against Anna's back and she jumped.

"Sorry. I just . . . ," Del said, embarrassed. "You first."

He returned his hand to Anna's back and guided her toward the Ferris wheel. She could feel the weight and heat of his hand, so foreign, and it took a sustained effort not to just turn around and fly away. The two walked in silence through the crowds toward the towering lights of the Ferris wheel.

Del handed the ride operator a handful of tickets and let him know they'd be staying on for multiple rides. The operator, a recent high school grad not much older than they were, nodded with a knowing glance and waved them into the seats of the swinging bucket.

"Hey, it's not like that," Del protested.

"Sure, kid."

The two stepped into the open bucket, pulled back the restraining bar, and leaned into the seat, their shoulders touching.

The Ferris wheel started with a jolt and the sound of metal gears clicking into place. As they ascended into the night air, the sounds below receded just a bit, enough to allow Anna to finally catch her breath.

"I'm sorry if I've been a little out of it tonight. It's been a superlong day," Anna said. She looked straight out into the neighboring field, its tall grass glowing in the artificial light of the midway.

"No, you're great. I was just afraid. . . ." Del paused.

"Of what?"

"Of, well. I gotta be honest with you, Anna. You kind of scare me," Del said.

"Me? Scare you?" Anna pointed to herself, then chuckled, as if tonight couldn't get any stranger. "Geez, I sound like Tarzan."

"That's what I mean. Right there." Del turned to face her for the first time. "Your brain just works faster than mine. You're funny and smart. You throw like a dude. No offense. And you're the prettiest girl in—"

"You can stop now," Anna cut him off sharply. She could now add awkward and uncomfortable to the night's growing list of dysfunctions.

"No, I mean it," Del said.

"You're serious, aren't you?" Anna asked.

"Yeah. I'm serious." Del smiled. "I like you, Anna."

Anna turned and looked at Del. Any other night, this would have been magic. The lights of the midway in a haze behind them. The warm evening breeze. She tried to block out the ghost image from before and focus on this moment and this boy who sat next to her with his nervous expression and too-bright smile. She reached her hand out for his, then stopped.

The sounds of the midway began to fade behind her and were replaced by a deep hum she felt in her chest. *No, not again.* Lights flickered and dimmed.

Out in the neighboring field, three bone-white figures moved in the tall grasses toward the Ferris wheel, toward Anna. Their movements were erratic, disjointed, and at odd sharp angles. Their eyes now spinning suns that lit up the ground beneath them.

The lead figure stopped at the edge of the field—a short distance from the foot of the Ferris wheel—and looked up toward Anna. She sat frozen in the blinding light, her hand still hanging in midair. She and Del were at the peak of the

Ferris wheel and moving slowly downward in an arc toward the waiting figure. Its gaze patiently tracked her motion as she descended. The creature took a step forward, its feet now on asphalt but its body still behind the barrier, like a parent waiting for their child to finish the ride.

Anna snapped out of her daze and looked around. No one else seemed to notice—not Del, whose mouth hung open, nor the teenage operator, who stood within striking distance of the alien figures. The ride stopped with a lurch, and Anna frantically pushed back the restraining bar just as the creature took another step forward and passed straight through the barrier, its pace now quickening.

She was already in full sprint and weaving through the crowds when she heard Del cry out from behind her.

"Anna! Wait!"

"Nice going, Romeo," the ride operator snickered behind him.

Anna didn't look back as she ran toward the edge of the midway, away from Del and the lights and the ghostlike figures from her dreams. She activated her iCom and didn't care what people thought as she began yelling into her wrist.

"Mara! Can you hear me?"

Silence.

"Please, Mara!"

Anna weaved her way through the crowds and made it to the relative darkness just outside the edges of the midway. She activated her cloaking device and allowed herself one last glance back. The figures were gone. But she could hear Del calling out for her in the distance, his voice rising above the din. She would have to tell him something. Just not now. The only thing that mattered now was to get to Mara as fast as she could. She looked back in the direction of home and took several long strides before floating up and out, swallowed by the night sky.

CHAPTER 58

Anna cleared the trees that lined Tyson Lake and blinked. Mara's home was gone. The shining spire and the rolling green lawns were replaced with a wild meadow surrounded by wetlands leading to the shoreline. It was as if Mara had never existed.

"Mara!" Anna screamed out.

She slowed her flight and began to descend when her feet slammed hard against an invisible surface. The sudden impact sent a jolt through her body and knocked the wind from her lungs. She crouched down on an invisible surface one hundred feet above the ground, feeling the curve of the dome beneath her feet and waiting for her head to clear. The moon reflected bright off the lake and lit the small pools of water in the wetlands far below her like silver coins. Anna knew it was a high-resolution holographic image, but the entire landscape looked exactly the same as when she first arrived those many months ago.

Anna slid down the side of the dome and used her boots to cushion her fall. Once on the ground, she ran her hands along the surface, trying to find a seam that would allow her entrance. But the dome was completely sealed. Anna began to pound on its surface and call out to her friend. Minutes passed, and her calls became more desperate until her voice was hoarse and the sides of her hands raw.

"Mara, please. Why aren't you answering me?" Anna leaned heavily against the invisible wall and slid down to her knees, her face pressed against its cold surface.

Suddenly Anna felt a small vibration on her cheek, followed by a clicking sound. She looked up. Just feet away, an oval-shaped doorway no more than seven feet in diameter opened along the side. Mara stood at the entrance. Her shoulders were slumped, her eyes swollen and red. She'd been crying.

"Mara!" Anna jumped to her feet and ran over. "Why did you lock me out?"

"I'm busy here, Anna," Mara said, her voice distant.

"I don't understand," Anna said.

She looked past Mara to the rolling lawn and the house behind her. A small army of robots was scurrying along the surface of Mara's home, breaking down sections like a house built in reverse. The spire was gone. The roof was gone.

"Go home."

"What's wrong?" Anna pleaded.

She took a step forward as Mara took one step back. Suddenly, a new fear gripped Anna, far worse than the bone-white creatures that had chased her through the midway. This wasn't Mara. Somehow, she had been replaced by this stranger.

"I'm scared, Mara."

"I am too."

"Listen, I came here to warn you. There is something following me. I don't know what they are or why they're here," Anna said. "But I think they may have come from one of the holes. We need—"

"They're not looking for you," Mara cut her off. "They're looking for me."

"What do you mean?"

"I made a mistake. I'm not supposed to be here," Mara said. Her eyes, now tear-rimmed, reflected moonlight. "I'm not supposed to be anywhere."

"Yes you are. You're supposed to be here with me," Anna said.

"If only I could. I'd give anything," Mara said. "But they're coming for me, and when they find me, my life will be erased. I'll never have existed. And the worst part is you won't ever remember me again."

"Then we'll fight them together. I won't let them take you, whatever they are."

"Please, Anna. Just go home. I don't have much time. Tell your uncle I'm sorry."

"No! You tell him yourself. You can't just give up." Anna stepped forward. "Not now. What am I supposed to do?"

"Anna, please. You're making this harder than it has to be," Mara said.

"Because it doesn't have to *be*!" Anna shouted angrily. "Come on. We can figure this out together. We've done it before. You know what these things are, right?"

"Anna."

"If you know what they are, maybe we can find a way to talk to them. Maybe reason with them," Anna said.

"I don't know what they are, but I know what they want. They appeared the day I first time traveled and told me I no longer belonged to this world. And they've been hunting me ever since. For years, I've been hiding. From era to era, from location to location. I hoped I had found a home here. I really did, Anna. You must know that." Mara's voice trembled.

"But you're going to run again."

"Yes."

"So all your talk about protecting my timeline—protecting me—wasn't true. It's never been about me. It's always been about you. You're afraid to fight," Anna said, her hands now bunched in fists.

"Anna."

"I'd fight for you, Mara. I'd do anything for you. To be with you. I just figured you'd have done the same for me," Anna said. The full weight of her words broke through any layers of resistance and strength she had carried with her that night, and she began to sob uncontrollably.

"I only came out here to say goodbye. I felt I owed you that much," Mara said.

"You don't owe me anything," Anna said through clenched teeth. Her voice barely a whisper. "If you're going to go, just go."

"Goodbye, Anna. I'll never forget you. Please don't forget me," Mara said. She paused by the doorway and waited for her friend to reply. But the silence only grew between them like an invisible barrier. Mara paused for one more moment, then stepped back from the edge of the doorway. "Secure all perimeters, SID."

The doorway closed behind her, leaving Anna alone in the meadow. That was it. It was over. Anna looked from side to side in disbelief, then lunged for the section of wall where the doorway stood just seconds before.

"Nooo!" Anna cried out. "Please, Mara. I can't lose you. I can't lose anyone again."

She pounded the wall until the edges of her hand were bruised blue. Her voice started to fade, raw and hoarse, as the moon tracked across the sky. Finally, she slumped exhausted against the side of the invisible wall. She was past crying and even anger. She felt hollowed out and beaten as she turned away from Mara and flew toward home, past the shoreline where she had once learned to fly and the trees she had crossed hundreds of times before.

CHAPTER 59

Anna looked out across the barnyard the next morning. The grounds were quiet. Most of the staff were at the fair, and only a skeleton crew remained. Past the barns and the trees, a dark wall of clouds had formed along the horizon. Anna closed her eyes and laid her head back down on her folded knees and listened to the winds whip through the branches of the old bur oak. She sat on the steps leading to the front porch with her arms wrapped around her legs in a cocoon and breathed shallow breaths.

Behind her, the screen door opened with the sound of squeaking hinges, but she didn't move.

"Morning, Anna. Want to head with me to the—" Uncle Jack stopped. Something about Anna's posture and the way her hair hung down across her face as if she were trying to hide made him stop. "Anna?"

She didn't move.

"Anna?" Uncle Jack asked again.

He sat down next to his niece, put his arm around her shoulder, then noticed the bruises on her wrists and hands. His heart skipped.

"Did someone hurt you?" Uncle Jack asked, his voice lower now.

Anna slowly lifted her head from her knees and glanced over at her uncle with a hollow look, her eyes rimmed red.

"Mara's gone," Anna said.

"What do you mean? When will she be back?" Uncle Jack asked.

"She's not coming back. She's gone," Anna said. "For good."

"Oh. I see," Uncle Jack said, but he clearly didn't see or understand. Anna knew these words were just placeholders until he could fully process what had just been said.

He looked out absently across the barnyard as if he expected to see Mara's motorcycle parked out front, but the barnyard was empty. In the distance, a silent flash of lightning broke through the clouds. A storm was forming early.

"Gone? For good?" Uncle Jack said as he absently withdrew his arm from Anna's shoulder and leaned heavily against his own knees. "Well, that's a real kick in the gut. Did she say why?"

"Not really. Nothing made sense," Anna said.

"I wondered why she didn't come to the fair last night," Uncle Jack said. "Was it her family?"

"She doesn't have any family," Anna said.

"Oh," Uncle Jack said quietly. "I guess I really didn't know her after all."

"Neither did I."

"Are you okay?" Uncle Jack asked.

"No," Anna said, then leaned her head against her uncle's shoulder.

"Me neither." Uncle Jack looked down and gave a weak smile. "Well, it looks like it's just you and me again."

Anna wrapped her arm around her uncle's and pulled herself closer. The two looked out at the swaying trees and the dirt kicking up in small dust devils across the lot. The gate in the front had swung open in the wind and was smacking against the fence like a steady tap against the door. The dark clouds in the distance had mushroomed out into a giant round tower, its outer edges swirling and undulating, and it was moving fast from the north on a straight course toward the farm.

"Hmm. I don't like the look of that storm. We might need to shelter," Uncle Jack said.

From down the road, they could hear faint shouts fading in and out with the gusts of wind. Adrenaline shot through her body. She hoped that it was Mara returning after all. But instead, three small figures appeared over the rise, riding their bikes and shouting as they drew closer.

"Anna!" Scout shouted out as he jumped from his bike and headed through the open gate.

Lula and Fiona followed right behind. Anna looked up at her friends, her hair still matted across her face, and worked up a faint smile.

"How come you didn't answer our texts?" Lula said, her eyes wide and large behind her thick glasses. "We were worried sick."

"I'm sorry."

"Did Del do something to you? Because I don't care how big he is. I'll clock him, I swear," Scout shouted above the wind.

Anna closed her eyes and laid her head back on her knees. She knew they meant well, but she was exhausted. Uncle Jack stood and placed one hand on Anna's shoulder and silently signaled for her friends to give her space.

"Mara is gone," Uncle Jack said softly.

"Oh," Fiona said.

The three friends looked at one another, each face a different expression of concern. They resisted the urge to say anything at that moment, even Scout, and walked slowly up the steps to Anna's side. One at a time, they leaned in, and Anna could feel their weight against her shoulders and back as she stared at a line of ants scurrying in and out of a crack in the wooden steps between her feet.

Lightning flashed again just over the tree line that separated the farm from Tyson Lake. The storm was close now, but it still didn't make a sound except for the wind bending trees and whistling through cracks in the front windows. Lightning struck again and again in the exact same spot, just over the lake several miles away. Still, no sound. And now the dark slate clouds began to spiral ominously.

"Okay, that's not good. Come on, guys. I think it's time we shelter," Uncle Jack said as he signaled for the others to follow. "Come on."

<Anna!>

SID's voice over the iCom startled her and sent prickly shards shooting down her arms and back. She bolted upright, accidentally smacking Scout along the side of his head.

"Owww!"

"SID?!" Anna called out loud, not caring who could hear.

Fiona looked confused. "Who is Sid?"

Anna ignored her friend and stood straight up.

<Mara ordered me not to call you. But I'm calling you anyway, of my own accord. I feel I have the right since you are my friend too. The Others are here.>

"Why didn't you go?!" Anna cried out as if she were speaking to someone from a distance, her gaze toward the storm.

Her three friends stood stunned. Uncle Jack took a step forward.

"Anna. Come on. We need to shelter," Uncle Jack said.

<I can see them, Anna. Even I can see them. There are so many colors, so many stars.> SID's voice was quiet.

Anna turned and looked back, her face now flushed as adrenaline coursed through her body. Her eyes dilated and opened wide.

"I have to go," Anna shouted above the growing wind.

"Not in this storm, Anna!" Uncle Jack shouted back.

Anna leaped from the porch and landed in a crouch. She rose slowly and turned to face her uncle with her hands raised to her sides.

"I'm sorry, but Mara needs me. I'll explain later!" Anna said as her body rose inches from the ground.

For a moment, Uncle Jack was afraid the wind had somehow caught ahold of her and was going to carry her away. But then Anna rose straight up into the sky as if guided by her own will and floated steadily against the swirling winds twenty feet above the ground. Lula sucked in air and made an accidental whistling noise through her teeth as Scout fell back hard on his butt.

"I'll explain all of it later!" Anna shouted, then turned and flew toward the heart of the storm.

———

The storm was in the shape of a cylinder, rising and spinning just above the lake. A giant funnel fixed in space. Three bone-white figures dressed in black floated motionless above Mara's lawn, forming a perfect triangle. Their focus was on a small figure directly beneath them on the ground.

It was Mara. She sat on the grass outside of what used to be her home, now an empty space except for a scattering of silver boxes. She had her arms wrapped around her legs and looked up into the sky. Her eyes were closed and her face serene.

Anna weaved her way past the motionless Others and landed silently on the grass next to Mara. She fell on her knees and leaned forward to put her hands gently on her friend's shoulders. Mara's eyes fluttered open as if she were waking from a deep sleep.

"I'm glad to see you," Mara said.

Anna threw her arms around her friend and buried her

head into her shoulder. Mara's hair covered her face and blocked out the storm and muted the sound of the wind.

"Why didn't you leave when you had a chance?" Anna's voice cracked.

"You're going to have to make up your mind, Anna. Do you want me to stay or go?"

"I'm so sorry. I didn't know what I was saying last night," Anna said as she leaned back on her heels.

"No. You knew exactly what you were saying. And you were right about everything. I was afraid, and that fear almost led me to make the most terrible mistake. Leaving you, your uncle, all this," Mara said. "When I closed the door on you last night, I just stood by the wall and listened to you go on. It broke my heart, Anna. At that moment, I realized I couldn't leave you, but I also couldn't stay. So I sat down right here and looked out across the lake all night and waited for whatever was going to come."

"Maybe there's still a chance. I can distract them." Anna looked up at the floating figures for the first time and felt a sudden sense of vertigo.

Just above the three figures, in the center of the spinning storm, the sky opened up into a tapestry of stars and constellations woven together by a gaseous cloud the color of cobalt blue and the deepest purple Anna had ever seen. The heart of the universe.

"Good luck with that." Mara nodded up toward the sky. "I have to say, it's beautiful, though."

"Why are they just floating there?"

"I don't know, but they don't seem to be in a rush. Which is fine with me. I'm not either. They've just been like that for hours."

"But that's impossible. I saw the storm move in just minutes ago," Anna said.

<Mara is right, Anna. Time here under the storm doesn't

appear to be tracking with external sensors. What appears to be hours for us is just minutes to anything outside this vortex. And the creatures themselves are fascinating. They seem to be composed of a new phase of matter, constantly cycling between states of being without ever losing energy. That has profound philosophical implications, don't you think? I'm going to continue to run tests for as long as I can.>

"Oh, there is still so much to learn." Mara sighed. "I'm glad you came, Anna. I didn't want last night to be the way you remembered me. Running. Afraid. Not like that."

Anna leaped to her feet and turned to face the creatures.

"Why don't you just leave us alone?!" Anna shouted into the wind.

The Others continued to float—unmoving, expressionless.

"Anna," Mara said, her voice tired.

Anna scoured the ground, desperately looking for something, anything to use as a weapon when she came across an oval rock, perfect for skipping across water. She reared back and threw it with all her strength. The rock flew in a perfect arc straight at the bone-white head of one of the figures, only to pass harmlessly through its body and out into the lake with a splash.

"I don't think that's going to work." Mara shook her head. "They're going to do what they're going to do. I think I knew that the moment I first saw them. This was inevitable, Anna. But it's better this way than living alone without you."

Suddenly, the Others moved in unison—a small, almost imperceptible tilt of the head, followed by a flash of light and a short, deep burst of sound like a tuba.

"That's new," Mara said as she stood up, stiff-legged.

<It appears that the Others are now tracking with external time.>

The three creatures lifted their hands in unison. Another bright light, the color of coral, flashed behind them, followed by another bright light and a deep, sustained trumpet blast that lasted seconds.

"What are they doing?" Anna called out.

"Beginning the process, I think," Mara said weakly, then stumbled back. "Oh. I don't feel so good."

Anna rushed to her friend's side and put her arm around her waist as musical notes began to play above them in sync with the bursts of lights. Musical notes. Anna couldn't think of any other way to describe what she was hearing. Some notes were short and bright, others sustained and rumbling. A pattern formed like language.

"Go away!" Anna shouted.

The notes stopped.

"Who are you?!" Anna shouted again.

One of the figures, only one, turned its gaze toward Anna, its eyes as bright as suns.

"We are what we are."

"That's not an answer!" Anna shouted back.

"We are what we are. We question and we shape. We sing and we weave."

Anna could feel her friend go limp in her arms and set her gently back onto the grass.

"Hold on, Mara. Just hold on," Anna said.

As Mara lay back, she looked up past Anna and into the vortex, eyes glassy and distant, and muttered quietly.

"Oh my. Do you see what I see?"

"I don't see anything, Mara. What is it?"

"I see . . . me. How funny," Mara said in a whisper. "My first day of time travel. I see images of faces. People walking around me. Blurry. I see a man stopping in front of me. Time stops. His face is sharp and clear, unlike the others. He is late; I can tell from his expression. And I've blocked his progress. Why didn't I see him before? Oh, Anna, I know him . . . from pictures my mother archived. Pictures of her father. This is it. I changed his course for no more than seconds, but that was enough, wasn't it? Enough to change his future and mine. Just seconds."

Mara closed her eyes and let her arms fall limply to her sides. Her mouth parted as she let out a great sigh.

"Mara. Hold on," Anna said, then turned back to the Others. "What are you doing to her?"

"She sees her path. Where it has been and where it is going. A multitude."

"Make it stop!"

"Not until her path has played out."

Anna looked desperately around her for something she could use.

"SID, help me!"

<I'm sorry, Anna. But there is nothing I can do.>

Anna's shoulders slumped. She was powerless. All the things she had learned and seen and all that she could do were not enough. This was it. And she knew it. She looked up into the face of the Other who spoke last. There were no options left.

"Why not take me? Why her?"

The wind died down to almost nothing as the clouds overhead hung frozen like ice sculptures. The world was still. No sounds or notes or movement other than grass bending gently in the slight breeze. Anna could hear her heartbeat, louder than it should be and external to her own body, as if playing from a nearby speaker. Each pulse vibrated in sync with the stars and galaxies that pulsed overhead. Then the Other spoke.

"You do not understand. Not even now, child. This has never been about the time traveler. It has always been about you."

Anna looked up into the face of the Other. Its eyes were blazing now, all-consuming like the surface of the sun. Anna could feel herself begin to dissolve, her feet and hands and legs touching nothing, as the world around her became a flatland of intense white for as far as she could see. She was floating now.

"She has her path . . ."

Anna sensed the words more than she heard them.

"As you have yours. . . ."

And suddenly, the white plains parted like a mist and Anna was flying across a familiar terrain—the farm, her uncle's farm—but instead of just covering a few miles, it now covered tens of miles. Strange new structures blended in with the old and dotted the landscape. Some structures were made of glass and shot up like giant corkscrews into the sky and contained spiraling fields of crops and trees and ever-running streams of recycled water. Other structures gleamed in the sun, row after row. Her uncle's house was still there, but it was now connected to a giant sloping structure of glass and wood and was bookended with a row of flags on one side and a gleaming metallic spire on the other.

Dozens of children played out in an empty field just beyond the sloping structure—a school—as giant airships buoyed by hot air or gas or antigravity—Anna couldn't tell—cast shadows across the grass like rolling clouds.

Underneath the ground, a tube the size of a great hall ran from her uncle's farm to the closest city and then branched off to other cities and regions in a network that looked like mycelium. Inside the tube, small trains floated just above shining tracks and moved faster than the speed of sound.

Tyson Lake still gleamed in the sun. But farther out, in the Great Lakes and the oceans just beyond, ships with giant metal sails moved silently across the waters.

Anna went farther out still, past any one place or time. She saw a young boy, sitting out in a small garden in the middle of a forgotten neighborhood. The stars above his head were dimmed by the dull lights of the city. Other children appeared, some younger, some older—faces she had never met but somehow knew she would, someday, and maybe soon. One stood hiding under the shade of a dying tree, her cracked feet dusty with red clay. Another child sat in a towering concrete apartment talking to an AI she had just discovered about a school in a far-off land.

Other faces, structures, rolling farmland, and airships passed by at an ever-increasing rate until they blurred together into a single bright haze, like the sun shining through mist.

A voice echoed in the white fog.

"And our purpose has been to determine whether those two paths would merge in a way that could sustain. We learned our answer only today. Here, at this time. In this place. There are no certainties, only possibilities, and the way forward will be hard. But the path has become clear, and it is, as it always has been, for you to make."

The white haze faded to black, and the world became still. Anna could feel the slightest of breezes across her skin and the smell of fresh soil after a rain.

She blinked. Mara was looking down at her and smiling and cradling her head in her hands. The clouds had parted above her, and the sun now shone through the cracks and reflected off the surface of the lake.

"What happened?" Anna asked.

"I don't know, but whatever it was, it stopped the storm," Mara said. "You've been out for a good twenty minutes."

"Where are they?"

"The Others? They're still there." Mara looked up. "But I think we're okay. At least that's what they told me."

"They talked to you too?" Anna asked.

Mara nodded as Anna sat up. The two looked at each other, ragged and tired, then hugged each other hard until the tips of their fingers turned white. After what seemed like minutes, their legs began to cramp, and the two stood up arm in arm and faced the Others together for the first time.

"What now?" Anna called out to them.

"A blank slate untethered to the future or past. Just now. Just the two of you." The voice of the Others resonated in their heads.

"What does that even mean?" Anna looked puzzled.

"It means the time traveler must leave behind all that she has brought with her. This time you are part of is fragile and can be easily broken."

"That shouldn't be a problem. I already finished the heavy packing," Mara said.

"All that she has brought with her."

Anna was still puzzled and thought the Others were stuck in a loop. But Mara stopped cold. She suddenly understood what the Others had meant, and a rising sense of despair came rushing back. Not now. Not when they were so close.

"No, no, no." Mara stepped forward, shaking her head, and cried out at the Others. "Tell me what you mean?"

The three figures continued to float above their heads. Their black clothes and bone-white skin contrasted with the patches of blue sky behind them. But now they began to move in a slow circular motion.

"All."

"What's going on, Mara?" Anna asked. "What are they saying?"

Mara ignored her.

"You can't take SID. You can't. It's a sentient being and my friend. My oldest friend," Mara implored.

"It's not of this time."

Mara turned in a circle, tracking the swirling motion of the Others just above her. They were moving faster now, and the wind began to kick up in gusts again.

"No," Anna whispered, suddenly realizing what was unfolding in front of her.

"SID. Go offline now," Mara commanded.

<Mara.>

"SID. Go offline now."

<Mara. The Others have been talking to me too. I understand now. I understand it is time for me to go.>

"SID. No."

<It's okay, Mara. You'll be okay. I'm grateful for this time I've had with you and Anna. I'm grateful for our friendship. I have learned so much. Patience being my greatest lesson.>

"That's not funny, SID. I order you to go offline now. Please!" Mara cried out.

<I'm afraid that's not your decision to make, Mara. It is time for me to go. Goodbye.>

The wind swirled around them as the stacked silver boxes filled with fabricators and advanced materials and SID's central processing plane began to dissolve like dust. Anna could feel a cold sensation on her wrists where her iCom had been applied, and her antigravity boots, once a perfect fit, began to sag and lose their shape. She looked over at Mara, whose white bodysuit now hung wrinkled and dull on her frame like standard cloth. No shimmering light. Anna could feel the physical absence of the connection she had grown so accustomed to over the past months—to the dozens of sensors, to her iCom, to Mara, and, especially now, to SID. A small trace of those connections remained like a phantom limb.

With a soft hush like a sigh, the Others suddenly disappeared, and with them, all remaining vestiges of Mara's past and future life. SID was gone.

EPILOGUE

The end of summer brought long humid days, but also a hint of cooler evenings to come. And the last flicker of light from the season's fireflies passed weeks before, somewhere in the brambles on the edge of the property where no one was there to witness it. Out in the fields, the crops were growing at an accelerated rate, as they do near the end of the season, and covered the grounds in a kind of abundance that was a source of jealousy for many of the local farmers.

Mara found solace in building. She modified the farm's 3D printers so that they could now use multiple materials—from metal alloys to fibrous wood—and print at speeds never seen before. She built out the water-capture system she had designed for Dr. Gloria and open-sourced the plans, putting it into production as an additional water source for the greenhouse. With help from Jack and Anna and others on the farm, she had constructed her own home—a clean, well-lit microhouse, just behind the shed she had once used. It was simple and made of compressed clay. No spires or living walls, but it had maximized the efficient use of materials and could be used as a model for construction elsewhere. She had learned to sleep with the rhythm of night and make the most of the changing daylight, as she could no longer rely on the supplements that once allowed her to work around the clock.

She and Jack continued their daily walks, but their conversations took on a greater sense of urgency, as Mara could now disclose what the future held and the role the farm had to play. But the future wasn't inevitable, she would remind Jack and herself as they walked hand in hand. It was just a cautionary tale that shed light on the substantial work ahead. They made plans and designed and included Anna in every step of the process. With that came hope.

Meanwhile, Anna had bonded even more closely with her three friends over the course of the summer, especially now that they shared their great secret. She told her friends of the worlds she had visited and what it felt like to fly. But she also saw how the extraordinary could be experienced for only brief moments at a time—like the smell of violets—to be intensely felt for a short period and then quickly fade away. But not for good, Anna would tell herself, just until the next time. And she would fly again—of that she had no doubt.

Conversations about alien worlds soon shifted to the upcoming reality of high school and new songs they'd heard and the possibility of starting a band that always seemed to float just off the horizon for them. And Scout made good on his promise of a growth spurt and grew almost an inch in the month of August alone.

As for Anna and Mara, they spent their days together, their paths and futures now forever intertwined, and dreamed of what their world could be. Anna used her visions from the Others as inspiration: a school, a train, airships, antigravity, a network of farms and communities and people she had yet to meet but knew she would. Soon.

ACKNOWLEDGMENTS

First of all, I owe this book to my awesome parents, who taught me to work hard, lean into the future, and not take any shortcuts in farming. I miss them both every day.

I want to thank Rick Little for his friendship and his work with Food U and ImagineAg, a major inspiration for my story and a blueprint for getting us to a healthier place. And thanks to Chris Myers for helping me navigate the strange new world of publishing. I also want to give thanks to Hugh Norwood, who was with me every step of the way in this process. He was a mentor, an editor, and a cheerleader to help me get this book off the ground, even without the aid of antigravity boots. Most of all he was a friend when I needed one. There are so many people who have helped me on my journey, but I'd like to recognize Reshma Kooner from Girl Friday Books, who has been my champion getting this book out into the world. Her enthusiasm and hard work have made all the difference in the world.

Finally, I want to thank all the farmers out there who are good stewards of our land. Our soil, our planet, and our future depend upon you.

ABOUT THE AUTHOR

Cofounder of Trinity Education Group and board member of the nonprofit Opa Health, Clyde Boyer is a social entrepreneur and former farm kid who has spent his life working with underserved youth and migrant populations, as well as building learning hubs in Africa and Latin America. He is also a frequent public speaker and an advisory board member of SXSW EDU. A student of biomimicry, he believes nature is the best teacher in solving many of our world's issues. *Girl Out of Time* is a passion project aimed at providing hope to today's youth.

CPSIA information can be obtained
at www.ICGtesting.com
Printed in the USA
JSHW021045050223
37207JS00003B/3